Center
OF
GRAVITY

K.K. ALLEN

Cover design by Sarah Hansen | Okay Creations
Cover photography by Perrywinkle Photography
Edited by Red Adept Editing
Book design by Inkstain Design Studio

For more information, please write to SayHello@KK-Allen.com

ISBN: 9781723829352

To my dance sisters and brothers from Suburban Dance Studios, RHS Dance Team, Western Hip Hop, Westlake Seattle, 24Hour Fitness, and LA Fitness. And especially you, Kristen. Sis. When I think about the happiest times in my life, I think of dance. And when I think of dance, I think of you. Love always.

BOOKS BY
K.K. ALLEN

SWEET & INSPIRATIONAL CONTEMPORARY ROMANCE

Up in the Treehouse

Under the Bleachers

Through the Lens (Coming in 2019)

SWEET & SEXY CONTEMPORARY ROMANCE

Dangerous Hearts

Destined Hearts

Center of Gravity

ROMANTIC SUSPENSE

Waterfall Effect

YOUNG ADULT FANTASY

The Summer Solstice Enchanted

The Equinox

The Descendants

SHORT STORIES & ANTHOLOGIES

Soaring

Echoes of Winter

Begin Again

Dear Reader,

In an effort to give you an interactive experience, YouTube links have been included throughout this book with no copyright infringement intended. All links point to their rightful owners, and all owners have been contacted regarding the use of video in this publication. Viewing the videos is not required to read, however, my intention is to bring you the inspiration that went into creating this story while you follow along.

Enjoy!
K.K.

Video Playlist

Heartbreaker | smarturl.it/Gravity_Heartbreaker

Confident | smarturl.it/Gravity_Confident

New Balance | smarturl.it/Gravity_NewBalance

What Do You Mean? | smarturl.it/Gravity_WhatDoYou

The Cure | smarturl.it/Gravity_TheCure

Wild Love | smarturl.it/Gravity_WildLove

Love So Soft | smarturl.it/Gravity_LoveSoSoft

Hanging On | smarturl.it/Gravity_HangingOn

Love In The Dark | smarturl.it/Gravity_LoveInDark

cen·ter of grav·i·ty

sen(t)ər əv ˈɡravədē/

noun: center of gravity; plural noun: center of gravities
The point at which the entire weight of a body may be considered
as concentrated so that if supported at this point, the body
would remain in equilibrium in any position.

Part One

THE AUDITION

Chapter 1

LEX

"I got an audition," Shane announced when he walked into the apartment, slamming the door behind him. A grand flourish if I'd ever seen one. Not even I would walk ten blocks in four-inch stilettos. But that was Shane, my six foot two inches of a man-friend whom I'd known since our very first dance class back in Seattle at age five.

His jersey bag landed at his feet, and his hands pumped the air as they often did when he was overly excited about something. "Sorry. Not *just* an audition. I got an *invite*."

My eyes grew wide, excitement flourished quickly, then anxiety ripped through me at the speed of a freight train. So many emotions all at once. Up until that point, everything had been good. We'd been living off our savings, spending as little money as possible, and taking a variety of classes at Gravity

Dance Complex, the premiere studio of the commercial dance world. No pressure. Just fun.

"An *invite*? For the Janet gig?" my voice squeaked. I scrambled to my knees. "But we've only been here three months. Is that even possible?"

He winked. "When your name's Shane Masterson, anything is possible, honey."

I fought back a groan. Shane had always been innocently cocky, aware of what his charm did to the human race. He was devilishly handsome, too, with raven-black hair cut short on the sides and always spiked in one direction or the other, rarely in the middle. But it was his personality that won everyone over. And yes, for Shane, *anything* definitely seemed possible.

Refusing to respond to his joke, I crossed my arms. "I thought we decided to wait. We're finally getting into a rhythm here. You can't—"

"Lex." He pursed his lips as if he were about to scold me. "I got an *invite*. I'm not going to turn it down. That would be career suicide, and you know it."

I was speechless. Professional gigs for music videos and stage shows came through Gravity all the time. It was the mecca of dance talent where A-list celebrities and casting directors nationwide frequently recruited, primarily for stage, television, and film bookings. Shane and I had talked about attending an open audition *one day* after getting our feet wet. The plan was always to take the plunge together. But getting an *invite* to audition was rare. He couldn't turn it down, not even if he wanted to.

My mind was still reeling as Shane started to raid the cabinets, though I wasn't sure what for. The only food remaining was the jar of peanut butter that sat half empty on the counter. He must have realized it almost as fast as I thought it, and he slammed the door shut. "We're ordering a pizza."

"Shane," I warned. We'd set aside money for one year of dance classes and rent. He knew we didn't have money to indulge.

"Lex," he warned back. "We dance eight to ten hours a day. You've still got that ass, but I will not be held responsible for you turning into a pile of bones. It's time to indulge in a big ole pie of heaven."

I let out a laugh despite the residual shock from the bomb he'd just dropped. Leave it to Shane to mask any tense situation with the topic of food.

"Look," he said, his sweet smile telling me he knew he'd won. "Just think. If I get this gig, we'll be better off. We can't take classes and live off Skippy and ramen while we wait for something to happen. Aren't you tired of waiting, baby girl?"

"Yes, but—"

He popped his hip and pursed his lips. "But what?"

"You'll get the job." I didn't mean for my voice to come out so whiny, but we'd just moved to LA.

"You don't know that."

"Maybe not this job, but it won't take you long. And then what? You might have to leave LA ... and leave me here ... alone."

He tilted his head and quirked his lip. "So dramatic."

I bit back my smile. The exaggerated pout was a little much.

"You could start auditioning too."

"Ha," I said on a sarcastic breath.

"C'mon, Lex. It's just like dating. You have to put yourself out there. Let them know you're interested. Check out your options." His eyes lit up, and he smacked the counter before leaning forward. "Speaking of dating options."

Oh no, here we go. My entire body cringed.

"There is this gorgeous hunk of man who teaches some of my classes. Do you know Reggie Maynor?" He fanned himself with his hand as his lids fluttered dramatically. "Dear Lord." But when he looked up and my expression hadn't changed, he threw his hand down while rolling his eyes. "Doesn't

3

matter. You'd know who he was if you saw him. Anyway. He was trying to be sly, but he was asking about you today."

I knew exactly who he was talking about, but I didn't come to LA to find a man. So I chose to ignore his second attempt at changing the conversation.

"You know I'm not ready to audition yet. I thought we *both* wanted to get some training first and—"

"We've been training our whole lives. This is why we're here. Besides, what better training than to audition and check out the competition?"

I snapped my mouth shut. He was right, but I wasn't ready to pay the ultimate price of my dream—losing my best friend. Not yet. Frustration shook through me. "Who gave you the invite?"

"Her name's Janelle. She scouts for a bunch of artists. Heard she's friends with that dreamy choreographer you love too. Theodore Noska." When his eyebrows wiggled suggestively, I picked up the nearest object and chucked it at him. My black-and-pink tennis shoe smacked him in the chest, causing him to shoot me a glare and stab a finger in the air. "I'm dragging your freckled ass to the next open audition just for that."

I wanted to scream. He didn't get it. In this industry, it wasn't enough to be the best dancer in the room. It was about friendships, connections, timing, and a little bit of luck. I saw the way the veteran dancers had looked at Shane and me when we first arrived, some with their side-eye glances or, worse, those who didn't see us at all. We were blips on their radars, passersby there for the experience, and immediately dismissed as contenders. I wanted that to change—I wanted to earn my spot.

And maybe somewhere deep down there was fear of failure too. Of getting rejected for the one thing I loved most in the world. I'd only ever had a plan A, despite my parents' wishes. And taking class was fun. Taking class didn't lead to the inevitable disappointment that came with this industry.

I was comfortable, but maybe that was a bad place to be. Still, the insecurities swarmed my chest, and I couldn't let them go.

"Do you know how many times I've been told I won't make it as a professional dancer? I'm not ready to hear it from the people who matter. This studio … those dancers … the choreographers. I need this community to accept me. If I ever get a job, I want them to know I earned it."

Shane's expression changed drastically from the happy-go-lucky man who walked through the door minutes ago to someone with only my best interests at heart. I cringed at the ass kicking to come.

"Don't let your father's words hold you back, Lex. That's all they are. *Words.* You're here because you belong here, and you'll see in time, it was the right decision."

His comment hit me in the gut.

"I will?"

"Yes." He leveled me with his eyes. "You're the biggest fucking rock star on that dance floor, Alexandra Lorraine Quinn, and I'm not just saying that because you bought me my first pair of stilettos."

I giggled, but his eyes remained serious.

"You think those dancers are going to respect you if they see you taking a million classes before you ever audition?" He shook his head emphatically. "Wrong, sweetheart. They won't even know your name until you slap a numbered sticker on those tight abs of yours, strut onto that dance floor like you think you're Beyoncé, and then fail—and then fail again. And third"—his eyes narrowed on mine, silencing my giggles—"the only person holding you back from your dream is you."

My eyes filled with tears as he made his way over to my air mattress, plopped down, then pulled me into his arms. I loved the closeness we'd maintained all these years. I loved how Shane had always been the one to push me toward my dreams and comfort me when things didn't go as planned. So yeah, I was terrified for all of that to go away. And I could feel it in the air; the time was coming.

Shane lived life full out. Nothing scared him. Nothing was worth backing down for. That might have been what I loved most about him. He'd faced all kinds of adversity, from his sexual orientation to surviving a toxic home life to always being considered freakishly tall compared to the rest of our peers. And all that was mixed with the ridicule he'd received for being a male dancer among our adolescent peers. He never let anything stop him from reaching what he wanted.

Shane and I were opposites.

Doer versus dreamer. Life of the party versus wallflower. And for some reason, we loved each other more for it all. We balanced each other. Or rather, *he* balanced *me*.

When Shane spoke next, my head was tucked safely under his chin.

"You might never feel ready, Lex. You just have to take a leap at some point. It might as well be now. It's time to fly, baby girl."

Chapter 2

LEX

The next audition didn't appear on the bulletin board in the community area at Gravity until a couple of weeks later. "You're coming with me to this one," Shane had demanded that night over a homemade platter of meats and cheeses.

I hadn't put up an argument. He was right about auditioning for the experience. When I thought about it like that, the outcome didn't seem so intimidating.

The Janet audition was a bust. Shane didn't even make it past the first round of cuts, but at least he had tried, which was a hell of a lot more than I had done since venturing with him to LA. That all changed today.

We were lined up in the hall, waiting to register for an upcoming audition—a music video for an up-and-coming urban pop artist, Dominic

Rivas—when a couple of girls in front of us started to whisper.

"Oh my God. He's here."

"Who?"

"Theodore Noska."

A gasp.

"Where?"

"He just walked in the front door."

As soon as the words left the girl's mouth, the world around me began to spin in slow motion. Voices played through a vacuum, muffled and quiet, conveniently drowning out their gushing. And my movements decelerated, as if I were being dragged through quicksand.

"Ho-ly shit." Shane's voice pulled me to the surface. He'd spotted Theo too.

Refusing to turn toward the rising commotion, I looked up at Shane just as he peered down at me. The sight of his whiskey eyes and jaw agape was enough to warn me that Theo Noska was every bit as delectable as he appeared in the media.

My body began to quake, a ridiculous reaction to a celebrity, but Theo wasn't just a celebrity. He was everything. He was all that I aspired to be and the one person whose opinion would mean the most, if I was ever lucky enough to have it.

Shane's warm fingers landed on my shoulders and swiveled me to face front. He turned my head toward the dance god himself.

The first thing I noticed was wild sandy blond hair—a perfect display of controlled chaos that one could happily sink fingers into in the throes of passion. Because clearly, there was only one good reason to have hair that sexy. Paired with the dark shades that masked his eyes, a leather jacket wrapped around his upper body, and ankle-length black jeans, he was every bit as intimidating as his choreography.

"Absurd." Shane groaned, and I could have sworn drool was pooling in his mouth.

Sure, Theo was all kinds of gorgeous, but it wasn't his looks that had made me fall in love with him from afar. I'd obsessed over his YouTube channel since its inception and had perfected every single one of his routines that I could lay eyes on.

He was hip-hop and contemporary fused with elements of ballet, jazz, tap, Bollywood, and every other dance style I could think of. His choreography could be epically dark and twisted or immensely beautiful and romantic, sending an audience to the edge of their seats while tears streamed down their faces.

All of America had watched the episode of *Dance Idol* where he came on as a guest choreographer and taught a contemporary partner routine to the finalists. The dancers executed the number flawlessly, but it was the emotionally charged choreography that made the video clip go viral. I remembered watching the routine and knowing that if Theo Noska wasn't a household name before that day, he would be after.

My heart beat like crazy just thinking about it.

Theo had put Gravity Dance Complex on the map, so it wasn't a complete surprise he'd shown up. I even hoped he would offer a class or two so I could mark that one off my bucket list. But I studied the weekly schedules as if that were my job, and Theo's name never appeared on any of them. *So, what is he doing here now?*

My eyes followed as he inched his way down the corridor in my direction then stopped briefly and collected a few fist bumps and one-armed hugs. He didn't stop for long or smile for anyone as he drew closer.

"Yo, Theo. What's up, buddy?" someone behind me called.

Theo was only a few feet away when he did a quick sweep of the line before giving an uptick of his chin to whoever had greeted him.

Then his head dropped slightly, his gaze connecting with mine—I thought. Theo's glasses hid everything, so I couldn't be entirely sure. It was just a second, a flash, but I felt it—a connection I don't think I could have made up despite my fierce crush on a man I knew only from his interviews. I wanted to stretch time to stay a little longer in the moment because the instant it was gone, I knew I would never get it back again.

I was lost in my thoughts when I felt fingers splay across my back. A shove thrust me onto my toes, tipping me off balance.

What the—?

I shot forward, my hands reaching in front of me, ready to catch my fall, when I realized only one thing was there. Or one man, rather.

Theo's arms reached out, his expression unchanged, as if catching me were the most natural thing in the world. My palms slammed against his chest just as his arms wrapped around me. Then he stood me up, his grip firm as I stared into his glasses, desperate to see past the reflection of myself.

All I could think about was the sturdiness of his form, the strength of his hold, and how absolutely consuming his rough, calloused hands were as they skimmed the bare skin of my shoulders and arms.

"Think you can be more careful next time?" He grumbled the words over my shoulder, snapping me back to the present.

Shane. A snare shot off in my chest. *He pushed me.* It had to have been him. But I didn't want to pull away from Theo long enough to confirm my suspicions.

"This is a dance studio, not a mosh pit." Theo's accusing tone was filled with raspy disapproval. He shifted me slightly, scenting the air with fresh apple cinnamon and leather, an intoxicating mixture that left me dizzy. "You don't want to be responsible for shortening this young girl's career. Apologize."

I turned then, ready with my glare as I caught the eyes of my best friend.

I'm going to kill him.

"I'm sorry, Lex." Shane's tone was sincere, but there was no denying the hint of amusement it carried. Theo's arms left me, forcing me to stand on my own. I turned around, ignoring Shane and offering my savior a polite smile. "Thank you for catching me."

He didn't smile. In fact, his brows stayed dented in the center. "Glad you're okay." He didn't ask whether I was, and he didn't wait for me to reply. Instead, he aimed one final look at Shane, the crease lines in his forehead expressing his annoyance.

"It was just an accident," Shane pressed, pulling me into his arms in what I'm sure was meant to be an apologetic hug.

But as Theo backed away and continued down the corridor without another pause, I was certain it wasn't an accident at all.

♥

"I should murder you."

I was patient enough, waiting until we'd left the dance studio later that day to let Shane have it. We had just started our ten-block walk to our place, and I felt as if I would burst if I didn't say something.

His laughter started, and I threw an arm out, knocking him in the stomach. He cringed and swooped me up cradle-style, despite my flailing limbs.

"Put me down, you big, giant asshole."

His laughter never ceased and only grew louder. "You should be thanking me. And I'm not letting you down until you promise to keep your hands to yourself. You heard what Theodore said about being careful. Oh, and what else? Shortening the life of this young girl's career." He burst into another fit of laughter. "He thinks you're twelve."

I was mortified and completely furious at my best friend.

11

"Let me down, or I'm moving back to Seattle."

"Oh, stop it. You would never."

"You have no idea what I'm capable of doing right now, Shane Masterson. And right now, you are not my best friend. You're this evil *thing* of a person sent to earth to destroy me. Right now, I hate you. I can't believe you did that to me. Why? I just want to know why you felt the need to embarrass me in front of the one person—*the one person*—I care about impressing."

Shane put me down, leaving a hand on my shoulder. I shook myself away, and his laughter finally silenced. "Oh, Lex. I'm sorry. If it makes you feel better, I think I'm officially on Theo's shit list. He was mad at me, not you."

"No," I squealed. "That does not make me feel better. We're in this together, remember? Don't make me regret signing up for tomorrow's audition."

"Okay, okay. But at least you got to touch him. How did he feel? Please tell me his skin is as soft and velvety as it looks." His head snapped toward me. "Oh my God. How did he smell? Like sunshine and roses? No. I bet it was more like dandelions after a warm rain shower."

It was Shane's heavy, dreamlike sigh that broke the spell. I laughed, because laughter was so much easier than staying mad at my best friend.

"Thank God," Shane said, clearly noting my amusement. "I cannot handle angry Alexandra. You remind me of your mother, all spun up and spewy, like a whacked-out sprinkler system." He shook his head as if disturbed by whatever visual had played in his mind. "Hey, let's go out to eat."

The change of subject happened so fast my brain did a complete three sixty.

"No. Not until you explain to me what the fuck you were thinking back there. You thought that was how to get Theo to notice me? Really?"

He gasped and held up a finger, tsk-tsking me. "Cussing sounds dirty coming from your mouth. Don't do it."

"Shane," I shot out. It was my final warning.

"Fine. He was standing right there in front of you, and I could practically see the little Theo and Lex babies running around in the background. It was this sixth sense. I pictured the entire epic love connection. You know, the ones you see all the time in movies, where the couple makes eye contact for the first time and these little stars and hearts start fluttering around the air."

"Yeah, pretty sure I've never seen a movie like that."

He stomped his foot and placed his fists on his hip. "Whatever. You've only been in love with the guy for the past decade. I was trying to help you out."

"How'd that go for you?"

He pursed his lips, as if deep in thought. "At least you can count on the guy if you ever decide to play 'Trust Fall.' He caught you, didn't he? And then he asked if you were okay."

I rolled my eyes as hard as I could. "Wow. Yeah. I think it's love. Maybe he'll fly me to his summer house in Spain and propose to me there."

Shane's eyes grew wide. "He has a summer house in Spain? Is it nice? I'm sure it's—"

"Shut up!" I growled.

Chapter 3

THEO

As soon as I was safe from the crowd, I hurried the rest of the way down the hall and closed—and locked—the staff room door behind me. "Holy shit, someone should have warned me there would be a crowd today."

Laughter filled the room while one of the voices yelled jokingly, "Did you check the schedule?"

"Nope." I had no clue who I was responding to. I didn't care. I never checked the schedule before making my pop-in visits.

Taking a quick look around the room, I found fellow choreographers, Gravity staffers, and Lifers, our name for the dancers who had found a home there, like me. None of them would fangirl over me like the crowd outside. I was safe.

Reggie knocked into me while opening the fridge and grabbed a water, his scheming grin stretched wide. "Got that worldly sex appeal thing going for you with those aviators and leather, man. Nice touch. You see anything out there you liked?" He stuck his tongue between his teeth and threw me a suggestive glance, as if we shared some secret language. "Lots of fresh meat lately."

I rolled my neck, the tension already building. I'd never been a Reggie fan. He was the epitome of a snake in the grass, just waiting for the opportunity to strike. And I felt inclined to egg him on.

"Yeah, some nice ones, Reg. If sloppy seconds are your style, head on out there." From the look he gave me, I knew my sarcasm was not lost on him.

"You're a chump, Noska."

"As are you, Maynor." I elbowed past him and yanked out a chair at Janelle's table.

She smiled, her expression playful as she leaned in. "That's Dominic's mob scene out there. It's gonna be a good one tomorrow. Hope the ladies didn't hurt you, though. Clawing and purring all over you and shit." She laughed. "That's about how it went, right?"

I tipped my head, considering her comment. "Pretty damn close."

Long, wavy blond hair, sapphire eyes with swirl of green near the center, and a smattering of freckles on a small button nose flashed through my mind. I had noticed her before that asshole boyfriend of hers shoved her into my arms. She had that "fresh meat" look Reggie was referring to. Doe eyes, flushed cheeks, timid smile. A girl like her would get eaten alive at Gravity.

When my thoughts turned slightly lewder in appreciation of the girl's ... assets, I swiped them away. "I really should learn how to check the audition schedule."

Reggie grabbed a chair near Janelle, swiveled it around, and sat on it. He leaned in, his arms folded on the table. "If you had taken a look at the schedule, hotshot, you would have seen that nothing's changed around here. In fact, things are busier than ever. Rooms are booked solid for the month."

"Shit," I muttered under my breath. My eyes turned away, my mind reeling at how much I'd managed to fuck up lately.

I could tell Reggie's curiosity was eating him alive. "You here to take a class? I've got a master class coming up later tonight if you want me to fit you in." His condescending tone bled through his words.

I would have rolled my eyes if a gesture like that weren't beneath me. "I'm good. Thanks."

His gaze hardened. He knew I was up to something.

"What brings you back to LA, Noska?"

"Winter." I blurted it out and watched every inch of Reggie's arrogant expression fall into something resembling annoyance then anger. I loved it.

He tensed further. "The Vegas gig?"

He and I were the only two in the room who knew what we were talking about. Winter, the one-name-only pop sensation with an obsession for the color white and anything Dior, had scored a six-month Vegas residency series that was nearly sold out. She'd recently been on the search for a choreographer, and Reggie wanted the gig. Badly.

I nodded and watched his expression settle into his natural "I don't give a fuck" face that I knew was a lie. Reggie had been a contender for the Vegas gig, and it would have been his big break into professional choreography outside the studio.

Unfortunately for him, I was the better choice. Apparently, he just hadn't been told yet.

"So, that's it, huh?" Reggie's nose flared. "Gig's yours? Officially?"

I shrugged. It wasn't my job to babysit Reggie's feelings. "Yeah, but you can still audition for backup." I knew I was being a prick. I just didn't give a shit.

Janelle snorted, and he shot her a glare. "Sorry." She threw her hands up but couldn't stop laughing.

"Oh, I will," Reggie said, shoving his spoon into his yogurt cup, most likely scheming about my demise. "And don't you worry, Noska. When you fuck up, I'll be right there to save the day."

My teeth ground, a completely unintentional response. It wasn't like me to let Reggie wind me up, but that comment did the trick. I had already fucked up. I'd fucked up with my last assistant, big-time, which started a domino effect of mess up after mess up. I was back in LA to pick up the pieces and somehow put on the award-winning show I had promised Winter.

I cleared my throat. It was time to focus. That was why I came to Gravity today. There was no better place for me to get back in the game. "Who's got the performance center this week?" I looked around the room, my question directed at anyone who would answer. "The studios are booked solid, but the stage should be open, yeah?"

Janelle reached for her phone and nodded. "It's all yours, baby. I'll book it for you right now."

I reached over the table and squeezed her arm affectionately. "Love ya, Nellie."

"Love you more."

I almost smiled.

Chapter 4

LEX

"I can't believe you talked me into this." I was squeezing the shit out of Shane's hand, making him wince, as we stood in line to collect our audition badges for Dominic's music video. Yesterday at registration, I hadn't felt this quick fluttering in my chest, as if my heart had just grown wings and I couldn't trust the flight pattern.

"Damn, Lex. I need those."

I pulled my hands away. "Geez, sorry. I'm just so nervous."

"Good. You always dance better when you're nervous." He massaged his hands. "Besides, the people in this room don't care about anyone but themselves. You're as ready as anyone else here."

"You don't know that."

"And you don't know that you're not. Not until you suck it up and go out there and try."

Sometimes, Shane could be so irritating. But I knew he was right, and my attitude deserved a swift kick in the ass.

The wide hallways were so crammed on our way into the studio, I could barely see the entrance. Dancers were shoulder to shoulder with no end in sight. And not a single one of them looked half as terrified as I felt.

We made it to the front of the line and slapped on our stickers that identified us as numbers eighty-six and eighty-seven. I wrapped my arms around one of Shane's to stay close as we followed the herd into our audition room. Or rather, *the* audition room.

Above the door, the sign labeled "Main Studio" did nothing to describe what existed beyond the solid mahogany double doors. The room was reserved primarily for bigger auditions—like this one—and rehearsals. I was well aware of the Grammy and Tony award winners who frequently graced the room with their presence. I was also aware of the groundbreaking choreography that was birthed in the very room we were stepping into.

Nerves lit up my body like rapid fire as Shane pulled me across the threshold. My eyes widened, immediately taking in every inch of the room. The walls were a shimmery light gray with black and red diamond accents, mirrors spanned the entire front of the room, and the light-wood floor looked so polished it could have been used as a Slip 'N Slide.

"Wow," I gushed. It was as if I'd just stepped into Theo's YouTube channel.

"Amazing, right?" Shane grabbed my hand and pulled me to the only free space in the room big enough for both of us.

The studio was packed already, wall-to-wall with dancers who were chatting, stretching, getting ready for what might have been the biggest opportunity of their careers. I should have been doing the same. Instead, my eyes connected on the center of the room. My entire body tensed.

Every dancer had their sweet spot, their special place on the studio floor where they believed they focused best. Some gravitated toward the right, some the left, some the front, some the back. My special place was the dead center of the room, and someone was already standing there.

Shane put an arm on my shoulder. "Sorry, Lex. There's no way you're getting in there."

With a heavy sigh, I knew I had to acknowledge he was right. "Damn it."

I sat, throwing out my legs in a V and leaning back on my palms. "Yeah, well. It's not like I'll last very long."

He gave me a lopsided grin as he sat facing me and mirrored my stretch. "Turn that bad attitude around. Or do we need to have the self-fulfilling-prophecy talk again?"

I groaned. "Ugh, no. Please."

"Then grow some confidence, and trust me when I say you've got this. I'm not going to tell you again."

Shane and his damn pep talks. I bit my lip, trying not to smile.

Another thing I loved about my best friend: he kept his promises. If he said he wasn't going to pump me up anymore today, he wouldn't. He wanted me to battle my insecurities as much as I wanted to. The funny thing was that having confidence on the dance floor wasn't my problem. That came naturally. It was the "getting there" I was having trouble with.

My thoughts were jarred by the sound of the main doors to the room clanging shut. I looked up to see Janelle weaving her way through the mess of stretched-out limbs as she walked to the front of the room.

"All right, all right," she said, her voice carrying over the excited chatter. "Let's get the party started."

A cheer rose from the crowd, and my heart thrummed a mile a minute.

I'd taken a few of Janelle's contemporary classes before, so I wasn't a stranger to her choreography. But it wasn't just her compositions that made her a star choreographer. Everything about Janelle's energy screamed sass and confidence—my favorite combination—and watching her filled me with a certain buoyancy just waiting to be unleashed.

I aspired to be on the other side of things one day. To create. To teach. To inspire. And being here at Gravity, especially in this room, was the biggest step I'd ever taken toward those dreams.

"I'm gonna lay it down real quick so we can get started, so listen up." Janelle clapped her hands, demanding silence.

In seconds, all eyes and ears were on her. Why wouldn't they be? Even I could admit she was hard to look away from. She had the most amazing hair—a pouf of dark brown with blond highlights situated in tight rings around her head. Her bronze skin was radiant under the harsh glare of the studio light, and the smile that lit her face also lit up the entire room. She was a star.

"There are over two hundred of you in here right now auditioning for one of eight spots for an upcoming music video." Her wide eyes drifted over the room. "So, if urban dance is not your thing, get the hell out now before I tell you it's not your thing."

Laughter shook the room, and she responded with a grin.

"We're going to need to keep things moving quickly so we can get into the meat of the choreography. Dominic will be joining us in one hour, and we'll only have room for fifty of you. That means cuts will be frequent, possibly when you least expect it. So, if you're asked to leave, please make your way out the door swiftly and quietly. Got it?"

Everyone nodded and muttered their agreement. When Janelle seemed satisfied with the response, she gestured for us all to rise.

After centering herself in front of the mirror, she delivered the first eight count, walking us through the fancy footwork a few times, letting us get the feel for the moves before we ran it with music. She didn't pause to reteach the steps as an instructor would in my studio classes. She blazed forward, moving through phases of music with a clear expectation—*Keep up.* Looking around the room, I noticed many dancers were struggling to do just that.

"Holy crap, she's going fast," I hissed to Shane when Janelle jogged to the front of the room and guzzled some water.

He was focused on his reflection, practicing what we'd learned so far. "Welcome to auditions," he said without stopping. He shot me a quick look. "Why aren't you running it? Your brain needs to be on hyper-focus mode now. Don't get distracted."

There was that ass kicking I needed again. It helped. Soon enough, I'd gotten into my own rhythm, and I started using the little down time we had to mark the steps with Shane.

When Dominic entered the room an hour later, the intense energy among the dancers was palpable. Everyone had reverted to competition mode, and I could practically taste their blood as Janelle proceeded to cut another fifteen dancers.

Fifty dancers remained.

My heart leapt, and I turned to Shane. "I'm still here," I hissed, looking around the room in disbelief. My eyes connected with the floor in the center of the room, and my heart kicked in my chest. "Shane." I grabbed and shook his arm. "Look."

He followed the direction of my stare and let out a booming laugh. The spot was empty.

"Well, what are you waiting for? It's time to slay the shit out of the competition."

❤

"Number eighty-six," Janelle called out. "You're up."

The last hour had been an exhilarating whirlwind of choreography, line critiques, and group performances so Dominic and Janelle could see how we meshed with other dancers. Cuts were nonstop and random, dwindling the group to a mere ten.

I jogged to the front of the room and took the only spot available on the end. And as soon as the music started, I felt it—the surge of energy that cycled through me at the start of every performance. I'd almost forgotten what it was like to totally let go and let my muscle memory take over. To attack each move with a fierceness that turned me into a superhero.

People often asked how I was able to perform with so much passion and confidence. My answer was always the same: "Know the routine so well, I don't need to think about the moves anymore." My job was to express with conviction everything my body already knew. So that was what I did.

WATCH: HEARTBREAKER
smarturl.it/Gravity_Heartbreaker

I spun out of a move and into a final pose, a giant smile plastered on my face. Janelle's eyes were focused on me. She was nodding, and I knew I'd impressed her. *I nailed it.* I wanted to burst with joy.

Shane's group went next, and I low-fived him as we exchanged spaces. "So hot, Lex."

"Kill it, Shane."

Shane was one of those dancers who popped and locked so hard, I wondered if my eyes were playing tricks on me. But it was his contemporary that had made me fall in love with his every step. The boy could have easily made it in professional ballet, but that wasn't where his heart wanted to take him. No. Shane's heart was in modern dance, which was why he easily outperformed all the other dancers in his line. Break dance was his specialty. I wasn't surprised that he annihilated the routine.

Shane returned to my side while Janelle paused, looked at a sheet of paper, then walked to the front of the room. "Let me see numbers eighty-six, eighty-seven, and one thirty-three, one more time, please."

My heart plummeted as she waved another girl and me forward into a line. Shane and I glanced at each other, as if realizing the same thing. The majority of the dancers must have already been chosen—which meant she wanted one more look at us before she made her final decision.

They were going to either cut me or keep me.

"Good luck," Shane mouthed from his spot against the back wall. Nerves rattled my face as I smiled in return.

The music started, and all my anxiety fell away. It didn't matter who was in the room or what personal problems I had outside the studio. When the music started thumping through me, I was a totally new person. A whole new *brave* person. And this dance was no exception.

Shane grabbed my hand when we were done, our breaths heavy and palms sweaty, but I didn't pull away.

Janelle leaned into Dominic, and they deliberated in hushed voices. Two of us had to go for them to have their final eight. Unless they made an exception. Hope flickered through me.

Janelle frowned, then Dominic shrugged as if there were some disagreement, but it didn't last long. Janelle faced forward and grabbed the microphone, her smile breaking through her serious expression.

"Numbers eighty-six and one thirty-three, thank you so much for joining us today. Unfortunately, you didn't make it through." Her kind eyes settled on me.

"You both made it a very tough decision, and for that, you should be very proud."
She beamed at the remaining dancers. "The rest of you, congratulations. We'd
love to have you in Dominic's next video. Please stick around for a few minutes."

A familiar hand settled on my shoulder. "I'm so sorry, Lex." Shane was so
sincere, it almost made everything worse.

If a heart could split in two, that was exactly what mine did in that moment.
Half of me was overcome with joy for my best friend while the other half was
completely brokenhearted for me.

That audition couldn't have been more perfect for him. I knew that, deep
down, from the start. I wanted him to get the part, and I was elated when
he did. There wasn't a single ounce of me that felt resentful toward him. But
damn, I didn't think rejection would suck this hard.

Shane wrapped his arms around me, and I squeezed him back. "You
deserve this. You killed it today."

"So did you."

I shook my head, refusing to let any negative emotion surface. This was
his moment, and he was going to enjoy every damn second of it.

"I'm holding out for something better," I teased.

He hugged me again, practically swaddling me, until he was called to the
front of the room.

So I left my first audition with a heavy heart and a jar of bottled-up feelings
that I still refused to release. Not there.

I looked around the crowded hallway while figuring out my next move. It
must have been the top of the hour because everyone was heading to a class.
I didn't feel like taking a class. Not after that audition. I didn't feel like going
home either. I didn't even feel like waiting for Shane to leave his meeting with
Janelle and Dominic. I just wanted to be alone with my thoughts and maybe
open that jar of bottled-up feelings I'd been holding onto so tightly.

Chapter 5

LEX

Curiosity seemed to take my mind away from the staggering disappointment I'd just faced, so I wandered the wide, mazelike halls of Gravity. I peeked through windows and open doors to spy on classes in session. I passed by the staff room and the community area, where dancers congregated throughout the day, and moved swiftly past the training center that held a gym, sauna, pool, and locker rooms.

There was a college vibe as I traversed the halls, unique from any other dance studio I'd been in. But the history embedded subtly throughout the facility spoke the loudest. It had awards dating to the mid-nineties and autographed photos that appeared to date back just as far. I stopped at a plaque with a gold plate and wooden frame, feeling an instant tug on my heart. I knew it was special, even before reading the words.

In Loving Memory
Rashni Kaur
1976 - 2010
Founder of Gravity Dance Complex

I had a heaviness in my chest for a man I'd never known but who'd created something so beautiful. I wondered if he realized the impact his studio had on the world, not just in entertainment but as inspiration to young hearts everywhere. Like mine.

I first learned about Gravity from going down the YouTube rabbit hole. One second I was watching adage exercises to help strengthen my center, and the next I was taking an inside peek at studio performances choreographed by none other than Theodore Noska.

If my parents had known their sixteen-year-old daughter was internet stalking a twenty-four-year-old guy, they would have changed the Wi-Fi password on me for life. Fast-forward six years. If they knew their twenty-two-year-old daughter was more infatuated than ever with that now thirty-year-old *man*, they would have driven me straight back to Seattle.

I couldn't let that happen. Living in a dingy apartment off Ventura Boulevard, sleeping on air mattresses in the living room, stealing Wi-Fi from our neighbors, and frequenting the laundromat down the road wasn't exactly what I pictured when Shane and I decided to move to LA. But so far, it had been the most liberating three months of my life.

As I continued down the hall, it was almost as if Rashni's spirit was with me, guiding me, encouraging me to explore. I had a newfound respect for the space where I'd been spending my days and nights—and a deeper respect for myself. I did it. I was doing it. Following my dreams, even if the current path was a little rocky.

I didn't even realize I'd hit the end of the last hall until I spotted a gold-textured sign above it.

Gravity Performance Center

The antique white French doors below the sign were closed, but when I pressed my ear against the entrance, everything seemed quiet. I pulled on the handle, halfway expecting it to be locked, but it opened easily, so I peeked through the dimly lit crack.

Empty. A sigh of relief escaped me as I entered the theater.

The first thing I noted was the theater's size. It looked large, but I didn't have much to compare it to. There were three sections of blue velvet seats, and each aisle had a runway of carpet and stairs with gold-wrapped banisters, all of it angled down toward a deep stage.

Scuff marks marred the stage floor, and a faded blue-velvet curtain was open. Small brass lamps holding dim lights were fastened to the floral-papered walls, emitting a comforting ambience despite the vastness of the space.

I made my way forward, down the wide aisle, detecting a light draft that brought a scent of fresh wood and paint. After untying my black sweater jacket from my waist, I slid my arms through the sleeves and zipped it over my breasts. I threw the hood of the fabric over my head to combat the frigid air and, with a sigh, sank into a seat at the front of the room.

My thoughts flashed between the failed audition and the constant look of disappointment on my parents' faces that always seemed to accompany anything to do with dance. They didn't get it, and I knew they never would. But as a college graduate who'd pursued all the internships and part-time positions offered at my parents' publishing house, I'd done everything they'd asked to stay in their good graces. My decision to move to LA had disappointed them, but at least they agreed it was my decision.

A loud clang from above jarred me from my thoughts, and a beam of bright light flooded the stage. I gasped, sinking lower in my seat when a figure dressed in white jeans and a leather jacket walked out from stage left. My heart galloped as I identified the man with one sweep of my eyes.

Theo.

There was no mistaking his lean but muscular build, his sexy hot mess of blond hair, and the square face that showcased the sexiest dimple in his chin. I couldn't see his dimple now, or his insanely hot lips—thick with a peaked Cupid's bow—but they had been embedded in my mind since yesterday. My cheeks heated at my thoughts.

He removed the jacket and slung it toward the curtain, revealing a loose white muscle shirt underneath.

Music streamed in from the surrounding speakers, but Theo just stood there, his eyes closed, his head down, and his jaw locked tight, as if he were taking in the words and imagining what he could do with them. Even I was imagining what he could do with them.

Rumors started traveling the moment he'd strutted through Gravity's main doors yesterday. It seemed his mysterious reappearance had been everyone's favorite topic. Talk in the community center gave me the impression that Theo was content on bouncing from job to job without a real break in between. Apparently, he hadn't taught a studio class in years, so the probability of him trying to find an open studio to teach in was slim. No one understood why he was back, though there were whispers of a hush-hush project for someone high-profile.

My eyes snapped to the stage when he started to move. First he rolled his neck and then his shoulders in slow and steady isolations as the unfamiliar song played on, save for the random lyric or beat that would inspire him to break out into a combination of moves. Was he choreographing in his head? He'd never talked about his creative process in any of the interviews I'd seen. He always made it seem as if it just happened.

I watched him for a long time, his focus inspiring. From what I'd gathered about Theo over the years, he was a deep thinker—quiet, serious, and not much of a talker. He kept a low profile when it came to his personal relationships and never got caught up in political warfare. He seemed … simple, yet there was nothing simple about the way he danced.

Track after track, he let the record play without stop. I heard more unfamiliar songs, but at some point, I recognized that the voice behind the sultry vocals belonged to Winter. The world's hottest pop icon—clearly, since she didn't need a last name—the pop and R&B-inspired singer from Canada had gotten her big break ten years ago when she was just sixteen. She was known for her knockout stage performances and catchy songs guaranteed to blow up the charts.

I held my breath when I realized I must have just listened to Winter's entire unreleased album. Suddenly, I felt I had gone beyond simply invading Theo's privacy. My head whipped around the space, my heart frantic. Had I trespassed? Could there be consequences for something like this?

Unease rattled me, and I would have snuck out right then if I hadn't thought I would attract attention. So I stayed put as guilt feasted away at me until, finally, Theo started to walk off stage.

I let out a deep breath as I quietly pulled myself out of the row. I was a split second away from making a run for the exit when Theo strutted back onstage.

My eyes froze on him, half expecting him to catch me in the audience, but his eyes were on fire and so focused on whatever he was trying to accomplish that he still hadn't spotted me.

I sat back down, my palms sweating and my heart hammering, and then watched as everything he'd been building in his head exploded onto the stage.

Theo laid it all out on the dance floor. His passion. His intensity. He practically shook the room. There was a litheness behind each glide and twist, the strong lines of his body as he rolled into a lock, and the tension he unleashed in each isolated movement.

Jesus. *Is this what an out-of-body experience is like?* I was weightless, transfixed at the scene before me. Dance was the language of Theo's soul. He bled in sweat. He breathed in the music. And he radiated passion through every square inch of his body.

I'd always been fascinated with how much emotion could be conveyed through dance. How the body could become an instrument and tell an entire story. Watching Theo dance proved it. He was my preacher, and I was his loyal disciple, two seconds away from worship.

A sheen of sweat coated his face and dripped down his neck, disappearing beneath his long white shirt. He was a beautiful man, but it was what he expressed through his body that made him a god. Some had even called him a modern-day Bob Fosse, with stunning technique and the fluidity that gave him a unique edge and limitless creativity. And it wasn't just the way he moved or choreographed a single piece but the way he put productions together, making the audience feel immersed in whatever world he'd created.

The longer I sat there, the worse I began to feel. I wasn't sure how much time passed before he took his next break and downed an entire bottle of water, his muscular chest heaving, his body a river of sweat.

The music still played, but nothing could disguise the sound of my phone when it started to ring.

Fuck.

I might have even gotten away with the one ring since the music was so loud, but when bling after bling sounded, like the annoying chime of a morning alarm, I knew I was screwed. I scrambled to steal my phone from my pocket, already feeling intense eyes watching me. I pushed the switch to silence my phone, but it was too late.

The room carried a heavy silence, and an inferno of heat washed over me. I could feel a confrontation looming.

"Who the hell are you?" The boom of his angry voice shook me.

I cleared my throat and stood, shakily, then stepped into the aisle. "I'm sorry. I didn't know you were going to be in here."

"I didn't see you come in." His tone was accusing. When I couldn't find the words to respond, his cheeks reddened. "You've been here the whole goddamn time? Didn't you see the 'Reserved' sign on the door?" He threw a look toward the main doors and raised his finger. "How did you get in here? The door was supposed to be locked."

I looked in the direction he was pointing, confused, then turned back to Theo with a shake of my head. "It was unlocked. There was no sign. And no one was here when I—" I swallowed the jumble of nerves in my throat. "I just wanted a little privacy." I began to back away slowly. "I'm sorry. I should have told you I was here the moment you walked in."

"Why didn't you?"

"I-I don't know. You looked ... focused. I didn't want to interrupt."

His breath came out in a rush, and he leaned in, trying to get a better look at me. "Take off your hood."

My hand shook as I lifted it to my head and slowly pulled down my hood, too nervous to just rip off the bandage, as I should have.

"What's your name?"

"Alexandra Quinn." I snapped my mouth shut then opened it again. "Lex, actually."

"You look familiar. Why do you look familiar?"

He doesn't even remember. I shrugged, trying to ignore the ache in my chest. "I'm just a dancer." It was true. I was a nobody to him. Invisible.

His eyes scanned the length of my body, I assumed to check out my attire. "Clearly," he murmured, and I wasn't sure if he meant for me to hear it. "I'd hate for anything you saw here to get leaked. I could have you sign an NDA, but I don't have fucking time for that right now."

My jaw dropped. "I won't leak anything—I wouldn't—but I'll sign it if you want."

He hopped off the stage and made his way toward me before stopping a few feet away. His heavy scowl caused my heart to leap into my throat and my pulse to pound through my veins, and I couldn't for the life of me find my next calm breath. I took in a ragged one instead as he assessed me.

A moment later, his eyes widened in recognition. "You're the girl from yesterday. From the registration line."

I nodded. "Yeah. Thanks again for, you know, catching me." My cheeks burned. *How much worse can this conversation possibly get?*

"Wasn't that audition today?"

I nodded.

"Janelle's choreo?"

I couldn't decide if I was being interrogated or if Theo was genuinely curious. My eyes flicked between his, and I nodded again.

"Well," he prodded. "Did you get it?" He spoke almost as intensely as he danced. I didn't know what to make of it.

"No. I didn't." Mortification snaked through me. It was bad enough to fail my audition, but to have to discuss that failure with the one person I'd always dreamed of working with was the absolute bottom of the barrel.

"What happened?" His voice wasn't one of a concerned mentor. He was definitely interrogating me—feeling me out—and I was afraid of what he was fishing to find.

"It was my first audition ... so..." My voice trailed off as I caught the way his brows turned down, clearly displeased.

"You're making excuses."

Shit. I shook my head. "I'm just—"

"Making excuses. You shouldn't do that. Justifying all the reasons you fucked up your audition won't help you improve. Own your mistakes and work to never make them again."

Wait a second. My head felt as if it was spinning on its axis. Mistakes? "But I didn't—"

He barked out a laugh, cutting me off again then pinning me with his eyes. "You did. That's why you tucked your tail between your legs and snuck in here. Am I right? Couldn't handle the rejection?"

"No," I shot back. "I handled it just fine, thank you very much."

He chuckled. "Good. Because it won't be the last time."

Jesus. Who knew a fantasy could be destroyed with a few angry words? Theodore Noska was an asshole. I couldn't find the words to respond. If I opened my mouth, I would be a sputtering idiot, giving him more to dig into me about.

He sighed then shook his head. "Look. I've been doing this a long time. I've seen this industry swallow up girls like you."

I crossed my arms. "Girls like me?"

"The newbies. The dreamers. The naïve souls without a clue what it takes to step into the professional world. Chances are, the reality will crush you, *Alexandra.*"

"It's Lex." I didn't care that I'd turned into a snapping turtle in reaction to Theo's harsh words.

His lip curled. "Whatever. Some people are better off keeping dance as a hobby."

In that moment, I hated him more than I'd ever lusted over him. Which was probably why my next words flew from my mouth like word vomit. "You're a jerk." I gasped, my lids stretched wide, and clapped a hand over my mouth.

His eyes flashed with amusement, then his head fell back as he laughed. "Did you just call me a jerk?"

My entire body shook as I narrowed my eyes at him and released a heavy breath from my nose. "Yes," I hissed.

He shrugged and narrowed his gaze. "I've been called worse." With a lift of his chin, he gestured toward the door. "Get the hell out."

So cold. So cutthroat. It was my first run-in with Theo Noska, and I hoped it would be my last.

Chapter 6

THEO

The leather seat felt stiff beneath my legs as I settled into my chair at Wicked Saints Records. Forty-five minutes. That was how long I'd been waiting for Winter to walk through the conference room doors of the downtown LA skyscraper. I sat in a boardroom full of investors, leading sponsors, venue managers, set designers, wardrobe specialists, and all the assistants and assistants' assistants imaginable. *In-fucking-sane.*

Since returning to LA three weeks ago, I'd been feeling … off. I'd have probably walked if this gig didn't mean something to me. And not just because Winter and I went way back—back to the first time she stepped foot into Gravity ten years ago and handpicked dancers for her very first music video.

I hadn't been hired only to choreograph Winter's Vegas show. I'd been hired to help produce it too, an opportunity I'd been striving for my entire career without even realizing it. Now that we were less than two months from showtime, I couldn't afford to fuck up more than I already had.

The door to the room swung open, pausing the happy chatter among my peers. In walked an entire entourage of familiar faces—Winter's label rep, her manager, her stylist, her hair and makeup artist, her assistant, her two bodyguards, and finally, Winter herself.

Her smile bloomed when she looked around the room and saw us all waiting for her. "I think this just may be my favorite sight since landing in LA." She turned to her assistant, Alison, and squeezed her arm. "Can you believe it?" She looked around the table and threw her hands up. "Vegas, baby."

Cheers broke out around the table, and I watched the group in fascination. Winter hadn't always been the puppet master of a room of this caliber. She was once the desperate sixteen-year-old who'd gotten her lucky break through family connections and "the look" the label was searching for at just the right time. It helped that she could carry a tune, but that wasn't why the label loved her. She was young, fresh, and moldable, and her innocence was extremely marketable.

She lifted her hand halfway and waved at me, her dimply smile as sexy as I remembered. I waved back, sans dimples, knowing it was best not to egg her on. There was a comfortableness between Winter and me that went beyond friendship, beyond business. With all the gigs she'd hired me for over the years, it was only natural for us to flirt from time to time. But that couldn't be an expectation. Not now. Not when I was months behind on my work. Not after Mallory.

When Winter pouted at my lack of affection, I shifted my gaze and my focus to the front of the room. Denise McDaniel, entertainment manager for the Zappos Theater at Planet Hollywood, was speaking, delivering the news we'd all been waiting to hear.

"First of all, as of this morning at eight a.m., the 'Love in the Dark' concert series is officially sold out. Congratulations."

The entire room burst into applause and mutterings of "Congratulations," all while Winter looked stunned in her chair. The tickets had been on sale for four months, but for a six-month series, that was pretty damn good.

"More great news." Denise spoke up as the cheering faded. "The permits came through on the set design, and you're fully approved to move into the venue to begin setting up next month. The space is yours for whatever you need. I'll just need you to send back the liability waivers for your staff. Also, I'm working on securing your residences in the hotel, but I'll need first and last names, phone, email, and a prepayment, at the very least, to get started. Are you fully staffed at this point?"

Winter shot me a curious glance. She was the only one in the room alert to my three-month absence, and I'd promised her that I'd make up the time. Unfortunately, even after being back in town for three weeks, I was still way behind on choreography and choosing dancers.

I cleared my voice and raised my hand to let Denise know I could respond to her question. "We'll be hiring twelve additional crew members. Dancers. But I won't have their information for you for another week." I scrunched my face and flipped my palms out, elbows still bent. "Maybe?"

"Another *week*?" Winter asked with forced politeness as she shifted in her seat. She let out an awkward laugh, her eyes darting around the room before returning to me. She leaned forward. "When's the audition?" Her head turned to Alison. "Is it on my calendar?" I heard her whisper.

Alison almost immediately shook her head, offering me an apologetic look. Winter's eyes turned cold and snapped back to me.

I sighed. The last thing I needed was a micromanager breathing down my back when I already felt the pressure. "It is what it is, Winter."

Shock registered on her face, as if she'd been slapped. Her spine straightened as she pushed her shoulders back and flipped a section of hair over her shoulder. "Let's discuss this after this meeting."

♥

"*It is what it is?* What the hell is wrong with you, Theo? I'm trusting you with the biggest show of my life."

Winter was always so melodramatic. I shut my eyes while she continued to spew her disappointment. She'd been able to contain her rage throughout our four-hour meeting, but as soon as it was over she dragged me into a private room on the other side of the building.

"I've got this," I said calmly, hoping my nonchalance would rub off on her, but my comment only seemed to wind her up. Her chest popped out as her eyes flashed red.

"We're two months from showtime, and I have no dancers, no choreography." She pressed her palms to her face and threw them back down. "I gave you time to deal with ... everything you've been going through."

Her eyes softened some but only for a second. "But Theo. You promised."

"And I've come through on everything so far." I placed my hands on her shoulders, desperately needing her to chill the fuck out. "The stage design, the music mixes, the backdrop, and costumes. I've overseen all of that."

She nodded, letting out a breath through her nose. "You're responsible for a lot, I know. But I need your choreography more than anything else. Please tell me you have a plan."

"I have a plan."

Her nostrils flared again. "Mind sharing it with me? There's no show without my dancers. You realize this, right? You realize I came back to LA to start choreography. Which means the dancers should have been trained by now. Hell, half of the dance crew is already a shoo-in. You just need to pick six. Six dancers. Why is that hard?"

"It's not. I'll schedule the audition for this week, and we'll start rehearsals the next day."

Winter's eyes narrowed, and she leaned in closer. "No. You will set the audition up for Tuesday. You have three days. Make it happen."

"There's no way." *Now I'm the one on fire.* "I won't find audition space by then."

"Gravity owes you. They'll do anything you say."

She didn't get it. I didn't throw my weight around like that. I wasn't her. "Even if I do find the space, there's no time to send out invites. You don't expect me to hold an open audition, do you? And have all the wannabe dancers waltz in thinking they have a shot? You want the best of the best, and you're not going to get that by throwing some crapshoot of an audition."

"Listen to me." Winter seethed, and I could practically see venom rising from her skin. "I'm not asking you. I'm telling you. There better be an audition on Tuesday. Invite only. I'll be there. Figure it out." She slammed her fists on the table and stood. "Got it?"

I raised my brows but knew there was no arguing my way out of this one. I'd made my own bed. "Got it."

Chapter 7

LEX

Something happened to me in that theater with Theo. I couldn't even explain it to Shane after I'd confessed what had happened, but for some reason, Theo's cruel dismissal lit a fire within me. For the next three weeks, I signed up for every audition and supplemented every other hour in the studio with advanced lessons, workshops, and master classes—all to push my limits.

I was slipping my dance shoes off on Monday night after one of Janelle's contemporary classes when she crossed the room and plopped down in front of me. My eyes shot up in surprise, then I laughed at the smirk plastered on her face. "What is that for? You're scaring me."

She scooted closer and pulled something out of her jacket pocket. The yellow paper had black words printed on it, words that I couldn't yet read.

She held it to her chest when I tried to sneak a peek. "There's this audition tomorrow, and I would like to invite you to attend."

My mouth went dry when her words sank in. "What? Really?"

She nodded then bit her lip before leaning in. "I can't say who this is for, Lex, but it's a big deal. It's also kind of last-minute, hence my approaching you tonight and not weeks ago."

I drew my brows together, curious. "Okay, well, when is it?"

"Tomorrow."

My heart leapt then slapped back on the floor. "Janelle, that's—"

"Don't turn this one down. It's perfect for you. I'm not making any promises or anything, I'm just saying, I've seen your work. I've seen how much you've grown in the past few months. I've seen how you shine when you take my fusion classes. You need to trust me on this one."

She was still holding the yellow slip of paper when I yanked it from her hands. She smiled, then I stared at the words written on it.

GRAVITY DANCE COMPLEX AUDITION
INVITE ONLY
CLIENT: Undisclosed
CONTRACT: 8 Months
TICKET: #24
ARRIVAL: 9AM
*Bring your own lunch

I looked up at her again, my chest a mess of flutters. *Eight months?*

Janelle was staring at me, clearly waiting for me to say something.

"When will they tell us who this is for?"

"The artist will come in once we've narrowed it down, just like Dominic's audition. That's typically the way it works since an artist's time is so limited."

I eyed her, hearing something I thought I didn't catch before. "Did you say once *we've* narrowed it down?"

She shifted a little, as if she didn't want to divulge more than she already had. "I've been asked to help judge." She held up her hands. "But that doesn't mean anyone is getting special treatment. You have to bust your ass, Lex. It's the artist who will have the final say. She's who you need to impress."

"She?" I grinned, and Janelle's eyes shone with amusement. "How many dancers were invited?"

"We're capping it at seventy-five. Twelve will be chosen, and out of those twelve, six are already guaranteed spots. I *still* think you have a shot." She watched my face as I thought over everything she was telling me. "Look, the choreographers here were asked to choose five to ten students they thought could handle this gig. You were the first dancer who popped into mind. That should mean something to you." She tapped the ticket in my hand and stood. "I'll just leave this here. Whether you decide to use it or not, it's yours."

She drifted out of the room, leaving me shocked and alone. I immediately reached for my phone to call Shane, but as soon as I glanced at the time, I knew he wouldn't be available.

Dominic's video shoot was only one week away, so Shane had left the apartment early in the morning for a costume fitting that was supposed to last all day. I only knew that because he'd left me a cute note in the fridge. It was taped to the carton of milk he knew I'd guzzle the second I woke up. The sentiment made me smile, but my heart was heavy knowing that the closeness, that familiarity we shared, would soon fade.

Ever since he'd gotten the music video job, I'd barely seen him. Rehearsals were all day, every day for the past three weeks, and his lunchtimes rarely fit my schedule. He was exhausted when he came home, and he frequently passed out during conversations. But he was happy. And as cliché as it was, his happiness made me happy.

I shot him a quick message, anyway. "I got an INVITE. Janelle wouldn't say who the artist was. Eight-month gig. I'm freaking out. Hold me."

He shot a text right back, making me smile.

"HELL YEAH, GIRL. Tell me more tonight. My arms are ready."

I fell asleep alone that night.

♥

The scent of bacon grilling on the stove woke me before Rihanna's "Umbrella" could sound from my alarm. My eyes flew open to find Shane dancing in the kitchen. Over his black briefs, he wore a ridiculous yellow apron with lace-edged frills. I laughed, drawing his attention. He grinned and proceeded to turn the music up as he danced even harder to one of my favorite songs by Winter, "Bring Me Flowers."

"That better be an apology breakfast," I warned as I lifted myself from bed and tossed on the closest shirt.

Shane gave me a pout before turning down the music and shuffling over. He wrapped me in his arms and buried his face in my neck. "It is. I'm sorry I wasn't here last night."

He'd already sent an apology text to tell me he got roped into a club event with Dominic and some of the dancers. Shane was at a point in his career when he needed to be immersed in the scene. I understood he needed that time to bond with his crew and Dominic. He'd even asked me to come, but with the audition in the morning, I hadn't wanted to risk the lack of sleep.

I smacked his ass and pushed him toward the kitchen. "Apology accepted. But burn my bacon and I take it all back."

He chuckled and turned to the stove. "You have time to hop in the shower. I'll get you fed and walk you to the studio. I have a meeting at Gravity this morning with Dominic and a few of the dancers." His head snapped to me. "Guess what?"

His eyes were so large, I knew it was going to be another opportunity. My heart couldn't help sinking for a split second before I realized how selfish I was being.

"Tell me all the things. After my shower."

My wake-up alarm was ringing when I stepped out of the bathroom, steam billowing after me. I pulled the towel snug around my naked body and walked straight to the closet Shane and I shared.

"Sexy boots, black leggings, black midriff, and wrap your plaid around your waist."

I looked over at Shane, who'd just shouted out what I should wear for the day. "Really?" I hadn't planned on wearing heels. "Janelle said this audition is perfect for me, which means sneakers might be better."

He seemed to ponder my words then nodded. "On second thought, black sneaks with red trim. Definitely the plaid." He cut me a look. "Hurry up. Breakfast's ready."

I shrugged and slid on my black leggings first, holding off on the shoes until I was ready to walk out the door. Out of my four black midriffs, I picked the one a little lower in the chest to show off my red sports bra. After brushing my hair and dabbing on a bit of makeup, I joined Shane for his apology breakfast.

I shoveled a huge forkful in my mouth. "So what's the exciting news?" Shane didn't seem to care I was mumbling past the food.

"Dominic's looking for a road crew for a club tour he's putting together since he's not planning a stage tour until next year. He wants to be more low-key, connect with his people, but still stay out there, so he thinks this is the perfect idea. We'll hang with him, perform a few songs, then move on to the next city. He's talking twenty-four US cities now, but it could grow. The clubs seem to be loving the idea."

"Wow, that's amazing. Dominic really likes you, too."

Shane threw me a look to tell me my comment was ridiculous. "Of course. Why wouldn't he?"

I laughed. If I had an ounce of Shane's confidence, I'd be set for life.

"Shit. We need to get you to the studio." Shane popped out of his chair. "Do something with your hair, and I'm going to pack you a bag for today. Trust me, you'll want some backups."

"Backups?" I called after him, but he was already on the move, packing my duffel full of extra leggings, shirts, and shoes. Then he went into the kitchen and added some snack bars and water.

"Aw, babe," I cooed when he met me at the door, my shoes and plaid fully intact. "You shouldn't have." I grinned, motioning to the bag he carried.

"This is the last of my apology. After this, we go back to even steven."

He locked the door behind him, and we started making our way down the hall. "All right, now tell me about this secret audition. Did Janelle give you any hints?"

I shook my head against the breeze that whipped strands of my hair into my face. I'd curled it a little, but I was certain it would straighten by the time we got to Gravity. "She's helping out with auditions. There are seventy-five dancers, and there are twelve spots, but six of those are already filled, unofficially." I made air quotes around unofficially, and he nodded.

"Janelle is the real deal. You're in good hands with her on your side."

I let out a deep breath. "I hope so. But whatever, right? It's just another audition. I'm either right for the part or not."

Shane wrapped his arm over my shoulders and kept me close. "No, girl.

This is the one. Don't ever be content with failing."

"But not getting selected isn't failing," I said, because it was what I'd been telling myself after every audition where I hadn't been chosen.

He laughed. "That's what losers tell themselves, Lex. Don't be a loser today."

Chapter 8

LEX

Shane walked me all the way into the studio and led me to my favorite spot in the center of the room.

I was used to open auditions—rooms packed to maximum capacity with barely any space to move. But after one scan of the room, noting all the serious faces, and bodies spaced out from each other, I knew this audition would be different. More intimate.

Every audition seemed to be set up in a similar fashion, and this one was no exception, with one or two folding tables placed near the mirrors at the front of the room and a microphone on a stand. Each judge was given a stack of papers and a manila folder that held our head shots and resumes.

The judges' tables were empty, yet I could still feel my heart pounding with the anticipation of finding out who I'd be dancing for today.

Shane turned to me, grabbed my face in his palms, and stared me dead in the eyes. "You're going to rock the shit out of this audition." Excitement was practically oozing out of him. "You're shaking," he noted with a gentle smile. "Stop. You've got this."

"How do you do it? How are you so calm and levelheaded about everything?"

"How are you so blind to your own talent? Damn it, Lex. You're the best dancer in this room, and it's time you started to realize it too. I won't be around to keep reminding you, so lock this conversation up in that brilliant brain of yours. You're going to tear this dance floor up. Take no prisoners. Leave their mouths agape—"

"Okay, I get it." I laughed and felt my heart swell at the same time. Leave it to Shane to put me in my place. It was why I'd kept him around all these years.

His expression remained serious, sobering me quickly. "Your only job is to give your all today, blood and glory, baby. Everything will play out as it should."

I breathed deeply, inhaling through my nose then releasing it through my mouth.

After my heart settled, my eyes locked on his—an endless sea of whiskey. And somewhere inside them lay my buoy, bobbing calmly in rough waters, where I could always cling if needed. I felt it. His words filling me. My confidence building.

And then something shifted in the room—an energy, a shuffle of sounds. I couldn't exactly pinpoint it, but whatever it was raised every hair on my body. Because somehow, I knew without having to look.

Shane's palms fell from my cheeks as my head turned and I spotted him, the dream crusher himself. Theo was walking the perimeter of the room toward the judges' tables. Meanwhile, all the confidence Shane had just worked up in me vanished in an instant.

I hadn't even danced yet, and I'd already completely failed the audition. I wanted to cry. I wanted to scream. I wanted to—

"What is it?" Shane asked, my discomfort on full display.

"I can't do this."

Shane looked genuinely rattled by my comment. "What the hell? You've got to be kidding me." Then he turned to follow the one my eyes were tracking. "No fucking way."

Theo had picked up the manila envelope and was pulling out the resumes. He hadn't even looked up. He started sorting through the pile, one by one, and reading quickly through them before flipping some over to see the head shots.

Then something else clicked in my brain and my heart squeezed.

"Shane." My voice shook. "Theo was listening to a bunch of Winter's new songs in the theater."

His face fell as if I'd just crushed all his dreams. Shane had been obsessed with Winter for years. Auditioning for her in any capacity was his dream too, more than anything Dominic could provide him.

"Are you sure?" Shane's eyes were glued to my lips, as if he couldn't believe the words coming out of them. He looked around the room and spotted something else. "You've got to be kidding me." He released me. "Janelle," he called.

Janelle had just walked into the room. Her eyes snapped to him, confused, and she made her way over. Her expression softened. "You can't be in here, babe."

I saw the devastation on Shane's face. "Nellie," he said, almost pleadingly. The nickname was new to my ears, but I knew they'd been close since the Dominic gig. "Why didn't I get an invite for this?"

Her face twisted into a genuine apology. "Oh, hon. I would have given you one, but you're on contract. You can't audition again until the video is over. And if you agree to the club tour, then you'll have to wait until that's over too. I'm so sorry, but that's the breaks of the business, I guess."

Shane groaned dramatically. "Shit."

Janelle reached for him, and I watched their hug with a small smile on my face. She patted his back after a few seconds. "Now you need to wish Lex good luck and get the hell out." She winked at me and backed away, pointing a finger at a still-pouty Shane. "We'll talk later. Get out of here."

He turned, a smile blooming on his face again, and wrapped me in a big hug that lifted me from the floor. "I'm going to ignore what you said when you saw Theo. If you leave this audition, I might actually murder you in your sleep tonight." He released me and backed away. "Remember what I said."

And he was gone. My heart grew heavy, and I faced front. As I did, my eyes locked on Theo's. He'd spotted me. And from the way he was squinting, his hazel eyes aflame, he didn't look pleased to see me. At all.

♥

Janelle did the intro speech, basically rattling off the things she'd told me yesterday, noting that the artist would be in later but adding the bit about Theo being the choreographer. Yeah, that piece of information would have been useful yesterday. *Why didn't I think to ask?* Not that she would have told me.

It was too late now. I was in my lucky spot, and I had Janelle on my side. I'd been studying Theo's dance style for six years. The odds were in my favor, and if I hung onto that thought, I might have even started believing it—if it weren't for Theodore "Angry" Noska glowering at me from the front of the room.

So I did the only thing I could think of. I tore my eyes away from him, focused on Janelle, and pushed away every ounce of insecurity. I needed to stop focusing on all the reasons I wouldn't succeed and start thinking about how well I was set up for success. Shane was right. There wasn't a single reason I shouldn't nail this audition.

When the room cheered after Theo's introduction and he jogged to the front of the room, I clapped too. I played the part. No one would have known that in one exchange Theo had tried to crush every single fantasy I'd ever had of him.

In that theater, he'd effectively kicked me when I was already down—a classless move. Still, I knew I'd become stronger for it, and he wasn't worth the nerves I'd once had in his presence. He was a brilliant choreographer, but that didn't mean I had to like him.

Just like that, my insecurities dissolved and I focused on Theo's intricate steps, completely losing myself in the zone.

If I'd thought Janelle's audition choreography was fast, I was sorely mistaken. Theo didn't spend much time repeating eight counts. And he didn't hold back with choreography either. Thanks to my superb Theo-video-stalking skills, I was well aware that he taught in sounds rather than music counts.

"Let's see it," he called as he turned around. He nodded to Janelle, who was controlling the stereo system from an app on her phone.

The music played, and I waited for him to see me. To judge me. But after the first two intro counts passed, his eyes had moved on to everyone except me. I shoved away my frustration, knowing we still had four eight counts to go. He would watch everyone at some point, I just had to be ready.

I nailed it. I hit every single odd count and offbeat of the four eight counts he'd taught us in less than an hour. His gaze never stopped on me. By the end of the routine, I wanted to scream.

Theo took a seat and turned to Janelle. She nodded in response to whatever he said and leaned into the mic. "Five-minute break, guys."

My water was sitting against the wall in the back of the room. When I reached it, a girl with long and sleek dark brown hair leaned down and grabbed her water too. We guzzled from our bottles in sync, and when we put them down, we faced each other and laughed at the awkwardness.

She stuck out her hand. "Hey, I'm Amie. I've seen you in some of my classes."

My mouth turned up at the sides. Someone actually recognized me, which was an improvement from just a few weeks ago. "I'm Lex," I said as I took her hand. "My friend Shane and I moved to town four months ago. We've been taking classes full-time." I laughed with a shake of my head and added, "Well, he got the Dominic gig, so he's been busy with that lately." And why was I still talking?

Her eyes shone. "That's incredible. And now you're here. I don't think I got my first invite until two years ago." She waved away her own comment with a swipe of her hand. "But I started when I was in elementary, so there wasn't much I could audition for, anyway."

"So you're a Lifer, then." I'd heard others use the term in reference to the dancers who had been there for years, ones everyone seemed to know.

She nodded, her eyes wide. "Oh yes. Stick around. You'll get there. I love Gravity. We really are a big family."

"That's the plan, hopefully—to stick around."

"Good." She leaned in and squeezed my arm. "Good luck today, by the way. I've watched you. You're really good."

"Thank you." Her words made me feel a little lighter in my chest. "Good luck to you."

We made our way to our spots on the floor. When I looked up, it was hard not to notice the conversation going on at the front of the room. Janelle and Theo were having an argument. Their expressions were heated as they took turns speaking, the exchange complete with tight jaws and finger pointing. I started to feel shifty in my skin, as if I were invading their privacy by watching them, when Janelle's eyes shot to me.

My heart sank. If her look alone didn't tell me that whatever they were arguing about had something to do with me, then the look that Theo threw my way absolutely did.

Chapter 9

THEO

"You are not letting Lex go this first round. Did you even watch her? She was the only one out of the entire group who nailed your choreography." Janelle let out an incredulous laugh, grinding on every one of my nerves. "Come on, Theo. This whole last-minute audition was bad enough, but you let her go and you're making the biggest mistake."

"This isn't your decision."

Shit. That was the wrong thing to say.

Janelle's eyes narrowed on me. "Fuck you, dude. I canceled my class for you. I handed you studio space that I'd reserved three months ago. I sought out dancers for you the day before your goddamn audition. I think you owe me just a little respect."

"Okay." I shrugged. "I'll give you *just* a little."

I knew Janelle wanted to scream. She probably would have punched me if she weren't surrounded by her peers and pupils. Why the hell was she fighting for this Lex chick, anyway? This was my call. My choreography. My production.

"What is your deal with her? You've been making snide comments since the start of this. She hadn't even danced yet and you shoved her picture in my face and told me to kick her out from the start. Why? What am I missing here?"

I let out a deep breath, knowing Janelle wasn't going to ease up. "She called me a jerk."

I didn't think I'd ever seen Janelle laugh so goddamn hard since I'd known her.

"News flash," she said through a fit of giggles. "You are the biggest jerk. And that's putting it nicely. So get over it, because everyone in this room who knows you would agree." She faced front, then it seemed she had an afterthought, because she turned back to me. "When would Lex have had the opportunity to say something like that, anyway? How do you know her?"

I crossed my arms and leaned back in my chair. "She was spying on me in the theater when I was choreographing Winter's set."

Janelle's eyes went wide. "What? Spying on you?"

Okay, so maybe that word was a little harsh. "I think it was an accident or something, but when I caught her, she called me a jerk."

Janelle shook her head. "Yeah, there's more to that story, clearly. Look, this is what we're going to do. I want to respect the fact that this is your gig. I really do. But you owe me. Have her line run it again and watch her. You can't let her go if you haven't even seen her perform."

She was right. I knew she was right, but something about Lex had crawled under my skin and festered for three weeks. I couldn't understand why, exactly. She wasn't the first chick to call me a jerk or some other nonflattering version of the word. In my mind, she was cut the moment I spotted her in the pile of head shots. And when I looked up and saw her staring back at me before auditions began today—in the arms of that same guy who had pushed her into me—she was definitely cut. So no, I didn't watch her perform. I refused to look at her. A little stubborn on my part, but I didn't want to waste my time since I knew she would be first to go.

I gritted my teeth. "Fine."

Janelle sighed. "Thank you." She leaned into the mic without wasting a second and asked the center row to come forward.

Lex knew we'd been talking about her. It was written all over her body. Nerves. Doubt. She was filled with it all. I couldn't wait to tell Janelle I'd told her so. I leaned in and got comfortable, and my eyes focused on Lex and only Lex. Just as I'd promised.

Her intro was shaky. I could tell Lex was rattled from the argument that was clearly focused on her. Hell, we'd looked right at her in the heat of it all. I felt a little bad about that. I was planning to cut her, not to let her know she was a problem, by any means.

Now that our cover was blown and Janelle had me by the balls, I watched Lex rid her nerves with each step.

Just before the first beat of choreography began, Lex shook her entire body, and with it went her nerves. I watched the transformation, transfixed by the look of calm confidence that washed over her, as if she'd been put under a spell. And so had I.

I was so used to showing choreography in a way that was comfortable for me. I wasn't a teacher. I'd never been able to *teach* someone how to glide and pop and click and lock or even follow the rhythmic score of a song the way I could. It was just the way I danced, thanks to years of learning alternate styles.

Those who'd worked with me knew to learn my choreography in small doses, to break down each step and study it. It was what I expected from the crowd today, but to fuck with them, to see who gave up the fastest, I gave it to them quickly, with every intention of going back and breaking it down until everyone was flowing in sync.

Lex not only hit every phantom beat but also performed the shit as if she'd done it a million times before. She had me literally gripping the edge of my seat and my heart beating as if I'd just run a 5K. *Where the hell did this girl come from?* The timid and awkward girl from the theater who practically cried when she called me a jerk couldn't have knocked me on my ass harder than the one dancing in front of me to Demi Lovato's "Confident."

Even her strut forward was hot as sin, with her sharp hits and strong isolations, giving away every detail of her curved and toned body. It was obvious she'd danced her entire life. Her precision, her timing, and not only that but the fact that she was able to let go so early in the day and perform the shit out of my routine. Yeah, my dick was so fucking hard.

WATCH: CONFIDENT
smarturl.it/Gravity_Confident

I shifted in my seat, commanding my body to control itself. Then she hit the last note, jutting her hip out and flicking her hand in the air, her eyes purposely set on me. On her pivot, she waited till the very last second to snap her head to the back of the room as she walked off, swinging her hips until she hit the back wall.

The room went nuts with applause. Looking around at the other dancers, I could clearly see who everyone's eyes were on. I sat back in my chair, refusing to meet Janelle's eyes. I could feel the hole she was burning into the side of my head.

"Ready to hear me say I told you so?" Janelle's sarcastic challenge came with a knowing smile.

Fuck. This is going to hurt. "Day's not over yet."

Chapter 10

LEX

S aved by the skin of my teeth. My name wasn't called in the first cut of the day or the second. When they'd dwindled the group down to the top twenty-five, I was still in. Though other than when our line was called out to perform, Theo hadn't looked at me again.

I hated that it bothered me. That I wanted Theo's eyes on me. To take me in. Hell, to critique me as he'd done with a few others. I wanted that attention so badly it shook me to the core.

We'd just gotten back from one of our longer breaks when Winter trailed through the door behind us. She looked every bit as amazing as she did on screen, with her long white hair pulled back into a high ponytail and her makeup drawing attention to her ridiculously long eyelashes and pouty red lips. She wore tight light-wash jeans, ankle-high heeled boots, and a see-through white button-down top that revealed a red lace bra.

Loud cheers and applause burst from the lot of us. My heart must have performed an entire gymnastics floor show by the time she made it to the front of the room. She stood in the center, waving, smiling, and laughing at our reaction until, finally, Janelle handed her a microphone.

"This is the best reception ever. Thank you all so much." She beamed at the next round of cheers in reaction to her welcome. "I just want to say congratulations for making it this far, and I cannot wait to see you all in action." Her eyes shot to the front of the room. "Theo's been treating you well, I hope."

A mixture of laughter, hoots, and claps erupted from our group. I hardly believed the other dancers thought Theo had treated us well, but it was the right reaction under the circumstances.

Winter squealed. "Great. Let's get started."

Amie and I made shocked faces at each other from across the room. We'd been chatting it up on our breaks, and I hadn't had the balls to admit who I thought the artist might be, because then I would have had to explain why I thought that, and I definitely wasn't going to confess to my run-in with Theo weeks ago. Shane was the only one who knew that embarrassing story, and it would remain that way. For life.

"All right, all right." Janelle spoke into the table mic, but my eyes were on Winter, who took a seat beside Theo.

I watched her lean in and hug him, a flirtatious smile on her face, and my stomach lurched. There was something too familiar about their embrace. It was public knowledge that they'd worked with each other before. But when she leaned into his shoulder and reached under the table to touch his leg, I knew something was off.

"Now that the guest of honor has arrived," Janelle continued, "and you all have the gist of the routine, we're going to switch up the music to something a little more"—she wiggled her eyebrows at Winter then turned to the rest of us and deepened her voice—"appropriate."

The entire room lit up with shocked gasps and excited chatter. But before Janelle hit Play on her phone, I knew what song she was going for—the same one Theo had on repeat in the theater when he finally began to let go. The same one he was dancing to when my ringing phone turned his attention to the voyeur in the audience and he proceeded to kick me out. I flushed just thinking of it.

As if he could read my mind, Theo's eyes dashed to mine, freezing me in my spot. Everything about him was so hard. His narrowed eyes, his jaw set like stone. But those lips—full, tinted pink against his lightly tanned skin—released a new feeling in me, one that didn't belong on the dance floor.

I shifted my gaze to Winter, but that wasn't any better. She was staring at Theo adoringly, clearly waiting for him to return the glance. I swallowed and looked away, this time to face Janelle, who was smiling through a familiar tune. Everyone around me was marking the steps, so I did too. We were instructed to perform the routine a few times as we rotated lines, giving everyone a chance to be up front for Winter to see.

She wasn't ready to make cuts until we started to perform in small groups. As I watched other dancers go before me, I paid attention to Winter's responses, her expressions, and those moments when she jotted something down. She was easy to read. When she liked something, she'd raise her brow, give a little nod, and take her pen to paper. I figured if I got that same reaction from her, I'd be set.

It was my turn, along with two male dancers I hadn't had a chance to talk to. Thank God my nerves weren't what they used to be when I was younger. Back then, they'd get so bad I'd feel as if I were sinking in quicksand.

I learned at a young age how to harness that anxiety and turn it into something powerful. Well, Shane had taught me that.

It was my first performance ever, and I was eight. In a theater of two thousand bodies, including peers and family, the lights were turned down, and the music was off. We were seconds from the start of our number, and I couldn't for the life of me remember the first step. I totally froze.

"How does it start?" I had whispered to Shane, who was standing beside me.

He shook his head as he always did when I said something ridiculous. "Focus on the music. Your body already knows what to do."

I would never forget that moment when the music started. It had to have been only a second before the stage lights switched on and the first beat of music pumped through the system. I didn't have to think of that first move, because my body already knew it. Shane was right. The dance flowed from me like magic. As if it had come straight from my soul.

That was the day I learned an important lesson I would always carry with me. *Choreography is 100 percent of the battle. The rest comes naturally.*

I didn't know how many times over the next half hour I performed in large groups, small groups, then finally a solo before Janelle made an announcement that they were getting ready to choose the final twelve.

While the judges deliberated, I met Amie in the hall, and we crouched against the wall. We pulled out our snack bags and chatted about what brought us to LA. Turned out Amie's parents were part of the Hollywood scene, though she wouldn't give up in what capacity. And she'd lived in Malibu most of her life, so driving to Gravity to take class was a short trip for her.

"You made a new friend, Amie. How cute." A guy sat down in front of us, leaning back on his palms, knees up. His eyes caught mine. "What's your name?"

Before I could respond, Amie jumped in. "Her name is Lex, and she's off limits to you." Amie's eyes twinkled when she looked at me. "This is Reggie. I'd say he's harmless, but I don't lie to my friends."

Reggie reached his foot out and nudged her leg. "Not nice. Not nice at all."

I smiled and flipped the cap open on my water. "I didn't realize Amie was the possessive type when we first started talking. I might need to reevaluate this friendship."

She gasped in mock horror as another figure approached. "Hi," the woman said. "We're asking the remaining dancers to fill this out. It's a commitment application, saying that if you're selected today, you accept the job based on the terms mentioned here. If you have an agent, please put down their name and phone number. We'll be contacting them shortly. It's the same salary for everyone, so feel free to discuss whatever you'd like among yourselves."

Agent? Am I supposed to have one of those?

"Wait, no tiered pay for veterans?" Reggie asked, looking slightly perturbed.

The woman frowned and shook her head. "I'm afraid not. It's an equal share. Everyone auditioned under those terms." Reggie opened his mouth as if to respond, but she continued talking to the group. "I've been asked to remind you that you're about to enter the final callback. We request that you're fully on board prior to returning to the studio. Please read over the terms carefully and hand the application to Polly on your way in if you choose to stay."

Polly was one of the assistants for the day and tended to the judges.

The woman whose name I'd never learned walked away, leaving the three of us to peruse our commitment applications. I was still stuck on the agent thing, so I tapped a quick message to Shane before flipping through a few pages of the document. I realized quickly it was like a contract. It was eight pages, with brief summaries of the terms we'd be committing to if we were selected to join the crew.

"Shouldn't they give us more time to review something like this?" I wanted to know what I was getting myself into. They still hadn't given us many details of what we were agreeing to other than the fact it was for Winter and that it was an eight-month contract.

Does it matter? I asked myself. For an opportunity like that, there wasn't much I would have said no to.

"Don't worry about it." Reggie took his pen to paper. "The pay is shit, but the food and housing are free, so if you're smart, you can walk away with a good savings in the end."

"I wasn't talking about the pay." I pointed at a line of text. "Like this, it says we're on a strict schedule, including curfews. And all my social media posts need to be approved? They stalk our social media?"

Amie chuckled and shrugged. "Reg and I are used to this, I guess. Yeah, they don't want you posting anything Winter wouldn't want out there in the public eye. You can take whatever pictures you want, but you need approval to post it if it involves anything to do with the show."

Reggie looked up as he placed the cap on the pen. "And the curfew isn't a big deal, honestly. It's only enforced on the eve of the shows. You'll be so tired most nights, you won't want to go out much, anyway."

My eyes traveled down to the next paragraph, section four. My pulse picked up at the words. "Really? No fraternizing with the choreographer?" I cocked an amused brow at both of them. "Who would want to fraternize with Theo, anyway? He's kind of an asshole."

Amie burst into laughter, and Reggie grinned wide. "You're going to fit in here just fine." He winked, and even though he was agreeing with me, something about it felt off.

Back in the studio, I looked around at the expectant faces, their eyes wide and hopeful. I'd always loved the energy in a dance studio. The buzz of the overhead fluorescents. The wall-to-wall mirrors where introverts came out of hiding. And while the competition was fiercer than I'd ever experienced, there was also an unspoken level of synchronicity, because we weren't just being judged on our individual performances but on our chemistry as a group.

"Welcome back, welcome back." We all joined in a collective cheer as Janelle spoke into the mic. "Before we get started on the final selection, we do need to see a few of you one last time. When I call your name, please come to the front of the room." The room grew silent. "Alexandra 'Lex' Quinn."

My heart leapt before I did. I didn't know if this was good or bad. It could go either way. Every emotion in me was wound up tight, ready to unleash at the start of the number. I'd never sensed such a fire in me before.

As I waited for the other dancers to join me, I looked up. Theo and Winter's heads were bent together. It seemed as if they were in deep discussion when he shook his head and leaned back in his seat, as if he'd given up on whatever war was brewing between them. I remembered then what Janelle had told me. It was the artist who had the final say.

Winter was the one I needed to impress.

That was all it took for the fire I'd sensed before to turn into a full-blown blaze.

Chapter 11

THEO

"I want her." Winter slid a head shot forward, and when I saw the face, my gut stirred.

ALEXANDRA "LEX" QUINN

Gender: Female
Age: 22
Height: 5'5"
Measurements: 34-24-36
Hometown: Seattle, Washington
Ethnicity: Irish American

Over the past six hours, I had become well attuned to all things Alexandra Quinn. I learned that she'd been taking classes at one of the better dance schools in the Seattle area since she was eight. She moved to LA a few months ago to pursue her dream of becoming a professional dancer. She picked up my choreography faster than anyone else in the room. And her dance preference, like mine, was hip-hop-contemporary fusion. And the kicker: she had zero professional experience.

I didn't care that she was the best one on the dance floor. She wasn't getting the job.

"Winter," I said, forcing out a gentle tone. "She's too green. No experience to prove that she can handle this kind of pressure. I don't feel comfortable taking her on." *That isn't entirely true.*

Janelle snorted. "Right. Since when does Theodore Noska not feel comfortable with anything? You're the cockiest son of a bitch I know."

Winter giggled, and I glared at Janelle. *Really? What the fuck is her problem?* Janelle had always been one of the better friends I'd made at Gravity, but today she was a giant pain in my ass. This Lex girl was spinning her all out of shape. And me too, apparently.

"Well, I like her. We're keeping her." Winter was set on her decision during the break, but I continued to argue my point as the dancers returned.

"Let's take another look," I suggested to Winter only. I pulled my head in close, slipping her a half smile. "Put up Lex with Leigh and Madeline. Compare them and make sure you're making the right choice."

Winter's chocolate brown eyes held mine. She was clearly beautiful, in a porcelain doll sort of way that had always drawn me in. I wished I could say it did something for me now. Perhaps Winter was exactly what I needed, but I felt nothing.

"Okay," she agreed, succumbing under my gaze. Like Janelle, she wanted to respect my position, even if she didn't agree. "Bring the dancers up."

Janelle had been listening to the exchange and sighed deeply before calling out their names. "All right, here we go. Full out, please."

I hated that my eyes were drawn to Lex. To her powerful moves, perfect technique, and sexy curves that made those inner stirrings I wished I felt for Winter come to life for Lex. Since watching her for the first time earlier today, I couldn't tear my eyes away.

I hated that she was good—more than good—and I would soon be forced to admit it. Because there was no way she wouldn't be selected. And I could feel it, the ultimate test of my willpower on the horizon. My self-imposed rules were simple: *Don't fuck a backup dancer.* Never had. Never would. But I'd soon be working with Lex every day for the next eight months—and it was a punishment that, deep down, I knew I wanted.

Winter had the pleasure of announcing the dancers who'd made it through. Lex's name was last. She was apparently so shocked that her jaw dropped, and her eyes immediately teared. Amie was the first to wrap her in a hug, effectively releasing a dam of emotion. Lex was practically sobbing, and I still couldn't tear my eyes away from her.

Janelle went to her next, surely whispering something supportive in her ear, then left her with a kiss on the cheek. I swallowed, my throat tight and chest hot. There was a time I'd felt that type of elation. When it was truly a surprise to land a job and my mind swirled with all the opportunities to come.

What happened to that *guy?*

I was still watching Lex when another figure approached her. My jaw locked, and whatever fondness I'd begun to feel over the newbie was quickly replaced by my annoyance over another man. Reggie pulled Lex into his arms, and I'd never wanted to punch him as much as I did at that moment. I didn't trust the guy, and I certainly didn't trust him with Lex, knowing how he felt about "fresh meat."

Janelle waved and got my attention. "Get over here," she mouthed.

I looked around. Winter was on the dance floor too, congratulating dancers and giving condolences to the ones who hadn't made it. I was the only judge still sitting.

After lifting myself from my chair, I moved around the room. I did my part, shaking hands, patting backs, saying the right things, until Lex was the only dancer left to congratulate.

She was wiping a tear and laughing at something Amie had said when I approached her from behind. "Hey," I said, coolly.

She swiveled quickly and faced me, her eyes lighting up as if in shock. "Hey."

Amie moved on to another conversation, leaving us alone.

"Congratulations. You worked hard out there." I could have told her what I really thought—that she was the best in the room and had shocked the hell out of me. But a part of me was still resentful she was there in the first place.

"Thanks," she said.

Her mouth opened then closed again, and I could tell she was struggling to say whatever was on her mind. I should have taken that moment to walk away, but my feet were rooted to the floor.

"Hey, I'm really sorry about that day in the theater. I never should have called you a jerk." She shifted and faced me completely. "If it's any consolation, it's kind of a dream of mine to work with you. I've been studying your choreography for years." Her blush was so deep, so red, all I could think about was achieving that same color by burying myself inside her.

I was a pig. I knew it.

"Don't worry about it."

Her shoulders seemed to relax.

Janelle clapped her hands, and Lex turned her body away from me. "All right, dancers. We're going to ask those of you who made it today to please stay for a few announcements. Everyone else, thank you so much for your hard work. Your efforts did not go unnoticed."

I was fully aware of how close Lex was to me, and it wasn't hard to appreciate what I saw. From this angle, I had an amazing view of her sunkissed skin and the deep crease of her spine that dipped into her tight waist. I could see how well her black leggings hugged her firm ass and soft hips and the way her sweat shone off her, as if she were a fucking diamond in the sun.

I'd always valued how dancers' bodies came in all shapes and sizes, but I'd never considered myself to have a favorite until that moment.

Lex flipped her hair, and a fruity scent caught my nose. It reminded me of the peach cobbler Granny Pearla used to cook up at the rec center every Saturday morning. I inhaled deeply and shut my eyes, taking in more of the few positive memories I had of growing up. The fact that Lex brought those memories to mind confused and intrigued me all at once.

When I opened my lids, my eyes fell on her bare neck. I couldn't help running my gaze up the length before stopping at her ear. I imagined my tongue journeying the same path next, and—

Fuck. I had to get away from her, but first, I needed to get closer.

I stepped forward, placed my hand on her hip, and leaned in. "I'll see you tomorrow, Lex." My words whispered against her ear, and I watched in amusement as her skin leapt to life. After another inhale, I moved away to join Janelle and Winter at the front of the room.

"You all ready to find out what you've signed up for?" Winter called out, earning a round of laughter and cheers. "Starting tomorrow, you will be rehearsing for a six-month concert series." She glanced around, suspending the news to play off their excitement. "In Vegas," she squealed.

Gasps, then more cheers, shot around the room.

"In addition to your salary, the show will pay for your board, food, dry cleaning, and you'll get a little something extra each week as a spending allowance." She glowed at the crew's positive response then turned to me. "Theo, do you want to talk about rehearsals?"

I took the mic from her, wondering why we needed the damn thing in a room filled with fewer than twenty people. Instead of questioning her, I decided to be a team player.

"Everyone needs to be here tomorrow at nine a.m. In this room. Expect a similar schedule as today. Small breaks throughout the day with a bigger break for lunch. You'll get two days off a week, determined by the studio schedule. And since Gravity is booked solid for months, they're doing their best to work with the instructors to get us the space we need. Some days we'll be in here, other days we'll be in the smaller studios. You'll get the schedule tomorrow."

"And pay starts tomorrow, as well," Winter cut in, her smile bright.

Again, everyone roared happily.

"You'll have six weeks to learn the choreography," I continued. "And two weeks to rehearse on the stage in Vegas. Don't let that time frame fool you. There's a lot of choreography. You'll be performing four days a week, so take care of yourselves and prepare for nonstop work."

"And fun!" Winter shouted out to soften my serious tone, I was sure.

I nodded. "Yeah, that too." Laughter filled the room, and I handed the mic back to Winter, giving her and Janelle a one-armed hug. "Now," I said to the crew with a slight wave of my hand. "If you'll excuse me, I have some work to do tonight. Congratulations." I slung my jacket over my shoulder and headed for the exit.

"Give it up for Theodore Noska, everyone, your choreographer for the 'Love in the Dark' Vegas concert series."

I didn't stop for the applause. I didn't even look back. Because what they didn't know would have shocked them all.

If I didn't get back to work, there wouldn't *be* a Vegas concert series.

Chapter 12

LEX

Diva Dive was a club in downtown LA that wasn't a dive at all. Reggie had invited all of us out to celebrate after auditions, and by the time I'd arrived, he'd scored us a table with bottle service. Shane came along too and brought some dance buddies. And there we were. Our first outing together in weeks.

"We both have jobs," I squealed in his arms.

He squeezed me tight before spinning me around and placing me down. "I am so proud of you, Lex. You must have lost your shit when they announced."

"She totally lost her shit," Amie confirmed with a laugh. She stuck her hand out and shook Shane's. "Hi. I'm Amie."

Shane grinned. "Amie. You took care of my Lex today, and for that, I am eternally grateful." He gave her a little bow, making her chuckle.

"You should have seen her. You would have been so proud."

Shane's arm wrapped around my shoulders. "Already am."

We slid into a section of banquettes at the table where Reggie had migrated. He'd already poured us a round of shots and started to hand them out. I refused mine while Shane and Amie took theirs.

"Where are your friends?" I asked Shane. I hadn't met any of his dance crew yet, and I was curious.

"I'll bring them over later," he said with a wave of his hand. "I want to hear more about your audition."

Amie threw herself on the couch next to me. "Theo's choreography was insane." She did a little couch-dance version of the routine that had the table howling while Shane practically salivated in his seat. I had to do a double take of Amie to see if she was already drunk but quickly realized it was just her personality—loud and proud. Like Shane. *No wonder I gravitated toward her today.*

"Oh. My. God." Shane was shaking his head and waving his hand over his face while he watched Amie's version of Theo's choreography. "I would swallow that man whole if he'd have me."

I giggled and nudged his side. "Don't get your hopes up. You'd be fired for even speaking about him under the contract we had to sign today."

Shane's eyes grew wide. "Say what? Tell me more."

Reggie slammed his shot glass down and pulled another one to his lips. "Trust me, guys, Theo is not someone you want to fuck around with, anyway."

Amie ignored him and leaned over my lap to fill Shane in. "There's a no-fraternization policy."

"But it would be so worth it," Shane groaned.

"She's serious," I added. "Backup Dancer shall not initiate, engage in, speak of, or entertain romantic relationship with hired Choreographer. In turn,

Choreographer shall not initiate, engage in, speak of, or entertain romantic relationship with contracted Backup Dancer." I recited the terms as well as I could remember them, but I knew there was more to it.

"Paying a little too much attention to Section Four of the rule book, aren't you, Lex?" Reggie narrowed his eyes at me.

Amie snorted. "Says the guy who knew which section of the rule book it was."

Shane and I laughed with her. Reggie remained stoic on his corner of the couch. "Doesn't matter, anyway. Theo has a rule about fucking around with anyone who works with him. Especially backup dancers. He won't cross that line. He cares too much about his job and reputation. But the artist, however"—Reggie threw up his hands—"that's fair game."

Amie's jaw dropped. "You're saying Winter and Theo?"

Reggie nodded, and something twisted uncomfortably in my gut. "Yup. How do you think he got the gig?"

Shane and I exchanged glances. I was sure we were thinking the same thing, only he was bold enough to spit it out. "Because he's one of the best choreographers *in the world*. He's choreographed for her before. It's not like the guy came out of the woodwork."

Reggie shrugged, looking unconvinced. "All I'm saying is there's something between them."

"Well"—Amie looked around at us—"I guess they'd be cute together. Right?"

"The cutest," Shane answered dryly.

I didn't say a word.

Chapter 13

THEO

I pulled into my garage around midnight after a full evening of choreography following the auditions. I was fucking exhausted. I'd been at it for three weeks, and the show still wasn't coming together at the speed I'd hoped it would. No way could I admit that to Winter. Up until tonight, I couldn't even admit that to myself.

Winter's set was twenty-four songs long plus a half dozen instrumentals, and all of that needed my attention. I'd created maybe a third of the show, and tomorrow, I would start unloading choreography to Winter's backup crew and Winter simultaneously. Somehow.

I still hadn't figured out how I was going to pull off any of the featured solo and partner routines since I was out an assistant. Janelle wouldn't be available, and I sure as hell wouldn't be asking Reggie to fill in. Except … he was beginning to look like the best choice.

To make everything worse, it was late, and I hadn't eaten a thing all day besides a bag of peanuts and a store-bought salad. I pulled out a few leftovers from the fridge. Chinese, Italian, Mexican. I warmed them all up and ate them in one sitting.

I should have been tired. I should have been asleep when the doorbell rang at one in the morning. And when I looked through the peephole and spied Winter standing there, a knee-length white trench coat pulled tightly around her, I knew I shouldn't answer the door. *Not now*, my inner thoughts groaned.

I propped the door open, catching her as she swayed a little on her heels while her high ponytail swirled and slapped her in the face. She giggled.

"Are you drunk?" It was a stupid question. It would have been a miracle for her to have shown up sober.

"Hey, Theo," she purred, or maybe slurred.

I kept myself wedged in the doorway.

"Can I come in?"

I held her stare with one of my own, mentally calculating how to approach the situation. This was already bad. The car that had brought her here was waiting in the driveway, and I had a feeling it would stay there until she decided to leave, whenever she thought that might be.

"Why are you here?"

A manicured hand reached for the tie at her waist. "I can tell you or I can show you." She slipped off one heel and chucked it down the concrete steps. Her next heel followed, then she turned to me with another drunken smile.

"Maybe you should tell me first."

"You want words?" She exaggerated a pout. "Okay. You seemed tense at the audition today. I don't want you to be tense working my show. So"—she popped a smile and dropped a finger down the opening of her jacket—"I brought you something to help."

I felt the familiar growl low in my belly, my groin tightening and threatening to spring to life if she made good on her threats. As much as I wanted her to leave, my body wanted the opposite.

"Whatever you brought me, I can't accept. Not right now. I have too much work to do, and it's late. And you're drunk."

"Don't you want me?" She pouted again, slipping her fingers over each button from the top down and popping her jacket open to reveal her expensive red undergarments.

Fuck. My cock pushed against my sweats, disobeying my desperate internal objections. Did I have the willpower to stop this? Sure. But did I want to?

She pushed her jacket completely open then slid it down her shoulders until it was a crumpled pile at her feet. I looked over her shoulder again. The driver's eyes glanced away. I sighed and pulled her into my house before slamming the door behind her to keep her out of view.

I'll grab her some clothes and send her home. This can't be the way rehearsals begin.

Winter didn't have the same thoughts. She pressed into me, her hands cupping my cock and squeezing.

Fuck me. A release would be nice. I didn't even want to think about how long it'd been since I'd properly fucked a woman. I refused to think of the last time. The memory was too painful. Yet here one was—the queen of them all—offering herself to me on a silver platter.

I knew that getting this job would put me in close proximity to Winter, closer than I'd ever been. I worried about it. About the expectations that came with the job. But not enough for me to turn down the biggest opportunity of my life.

I didn't have time for expectations in the romantic sense. And I certainly didn't want to give Winter the wrong idea. Nothing against Winter. Those were my rules. No cuddle sessions, no daily repeats. No cravings for deeper connections. And definitely no public appearances.

But then again…there was something amazing about letting a powerful woman sit on my cock and watching her fall apart on top of me, but that was where the intimacy ended.

Her lips met my collar as her hand moved beneath my shirt, scratching my abs with her nails. "Ah," I hissed, pushing her hand down and out of my shirt. "Winter. We can't do this."

She pressed against me again, dipping her free hand into my pants and boxer briefs, stroking me before I could protest again. I groaned and thought about moving her. I thought long and hard about how I should send her back to the car and tell her driver to take her home. And I thought about how pissed she'd be at me in the morning.

But when she sank to her knees and put her wet mouth around my cock, I decided that turning her away would just be rude.

Part Two

REHEARSALS

Chapter 14

LEX

Theo was an asshole. A tyrant. A relentless perfectionist. A far leap from the man who'd captivated me from behind the computer and television screen for so many years. He didn't even smile. What kind of person living the career of his dreams wouldn't even crack a smile?

We'd been in choreography for three weeks, from eight in the morning until eight at night, with just enough breaks to grab quick snacks and water and take bathroom breaks. That was it. We were learning one dance every two days, which would have been fine if Theo were happy with anything.

He wasn't. Every other hour, he asked us to change a direction or a step without letting us in on any of the reasons why. I wasn't the only one in the class who was frustrated. Rumors about Theo percolated in the halls and lunch spaces. Comments about him "losing his goddamn mind" were not surprising to hear.

Theo was looking at his phone in the front of the room when he shouted. "Lex! Can I borrow you?"

Borrow me? I approached him, a little put off. And a little nervous that he would call me out at this stage in rehearsals. Had I been doing that badly? If anything, I'd been picking up choreography faster than anyone else. And he hadn't picked on me one bit as I'd expected. He looked up with his crinkled forehead and tired eyes, the spark that I'd thought lived in him completely gone. This couldn't be the Theodore Noska I had adored from afar. This man was miserable.

"Lead them from the top, okay?" He stood to face me. "Winter's in the other studio waiting for me. She's behind on choreography. I'm not ready to bring her in yet." He glanced at me again, our eyes connecting. And what I saw scared me. Exhaustion, unhappiness, emptiness.

So I did as he said, surprised by the level of responsibility he'd just given me. Leading the class while Theo tended to his girlfriend in the other studio? Would that become a regular thing?

But the optimist in me shouted, *He can't possibly be in both places at once. And I do pick up the choreography faster than anyone else.* As sick to the stomach as it all made me, I felt a little honored too.

"Sure thing," I told him.

He walked forward and addressed the class. "Lex is in charge for the next four hours. If I hear a peep of disrespect, you'll answer to me."

He left without another look back, leaving me red-faced and creating an ache in my gut that I didn't understand. But as soon as the door shut behind him, I stepped to the front of the room and started marking the moves to "Rip My Heart Out," without music. I broke it down, step by step, until it seemed as if everyone had an entire eight count down, then we'd combine what we'd done with music to get them comfortable with the pacing.

It all seemed to be working out well, but my anxiety level rose when I turned around to watch the crew and mentally critiqued them.

Should I give them feedback?

Theo expected more from everyone at all times, but he wasn't around to demand it. And I wasn't their choreographer. The responsibility of perfection shouldn't be on me. They were learning from me because that was what Theo had directed, but I could already feel a wedge between me and the other dancers, the jealousy floating through the air.

When the clock hit five that afternoon, no one waited for Theo to come back into the room to run the routine again. Most of them left as soon as the time changed, while I found a place on the floor to lie. Amie joined me. "Girl," she started. "I am more than ready for our two days off this week."

"Ha," I blurted out with a smile. "Me too."

"I don't know why he asked you to lead like that. Are you okay with it?" Amie asked sympathetically. She must have noticed the tension among the other dancers too.

I shrugged. "I don't know. It's fine, I guess. It's not what I expected."

She chuckled. "Not the glamorous life of a backup dancer you'd always dreamed of?"

I grinned and turned my head to look at her. "Not that. I've just looked up to Theo for a long time, since before coming to LA. I wanted to take a class from him, not fill in for him when he disappears with Winter. It's a little weird."

A strange silence filled the air and made me want to crawl right back into the turtle shell I'd popped out of.

"Then don't do it," boomed an approaching voice.

How I felt his presence before I knew he was there was a complete mystery.

My entire body cringed.

Amie's eyes went wide. She mouthed "Oh shit" and pulled herself to standing. "Hey, Theo," she called out with a wave. "Bye, Theo." And she ran out the door like the worst friend in the world, leaving me with a look of horror on the way out.

I moaned and pulled myself to a sitting position to face him. "It's not what you heard."

He stood above me, hands on his hips, his naturally stoic look intensifying. "So, it's not weird when I ask you to take over rehearsals when I disappear with Winter?"

An awkward smile spread across my face. "It's a little weird. But I'm not complaining. I'm happy to help."

"Good," he responded dryly. "You should be."

I stood up, heat snaking its way through me at his totally insulting reaction to how I'd helped him. "Excuse me?"

He shook his head and began to back away. "Lex, I'm fucking tired, and I'm not going to do this with you. I won't ask you to lead again. End of conversation."

I followed him as he walked toward the mirrors, where his belongings were. "I said I would."

"Yeah, well, you made it clear how you felt about it." He snatched up his leather jacket and started to slip it over his arms, his face toward the mirror. "And to think you almost didn't even make the crew. You should be a little more grateful." He muttered it almost as though I wasn't in the room with him.

I'd never been so fired up. Not even on the day I called Theo a jerk. He turned around as he was shoving his keys in his pocket and began thumbing through his phone. I stepped closer, forcing him to look at me.

"You think you did me a favor by putting me on this crew? You think it's a secret you didn't want me here? That it took Janelle and Winter to convince you? Wrong. But you know what I find pretty amusing about all of that?" I narrowed my eyes, jamming my toes against his and forcing his eyes to mine. "You need me. You needed me today, and you'll need me tomorrow. You'll never admit it, but I see right through you."

I pushed off his chest and pivoted, beelining for the door and sweeping up my bag from the floor.

"Lex," he called out.

I shouldn't have stopped, but something in his tone, something raw and vulnerable and new, gutted me on the spot. He was desperate. For what, I didn't know, but I couldn't leave before finding out. I turned around again.

"I do need you."

Just like that, the fire that raged inside dissipated into a fog of hope. My heart started to thump harder, and my mouth went dry. He stayed on his side of the room and I stayed on mine, but my staying was enough. He'd extended a hand, and I took it. Now what?

"What's going on?" My tone was softer, to match his, but still shaky with nerves. "I know I'm new to this and all, but I get the feeling this rehearsal schedule isn't normal."

He swept both hands through his unkempt hair, messing it up even more. "What's your definition of normal?"

"Theo," I warned. I wouldn't accept his vague answer this time. I deserved to know the truth.

He pulled his hair again and gritted his teeth before throwing his arms in the air. "It's ... unusual, yeah. I'm behind on choreography, okay? It's my fault. I lost my assistant before I came back to LA, and she was supposed to have set all this shit up. But she—" He shook his head. "She did none of it."

"Why not?"

His eyes shot to mine. "That's none of your business," he snapped.

Discomfort rattled my chest, and I folded my arms, as if that could fix my insides. Nothing could, not when Theo talked to me like that. I wished it didn't get to me. I wished I didn't care. But I did.

"Anyway, the point is I'm behind. Winter's behind. The dancers are behind. And the stress, which usually doesn't bother me, is fucking killing me right about now. I haven't slept in weeks. So yeah. None of this is normal. I'm just trying to manage the best way I know how."

"I can help." The words were out before I could comprehend my thoughts. *What am I offering, exactly?*

He laughed, digging into the wound he'd already created in my chest. "You pick up the choreography faster than anyone. I trust you to help the group. You have been helping me, Lex."

I swallowed, not wanting to elaborate on my offer. I wasn't talking about leading the group. I was talking about the choreography, but it was clear he wasn't ready to accept that kind of assistance.

"Okay." I nodded. "Then I'll keep helping."

"Okay." He didn't argue about it again. A deadness rang through the air. A finality to his agreement. It was all he was going to give me.

And with that, I stepped into the hallway and took my first deep breath of the day. As I walked through the halls of Gravity and passed the community center, I thought about how much I was looking forward to the next two days off. Though with Shane out of town, I had no clue what I was going to do with myself.

"Hey, Lex." Amie's voice surprised me. I looked over at a cluster of couches, where most of the crew was congregating.

"Hey, thanks for all your help in there," I chided, following it up immediately with a smile, because I wasn't all that upset she took off and left Theo and me alone. "I didn't realize anyone was still here." I looked around at the group. Some acknowledged me, but others shifted their gazes.

Reggie stood from his seat and walked over. I wondered whether it was his attempt to bring me into the group and help me fit in. I couldn't be sure, but I appreciated how he and Amie always let me know I was one of them.

"We wanted to make sure you knew we were heading for dinner." He gestured at the dancers behind him. "Nothing fancy. There's this hole-in-the-wall bar down the street. Thought we'd grab a bite, maybe a drink, and unwind a little. It's been a rough couple of weeks. Today especially, yeah?" His arm wrapped around mine sympathetically.

I shot a look at Amie, and she gave me an amused shrug.

For so many reasons, I couldn't say no. "That sounds great."

♥

The chatter on the way to the bar was lively and carefree, the complete opposite of the energy in the studio with Theo. Was he that intense all the time? That had to be exhausting.

Amie slid in beside me in the booth. Reggie and another dancer, Wayne, sat across from us. The rest of the dancers grabbed a nearby high-top table and dragged it over so we could all be within earshot of each other.

"How's your buddy doing? Shane, was it?" Wayne asked.

I cheered up at the sound of my best friend's name. "He got offered another gig with Dominic. They're doing a club tour around the US. Sounds pretty cool. He left last night."

Reggie looked genuinely impressed. "That does sound cool. Shane's hooked himself up with the right crowd, that's for sure. Dominic takes care of his people. I imagine your friend's happy."

I shrugged. "He is. He was bummed he wasn't able to audition for Winter's show, but I think he got over it quickly."

Laughter filled the table, and my guess was they all agreed Shane was better off elsewhere, away from the torturous schedule and demands of Theo.

"You holding it together okay?" Concern streamed from Reggie's voice, but I detected an edge too.

Amie pressed herself into my shoulder. "I told the crew what you were saying when Theo walked into the studio." She laughed good-naturedly. "Was he still pissed after I left?"

I understood now why the crew waited for me. Why I was invited here tonight. Why the tension with the other dancers felt as if it had eased. Amie made me the victim, and I couldn't hate her for it. Considering the circumstances, it was actually quite smart.

"He was pretty pissed." I shrugged. "But I don't think he'll let up on me anytime soon. It sounds like Winter is behind on choreography. He can't possibly be in two places at once."

"I'm sure he appreciates it," Amie chimed in, looking around the table. "I'd rather you lead class, anyway."

"Yeah, me too." Chaz joined in from the high top closest to Amie. "What's been up his ass lately?"

Wayne snorted from across the table. "I'll tell you what's up his ass. Winter. They're a thing now, which means she's got him by the balls. I've seen it before. When she digs her hooks into someone, she bleeds them dry. No wonder he's tired."

Amie rolled her eyes and leaned into me. "But you talked to him, right? He must have given you a clue as to what's going on with him?"

Reggie let out a deep chuckle. "Getting Theo to talk is like yanking a horn off a bull. Not going to happen, sweetheart."

"So." I smiled, looking around the table and intending to change the conversation. "What are you guys doing on your days off? I think I might not move. At all."

"Me too, girl," Simone shouted from the other side of the table. We gave each other an air high-five.

"Flying home," Brenda noted.

"Spending the weekend in my garden."

"Teaching a class."

"Taking my son fishing."

The responses were so diverse, I realized how little I knew about the other dancers. I'd heard how close crews became on a show site. How there was a family-like intimacy created between dancers. While we all wanted to be the best, we still needed each other, because when the music started and our hearts were thrown on that dance floor, we became one.

Conversation flowed over a meal and some drinks. I stuck with water, knowing I wouldn't be able to sleep a wink if I had any alcohol. I'd never been a big drinker, anyway—not since I learned what it was like to lose control of my body at only seventeen. After that, liquor just made me feel anxious—on edge and helpless. I swore I'd never feel that way again.

I hadn't learned my triggers well enough to prevent the darkness from claiming me and transporting me back to the party on the lake. To the night I became helpless in the arms of a monster. But when the darkness came, it washed over me the way water rushed the shore. And every sensation from that horrible night seeped through my pores and weighed me down like wet sand.

I remembered my body rocking above the waves, the heavy breathing above me, my cries for something, some*one*—*any*one—and hot tears sliding down my face as I prayed to the full crescent moon.

Snippets of a night I wished I could forget seemed to invade my mind at the worst possible times. Like now.

If Shane had been there, I wouldn't have been forced outside my comfort zone, which most likely triggered my last memory. Social events gave me anxiety. Having a friend who was so bold and relentless in his pursuits was a blessing in so many ways. He was always there to pull me out of my shell. Because of him, I didn't miss out on much. We were a package deal, and no one questioned that back home.

But we weren't in Seattle anymore. LA was a different beast, a bigger pond, with everyone driven and passionate about the same goals—and Gravity Dance Complex was the epicenter of it all. The hub for dance talent. And he wasn't there.

After we paid our bills, Amie and I slid into the back seat of Reggie's sports car. He drove toward my place first since it was closest. I dreaded that I would be sleeping alone in my dingy apartment that night. With its questionable security system, thin walls, and tattered blinds, I couldn't help feeling more on edge than ever before.

Shane and I had opted to live in a questionable area of town because it was the only way we could afford classes at Gravity in addition to a year's worth of rent. We never talked about what would happen when one of us found work and left the other alone.

I took a deep breath as we pulled up to my apartment complex. "Thanks for the ride," I called back to Reggie, shutting the door behind me. I blew Amie a kiss and jogged up the steps to my apartment, then I waved goodbye as I punched in my code and slipped through the main door.

My body was leaded with exhaustion as I took the stairs to the second floor. And while my heart was beating triple time, I knew it wasn't from the journey upstairs. As I walked the narrow hall, I took in the peeled orange wallpaper and the overhead lights flickering, startling at every strange creak and moan of the floorboards. When I finally got to my apartment, I dashed inside and locked the door behind me.

My gaze floated around the space. Nothing was out of the ordinary, not that it should have been. But I still felt jumpy, even with the overhead lights on.

I pulled off my shoes and wandered around, checked behind the doors and shower curtain, then fastened sheets to the windows with clothespins. It was weird to see Shane's side of the studio vacant except for his mattress. I frowned at the vastness of it all.

After tossing myself onto my bed, I curled up with my pillow, forcing my thoughts to turn in any direction but the darkness.

And then I thought of him—Theo. Why? It made no sense. Theo was the epitome of dark and disturbed, and he was exactly the sort of man I needed to stay away from. Yet there he was, etched into my mind—the vulnerable man who'd given me a piece of himself today.

My mind settled some, but my eyes were glued open. I was restless, my heartbeat stubbornly hammering away. There was no way I would last all night in this apartment alone. Not when I felt as if someone were feeding my veins caffeine.

But where could I go?

The answer was so obvious. *Gravity*. It was the first thing that entered my mind.

The Center was open twenty-four seven, and most likely there'd be an empty studio I could hop into.

But it's dark. I can't walk there now.

Our apartment might have been in a creepy part of town, but Gravity wasn't. Still, the idea of walking there at this hour didn't give me the warm fuzzies. I picked up my phone, found the car service app, and scheduled a pickup.

Chapter 15

THEO

The sound of a drill pierced my ears when I entered the side door of my three-story house. I lived on the outskirts of LA with privacy and land not normally found on this side of town. It was quiet and homey—the perfect getaway from my normally crazy life. Talk about an inconvenient time for renovations. Especially on a day when I could use some major shut-eye. The past few weeks had caught up with me. But the construction was almost finished, and it would be a lifesaver when it was.

As I moved through the foyer and down the hall, specks of sawdust caught the light and floated in a cloud around me. I entered the room where the ruckus was coming from and someone cut the engine to the machine. In seconds, the dust cleared, giving me a better view of the open space.

My mood was instantly lifted. My own personal dance studio. It'd always been a dream of mine, and after I'd bought the house three years ago, the studio was the first update I planned to make. The time had never been right before, but after officially getting the gig with Winter, I decided to make the move.

My plan was for the studio to be finished two months ago, but that was another project my ex-assistant had been responsible for.

"Coming along, boys." I greeted the four men with a handshake as they proceeded to run down the list of remaining work.

"I'd say we're about two days out. Walls get fresh paint tomorrow. Floor sealant goes on the next day. You'll want to give it a few days to dry. Then it's all yours."

"Thanks, man. I really appreciate the rush job here. Finding studio time at Gravity has been a bitch."

The men chuckled, though I knew they hadn't a clue what I'd been through, nor did they care. After a final perusal of the space, I jogged upstairs, strode past the kitchen and living room, then made my way to the top floor, where my bed was waiting.

The studio would be soundproof, but since the door was open, I could still hear faint sounds of the machines. Luckily I was too tired to care as I threw myself on my bed, intending to nap for just a few hours.

❤

It was dark when I woke, my eyes sprinting open and my heart lunging straight through my throat. "Fuck. Fuck. Fuck." I'd slept too long.

I threw off the covers and dove for the bathroom to rinse off and change before I headed back to Gravity. I had five more dances to choreograph. I'd been stalled for the past few days, which set me back. And Monday was going to be a big day. The crew would not only learn an entire routine but also Winter would be joining them for "blends," which was when backup dancers and the artist began rehearsing together.

Blending was always the trickiest phase of show prep. For artists, it was like a whole new world, being surrounded by dancers who were ultimately better than them. But at the same time, it empowered the artist to know they were backed by a chorus of talent to help them shine. The glittery costumes and fancy lighting didn't hurt either.

I stuffed my legs into a pair of sweatpants and a muscle shirt, strapped on my sneakers, and busted down the stairs like a tropical storm ready to destroy anything in my path. The center was only twenty minutes from my house, and luckily LA traffic was avoidable along the backstreets.

I parked along the curb in my usual spot at the front of the building and entered the dimly lit facility, no key required per the twenty-four-hour policy. The only person there was a security guard, Fred, who watched over the place every night. He walked the halls and the perimeter nonstop, and he'd been doing it for years. Hired by Rashni when Gravity opened, he was now the longest-standing employee in the entire facility.

I walked the long hall until I reached a room with light streaming through the rectangular peep window in the door. It wasn't completely unusual for someone to be here training after hours. I did it every night. But it always made me curious to see who had that same kind of drive.

When I reached the window and looked inside, my heart kicked up a beat. Lex was there, her caramel blond hair thrown into a messy pile atop her head. She was barefoot and wore gray sweats and a white tank that exposed her toned middle section. And from the amount of sweat on her body and her heavy breathing, I guessed she'd been there for hours.

Something about Lex's style made her stand out from the other dancers.

She had a brilliance to her movements and transitions that she probably didn't even understand in her young career. The way she was able to move from hard and athletic to heartfelt and lyrical made every move—even the moments when she was standing still—mean something.

Every move mattered. Every emotion on her face felt authentic, to the point it reached me deep in my bones. When she danced it was as if she were speaking directly to me. It'd been a long time since watching someone dance made me feel that way, as if my heart were moments away from being yanked from my chest.

When the song ended and her head began to swivel in my direction, I stepped away from the door so she couldn't see me. I couldn't let her catch me spying on her like some creep.

Kinda like the way she spied on me in the theater.

Yeah, well. I guess we're even now.

Chapter 16

LEX

My heart lurched when I saw a figure cross the window. It was probably Fred making one of his rounds. He was one of the reasons I felt safe here instead of back at my apartment. I had grabbed the first studio I saw, and since I didn't have Winter's set-list music, I used my own playlist of singer-songwriter tunes to freestyle to.

As the music played on, I found myself moving more lyrically than what my body was used to lately. Hip-hop was so hard-hitting at times. While I still felt every hit and roll, there was something about slowing it down and stretching my limbs into arabesques and relevés and inverted turns that helped me connect with whatever darkness still swarmed inside me.

I could let it all go through dance. *At least I would try.*

LEX, SEVENTEEN YEARS OLD

Shane and I arrived together to the party on the lake. The sun had dipped below the horizon, and a beautiful purplish-orange glow lit up the sky. We'd marveled at it, taking our time to join the growing crowd that began filling the porch and yard of my longtime crush's house.

Justin Windsor, the boy with the shaggy chocolate hair and easy smile, hadn't so much as borrowed a pencil from me since the sixth grade. He was the first boy to make my heart beat fast, even when he hadn't noticed me. But something had changed recently. Flirtation rippled between us in the halls between classes, and at lunch one day, he finally asked me out.

We'd shared our first kiss—*my* first kiss—the weekend before. I couldn't even remember the plot of the action movie we'd been watching when his arm slipped over my shoulders and he practically burned a hole through the side of my head. Exactly one hundred heartbeats later, I drummed up the nerve to look back.

"You're so beautiful."

I watched his lips move while my chest felt as if it would explode. He leaned in—pausing an inch from my lips, as if in warning—then kissed me. And he *kept* kissing me until the credits rolled and the theater lights flicked on. My heart never left my throat.

I never fit in with a specific crowd in high school. It was always Shane and me and whoever we chose to surround ourselves with. We didn't believe in cliques or popularity. We were smart enough to understand that high school politics was bullshit, and all that mattered was where we went once we graduated.

But that night at the lake, staring at Justin's sky after Shane snuck off to mingle with the crowd, I became a version of myself that shouldn't have ever existed. I wanted to be one of them. To feel as though I belonged somewhere.

To be accepted. So when Justin appeared beside me, with the red cup in his hands and that easy smile that swept my heart away, I accepted the drink and took my first swig.

It was cold and bitter going down my throat. I hated the taste, and if it weren't for the dimply boy beside me, I would have spit it all over the dock. But as we fell into awkward conversation, I found myself using the drink as a crutch to ease my nerves. It seemed to work. My head felt light, conversation flowed naturally, and when he kissed me again, I kissed him back with confidence I had lacked the week before.

I didn't remember how we ended up on the bed in his parents' boat or how my clothes wound up on the floor. But when I started to sober and my eyes opened to the moonlight that poured in through the skylight, my lungs burned with fear.

Then I felt his hands. They were exploring my body as if I were his playground. Gripping me, stroking me, he acted as though he had all the time in the world. I moved my arms to stop him, but he batted them away. I turned my body to roll from under him instead. He smashed his chest down on mine to stop me.

"Shh," he kept whispering. I didn't know why. No one was there. Every cry and every scream that tore from my throat was drowned by the sound of water rocking beneath the vessel.

A tear slipped from my eye.

He hadn't entered me yet, but I felt him, bare and hard, as his erection dug into my stomach. My wrists were pinned to the bed with his hands and my thighs wedged wide with his knees. Then he started his descent from my neck to my breast, dropping sloppy kisses on the way. He bit down hard, and my eyes squeezed shut at the pain.

I continued to fight back, my head still fogged with a drunkenness I would always regret. But I was pinned there, my struggle useless beneath his strength, so I howled.

Shane had been searching for me for a long time before his six foot two inch frame came crashing through the bedroom door. He'd seen my shoes on the dock and put two and two together. It didn't matter if I'd made a choice to be with Justin that night. Shane knew I'd been drinking, and that was enough for him to put a stop to whatever was going on.

But when he entered that room and heard my cries then saw Justin's naked body on top of mine, he lost it. Shane flew to the bed and ripped Justin from me, pinning him to the wall and holding him there as I scrambled to gather my clothes.

Just before we left, Shane drew back his fist and slammed it into Justin's cheek, knocking him out cold.

♥

As "New Balance" by Jhene Aiko played on, I gave myself over to the intimate lyrics. The song was chilling yet soothing against a backdrop of light instrumentals, a combination that worked well since I was spilling my emotions all over the dance floor.

It had been awhile since I'd moved like that. Freely, unchained from someone else's choreography and rules. Dance was my light in a world that held so much darkness. It was the only way I knew to combat the memories of Justin and that night on his boat.

I didn't dance to dwell in it. Instead, I lit up the floor with hope.

WATCH: NEW BALANCE
smarturl.it/Gravity_NewBalance

Chapter 17

LEX

I t was well past two in the morning when I stepped out from the studio, flicking the light off behind me. I crept down the hall, finding the silence deafening after hours of blasting the stereo. Dancing had always been the best form of therapy for my body, for my mind. It was exactly what I'd needed tonight.

Pulling my duffel over my shoulder, I pushed my way through the staff doors and walked across it to another room equipped with a full bathroom and bed. Reggie had made the mistake of mentioning it to me the other day, and I was about to take full advantage of that knowledge. Fred would kick me out of the community area with the couches before I shut my eyes, so I didn't even attempt to go there. And the thought of spending another dime for a ride service to take me home didn't sit well with me.

After brushing my hair and putting on cotton shorts and a tank, I set my alarm and slipped between the sheets of the large cot tucked away in the corner of the room. *My salvation.*

Just as exhaustion began to take hold of me, the door to the staff room creaked open and yanked me out of it. As I heard the faint sounds of footsteps padding toward me, I looked around the small space, frantically searching for an escape. There weren't any windows—just a bathroom and a cot. I groaned inwardly as I assessed my situation. The countdown clock ticked loudly in my head, taunting me.

Tick-tock.

The footsteps stopped outside the private room, and the handle began to move.

Time's up.

The door opened, and my eyes flew wide as the staff room light spilled over the figure. Fiery eyes stared back at me as his face contorted into confusion then anger. Oddly enough, relief snaked through my veins. It was just Theo.

He swung the door open then switched the overhead light on. I gasped and sat up, bringing the top sheet with me.

"What the fuck?" Theo was standing in the doorway, sweating from head to toe as if he'd just finished dancing. My mind reeled, thinking back to when I'd arrived at the center earlier. I was the only one here. None of the other studios' lights had been on.

He must have come in after me. My heart sped up as I remembered the shadow that crossed by the door's window.

Was he watching me?

"Jesus," I said, clutching the fabric to my tank. "You scared the crap out of me."

Theo squinted as he gripped the door. "You aren't staff. You aren't allowed back here."

Is this guy for real? I rolled my eyes and lay back down on the bed. "Try to kick me out. I've had a late night. I need to get some sleep."

His jaw dropped. "That's *my* bed."

"Pretty sure it's the *staff's* bed."

"And once again. You. Are. Not. Staff." He stalked over and ripped the top sheet from my body. "Get out."

"No." I pulled the sheet back.

"Yes." He tugged on the sheet again, forcing it out of my hold. "What the hell, Lex? Are you trying to get on my last fucking nerve?"

I let out an amused laugh, my energy depleted from dealing with Theo's demands over the last few weeks. "Nope. But I don't really care if I do."

He growled and shook his head before walking into the bathroom and slamming the door behind him. When the shower started, my heart began to pound. He wasn't going anywhere. The defiant voice in my head huffed and stomped her foot. And neither was I. No way was I going to let him shoo me away. Theo would have to find another bed.

I shifted, wrapping my arms around the pillow and trying to get comfortable. It was useless. Of course, I couldn't sleep now. Not with Theo's naked body showering in the next room.

When the water shut off and I knew Theo would reappear at any moment, I forced my eyes shut to make him think I was sleeping. Maybe then he'd finally leave me alone.

My thoughts were loud. My heart crashing against my chest was louder. But when a movement rocked and dipped the bed near my feet then worked its way up behind me, I knew Theo wasn't backing down.

I was frozen as I felt his warm body pressing against me from behind. The weirdest sensation snaked through me, as though I wanted him there when I should be terrified.

"Comfy?" Theo asked, amusement percolating his tone.

My body burned hot with anger, rage filling my veins and tensing my muscles. I flew out of the bed then tripped at the edge and tumbled onto my ass, my palms pressed to the linoleum floor to steady me.

I looked up. My blood boiled. He had the widest grin plastered on his face. And then he laughed. *What in the world? Did Theo Noska just smile and laugh?* I thought I might faint.

"What's wrong, Lex? I thought you weren't moving from this bed."

I sat up straight, dusting my hands together and narrowing my eyes at him. Without windows, the room's only light came from the bathroom.

"Yeah, that was before you crawled into bed with me and infested the sheets, thank you very much."

"You do have a brave mouth lately. You'll want to be careful with that thing. Wouldn't want anyone getting the wrong idea."

I fumed and blew a piece of hair from my face. "I think it's pretty clear how I feel about you. I can't believe you just kicked me out of a bed when I was asleep."

"You were not asleep." His grin spread.

Ugh. Why did he have to be so adorable?

"Well, I was getting there."

"Go home. You do have a home, don't you?"

It wasn't a serious question, but it gave me pause. I let out a breath, debating how much to tell him. "Yes. I have a home, it's just—being fumigated right now. I can't go back until I get the all clear." I swallowed my lie. It tasted awful going down.

He seemed to think about that for a minute. "Okay, then a hotel. There are tons nearby."

If he expected me to walk to downtown LA in the middle of the night to find the nearest hotel only to have to haul myself back here Monday morning, he was out of his goddamn mind.

"We just started getting paid. I can't—" I stopped the truth from falling out of my mouth. The fact that money was a problem was not something I could tell Theo. It was none of his business.

"Then that boyfriend of yours. What was his name again?"

It took me a second to understand who he was referring to. "Shane?" *He thinks Shane is my boyfriend?*

Theo shrugged, clearly trying to play off his question with nonchalance.

I bit back a smile. "He left town for a gig." I paused and assessed him. His eyes were on me, listening, studying. I would have loved to know what was going on within that beautiful brain of his.

I released a heavy sigh and decided to tell Theo the truth. "Shane and I have been living off our savings for the last four months. We prepaid for rent and dance classes for a year. Remaining funds aren't that great. Let's just say this job came at the perfect time. Anyway"—I shook my head, knowing I was drifting off topic—"I can't go back there tonight."

"Shit," he muttered. He sat up, and I had to suck in a breath. The comforter fell away, revealing his shirtless upper half. My body grew warm as he ran his fingers through his hair, his head down, his muscles flexing. He looked up, catching my stare. "C'mere." He patted the spot beside him, but I didn't move.

Panic shot through my veins. "No." I scrambled from the floor to stand and search for my things.

"Why?" He asked as I flew around the room, his eyes tracking me.

"Because," I exclaimed, stopping to stare at him. "Do I really need to explain?"

He nodded slowly. "I'm intrigued by your reasoning."

I let out a sarcastic laugh. "Because it's weird. We don't even know each other. And if someone were to walk in here, I'd be fired instantly."

"So then lock the door." He said it so casually, as if he didn't even have to think about it.

"No. I'll go." I reached for my duffel and slipped on a pair of flip-flops I'd brought. My throat was thick with emotion as I considered my options.

Theo flew from the bed before I could open the door. He slammed his hand against it and locked it. "Stay." His breath hit my neck.

I should have crawled into my dark hole as I'd done so many times, especially when I felt trapped in any way. But all I could think about was the scent of fresh mint, as if he'd just brushed his teeth, and the heat that radiated from his body like a furnace. I couldn't help thinking about how perfect it would feel to lie beside him, considering I was always cold at night. I stacked pillows over my legs for extra warmth, but I wouldn't need them with Theo.

Oh my God. *What am I thinking?*

"No one will come in here, Lex. If they try the door, they'll walk away. I've done this plenty of times to know for sure. Just stay."

His words hit me like a dart in the chest. I swiveled to face him, my eyes locking on his. I didn't want to be one of his "plenty of times," even if he was just talking about sleeping.

His eyes moved back and forth between mine, then he gave me one of his half smiles. "That's not what I meant." *Of course he could read my mind.* "I just meant that I've slept here plenty of times, enough that it's expected, and the staff here know not to bother me. Okay?"

My shoulders relaxed, and I looked away. His eyes were too intense. The heat coming from his body was even more so. Theo and I hated each other for the most part. Sure, maybe there was a smidge more respect after our conversation earlier today—er, yesterday—but this wasn't the next step in whatever partnership we'd agreed to. What he'd proposed was ridiculous.

"Stay," he said again, this time releasing his hands from the door in a gesture that let me know it was my choice. Something thick made its way up my throat. He was letting me decide to stay or go, but he wanted me to stay.

"We're just two dancers who need a place to crash. We'll share a bed. We'll sleep. And you have my word that I won't try to grope you or anything ... jerklike." There was that smile again.

My heart leapt as I focused on his words. His honesty. I didn't want to turn him down. I wouldn't.

So I went to the bathroom, turned off the light, then stepped over to the bed and slipped off my flip-flops. When I lay down and put my head on the pillow, I closed my eyes, anticipating the darkness. Theo was too close to me. I could feel heat radiating from his body. But surprisingly, the darkness never came.

Theo shifted, as if trying to adjust his body and not violate mine in any way. It warmed my insides more than I liked to admit. "Tell me if this is too weird." He moved closer, pressing his front to my back. My heart shot into my throat and my lids squeezed together as I focused on steadying my breaths.

I knew my voice would fail me, so I remained silent.

Everything was still for a few minutes, and I thought maybe I could get used to Theo cupping my body with his, his hand crushed awkwardly between us. But then he groaned and moved his arm around me, his fingers lingering just inches from my belly.

"How about this? Still okay?" His words were a gruff whisper on my back, wrapping me in chills. "I'm kind of a big guy to share this little cot."

Something about his tone lit my core on fire. "It's fine." My voice was strained. I shifted, aiming for comfort, but when I accidentally rubbed my ass against him, my entire body cringed.

He let out a grunt and pressed his hand against my stomach. "Don't do that," he warned. "Don't move. Not unless you want me to break my promise."

I froze and tried to ignore what was now hard and wedged between my legs. "Sorry," I whispered. I practiced breathing slowly in an attempt to calm my racing pulse. My lids fell shut, and I drowned my chaotic thoughts by repeating gentle commands. *Go to sleep, Lex.*

Minutes passed before my body finally started to relax.

"Lex," Theo muttered sleepily.

"Hmm."

Silence hung in the air and for a second I thought he'd fallen asleep.

"I've never seen anyone dance like you. You were incredible tonight."

He was watching me.

And there in the arms of a man I'd quickly grown to despise, I smiled and drifted off into a deep and restful sleep.

Chapter 18

THEO

"Wake up, sunshine."

The deep singsong voice reached into my slumber and yanked me out of it. I jumped without understanding why at first. Then I searched the bed, my palm skating across the sheets for another body, one I became far too comfortable with overnight. Where was she? *Where the hell is Lex?*

I looked up at the door where Reggie stood, a smirk plastered to his face. "Another late night?"

My eyes were still heavy, and for the life of me, I wasn't sure if I'd slept well or not. It wasn't easy to drift off to sleep with Lex in my arms, every shift of her curves quickening my already racing pulse.

God, I wanted to touch her last night. More than touch her. I wanted to slide her shorts down and press my cock between her thick ass cheeks, like a horny teenager with the bluest fucking balls. Every time she shifted, I looked at her to see if she'd meant to move against me.

What the hell am I thinking? I don't fuck backup dancers.

"What are you doing here on a Sunday?" Sundays were the only days Gravity didn't hold any classes.

"Went running and stopped for a water. Thought I heard something back here." He squinted at me then walked into the main staff room toward the fridge. I followed him, my eyes scanning the room for signs of Lex. When I looked back at Reggie, he was eyeing me over the fridge door. "What are *you* doing here?"

"Working." I shrugged. "You know how it is. I'm behind on some of the tracks. Nailed one last night and started another." I didn't think it was worth hiding that much. The team knew I'd been stressing.

He tapped his wrist. "Time's running out, Noska. Let me know if you need help." He winked, pulling out a water and slamming the fridge door.

No question, no discussion. Just a comment, a jab, then he left.

Growling out my frustration, I stormed into the back room and slammed the door. Not a minute later, the bathroom door flew open, and out sprang a flustered Lex. I couldn't believe I was seeing her there. Morning after, hair unkempt, white shorts, a black sports bra, and one of those weird shirts girls wore that just covered the arms and neckline. I could still see the swell of her breasts—a generous size for an athlete—and her toned abdomen. But it was the dip of her waist and the way her hips poured into her shorts that made me want to bend her over.

Fuck, my mind groaned. *Does she have to have the best ass I've ever seen too?*

"I thought you left."

She threw her duffel bag down, the fire from last night still evident in her eyes. "I was in the bathroom changing when I heard Reggie barge in. I thought you locked the door. Are you *trying* to get me fired?"

I looked at the door, confused. She was right. How did Reggie get in? "Maybe he has a key or something. I don't know. But it's all good. He's gone." I eyed her attire and the black sneakers she was putting on. "Where are you going?"

"For a run." Her tone was dry and riddled with annoyance. *At what? Me?* She was the one who snuck into the staff room last night. She should have thanked me for letting her stay.

I couldn't make sense of the panic I felt at the thought of her leaving. "Are you coming back?"

She shot me a confused look. "Do you really care?"

I reeled back as if she'd slapped me. "I asked, didn't I?" I rubbed my face and decided to try again. "I mean, you probably can't go back to your apartment yet, so I thought—" I shook my head, realizing the question I wanted to ask would sound stupid. "Never mind."

She stood, and I had a vision of her running around North Hollywood, dudes gawking at the perfection passing by. I stood too. "I'm coming with you."

I expected an argument, but instead she stuck a set of earbuds in her ears, tapped into the playlist on her phone, and started for the door. We didn't run beside each other for the entire five miles. But when we were rounding the corner of the building a few blocks from Gravity, I caught up to her and pulled her into the nearest café. "Food."

Again, she didn't say a thing. It wasn't until we were seated and had ordered our food that she looked across the table at me and opened her mouth. "Last night was bad. I shouldn't have gotten into that bed."

If she only knew how great "bad" could be. But I couldn't say that. Not to Lex. Not to Winter's backup dancer. Instead, I aimed for nonchalance. It seemed to be working for me. "Nothing happened. What are you all twisted up about?"

I watched as her cheeks turned pink, a sight I'd found to be quite addictive. Her blush was almost as sexy as her ass. She seemed at a loss for words as she chugged her water.

"When will your apartment be ready for you to go back?"

Setting down her drink, she looked at me. "It'll be fine tonight."

With those quick words, there was something she wasn't telling me.

"And this apartment you share with your..." *Boyfriend.* I couldn't even say the damn word. "Shane." I couldn't believe she lived with that douche.

"My *friend* Shane." She swallowed. "He's touring with Dominic."

So Shane was her friend and roommate, not her boyfriend. And he was out of town. Which meant she was alone. *Is that it? She doesn't want to be alone in her apartment?*

"I guess I should thank you for not kicking me out of the staff room last night. I wouldn't have known where to go."

"I'm not that big of a jerk."

"You kind of are," she said, a smile cracking her beautiful lips.

Her insult probably shouldn't have turned me on, but it almost felt as if we were flirting. I liked it too much. Clearing my throat, I contemplated how to make my next proposition. It had played on my mind all night as I drifted in and out of sleep, but after I watched her dance, I couldn't stop thinking about it. Her haunted movements were so controlled, like an athlete and ballerina molded into one perfect specimen. I wanted to do something with her gift. Or rather, I wanted *her* to do something with her gift.

"Now that you know what's been ailing me these past few weeks, I wondered if I should take you up on your offer to help."

She tilted her head, curiosity blooming across her bronze skin and bright blue eyes. "I'm not following."

I wrung my hands together, my gaze on the table as I drummed up the courage to ask for the help I needed. It wasn't like me, but I was desperate, and I'd never felt as inspired as I was last night while watching her move. She was poetry in motion, and I wanted more of it.

"A few of the final pieces I need to create include partner work and solos. What you did last night—I think that's what 'Moonlight' needs."

"Is that the ballad?"

I nodded.

Her gaze drifted as if she were in deep thought. She'd heard the song by now. From the way her face glowed at the familiarity of it, I knew she was interested. She looked at me. "Are you asking me to solo? Is that okay with the others?"

What am I asking her, exactly? "I don't know how the others will feel, but at this point, I don't have time to care. It's one less piece I'd have to choreograph." I let out a breath. "You can turn it down. But Lex, there comes a point in your career when you'll have to put yourself first. And those who don't support your success may not be the right friends to bring with you on your journey."

She let out a laugh as she stared at me. "Is that why you have so many friends?"

It was my turn to squirm in discomfort. "I have my reasons for keeping my circle as tight as I do."

"Oh," she teased. "You have a circle?"

I narrowed my eyes at her as the waitress brought our food—two baskets of breakfast burritos. When she walked away, I leaned in. "My circle is very small, but yes, one exists."

She eyed me curiously, as if she wanted to know more, but she began eating instead. I couldn't help watching the way her face lit up at the first bite, as if she hadn't eaten a real meal in years. It was a ridiculous thought. Lex was built the way she was and not for lack of nourishment. Still, I wanted to know more about her. Not just about where she came from or where she lived but *how* she lived.

"So that's it? You want me to solo 'Moonlight.' That would help you?"

I swallowed my food then drowned it with a chug of water. "I want you to freestyle to 'Moonlight.' Show Winter what I saw. And I want you to help me choreograph the partner routines."

"I don't partner." Her response was so quick it gave me whiplash.

"I'll teach you."

"No," she said, her eyes digging into mine. "I don't partner. I've never been into letting guys move me around the floor like I'm some kind of … object." Her cheeks burned red, but she wasn't playing around. She seemed almost angry at my proposal.

Shit. "Okay, we don't have to do any lifts. A lot of what I'm picturing in my mind is mirroring, anyway."

She let out a frustrated breath. "How many?"

"There are two."

"How many other dances do you need to choreograph after that?"

"I finished one last night and started the next. Once I finish, that's all of them."

She seemed to be assessing the work to be completed. Then she nodded. "Okay, I'll help you. On one condition."

I cocked a brow, waiting for the terms of her agreement. Everything about her seemed so different than the day we'd met. She'd been a scared little newbie who'd been caught in a precarious position. She'd reacted on emotion and shock and tucked herself away under her shell, as if that would save her. I noticed the way she'd spot me walking the halls at Gravity and change direction. And how her entire body shook at the sight of me at the start of that audition.

Who is this little firecracker sitting in front of me now? I liked her. A little too much.

113

"What's your condition?"

"I need this job. Which means, I can't take any risks in losing my place here. My reputation, my contract, all of it was at stake last night. That can't happen again. If we dance together, there can't be more. I'm not saying that's your intention or anything, I just feel the need to put that out there so we're clear. Are we clear?"

I probably hesitated a little too long.

"Theo." So stern. So fucking sexy. But she was right.

"You have my word. No more sleeping together, not even a daytime cuddle session."

She shot me a serious look while she laughed. "You're impossible."

I shrugged. "Everything's possible. You just have to play your cards right."

Chapter 19

LEX

Back at the studio, Theo played the two tracks he'd tasked me to help him choreograph, asking that I get a feel for them and choose which one we'd start with. I chose the more upbeat of the two, shying away from the emotional one—for now.

There was something incredibly endearing in how Theo had asked for my help. How the tables had changed so drastically from that first day we met. And now we were sharing a studio with the intent of working as one. I still didn't know how it was going to play out, but I did my best to keep my nerves in check.

"Set the mood for me. Where's Winter on the stage? Is she the focal point, or are the dancers?"

Theo replayed the song and explained the placement onstage and all its transformations throughout. "Here's what I think so far." He showed me the first few eight counts. "What do you think?"

I was shaking my head, blown away by what Theo could put together in only minutes from what he dreamed up. "I think you don't need me."

The side-eye he shot me next made me laugh. He reached out, grabbed my hand, and pulled me toward him. "Mirror me to start, but after the intro, you'll be here, like this." He turned me so we were both facing the mirror. "Now move left so you're diagonal." He placed his hands on my hips, fingers pressing into my hip bones just enough to make me gasp. I ignored the hint of a smile that crept onto his face. "Right there. Perfect."

"I thought you said there would be no touching."

He stopped, and his face crumbled. "Shit. I thought we agreed no lifts. You're going to have to spell this out for me, Lex."

I bit my lip to stop my smile. "I'll be fine. Just warn me before you move me."

The truth was, I didn't think I'd mind doing partner work with Theo. After he'd respected my space last night while it was very obvious he didn't want to, a trust had blossomed for the *jerk* standing behind me. I didn't know how I'd fallen asleep in his arms like that. In fact, I hadn't slept that soundly since moving to LA. That wasn't something I could ever admit to Shane. He'd feel awful. But there was no denying I felt safer in Theo's arms than I did under my own roof.

We marked the steps even as he began to add new choreography. To any outsider, it would have looked as though I wasn't much help other than being there for placement, but I knew different. He watched me as he contemplated every next move, as if he were feeding off me and I were somehow empowering him to move forward with a confidence that maybe he'd lost.

Theo's first touch was cautious and gentle. "Is this okay?"

"Yes." Everything about him was on fire at that moment. We were on our knees, him behind me, demonstrating the next step. I was wrapped in his arms, his fingers threaded through mine, and he was dragging our arms across my chest before breaking free. It was raw and gritty and powerful, and like a sledgehammer, it hit me as all the feelings from last night came rushing back.

"I think we can call it quits for today." Theo laughed as he lay back on the studio floor.

I tucked my knees under my chin and smiled. "That felt incredible."

"Yeah," he agreed. "It did. And we knocked another one out. Thanks for your help today. I think the crew will love it."

"Who will dance it?" The entire day, I'd been wondering. It almost felt wrong to give the piece to someone else after we'd put so much effort into it.

"I don't know." Theo had been watching me, probably trying to figure out why I asked the question. "Winter will want to decide that sort of thing. She might want to hold an audition for the featured spots. At the end of the day, it's her show, even though it doesn't feel like that sometimes. But you'll be the first one she'll see since you'll help me demonstrate it." He smiled and reached out to touch my knee. "You okay?"

My excitement blossomed at the thought of getting any of the solos or duets. "Yeah, of course. Today was fun. Guess I'm feeling a little possessive. It's silly, right?"

The look Theo gave me next made me feel as if I'd just gotten the wind knocked out of me. I wasn't sure what he was thinking, but my imagination was going wild. *Is Theo feeling a little possessive of me?*

Then he shook his head. "No, not silly at all." He sat up and rolled his neck. "You should probably get some rest. Today was intense, and Monday will be worse."

My head cocked to the side. "What's Monday?"

"Blends." He made a face I couldn't quite decipher. "With Winter," he added.

I smiled knowingly. "Oh."

He stood first, reaching a hand out to help me to my feet. I thought he was just going to walk me to the door, but when we reached the sidewalk, he gestured to a sleek black Ferrari convertible. I looked at him as if he were crazy. "What?"

"Get in. I'll drive you home."

My heart hammered. *Is he for real?* The sun was still shining, which meant it would be daylight for a while. There didn't seem to be a risk in walking home at that hour. "It's okay. I'm going to walk. I'm only a few blocks away."

He pulled his leather jacket over his shoulders and gave me an exhausted look. "Do what you want. But just so you know, if you don't get in this car, I will follow you home like a goddamn stalker so I know that you made it safely."

"Seriously?"

"Seriously."

I waited until he'd made it into his driver's seat before scrambling in beside him, fuming. Didn't we discuss this? Anything that could jeopardize my contract shouldn't even be considered. Yet he was making it impossible to stay away.

Everything's possible, Lex. You just have to play your cards right.

I bit my lip, trying not to smile at his words from this morning. There were so many ways I could interpret that sentiment.

"Hey, Lex."

I turned to face Theo. He had the car running, but it wasn't moving. "Yeah?"

"I don't know where you live." He flashed me a grin, effectively stopping my heart. *Why doesn't he smile like that more often?* My heart somersaulted. *Or maybe it's a better idea if he doesn't.*

"West on Ventura, right on Laurel Canyon."

I faced the passenger window the entire way home and reached for the handle as soon as he parked. I had a moment of hesitation as I stepped out of his car, hating the thought of sleeping in my crappy apartment alone. The studio wasn't an option. Not after last night. I would suck it up—thin walls, empty fridge, and all.

Speaking of an empty fridge, my stomach growled as I pressed forward.

"Wait," Theo called as he climbed out of his car. "I'll walk you up."

I turned and continued to walk backward. "Thanks for the ride. I got it from here."

Theo stepped forward again as his eyes scaled the exterior of my apartment complex. It was nothing to look at, but he couldn't guess from the outside just how bad the inside was. I could feel the judgment that accompanied his frown.

"Nine a.m. Monday," he reminded me. He finally stopped walking when he reached the top of the stairs. I was entering my code at the lockbox.

"Yeah, I remember." I threw him a smile over my shoulder. "See you then. Thanks again for the ride."

I didn't wait for him to respond. Instead, I slid my body through the narrow opening of the doorway and pulled it shut behind me. The click of the latch sounded before I looked up, meeting Theo's gorgeous hazel eyes against the glass. I got the distinct feeling that he wanted me to let him in—but I was afraid of what that might mean.

Chapter 20

THEO

Day One of blends began almost as shitty as it ended.

Winter was two hours late, but we made it work since I had another routine to break down for the group. And it wasn't as though I was surprised. Winter was perpetually tardy. It would have been stupid of me to overlook that while scheduling. But from the moment she strutted in the door with dark shades and a huge yawn stretching her face, we had our work cut out for us.

She'd learned every dance the backup dancers knew so far, but without her focus, she was forgetting all her placements, stumbling around the room, half-assing her movements.

We were struggling through a song when Lex caught my eye. She tapped her wrist and pretended to drink from an empty water bottle, motioning me to give everyone a break. We didn't have time for a break. The last thing we needed was another wasted day. But fuck it. We were screwed, anyway.

"Five minutes. Grab water, stretch. Snack. Whatever. We'll run it from the top when we start again."

I was a boiling pot of rage as I watched Winter excuse herself for the bathroom, and I didn't hear Lex when she approached a few minutes later. Instead, I smelled the peach lotion I'd seen in her bag Saturday morning, its scent relaxing my shoulders. No matter how hard Lex danced, she always smelled good.

"Maybe you should teach the new routine instead of the blending. I know that wasn't the plan, but"—her head turned toward Winter's exit—"it doesn't look like everyone is picking it up today."

I ran a hand through my hair and grabbed my neck, too irritated to admit she was right, or to think logically. "And what? Give up an entire day? We're on a schedule. Those who are falling behind will just need to pick up the pace."

Lex raised her brows in a challenge. "C'mon. You're smart enough to see a wasted day when it stares back at you in the mirror. Don't let this be one. There's still time—"

"This isn't your call," I snapped. The second the words flew out of my mouth, I wanted to pull them back. They sounded cold and harsh, just as I'd spoken to her that day in the theater.

"Hey, lovers." Winter approached, looking as though she'd freshened up a bit. Her shades were gone, her makeup pristine, and her eyes sparkling. "What are you two chatting about?" She snaked her arm around me, pressing herself close in a side hug. Her other hand landed on my abdomen, and I immediately tensed.

I watched as Lex's cheeks turned pink, and her eyes moved from Winter to me then back again.

"Lex was just asking for some help on a few transitions. I told her we'd run them again so everyone who hasn't caught on yet has the chance."

Winter made a much-too-dramatic sympathetic face at Lex. *Condescending as fuck.* "Oh, honey. You'll do just fine. Theo is the best teacher, and he'd never let you fall behind." She rubbed her palm up my abdomen, stopping at my chest, and all I could do was stand there like an idiot as Lex shifted uncomfortably in front of us.

Lex gave Winter a pinched smile. "I'm sure he won't." Then she turned away and didn't look back.

Chapter 21

LEX

"Rooftop Club tonight, Winter's Ravens," Winter hollered as soon as rehearsal ended.

I shivered, repulsed by the nickname she'd branded upon her backup dancers, and frankly everything Winter-related. She irked me, and I knew damn well it had everything to do with Theo.

Winter's bodyguards were escorting her out as she blew kisses to the dancers who remained. I was taking extra time removing my dance shoes and replacing them with sneakers I could walk home in when Amie nudged me from the side and stifled a laugh. "Hey. You okay? You've been kind of pissy all day."

Her statement probably should have bothered me, but *I had* been pissy all day. I could feel the negativity spiraling through me, and I was in desperate need of an attitude adjustment. "I'm fine. Just one of those days, I guess."

"Well, snap out of it. Come to Rooftop tonight. Let loose a little. Reggie offered to drive if you're in."

I opened my mouth to back out, but Reggie's voice carried from a few feet away. "Don't even think about saying no, Lex. You're coming. I'll pick you up at ten." He didn't wait for me to argue or even agree. He just walked out of the room.

"Everyone's coming," Amie added as she slung her bag over her shoulder. "It's kind of a bonding thing. As a newbie, you should definitely be there."

Everyone's coming. Her words echoed. Did that 'everyone' include Theo? Because if I had to sit in the same room as him and Winter while they made out in front of me, I would die a slow and painful death.

Amie pulled me to my feet. My muscles screamed in response. "C'mon." She smiled. "Go home. Take a hot bath. Grab some dinner. Take a few shots." She winked. "Or hell, take a nap. Either way, you better be ready for tonight. And look fresh." She pointed at me in warning as she slipped past the door.

I nibbled on a snack bar as I waited for the rest of the dancers to leave. Soon enough, it was just Theo and me. He'd been on edge all day, and while I was pissed at him for snapping at me, I still wanted to help if I could.

"Lex," Theo's voice shot out almost as soon as the door was shut.

Something about his tone frightened me. Not in the way that made me fear my life but in a way that made me want to lock up my heart.

He glanced around the room, obviously making sure I was the only one left. And then he looked me dead in the eye. "Don't come tonight."

Three words. And they gutted me, but I didn't completely know why. His tone was more pleading than demanding.

"Why?" As much as I hated myself for asking, I had to know.

"The same reason you didn't want anyone to see us together in the staff room. It's just better this way. It's work."

It wasn't *just* work, and we both knew it. My heart felt heavy even though he hadn't done anything wrong. Except … part of me felt as though he had. Something was going on between him and Winter, that much was obvious. She clearly wasn't hiding her affection for him. But how did he feel about her? Although, it didn't matter. Theo didn't owe me a thing.

"That's a pretty shitty thing for you to ask me."

His jaw hardened, and he looked away.

I was a fool. Theo and I weren't in a position to play these games. But one thing was clear after today—I'd have to learn how to deal with these feelings without sacrificing my relationship with the crew. They were all I had left since Shane was gone, and for Theo to ask me to give that up was unacceptable.

I didn't give him the satisfaction of sticking around and waiting for his apology. Instead, I crumpled the wrapper of my snack bar and walked away. Even after he called for me, I didn't stop walking until the door to my apartment was shut and locked.

Chapter 22

LEX

We approached an old brick building in downtown LA, and Reggie knocked on a door with peeled paint and rust peeking through. An insanely large bald man opened the door and narrowed his eyes.

Amie and I lingered at the curb while Reggie held up his phone to show the man our invite. After close inspection, he let us through with a flip of his hand.

We rounded a corner to reach the main landing where the elevator pinged. Another group of partygoers had already pushed the button. The door slid open, and all of us gathered inside.

"What is this place?" I whispered to Amie as we rode to the top floor.

She grinned and leaned into me. "It's a speakeasy—kind of. It wasn't actually one of the establishments created during Prohibition, but there's this cool retro vibe. And it's totally exclusive to the Hollywood elite."

Amie's excitement was infectious, and when the elevators opened, I was already drinking the Kool-Aid. Shane would die when he found out where I was spending my evening. And when we stepped onto the main floor of Rooftop—located on, well, the rooftop—I gazed around and saw that the club wasn't anything I'd expected. It wasn't wall-to-wall with sweaty bodies, and it wasn't loud and filled to the brim with couples practically humping on the dance floor. The 1980s décor was classy.

The entire floor was sectioned off with tall bushes, gazebos, and walls made entirely of brick. A chandelier hung from above the dark wood bar that sat in an alcove. The only thing that made the place seem like an actual club was the way everyone was attired—short dresses, big jewelry, expensive suits, and the tallest heels I'd ever seen.

Suddenly, I was happy Amie had nixed the outfit she'd seen me in when she picked me up. My black jumpsuit was fine, but it was obvious she'd understood the vibe of this place better than I. She had rummaged through my closet and pieced together a skintight nude stretch top with a low-cut rounded neck, light-wash ripped denim jeans, and ankle-high strappy gold heels.

Reggie pulled me away from Amie and gave me a tour of the place. He kept his palm on my back and stayed close. I knew he was just being friendly, but the gesture twisted something in my gut. As I walked with him, my gaze traveled around the perimeter. I liked it. I liked the ambience, the city lights over the edge of the rooftop, and the calmness of the busy city at this height. I'd been transported to Los Angeles's greatest illusion—glamour and wealth, mixed in a bottle of glitter.

Over the next hour, I felt like a new person. A confident new person, smiling and laughing, socializing, and connecting with dancers who hadn't yet given me the time of day. I felt as if I were on top of the world.

Until the elevator opened and revealed Theo, with Winter on his arm.

I swallowed against the thickness in my throat, my eyes betraying me as they stared at the gorgeous couple. Winter looked like a sex kitten in a knee-length white dress that clung to her skin like a press-on tattoo. Fake, but it looked good for the occasion. And Theo looked perfect by her side, wearing his typical leather jacket, a white V-neck underneath, and jeans.

Like Bad Boy Ken and Rock Star Barbie, they strutted through the crowd, attracting attention from every single person in the room—or so I imagined. Why wouldn't they? They were beautiful.

I sipped club soda then bit my straw before finally turning away.

"Hey, Winter just ordered a shit ton of appetizers. Let's devour," Amie said, her hand already tugging my arm.

I let her pull me along, knowing good and well my stomach could use the nourishment. Shane was always the one who ran to the grocery and cooked for us. I knew it was time to get my ass together and do those things myself, but I never had the time, and while I still had money for food in my savings, I didn't like spending it.

We piled our plates high, giving ourselves away as outsiders among the ritzy and classy. We found a high top near the edge of the roof, far from the majority of the crowd. I stared out at the city sky while I chomped on stuffed mushrooms and bacon-wrapped asparagus.

Amie turned to me after a few minutes. "You happy you moved to LA?"

"Yeah." I glanced at her. "I am. It was a bit of a culture shock. This place is nothing like what I expected, but it's growing on me, fast."

"What did you expect?"

When I decided to move to LA with Shane, I knew nothing about the city except that it included Hollywood and was near Gravity. Those were the only things I paid attention to at the time. I didn't realize it would be an entirely different world. Cutthroat and busy.

"I knew it would be a change. People said life would be faster, but I didn't really know what that meant."

"Do you know now? I mean, I'm not really sure I know what it means, and I've lived here my whole life." She chuckled and took another sip of her whiskey.

"It's just ... different. Even out here." I waved around the rooftop. "Everyone dresses to be seen." I gestured at myself. "I never would have worn anything like this in Seattle."

Amie grinned, her eyes squinting. "It was in your closet, Lex."

"Yeah, for dance attire, not clubbing attire. It's different." I felt the need to explain. "I swear, the moment Shane and I landed, he took me shopping and bought me a whole new dance wardrobe. Part of me wonders if he wanted to move to LA more for me than for him. To get me away from my parents so I could breathe, you know?" Then I laughed before Amie could say anything. "Probably not, huh? Having parents in the industry, you probably had free reign to explore all that creativity."

Amie shrugged. "Yeah, but we had other problems. I almost had too much free reign. My parents were always busy, and I got myself into a lot of trouble as a teen. I guess I was desperately seeking their attention or some shit like that."

I understood all too well. "I'll be honest. I'm lost without Shane. He always pushed me to be this brave person, and I could almost feel like that was real. Now, I'm here, which is a dream come true, but I feel like it could all just crumble to pieces any minute. He was always there to fall back on if I messed up. I know that sounds pathetic."

"It doesn't sound pathetic. But you know what I think?" Amie's smile was warm and trusting as she held my gaze. "I think Shane leaving was the best thing for you."

I wasn't expecting that. The words echoed through my mind, and I wondered how I could ever benefit from my best friend's absence. She was wrong.

"It's funny. I didn't see it the first day I met you, when you rocked it on that dance floor. You seemed so centered, so in control of every emotion in your movements, to the point I was fucking inspired. You should have that same confidence every single day, Lex." Her tone was gentle, comforting despite the truth of her words. "You don't believe in yourself enough. You should feel as centered in life as you do on the dance floor."

Shane would have told me the same exact thing, which was another sign that I should trust Amie. "How do you suggest I change that?"

She smiled. "Ah. I'm afraid that one's on you, girl. I will say this, though. Gravity is and always has been a tight-knit community. A family. And you're a part of that family now whether you realize it or not."

"A family that competes with each other?" That was absolutely the impression I'd gotten since Day One.

Amie chuckled lightly. "Even family has its ups and downs. But you need to change your perspective. Sure, there are some dancers out for blood. I won't deny that, but you can't think about them. They won't succeed with that mentality. They may win a few battles, but their own insecurities will bring them down in the end. Successful people never use their peers as their goal markers. Never." Amie shook her head adamantly. "The illusion of failure is real. The moment you start comparing yourself to someone else, you've already lost."

We shared the silence as we gazed out at the city. It was in those seconds of silence that I realized I'd gained something immensely valuable since Shane had left, something I hadn't even considered needing—another friend.

Amie's laughter brought my focus back. "I hate to break up our little bonding moment, but I'm ninety-nine percent sure our friend Reggie has the hots for you. He keeps looking over here, like he's waiting for the moment when he can pounce."

"What? You're joking. It's Reggie." I crinkled my face and let the information simmer. Romantic thoughts of Reggie had never even crossed my mind. Not even after Shane's passing comment about him weeks ago. I hadn't thought about much other than dance—*and Theo*—since getting the gig.

"I didn't know if that would intrigue you or make things awkward, but I figured I'd throw that out there."

Reggie stood farther down from us against the rail, his back turned to the city. He was making conversation with a couple I'd never met before, but I recognized them from Gravity. Reggie was cute in a bodybuilder sort of way, with gigantic biceps and thick thighs. I was amazed at how light on his feet he could be when required. And his laughter was always infectious, with the power to fill a room and spread joy. But there was something dark about him too. An anger he'd let slip a few times. It drew chills up my spine.

I stood, my throat dry from not drinking enough water during rehearsals today. "I'm heading to the bar. Want something?"

Amie raised her almost empty glass and nodded. "Please."

"You got it."

As I made my way across the rooftop, I purposely kept my eyes focused on the corner bar so I wouldn't slip and find myself gazing at Theo and his *client*. Still, white practically blinded me in my peripheral. I hated that he was here with her. I hated the way he spoke to me today. I hated the way I'd broken so many of my own personal rules with him—letting him sleep next to me, partnering with him. I was in way over my head with no clue how to turn back.

"One club soda and then an apple whiskey, please." It was open bar, but I was rifling through my purse to pull out money for a tip when someone slid up behind me.

"I got this," Theo's voice rasped behind me.

My body locked up tight, and all hair stood on end. My eyes flashed as he slid the bartender a twenty, a whole eighteen dollars more than I would have given.

I thought about pivoting to let him have it, to push away from him and walk off as I'd done earlier in the day, to do anything to be rid of the intoxicating scent of leather and mint that I already craved. Then I felt his chest press against my back, his arms set on the bar on either side of me, effectively trapping me. I should have hated being confined to so little space. I waited for the darkness to consume me. But once again, my body and brain didn't work as they normally did when it came to Theo.

My neck tingled as he leaned forward.

"I told you not to come." His words wrapped my bones and shook them.

I had to squeeze my lids shut, my muscles tightening to quell the ache between my thighs. Only Theo could have that effect on me. To tell me he didn't want me around then make me feel the complete opposite. Yeah, it was fucked up.

"Anything for you?" the bartender asked Theo as he started to make my drinks.

"Yeah, a scotch on the rocks. Thanks."

"Don't forget your girlfriend." My voice mocked with an innocence I didn't feel, and when I turned to look at him over my shoulder, I regretted it instantly. The sight of him hit me harder than when he'd first walked in.

His eyes were narrowed, his thick lips full and shiny, as if he'd just wet them. I had the immediate desire to take his bottom lip between my teeth and suck.

"I knew you'd be jealous."

The way he said it, so cocksure and angry, made my chest burn and my mouth turn up into a smile. "Trust me," I purred. "I'm not jealous."

His eyes flashed. "Bullshit."

"Why would I be jealous? Because you're here with your *boss,* pretending to be something more. Yeah, I'm not buying it. And I'm not impressed."

He tipped his head to the side, tightening his jaw.

I breathed out a laugh and turned to face front. Just then, the bartender slid my drinks across the bar. I lifted them over my head and turned in the tight space between the ledge and Theo, locking gazes with him one last time. "Enjoy your night. Excuse me."

With that, his arms fell. He took a step back, and I walked away.

Chapter 23

THEO

Lex stood with Reggie against the rooftop rail, sharing a laugh, a smile, probably a private joke. I couldn't tear my eyes away all night, not even when Winter began showing signs she'd had too much to drink. The leaning, the pawing, the giggles that manifested in cackling sounds. Lex's laughter was much sweeter. Lighter.

I looked at my watered-down scotch, the same one I'd been nursing for the past hour. That was about how long Lex and Reggie had been chatting. I couldn't help wondering if their conversation was any good or if Lex was just being polite. But the look on her face didn't tell me she was just being polite. It said the opposite, in fact. What I saw was deep conversation, heads bent low, and smiles. Too many smiles.

Lex excused herself, finally, and weaved her way through the thin but still-growing crowd toward the bathroom. I stood, hoping to catch her again and not knowing why. The terms were clear. My promise to keep things professional was still fresh. But it was more than that. In the little time I'd spent with Lex, I'd grown somewhat attached. She was interesting and funny. I was allowed to feel those things, even with her. Was it crazy of me to want to salvage whatever friendship had been building between us?

Except I fucked up whatever chance I had at friendship today. I should never have taken my frustration with Winter out on Lex. But I didn't regret asking her not to come. I knew what the night would be like the moment Winter invited me here and then the crew. I'd said yes for business and only that. But Winter wanted to make it more, so she made it appear like more. By arriving together, flirting, clutching me at every opportunity.

"You can't limit me." The shriek came from Winter, who was sitting where I left her on the couch. "I'm paying the goddamn bill, and we want another round of shots." She stamped her foot and slammed her ice-filled glass on the table. "Now."

The waitress had her tray against her chest and her eyes wide while searching the crowd. I jumped in, knowing Winter enough to see the signs were there. She was done for the night. "Sorry, ma'am. I've got her. We're ready to sign."

Winter growled at me and punched my leg. *Fuck, that hurt.* I sat down, wincing at the bruise she'd surely caused. I leaned into her ear. "Let me take you home."

"But I'm having fun," she whined.

I looked around, noticing that most of the eyes on the rooftop were on us. God, I hated that moment. She'd asked me to accompany her, and I couldn't exactly tell her no. She was my client, and kissing ass was part of the gig. But the thrills of kissing Winter's ass, in particular, had begun to wear off.

Is this what Winter has become? Messy. Emotional. Unreasonable. And she was too goddamn rich to care.

The bill came minutes later, and I watched as she scribbled her name as if she were doodling in the back row of a high school English class, taking her time, giggling. I was running out of patience.

"Let's go, Winter."

She was wobbly when I helped her stand. "I need to pee," she whined.

Cursing under my breath, I veered her toward the bathroom and gestured for her assistant to help. "Can you go with her? Just make sure she doesn't fall over."

Winter shoved me away and clung to Alison. "Thanks, boo," she purred while nuzzling Alison's cheek.

Alison gave me a big eye roll and nodded. "Nothing I haven't done before. We'll be right back."

With all the ruckus, I'd forgotten Lex had just walked into the bathroom until she came out, her neck twisting as she looked behind her. She seemed absorbed in thought, her expression a mixture of confusion and worry, completely unaware of where she was going. I stepped slightly left so she was now moving directly into me.

Just like the first time I spotted Lex Quinn, I was ready for the impact. "Oh," she said as she slammed into me. My arms wrapped her upper body, then I waited until she steadied herself before I let go.

She looked up, becoming flustered when she saw it was me. "I'm sorry." She raised her hands from my chest as if they'd burned her and placed them at her sides. "I wasn't paying attention."

"It happens." I refused to look away even though she already had.

Her face twisted again, then she stared at me, pointing behind her at the bathroom. "Is Winter okay? She didn't look too good."

"She had a few too many. She'll be okay." My gaze traveled the length of Lex's attire. Did she realize how stunning she was? In a room filled with LA's finest, Lex shone above them all.

She peered up with a frown, doubt flickering across her features. "It didn't seem like it in there. Maybe she should go home."

Her concern was cute. Maybe that was what drew me to Lex. She was different from the others—genuinely sweet in such an innocent way. I wanted to bottle her up to ensure she never lost her innocence. Maybe I'd splash a dose or two on me when needed.

"We're leaving when she comes back from the bathroom." As soon as the words flew from my mouth, I realized what I'd said and how it probably came across. "I meant to say—" I jumped in to correct myself. "I'm going to help her downstairs, to her car, and then I'm going to go to my own home. By myself."

Lex gave me a pinched smile. "I told you before, I don't care. I was just concerned about Winter."

This little game Lex was trying to play was starting to grate on my nerves. "You're not a very good liar." I bit into my bottom lip, waiting for her face to change color. It had become a mission, to turn her cheeks every shade of red imaginable.

"I'm not lying." She tilted her head, her eyes filling with a fiery challenge. "But I am curious why you do it. Pretend the way you do."

The clarity of her insinuation was flawless. It relaxed something in my chest and cleared a passageway for me to breathe a little better. If it were any other pupil of mine, I wouldn't put up with them speaking to me with such disrespect. But knowing Lex saw through the bullshit was refreshing.

I wanted to confess everything that came to mind—the fact that I didn't like myself very much anymore and that pleasing the industry to follow my dreams had made me sign away my soul. That at some point along the way, I'd

137

lost that deep inner desire to free my soul through dance, and it wasn't until I saw her dancing the other night that I'd found it again.

Lex might have even listened to it all without judgment, because that seemed like the kind of person she was. But before I could say anything, a commotion came from the bathroom. A few seconds later, Alison and Winter emerged from the open doorway.

"Shots!" Winter screamed, tripping forward and taking Alison with her.

I couldn't possibly have gotten to her in time. Not with Lex already standing in front of me. Winter hit the floor face-first. I heard the smack, and I prayed it was just her hands. But when she pulled her face from the floor, her eyes dazed and halfway rolled into her head, I saw the blood.

"Shit." I darted from Lex and dropped to the floor.

Alison slid out of Winter's grip and kneeled beside me, her hands moving over her mouth in shock. "Oh my God."

Stanley and Marcus, Winter's bodyguards, ran over as the crowd gathered around. They each took an arm and picked Winter off the ground. Marcus cradled her and started toward the elevators. The crowd made it hard for them to go anywhere.

"Everybody move back," Stanley boomed as he cleared the way. "We need access to the exit." He looked around at the stunned, unmoving faces. "Now!"

That did the trick.

Everything was happening so fast. Alison and I followed them into the elevator and listened to Winter's sobs for the entire ride downstairs. By the time we made it to the sidewalk, sirens were already approaching. I didn't know anyone had called them. We could have driven her, but with someone like Winter in our possession, they probably didn't want to take risks.

As she was being hauled onto the stretcher and hoisted into the ambulance, Alison faced me. "Maybe you shouldn't come."

My eyes darted between the ambulance and Alison. "Why?"

"You know Winter. She won't want you to see her like this. Stan and Marcus will be with us. And you've got rehearsals in the morning." She placed a hand on my shoulder. "Go. I'll handle this. And I'll give you updates."

Maybe I should have fought to go with them. Even if I hadn't, I could have driven to the hospital myself. I must have debated it for the next forty-five minutes. But I couldn't make myself actually get in my car and drive—anywhere. My eyes floated in the direction of the roof.

I wouldn't go back upstairs. I couldn't imagine facing our peers, who were most likely already whispering about the events that had just gone down. But I wanted to see Lex. Maybe if I got her alone... *Then what? What good could possibly come from getting Lex alone?*

I didn't stop to answer my own question. I pulled out my phone and found the number of the only person I felt like dealing with at this moment. I just hoped she'd respond.

"Need a ride home?" I texted.

Five minutes passed before I saw the bubbles by her name, notifying me that she was responding.

"Be down in a minute."

Chapter 24

LEX

I didn't tell Amie and Reggie I had left until Theo and I were already on the road. When I sent the group text, I told them I'd called a ride service and was already in bed. The fact that being with Theo forced me to lie should have been enough for me to change my mind and have him take me home. But as my gaze slid to his profile, his jaw locked tight, arms stiff on the wheel, and his focus set forward, I knew I couldn't leave him and whatever internal battle he was fighting.

I didn't ask where he was taking me. I didn't really care. It was nice to be free from the heavy city traffic for once, to feel the warm breeze whip against my hair and cheeks, to know there was more to this place than secret clubs and dancing. Before us stretched miles of road lined with city lights and palm trees and beach. There were rural areas and parks. And thirty minutes into our drive, I started to see hints of the most beautiful beach, set below a sparkling, moonlit ocean.

A familiar pier came into view, illuminated by multicolored lights, its reflection bleeding into the water below. A Ferris wheel towered above the smaller rides and buildings. And even at this midnight hour, foot traffic was heavy throughout. The faint sounds of laughter and screams came from the game booths and rides, and something about the entire scene made my cheeks lift in a smile.

Theo parked and looked at me. "You ever been to Santa Monica Pier?"

My eyes followed the giant wheel as it circled. "No. I haven't left LA since coming here."

He put the top up and stepped out of the Ferrari. I followed and met him at the hood. "I don't like the crowd, but I put up with it for the pier. Walk with me?" He held out his elbow, and I eyed it for a second, contemplating whether I should or shouldn't before sighing and taking it.

We walked through the crowd, past a burger place and an arcade, along with the typical mouthwatering carnival vending booths—caramel sour apples dipped in crushed peanuts, rainbow-colored shaved ice, pink and blue cotton candy, freshly dipped corn dogs. I wanted it all. I laughed at the screams coming from the slowest-moving roller coaster I'd ever seen and smiled at the giant multicolored Ferris wheel.

We continued down a dock lined with white lights, the Pacific wrapped around us. Couples strolled along, holding hands and stopping to peer over the rail into the ocean or pausing for a meal at the umbrella-covered hot dog stand. Music from the main pier played through a speaker system and followed us past a Mexican restaurant as we made our way to the final section of the last wharf.

The pier was loud, and traffic was heavy, but quiet filled the air between us.

It was sacred and intimate, and I felt selfish for not asking about Winter. When I was with Theo, I was present in a way I'd never been before. In a way that sent a quiver through my bones and rattled my chest.

When we paused at the end of the pier, our hands on the ledge in front of us, Theo finally spoke. "This tour means a lot to me."

His voice caught in the wind and whipped through the air so faintly, I thought I might have made it up.

"I've always thought a concert like this would be the pinnacle of my career, an opportunity few are given. But with that attention comes a responsibility to not fuck it up." He glanced at me, sending chills through my body. "I've already fucked up in so many ways, Lex. There are things that can't be undone—mistakes I've made, people I've hurt along the way. It's easy to get caught in the game of it all, but I don't want to do that with you."

I swallowed, fighting my subconscious not to dissect his words and make more of them than I should. "You don't have to pretend with me."

His eyes softened. "You're good. Too good. You were right about me. I am a jerk. I've used people my entire career to get where I want to go, but after this tour, I'm not sure what's left."

My heart squeezed. "What do you mean? You can't stop dancing."

He looked up and chuckled lightly. "Nah, I could never stop. Not even if I tried."

My brows bent in. "Then why would you be unsure of what comes next?"

"I don't know if I want to keep doing this. Schmoozing, partying, giving my soul to this industry when no one gets it. Dance saved me once, but it's killing me now. Rashni, the owner of Gravity back in the day—he was my mentor—he took me under his wing and introduced me to the dance world, a community I gave my everything to. What he did for us kids, it meant something. I feel like I've tarnished the gift he gave me."

My pulse raced as I leaned in. The jigsaw puzzle of Theo was clicking together in my brain, and I was starting to understand him, at least a little. "Have you ever thought about taking a break from the scene and maybe going back to your roots? You do have a gift. A beautiful gift, and what you do with it is still within your power. You haven't tarnished anything. You're just at a crossroads."

His neck twisted as he looked at me. The seriousness in his gaze warmed my cheeks.

"You're beautiful, you know that?"

I tore my eyes from his and focused on a light reflected in the water. "You shouldn't say things like that."

"Why? It's true. And you told me I didn't have to pretend with you."

My gaze clicked back to his, our smiles spreading at the same time. "You're ridiculous."

"But you like me."

I swallowed. "I shouldn't." My honesty felt surprising out in the open like that. "This tour means a lot to me too. It's everything, actually. My first break. I understand the need to play by the rules to get what you want. So whatever you're doing with Winter, I don't judge you for it."

His head rolled back in clear frustration, and he faced me. "I've never cared before. I do what it takes to make my clients happy. It's the only life I've known since I was a boy trying to get noticed by women choreographers. But I saw the way you looked at Winter and me today. I saw the disappointment in your eyes, and it makes me hate what I've become."

I felt shaky. "Why? I'm just a dancer." I said the words without believing them. I would tell him whatever he wanted to hear to dissolve his pain. "I meant what I said earlier."

His hand cupped my cheek, and I turned into it instinctively. My heart beat fast, and I closed my eyes.

"You're not *just* a dancer, Lex."

I opened my eyes.

I shouldn't have opened my eyes.

His head dropped down, his thick lips merely inches from mine. His eyes closed. And I knew any moment I would be kissing Theo. Blood sped through my veins at lightning speed. Wasn't that everything we had said was wrong? Career-ending wrong? I couldn't do that to him, or me. I slid my cheek to the right, feeling his mouth graze my skin.

My insides screamed—lungs bursting, muscles quivering. I wanted to cry.

Theo looked at me, his face crumbling. "Shit, Lex." He tugged my body toward him, growling and burying himself in my shoulder. "I'm sorry. I'm so fucking sorry."

Chapter 25

THEO

We'd managed to get through the next two weeks and stay on track. Winter made it out of the incident with only a bloody nose and a loose tooth the doctors were able to repair in surgery. She missed two days, and thanks to Lex, I was able to spend enough time with her to get her up to speed. She seemed back to her normal self. Flirty. Carefree. As if that night at Rooftop hadn't even happened.

It was Thursday, and the group, along with Winter, had just completed a run-through of most of the show when Chaz spoke up. "Do we know what's happening during 'Moonlight' yet? Or the cover for 'What Do You Mean'? What about 'The Cure'?"

The energy was electric, and I could feel the fruits of our labor coming together into one congenial celebration. But the show wasn't complete yet. There were three dances I'd yet to introduce.

"You're about to find out," I said with a grin, my eyes falling on Lex. I waved her over then turned back to the group. "We'll show you one of them now."

"'What Do You Mean?'" she asked as she made her way to me.

"Yup."

After the almost-kiss we never brought up again after leaving the pier, Lex and I hadn't met in the studio again. But it didn't matter. Her brain was like a sponge when it came to dance. She'd remember our choreography.

The crew shuffled around to the front of the mirror where they could see us best, hooting and hollering and pumping us up. Lex's bashful smile was worth the attention.

"Kill it, Lex," Amie shot out.

"Looking good, Theo," Nick called out with a laugh.

I raised my brows at him, humorously, and pointed at Lex. "It's all her, dude. Watch."

Winter took a seat in the middle, her expression somewhere between curious and cautious. I ignored it, positive she'd love what she was about to see.

I queued the song and took Lex's hand to position her in the center of the floor with me in front of her. With my head tipped down and hers up, our eyes connected, and it was impossible not to smile. We might have been surrounded by twelve of our peers, but this moment was ours.

Anticipation filled my chest as our fast footwork brought us out of the intro and into the rest of the choreography. Dancing with Lex filled me with an energy I didn't know I'd been missing—a void that I'd masked for so long. It was easy to feed off her strength, her passion, and every time our eyes connected or our bodies touched, I knew it wasn't a one-way thing. I'd felt our connection from the moment she fell into my arms back in that audition line.

WATCH: WHAT DO YOU MEAN?
smarturl.it/Gravity_WhatDoYou

The cheering that exploded through the room when we finished gave me the best high I'd had in two weeks. After all the stress, the issues with Winter, and unexpected feelings for Lex, I needed this. I needed to feel the lightness, the desire, and the blood-pumping satisfaction of performing. And I couldn't have done it without her. I pulled Lex into a hug, and her eyes went wide with surprise, but I didn't care. I wanted to thank her for reminding me of the old feelings I got when I first started dancing at Gravity.

"So what's the deal, Theo? How are we coupling up?" Reggie asked when the applause finally died down.

I pointed at Winter. "That's up to the boss. I'm just here to supply the choreo."

Then I noticed Winter's expression. Her eyes seemed glazed over as she looked between Lex and me, but she shook it away when a smile burst from her lips. "Yeah, okay. I'll think on it and get back to you tomorrow. Do you have another one to show us, Theo? I can't wait to see 'Moonlight.'"

Flirty Winter was back, and this time the flirting was aimed straight at me.

"Sure," I said to Lex. "Ready?"

She nodded, but her eyes shined with something else. Fear? Nerves? I couldn't make sense of it, and there was no time to stop and ask questions. Everyone was watching.

I stepped off the floor, catching Winter's eyes as they followed me, confusion bleeding through them. Tension wrapped its way around my middle, and I had an awful feeling that I'd done something wrong. I shook off the feeling and used my phone to control the overhead lights, dimming them to give the crew the full effect. They needed to see Lex the way I saw her that night. Lights low, a haunting track, and a solo that captivated and inspired.

If Lex got a solo spot, it wouldn't be my decision. All I could do was set her up for success.

I sat down in the front, knees bent in front of me. I waited for Lex to get into position, and when she looked ready, I hit Play. Winter shuffled over next to me as the first few notes came through the speakers. "What's the deal with the new girl, Theo?" she whispered. "Why is she dancing your choreo?"

I shot Winter a quick glance, not wanting to take my eyes from Lex. "This isn't mine." When her eyes went wide, I realized I should have explained that to Winter earlier. "Just watch." I whispered the plea. "It's perfect for 'Moonlight.'"

Lex was already taking over the floor, and she didn't hold back, putting passion and vulnerability into every step, never rushing her turns and leaps, fully extending her body until the last possible second, when she'd contract and catch the crew off guard by moving in a different direction. She danced as if no one was watching and I couldn't tear my eyes from her.

When the music faded and Lex began picking herself up off the floor, I noticed the room's reaction was the complete opposite of what it was after we'd performed "What Do You Mean?" Mouths were hanging open, and the start of the applause was faint and slow, as if no one knew what to make of what they saw.

Lex searched the crowd as she came out of her dance coma, and I watched with guilt as her face turned pink. Only a few of the Ravens clapped, and jealousy permeated the air. I hated them for it, for making Lex feel as if she'd done something wrong when she'd just killed it. They knew it too.

So I started clapping loudly, and eventually the crew joined in too, but the damage had already been done.

"What was that?" Winter asked me, her eyes on fire.

I tilted my head, taken aback by her rudeness. "*That* was the featured dance that will take center stage while you're in the swing below the three-D moon."

"Is Lex soloing that?" Brenda asked, her tone carrying a hint of anger.

Discomfort chewed away at me. I'd fucked up.

"Are we supposed to learn *that*?" Simone shot out.

Questions were being thrown at me left and right, so I stood to take the hits, one by one. Lex was walking briskly from the center of the floor when I stopped her and placed my hands on her shoulders from behind. "All right, let me explain," I called out, knowing I owed the group an explanation. "Lex was freestyling late one night, and what I saw inspired me. I immediately thought of 'Moonlight.' The lyrics speak to a loneliness that comes with falling in love when your feelings aren't reciprocated. It's deep, it's emotional, and the only way the audience will believe any of it is if you dance the truth. What Lex just did was truth in its simplest form." I looked at Winter, a new challenge in my eyes. "What do you think?"

"So," Amie asked, her eyes darting between Lex and me. I could tell she was trying to choose her words carefully. "Will there be an audition? Or is the solo Lex's?"

Lex tensed beneath me, and I squeezed her shoulders. *I've got you,* I wanted to say.

"I think it's only fair to give everyone a shot." I looked at Winter. "What do you think, Winter? Want to add this to your list of decisions to make tonight?"

"Will you be making it with me?" She shot back, and I knew she was pissed. It wasn't like Winter to have outbursts in the middle of rehearsals.

I didn't want to respond, and when I hesitated for too long, she stood and started walking toward the door. "Foyer. Now."

The room quieted, and I released my hold on Lex. "Run one of the new routines. I'll be back." Then I shot Lex an apologetic look when she turned, and I mouthed "Sorry" as I left.

I *was* sorry. Sorry that I was practically feeding her to the wolves as I

149

was leaving with Winter. Sorry that I'd put her in that position to start with. I should have considered how the others would react to Lex's solo. Of course they'd felt threatened. They didn't even have a chance after what Lex just did.

Winter didn't even wait until the door was shut to tear into me. "Mind running these brilliant ideas by me before pissing off my crew?" Her voice started escalating, drawing attention from a nearby crowd.

I shoved my finger in the air, gesturing at the empty studio down the hall. She refused to budge first, so I led her through it then shut the door behind us. "Mind not pissing all over me in front of my peers?"

She rolled her eyes. "Oh, come on. Since when did you start caring what others think of you?"

I didn't. I didn't care about anyone's opinion except Lex's. But I couldn't exactly say that to Winter. "Why are you blowing up at me? It's not like I handed the solo to Lex. I should have, because she deserves it, but the decision is yours. Do what you want with it."

"I'm not worried about the solo. I'm worried about you. You've already been letting Lex run your classes, and now she's doing your choreo too?"

"She's not *doing* my choreo, she's *helping* me with choreo."

She tilted her head, accusation in her eyes. "Don't be dumb. I can't afford another Mallory situation. Neither can you." She stopped, apparently to think about what she'd just said. Meanwhile, I was sizzling with rage. "Oh my God, you've already fucked her, haven't you?"

The laughter that bubbled inside of me was ferocious. I was ready to explode. It took everything to contain the pending eruption. "No, Winter. I haven't fucked Lex." I backed up, knowing I had to get the hell out of there before I said anything I regretted. "I think we're done talking."

"Oh, we're not done here." Winter crossed her arms across her chest. "Tell Lex you don't need her help anymore. I hired *you*, Theo. Not some amateur dancer. This is a *multi*million dollar production. You can't just make huge decisions like you did in there without consulting with me."

I huffed out a breath. "Look. I should have consulted with you, you're right. But as for Lex running classes, she was the best option to step in and help. I'm not going to tell her to stop. Not if you want to keep this show on track."

"What more do you have to choreograph?"

"One more."

She seemed to be processing my words. "Okay, that's not bad." She let out a breath and placed a hand on my arm, her lashes flipping up as she stared back at me. "Come over tonight and help me go over the featured spots. We can pick the dancers together. And if you need a partner to run the last dance with, I can help."

The idea of spending an evening alone with Winter made me cringe. "That's not a good idea."

She raised an eyebrow. "Because you'd rather work with Lex?"

My head spun with confusion. "I can't tell if you're concerned for me because of what happened with Mallory or if you're jealous because you want something to happen between you and me."

Something flickered in her eyes, but it was quickly replaced by a glare. "We flirt. I'm not stupid enough to want anything more with you." *Ouch.* "But Lex might not be so smart."

This conversation wasn't going anywhere good. "I have to get back in there. I'll send the crew's head shots to Alison so you can start thinking about the featured spots. We can easily give everyone an opportunity to feature. Let's regroup tomorrow and maybe try some pairings to see who works best together."

When Winter's expression gave nothing away, I started to walk through the door. "Theo," she called behind me.

I stopped and turned to see doubt spread across her face. "Just ... be careful. I don't know what's really going on with you and Lex, but there are rules for a reason."

"I know about the rules, Winter. I'm the one who wrote them."

She nodded. "Right. And I'm the one who'll enforce them. Believe it or not, I'm only trying to protect you."

Funny enough, Lex was the one person I didn't need protection from.

Chapter 26

LEX

The moment Theo ended class, I grabbed my things and headed for the door. To say it had been the worst day in LA since getting the job as one of Winter's Ravens was an understatement. After my solo performance, the tension in the room remained at an unbelievable high. Even Amie and Reggie were on edge with me. And Winter's sugary sweet demeanor after she'd walked in from her chat with Theo made my teeth ache. Whatever they'd talked about had pleased her, and I hated that I wondered what he'd said or done. Because it didn't matter. He wasn't mine.

I made it to the front door of my apartment building as Theo's black Ferrari pulled into the lot. I caught the reflection in the front door and debated dashing inside before he could get to me. But like an idiot, I released the door and turned to catch him jogging up the steps.

"Hey," he said, shoving his hands in his pockets.

My heartbeat quickened, and my anger immediately began to dissolve. His expression was genuine and more of an apology than words could have conveyed. I couldn't turn away. There was something lost in his eyes, something I wanted so desperately to find.

"Hey." I would hear him out, with open ears and a stubborn heart.

"Today was … unexpected."

"You could say that."

"I'm sorry. It should have never gone down like that. To put you in the spotlight … I hadn't thought it through."

I let out a breath. Only in those few moments before I walked to the center of the floor to perform had I gotten that icky feeling. Something had felt wrong. When I opened my eyes, I knew that despite my good intentions, helping Theo was the wrong thing to do.

"You couldn't have known they'd react like that."

He nodded, and silence hung between us. I could tell there was another reason he'd come here. Then he said, "After today, I feel pretty shitty asking you this, but—"

He looked up, and I already knew where he was going. He still wanted me to help him with choreography. Why?

Emotion swarmed my chest. "No," I blurted out. "I can't."

"C'mon. None of that was about you today. The dancers were pissed at me. Winter was definitely pissed at me. It's just one last dance. That's it. I need a partner for this. I need you."

A thickness was building in my throat, the pressure growing with each second. I crossed my arms over my chest and shook my head again. "Ask Amie or Brenda or any of the other girls. Ask Winter. But it can't be me."

"It has to be you." His voice was shaky, rising.

"Why?" My voice matched his in volume.

"Because," he spit out, his words continuing to rise in volume and emotion. "I can't dance with anyone else. Just you."

I hated how I loved his words. I hated how I needed them. How they filled me. How they seeped through my pores and clung to my soul as if they were the center of everything. The center of us. Because what he now had the courage to say, I had failed to believe until that moment.

He stepped forward, bending slightly so our eyes were level. "Come with me, Lex. Forget about what everyone thinks, what you fear they're saying behind your back. Forget it all just like you do when you dance."

His words felt like a gut punch. What was Theo asking, exactly? To pretend the world didn't exist when we were together? To pretend there were no rules? No consequences?

We'll just be dancing. I repeated the words in my head, as if one day I would be convinced. "Okay."

He didn't smile. He simply reached for the handle of my duffel bag then waited for me to walk down the steps.

"Hungry?" he asked when he started the ignition.

My stomach chose that moment to rumble, and my gaze floated to his. "I could eat."

We pulled up to Mel's, an old-fashioned drive-in diner with a speaker box for placing our order.

"You like shakes?"

"I shouldn't." I threw him a grin.

He chuckled. "Not what I asked."

I twisted my lips as if I were deep in thought. "Then yeah."

"Strawberry?"

"Vanilla. And don't you dare call me boring."

A hint of a smile appeared on his face. "Two boring vanilla shakes," he said into the speaker. "Two fries and two double burgers." He looked at me. "Anything else?"

"No, that's fine." I wondered why he'd taken me to a fast-food joint when we were planning to dance right after, but I didn't dare ask and ruin the heaven I was about to pour down my throat.

Silence sizzled through the air before Theo's quiet voice spoke up. "I slept with my assistant last summer."

The warm air billowing around us did nothing to thaw the slap of cold I felt in my chest. I took a breath and faced the windshield, bracing myself. "Okay." What this had to do with anything, I didn't know.

"Mallory had only been my assistant for a few months, officially, but she danced backup to some songs I choreographed for an awards show in New York. That's how we met. One day we got to talking, and she convinced me I needed help. With errands, dance steps, anything. I knew she had a crush on me, but her offer was appealing. Winter's Vegas gig was a possibility at the time, and I was still tying up other contracts, so I hired her. It was kind of on a whim, and she was great at first."

At some point, my eyes had slid back to him. His Adam's apple bobbed, and his hands tensed around the wheel. "A few months later, we were in New Orleans for a gig, and she somehow managed to get a key to my hotel room. She snuck in late at night and hopped in my bed naked. I didn't turn her away."

"Theo," I said, my gut churning. "Is there a reason you're telling me this, because I really don't think I want to hear it."

He threw his head back against his headrest and turned to me. "I'm sorry. I'll cut to the chase." He faced front again, speaking to the windshield. "I fired her the next morning. I was pissed and didn't think twice about letting her go. She started calling me obsessively, showing up at my house, sending me threatening texts, killed my old car with a bat, claimed she was pregnant … It was a fucking nightmare."

My eyes widened, and I no longer tried to block his words from my mind. "Oh my God, Theo. She was pregnant?"

He squeezed his eyes shut. "I didn't believe her, so I made her book a doctor's appointment to confirm. She didn't want to go, but it was the only way I was going to support her pregnancy. And I would have." He let out a breath. "After the doctor confirmed what I suspected, that she'd never been pregnant, I offered to take her to see someone who could help her." He shook his head. "She refused. Had me drop her at her hotel. That was the last night I saw her."

"Do you know where she is now? Is she okay?"

Something clutched my chest the moment I caught the flicker of pain in his eyes, telling me I shouldn't have asked. "This all happened three months ago, Lex. She committed suicide that night. Slashed her wrists in a hotel bathtub. She sent me a message before she did it, but I got there too late."

He faced forward then, but I'd already seen the red in his eyes and the sheen of tears. His knuckles went white when he tightened his grip on the steering wheel. "I, uh, went through a pretty rough time after that. It's safe to say I'm not completely over it. But that's why I'm scrambling to finish this choreography."

I swiped at the first tear that fell from my eyes, hoping to remove it before Theo could see. I didn't want him to feel worse than he already did.

His eyes latched onto mine. "I'm sorry."

I shook my head. "Don't be. I'm glad you were able to tell me." I swallowed, not knowing what to say or if he even wanted me to say anything. Maybe he just needed to get it off his chest. "That must have been awful."

He nodded. "Yeah, well, Winter knows the whole story. I was concerned the media would get ahold of the news and twist it into something it wasn't, so I asked for her help. That's part of the reason she flipped on me today. She, um, thought you and I had something going on." He let out a light chuckle.

Something dark and ugly swept its way through me. Did Theo really find it that appalling of an idea? I felt defensive and flushed in embarrassment. "I just wanted to help."

His eyes widened. "You have been helping," he said. "But I understand if you can't do it anymore. I mean, after today, and now that you know everything, I'd completely understand. I just thought I should explain."

He was giving me an opportunity to back out, and as much as I knew I should run for the hills, something stronger made me want to stay. "I'll still help. If you want me to."

We were silent for the next few minutes, my mind on his assistant. When the food came, Theo thanked the guy, paid, then set the greasy bag between us on the console before starting the car. "There's a park down the road. We can eat there."

Light was already fading from the sky. I didn't realize it had gotten so late. "Are we going to dance there too?"

He smiled. "We'll get to that. Food first. Never come between a man and a good meal."

I bit the inside of my lip, thinking fondly of my best friend. "Yeah, I've been well educated."

"By *Shane*?"

"By Shane," I confirmed.

"Sounds like a good guy."

I laughed. "He's all right, if you're into bossy control freaks with stiletto fetishes. I swear he has a better shoe collection than I do."

"Ah," Theo commented with a hint of humor. "Bossy control freak, eh? Sounds like he prepared you for someone like me."

I wasn't quite sure that was the truth. No one had prepared me for anyone like Theo. But as he was backing out of the lot, I turned to get a better look at him. His cocky expression was back—shaded eyes, small smirk, cool and concrete posture—and for the first time since I'd met him, that made me happy.

"Someone like you?"

"Yeah." He shrugged. "Someone who believes in discipline and taking control." His glance slid to mine at the word "control," making me blush. "I get what I want out of life, Lex."

I wasn't sure that was true either. I wasn't sure Theo completely knew what he wanted out of life. Sure, he'd succeeded in becoming the best dancer he could possibly be, and a household name. But there was so much more to life that I wasn't sure Theo was even aware of. A fulfillment he'd yet to grasp. Our conversation at the pier had clued me in to that.

"Is that why you wanted to be a choreographer?"

He tipped his head. "What do you mean?"

"The control aspect of it. Setting the rules. Telling others what to do. That's your specialty."

He grinned as if I were complimenting him. "You don't exactly play well with others," I added, watching as his grin slipped. "I can't imagine you taking direction from someone else. There's just that brilliant vision in your head."

"Did you just call me 'brilliant'?"

I rolled my eyes. "Of course that's the only thing you got out of that."

He shot me a look as he drove. "I'm a control freak. Born that way, I guess. Who cares? It gets shit done, and people take me seriously."

"I suppose," I said, amused. "They also call you names behind your back."

"And some call me names to my face."

My cheeks burned, and I turned my head toward the window as he veered into a lot for King's Road Parkland. It wasn't what I expected, just a small grassy area tucked among the residential neighborhood. The only signs of life were a couple walking a dog, and a child and his mom running around the playground.

"What's your weakness?"

His voice almost surprised me, then I repeated his question in my mind. A laugh burst from my throat. "And why the hell would I tell you that?"

He shrugged. "Figured it was only fair since you think you have me figured out. I have you figured out too, Alexandra Quinn."

"If you had me figured out, then you wouldn't be asking what my weakness is." I winked.

His lip curled up on one side. "I didn't need to ask. You're as transparent as they come."

I shot him a glare, my lips pinched in an effort not to laugh. "Am not."

"You are."

"How so?"

"You're shocked when anyone compliments you. You never think you belong—anywhere. And you're completely blind when guys check you out."

My heart galloped. *Has he checked me out? Have I missed that too?* Those were questions I wouldn't allow myself to entertain, so I scrubbed them from my brain. "You should have seen me when I first arrived in LA. I've adapted well—I think." I was hopeful, but I was still unsure. I knew I *had* changed. There was no way I would have had the nerve to audition for Winter's Vegas show when I had first arrived. But I still didn't feel as though I fit in completely.

"You have. But you're still adorably naïve."

I didn't know whether to take that as a joke or a compliment. Instead of figuring it out, I grabbed the greasy bag from the console and fished around for my meal. He parked just as I had everything ready to hand him. We stayed in the car and ate in silence while we watched the sun drop between the trees.

"In high school, my parents were adamant I quit dance. They believed it was ruining my future as their little protégé." I threw him a look, knowing I had to tell him more. "My parents own a publishing company in downtown Seattle. My moving to LA and dropping out of college was a big deal. They didn't understand why I was destroying my future for something that was only temporary. A hobby. Not to mention, once my body started changing, so did the rules. My father thought dance was corrupting my soul. He would have killed me if he ever saw me wear this." I gestured at my bare stomach and cleavage that peeked out from my sports bra.

Theo got quiet as his eyes traveled the length of my body, heating my insides.

"Shane helped," I added, trying to steer the conversation back to safe territory. "He was the only person in my life who didn't tell me my dreams were childish or sinful."

"As someone who's been doing this professionally since I was eighteen, I can tell you your dreams aren't childish. And there are certainly more sinful activities than dancing. This is your purpose, Lex. You were put on this earth to be exactly who you are right now, exactly who you were yesterday, and exactly who you will be tomorrow. I'm so glad you didn't listen to your parents. And give yourself some credit. You're doing just fine on your own."

My gaze traveled the features of his face. I couldn't help it. Theo was sculpted like a blond James Dean with his perfect proportions.

He smiled, and my heart caught. "You're the only one that gets to wear your skin, Lex. No one else. You might as well feel good in it."

There was something so incredibly warming about his words, his tone. So similar to the pep talks Shane gave me but without the sass. It didn't hurt that I could stare at Theo's incredibly sexy lips as he spoke. Damn my heart for wanting him in that way. And damn the rules for ensuring there was never a chance.

"It is nice skin, though," he added. "Whatever you decide to do with it." His tongue shot between his teeth to tell me he was teasing.

I scrunched my nose. "Maybe we should go back to talking about you."

"Oh no." He popped a fry into his mouth and continued talking. "I confessed enough today. Besides, I didn't buy you dinner so you could psychoanalyze me. You chicks love that, don't you?"

I laughed. "Well, how about you *don't* buy me dinner again?"

The way his gaze searched my eyes next caused a rush of heat to pool in my belly. "Try to stop me, Lex."

I was hot everywhere just from the way he said my name, so calmly, with a tinge of warning. A tease. I couldn't ignore it even if I tried.

For once in my life, I wanted to break the rules, just to find out how good the consequences could be.

Chapter 27

THEO

My house was in West Hollywood, not far from the park we'd just left. From the outside, it didn't look like much. Just a 1920s Spanish-style home in the Hollywood Hills. Thanks to the hedges that surrounded the oversized lot, there was even a little privacy, a rarity in LA.

I didn't tell Lex where we were headed, but from the stillness in the air and her stiffened posture, she'd figured it out.

"Before you get the wrong idea," I said, immediately defensive. I could feel a fight about to start. "I have a studio here. Downstairs, so we don't even need to go inside my home. Technically."

"Is this studio *attached* to your home?" she asked, her tone on edge.

I hesitated. *Fuck.* "Yes."

"Then it's technically in your home. Why did you bring me here?"

"Why are you freaking out?" I knew why.

"Theo," she warned.

"Okay, fine. Let's just leave. We can find studio space at Gravity." I tested. She just needed a minute to realize we weren't here for me to seduce her, since that was against the rules and all.

She let out a heavy breath as she relaxed against the seat. "You have a studio in your home?" I could almost hear the wheels turning in her head.

"Downstairs. It was just installed recently. Fresh wood floors and everything. I've barely stepped foot in it." I grinned, already feeling her caving.

A smile poked through her pursed lips. "That's got to be nice."

I left my finger hovering over the push button to cut the engine. "You think you'll be okay in there alone with me? You won't try anything, will you? Cause I can't have you in my home if you're going to try to grope me."

"Oh my God," she laughed. "Shut up and get out of the car."

I took her bag and led her around the corner of the house, along a cobblestone path that reached the side door to the downstairs, then continued on to the back.

"This is nice, your home." Lex spoke up behind me, sounding surprised. "I pictured you somewhere more ... uppity, to match your fancy car. This is refreshing."

"Yeah, well," I said, turning the key in the lock. "I like the privacy. When I come home, I want to feel like I have some semblance of a normal life, you know?"

She shrugged. She didn't know. She had no idea what a crazy life I led outside of rehearsal time. The appearances. The award shows. The interviews. The photo shoots and video productions. The consultations. And the touring. I was never off. Only in my home could I tuck away and enjoy a slice of sanity in the pie that was my life.

I held the door open, letting her walk into the foyer first. With a busy week of rehearsals and getting Winter caught up, I'd had only a few minutes to inspect the completed work. But as soon as Lex pushed through the double doors, I felt it. It was the feeling I'd strived for when requesting the remodel. A dance studio of my own. One that I didn't have to book and where I didn't have to be gawked at through two-pane windows. Just mine, and only Lex and I knew about it.

"Holy—" Lex stopped and gazed around. The room was almost as big as Gravity's main studio. Only the dim lights above the mirrors were on, so I flipped the main switch, illuminating the room. It had gray hardwood floors and, in a corner of the room, a speaker system that controlled the surround sound. Long panels of glass lined the front wall, with high arched windows above revealing the dim night sky. To the left was a simple lounge area with a small fridge and a couch pushed against the wall.

"This is insane. I can't believe this is yours." She flipped to face me.

I loved her reaction. Most dancers would react the same, but for some reason, when Lex lit up, so did my insides. I shouldn't have wanted to impress her, but I did. Something stirred in my chest. For the first time in a long time, I felt a sense of peace wash over me.

"Make yourself comfortable. Fridge isn't stocked yet. I'll grab some water from upstairs, then we can get started. Bathroom's down the hall." I pointed at the door we'd walked through.

She nodded, almost robotically, but I wasn't sure my words had even registered. Her eyes were still crawling the space, as if she'd just stepped through the wardrobe and into Narnia.

When I walked back through the studio doors, Lex was stretching in the middle of the room. *Her center.* I'd noticed. "You take the center often."

She looked up, then that beautiful blush spread across her cheeks, as if my presence surprised her. Or maybe my words did.

"It's my go-to spot. Started when I was little. I don't even notice it anymore unless I'm forced away from it. I think it makes me feel—" She laughed and shook her head. "Never mind. It's stupid."

"No, not never mind." I sat and faced her then pulled my legs into a wide V position to mirror her. "Tell me."

She let out a sigh, a smile lingering on her face. "It makes me feel centered, I guess."

I felt a tug at my heart when she cocked her head as though she was questioning her own feelings. If Lex had a smidgen of knowledge as to how fucking adorable she was...

Her shoulders lifted and released dramatically. "I blame it on my preteen years, when I started developing. My body was changing, and my little dancer body didn't know how to keep up with it. I was curvier than the others, and balance became a big challenge. My ballet instructor would call me out in class, make me stand in the center of the room, and demand that I execute fouetté turns until she instructed me to stop. It was humiliating. I couldn't even hide the fact that my body was different from the others."

It was the wrong time for me to check out Lex's curves, but just as in the car, I couldn't help glancing down. She wore white cotton shorts and a pale-pink sports bra. Simple, but combined with the bend of her curves, it was enough to know I couldn't look at her again. Ever.

"Your balance is perfect now."

She nodded and lay back, sprawling out as if she were about to make a snow angel. "It took a lot of work. Shane helped me. We started doing these workouts to help strengthen my core and doing a crazy amount of cardio. I don't necessarily believe fourteen-year-olds should become health nuts in the way I did, but I felt so helpless at the time. I remember thinking that my body was cursed and that the one thing I loved most in the world was unreachable because of something I could never change.

"Sometimes I wish I could go back in time and tell my younger self that it will all be okay. That I was beautiful and perfect just the way I was. That my dreams wouldn't be crushed because I was a little heavier in the hips or in the chest. I was me. And my dreams were my dreams. Sometimes the things that make us different are what make us great. You know?"

A lump formed in my throat, and a rush of heat spread through my chest. "What about your parents? I know you said they were strict and all, but didn't they know your insecurities?"

"Don't get me wrong, Theo. My parents loved me. Still do. They just never understood the whole dance thing. It wasn't what they envisioned for me, and they've never been able to let that go. My mom heard me crying about my body, and she offered to help me fix it instead of telling me the things I really needed to hear. I didn't need fixing. I just needed to learn how to love myself."

I followed her lead and lay back on the floor beside her. The ceiling fans were on full blast, and the AC was blowing cold air, but the room still felt warm next to Lex. "What about now? Do you love yourself?"

"I'm getting there."

I slid my hand across the floor until I felt hers and enveloped it with mine. "You know, it makes sense after hearing your story about the fouetté turns."

She turned to me. "What does?"

I nodded. "That you find your center in the center of the room. It's where you got comfortable with it. And I'll admit, balance is one of the hardest things to grasp as a dancer. It takes immense strength, so for you to recognize that at such an early age and make healthy changes to your body is not necessarily a bad thing. I've heard worse stories."

She nodded, then as if another thought crossed her mind, she let out a little chuckle. "I swear my body was made to defy gravity."

Every time Lex referenced her body, I couldn't help appreciating it more. It seemed she was tempting me—daring me to look. I lost every single fucking time. Her trim frame and sexy curves wouldn't normally work well for balance, but it was clear she worked hard on her core. I just never would have guessed that the work stemmed from insecurity. It made sense now. All I knew was that I couldn't take my eyes off her.

She sighed and sat up, looking refreshed with her hair down and her eyes soft on mine. "Now that story time is over, are we going to dance or what?"

This time, Lex held out a hand to help me up. I grinned, amused that she thought she could lift me from the floor. All six feet and hundred and ninety-five pounds of me. Using my quads, I stood and tugged on her hand, sending her flying into my chest. I narrowed my eyes on her when she looked up. "This one is a bit more intimate. Think you can handle it? I know you have trouble keeping your hands off me."

Her smile turned playful as she pushed me away. "I'll do my best."

I had been teasing, but I adopted a more serious tone with my next request. "Can I lift you? We can talk through the moves first. But this one will require me to move you a little."

I wasn't sure what her issue was with partnering, but we had worked well together before. She had seemed so freaked out about it at first. I watched her ponder my request, then she nodded slowly. "Yeah." Her eyes met mine. "I trust you."

Her words wouldn't leave me, not when I walked away to switch on the stereo. Not when I paired the Bluetooth on my phone and scrolled through my song playlist to find "The Cure," one of Winter's more personal tracks.

"All right, so you want to stand"—I searched the space then moved to

her, placing my hands on her shoulder and turning her to the side—"here."
I took my spot behind her. "The first two eight counts are me, guiding you,
almost like I'm puppeteering you to move. The feeling should be that you're
manipulated by what I want you to feel, so you move as I control you."

"Sounds a little creepy."

"Have you listened to the words of the song? It is a bit. But it's also emotional
and devastating and tragic." The tragedy that had entered and exited my own
life crossed my mind before I grounded my thoughts back in the present.

I was choreographing on the spot, repeating the start of the song to make
sure it looked as good as it did in my head. As always, Lex followed me, her
eyes in the mirror, picking up every intricacy and offering suggestions when
something felt more natural for her.

"Yeah," I commented as we ran four entire eight counts from start to
finish. "That felt good. Do it again from the top."

By the end of the song, I was bending her back, her body wrapped in my
arms and her hair tickling the floor, and my nose pressed against the spot just
below her chest. I never wanted to let her go. Not when she smelled so damn
good. I wanted to search for the origin of the fragrance, bury myself in her. All
night if that was what it took.

Fuck, I'm hard. I stepped away from her, reached the other end of the
room, and grabbed a hand towel from one of the cabinets near the fridge to
wipe my face with.

"That felt good," Lex said, approaching me from behind, completely
unaware of the effect she had on me. It was better that way. "Whoever gets to
dance that will be lucky."

I looked over my shoulder and stared at her throat as she spoke, not daring
to turn my body until the swelling between my legs relaxed again.

"Do you know what Winter wants to do with the songs? Did she say?"

I didn't know how to respond since I hadn't checked my phone all night. It was right there on the counter, so I grabbed it and started scrolling through my messages and missed calls. "Shit," I muttered when her name appeared a few times. One missed call and two text messages.

Winter: I just tried to call you about the features. Don't make me do this alone.

Four hours later.

Winter: It's done. See you tomorrow.

Lex's forehead wrinkled in the middle. "What is it?"

I let out a heavy sigh. "Winter asked for my help and I didn't see it. She's pissed at me."

"I'm sorry, Theo. Do you need to call her?"

No, I wanted to say. But I knew I should. Nodding, I pressed on Winter's name and waited for it to ring. It went straight to voicemail. "She's probably asleep." I stuffed my phone back in my pocket, hating the discomfort whirling in my gut.

"It'll be fine. Just talk to Winter in the morning."

Lex sounded so calm, so certain. I wasn't so sure it would be that easy. I hadn't told her what Winter had said this morning. Lex would lose her shit if she knew that Winter compared her to Mallory, and I could never tell her.

"You ready to go home?" I said, my mind twisted with worry. I shouldn't have brought Lex here. My intentions were pure, but my feelings for her clearly weren't, and that was enough to get us both in trouble.

Too fucking late, Noska.

"Yeah." I could hear the hesitation in her voice, as if she thought I was kicking her out. I guess I kind of was. "I'll grab my bag."

When we got to her place, I offered to walk her up, but she refused again, sliding her curves through a slit she'd created in the door entrance.

But I'd already caught the worry in her eyes as she glanced around the space, apparently making sure the coast was clear before she entered.

Something churned in my gut then—a suspicion that she was hiding something from me. Whether it was someone or something, I didn't know.

But I was damn well set on finding out.

Chapter 28

LEX

My phone was ringing when I got out of the shower. I threw a towel around me and ran into the kitchen, where my cell phone sat on the counter.

When I saw the ID flash Shane's name, my heart nearly jumped out of my chest. "Shane!" I squealed before walking into the main room and tossing myself on my air mattress.

Shane and I had moved in sans furniture, with the intention of buying a couch first. That was the plan until we were required to pay an entire year's rent up front since we didn't have credit. Who needed furniture, anyway?

"Hey, baby girl."

I grinned at the familiarity of his voice. Ugh. I missed him.

"How are things with the Grade-A Tyrant, aka Theodore Noska, and that hottie pants, Reggie? Please tell me you let Reggie pass through the golden gates. That boy is fine."

"Ha. Count on you to expect a man to treat me like a queen."

"That's right. He better treat that pussy like gold, baby girl. So, fess up."

I rolled to my side and laughed. "Sorry to disappoint, but these gates are locked and chained for maximum security. Besides, there's no time. We're in the studio day and night."

He sighed heavily as a form of protest. "Girl, you are killing me."

"Ugh. Let's not talk about it, then. Tell me about you. The gig. I need all the dirt. How's the club tour?"

He cackled and began to detail his days from start to finish. Constant traveling, working, and partying. He sounded happy and a little exhausted. As much as I would have loved the experience of a caravan tour, I was quite happy to know I'd be set up in a Vegas hotel, bunking with another dancer. I hoped they'd pair me with Amie.

"Shoot," I said apologetically when my door intercom beeped.

"What is it?"

"Nothing. Someone's at the apartment. Are you expecting a package or something?"

"Nope."

"Hold on a sec."

I held the phone to my chest as I walked to the front door and reached out my finger over the intercom receiver, suspicion crawling through me. It beeped again, and after a smidge of hesitation, I pressed the button and leaned into the receiver. "Hello."

"It's me. You ready?"

My heart took off at a gallop. *Theo. But why?*

173

I pressed the button again, waiting for the crackle to die off before I spoke. "Um. Ready for what?"

"I'm driving you to the studio. Want me to come up and wait?"

Shit. "No," I barked, wishing I had taken a second to respond. I swallowed a flurry of emotions to quell them from rising to the surface. "I'll be down in a minute."

"Who, dear girl, is that?" Shane asked, his detective spirit fully active.

I laughed, knowing it would kill him, but I refused to share details. "I'm so sorry, but I need to go. I'll call you tonight, okay? I love you."

"Lex. Don't you da—"

Cringing, I ended the call and unwrapped my towel as I ran to the bedroom on a hunt for fresh clothes.

After ripping my closet apart, I threw together an outfit for today's rehearsal—red shorts, black-and-white-striped leggings, a red sports bra, and a backless white crop top. I also managed to find a matching ball cap as I was jogging to the door.

I slid on my shoes and grabbed an extra hair tie before flinging the door open and shrieking. Theo was standing there, a hard look on his face as he searched the space behind me.

Mother fuck. No. My heart slammed into my throat, and I instinctively pulled the door handle behind me. It clicked shut, but the look on Theo's face told me he wasn't about to leave it at that. His hand shot out, and he pressed his palm against the door, caging me in.

Double fuck.

"Aren't you going to invite me in?"

I let out a breath of frustration. "No. It's a mess—"

"You're a shitty liar," he challenged. "What are you hiding in there?" His eyes narrowed.

"N-Nothing."

Fury was building behind his eyes with my every response. "You realize it would have taken me two seconds to open this door without it ever looking like someone forced their way in?" He slid his free hand around my waist to get to the handle, then he jiggled it behind me to demonstrate how loose it was. I was distinctly aware that he was jiggling me too. "And no one stopped me from trailing someone in downstairs. I could be a thief. Or a murderer."

"Or a nosy boss who asks far too much from his dancers," I quipped.

"Don't push me right now, Lex. I'm not in the mood."

I swallowed. He was so close, and his expression was intense. I didn't know if I wanted to smack him or yank his mouth to mine.

"Let's just go."

"Not until you show me what you're hiding."

I was shaking, but not with fear. Theo cared about whatever was behind my apartment door, and maybe he cared about me. Would he take no for an answer? Probably, but he'd walk away pissed. I didn't want that either.

Finally, I sighed. "Fine. Knock yourself out."

He wasted no time turning the knob and pushing the door open. I didn't move as he scanned the small space of my apartment from over my head. His jaw tensed again. "Grab your things."

I didn't understand. "I'm already dressed. Let's go."

He peered down at me then, and something fluttered where it shouldn't. "No. Grab a bag and pack your things. You're not coming back here."

My jaw dropped. "Are you insane? This is my home." Tears threatened to burst from my eyes as shame slithered through me. I was certain I'd just encountered the most humiliating moment of my life. My childhood crush had just seen me for who I really was—a poor slob with no furniture.

"This isn't a home. This is a step up from the overflowing trash bin outside."

I glared at him. "It might not be a million-dollar mansion in the Hollywood Hills, but it's mine."

He squeezed his eyes shut, and when they opened again, they were blazing on me. "It's not safe, and you know that too, or you wouldn't have anything to hide."

"What are you doing here, anyway?" My voice shook.

"I came to give you a ride. And now I'm helping you pack." He slid around me and started to move through my apartment.

"My legs work just fine."

Theo raised an eyebrow. "Looking at this place, that's quite the miracle."

He was being ridiculous. Sure, the apartment wasn't in the best neighborhood and wasn't exactly clean thanks to my habit of flinging clothes across the room when I was exhausted at the end of the day, but it was still a home with a bed and electricity. It was fine.

I humored him, shoving clothes and toiletries in a bag, enough to make him think he'd won this one. But there was no way in hell I would allow him to entertain his hero mentality. What did he think I would do? Camp out at the center every night until we left for Vegas? No way. We both knew what had happened last time.

We pulled into a parking lot a block from Gravity, where Theo was going to let me out so I could walk to the building unobserved. But I remained sitting, my mind still spiraling from his intrusion.

I turned to him, my chest rattling with emotion. "You can't do things like this. You can't come to my home uninvited and start packing my bags. You can't make decisions for me, and you sure as hell can't tell me where to live."

He let out a sigh and moved his fingers through his hair. He was obviously frustrated, but it wasn't his place to feel that way. "You should know I've felt off about that place since I first took you home. Seeing it up close—" He shook his head. "You can't stay there. I'll talk to Winter. I'm sure she'd put you up in a hotel."

"And what will you tell her? That you've been taking me home after secret rehearsals at your house and sharing a cot with me in the staff room of Gravity? Oh! And that you just decided to swing by my apartment and proceeded to demand that I show you my living conditions? I'm pretty sure any or all of that would get us both fired."

He cursed under his breath and faced forward. "You can't go back there. You can stay with me, then. There's plenty of space—"

"No," I said with a shake of my head, but I wanted to scream. Because all I really wanted to do was say yes.

"Then I'll pay for a hotel. We'll go after practice."

"I'm not going to let you do that either."

He slammed his palms on the wheel. "Fuck, Lex. Why won't you let me help you?"

"Because it's not your job to *help* me. I'm not your project."

"You think I'm treating you like you're my project? Really? Did it ever occur to you that I might have developed feelings for you over the past few weeks and that I might care about you—a little? That seeing you in that rat-infested apartment in a shit area of town might worry the fuck out of me? I'm not trying to be your Prince Charming. Trust me, I know I'm not good enough for that. I just want to know you'll be here when you wake up in the morning."

My breaths were deep and uneven. Moisture was brimming in my eyes. My bones were shaking, and my skin felt cold. I didn't know what was happening to me. I didn't know why my heart felt as if it were going to burst. So I did the only thing I could think of. I grabbed Theo's shirt and yanked him to me, planting my lips on his.

He gasped, and I felt him hesitate. I could smell the fresh mint on his breath from his toothpaste. And I could feel the heat of his body as it gave in to mine, letting me hold his face with my palms as I wrapped my lips around his until he kissed me back. I felt his groan deep in my chest, the effects traveling deeper and reverberating off my bones. I'd never felt so alive.

He pulled me toward him, over the console, and shifted my legs around his hips so I could feel him. So I could grind on him and work to relieve the ache between my thighs that had been there for days if not weeks. His hands moved around my ass as he pressed his pelvis into me, but nothing seemed to quell the need burning within.

I focused on our kiss, on every inch of his lips, the warmth of his mouth, and the gentle way his tongue ran against mine. He groaned again and looked up, his chameleon eyes blazing. "No turning back now, Lex." He kissed me again, this time gentler, pulling away lightly to speak directly against my eager mouth. "Please tell me you want to fuck me as bad as I want to fuck you."

Reality hissed at me through his words, my desire to strip right there stronger than anything I'd felt before. But we were one block away from Gravity. One block away from destroying everything I'd worked almost two decades for.

I looked over my shoulder and caught the time on the dash. I sighed, my forehead falling onto his shoulder. "We have to go."

"The fuck we do," he rasped in my ear. "I'm canceling rehearsal for the day." His hand slid up my back and tugged at my top. "Take this off. Let me see you." His thumb moved around my sports bra, running a finger between my skin and the fabric just beneath my breast.

My lids squeezed shut as the darkness rushed over me, shading everything I wanted. I shoved his hand away. It was the first time Theo had triggered thoughts of Justin. As much as I wanted him to touch me everywhere, I couldn't let him.

He didn't make another move for my breast, respecting my rejection. A calm rushed over me. I opened my eyes to his hooded gaze drifting up my body.

I swallowed every desire to yank off my top and tried desperately to clear my mind. "Rehearsal starts in five minutes." I was proud of the serious tone I'd adopted, my willpower winning. Too much was at stake to risk it all for a mind-blowing kiss.

He shifted me on his lap so I could feel him again. I sucked in a breath. "We need to go," I tried.

The disappointment in his eyes weakened me. I leaned down, pressing my lips against his with the intention that it would be our last. His palm cupped the back of my head and held me to him, deepening our lip-lock.

"We should go," I whispered against his mouth.

He nodded without releasing me.

"Winter's coming today, remember? We can't both walk in late."

That did the trick. He released me with a groan, his eyes flashing in obvious frustration. He breathed through his nose, shoved his fingers through his hair, slammed his eyes shut, then nodded as if the effort were painful.

I took that opportunity to slide off him, then grabbed my duffel and opened the car door. Theo caught my arm before I could step out of the car.

"Wait."

I turned to face him as he was leaning across the console. He took my face in his palms, his eyes intense, and kissed me breathless.

When he pulled away, it was just enough to murmur against my lips, "That was only the beginning, Lex."

The crew's boisterous voices died when I walked through the main studio doors. Tension filled the room as heat crawled up my back at their stares and whispers. I quickly found Amie and sat down in front of her. "Is everyone pissed at me?"

Her eyes darted around the room and back to me. She shrugged. "Maybe. Fuck 'em. You didn't do anything wrong."

A wave of shame washed over me at what had happened outside. I'd broken the rules. I'd just had an intense make-out session with our choreographer. And though Theo and I had acted only innocently before today, feelings had been building.

No one has to know about the kiss. I tried to calm my nerves by reminding myself of that simple fact, but it wasn't effective. If the others knew what I'd done, I would no longer be the talented newbie who had been handpicked by her choreographer to help move rehearsals along. I would become the other woman, the rule breaker, the one who used sex to get ahead.

Reggie strutted over and took a seat beside Amie, a grin plastered on his face. Something about him looked … off. "Hey, Lex, Amie."

Amie shot him a curious look. Even she appeared to notice his strange demeanor. "What has you so giddy today?"

He shrugged and threw his legs out in front of him. "One more week until Vegas. Things seem to be going well. Right, Lex?" His pointed stare made my insides twist. He exchanged his stare for a glance between Amie and me.

"Uh, yeah. Sure." I couldn't hold back my unease at his nonchalance. Something was definitely up.

He raised his brows, eyes pointed at me. Something about it felt like cold fingers gripping my stomach. "Do anything fun last night, Lex?" His question wasn't a question at all. *He knew.* But how?

Theo walked through the doors then, shades covering his eyes and leather jacket in place, wearing his famous hard jaw. The entire crew's eyes were on him, effectively saving me from responding to Reggie.

My heart stuttered as I remembered the way Theo's lips felt against mine, the way his arms felt around my body. So strong, so natural. Despite every ounce of guilt I felt as soon as I'd walked into the studio, I wanted him again.

He walked straight for the stereo and set his jacket and glasses down. He didn't turn around until he'd set up his playlist and started the show's intro track. "Get up. We'll mark it from the top. We'll run it full out when Winter gets here."

He sounded and looked ready for whatever the day would bring.

I wasn't sure I was.

Chapter 29

THEO

By the time Winter finally made her grand entrance, the crew had already finished marking the set top to bottom.

"Afternoon, Ravens," she greeted without her normal chipper demeanor. She appeared serious. Focused. And clearly still pissed off from yesterday. Winter didn't like surprises, and neither did I.

What is she up to?

She walked straight to me and handed me a manila folder. "Here. I assigned the features, no thanks to you."

I ignored her terse tone and held the folder. She hopped up on the speaker box and gestured for me to open it. "Go ahead. Announce the names. I know how important it is to you that we finish choreography next week."

I turned to the group as I pulled the sheet out. "All right, guys. Winter was generous enough to select the dancers for the three remaining numbers."

The cheers were present but faint. When I looked down and saw what was written, my blood ran cold then boiled almost immediately. *What the fuck?* I looked at Winter, appalled at the selections. Her lips curled knowingly at the sides.

"What are you waiting for, Theo? You're wasting time." Sugary sweet venom dripped from her words.

I snapped the folder shut and approached her, making sure to lower my voice. "Look, I know you're pissed at me, but can we at least talk about this?"

She crossed her arms and shook her head. "It's a done deal. Now smile and read off the names. You don't want to keep them waiting."

Turning back to the crew, I stifled my rage, cleared my throat, and read the sheet verbatim. "The 'Moonlight' solo will be performed on rotating nights by Contessa, Brenda, and Simone. And the choreography will be your own, not the one showcased by Lex yesterday." It took everything in me not to look at Lex and apologize in whatever way I could without words, but everyone was watching.

"'The Cure' will be performed by Amie and Wayne. Zaira and Nick. And—" I swallowed. That next pill was the hardest to go down. "Lex and Reggie." This time I did look up, but my eyes didn't catch Lex's. They caught the beaming smile of Reggie, who I was now convinced had everything to do with this lineup. I shot a look at Winter, who nodded for me to continue.

"Dancing to 'What Do You Mean?,' which is now a male rotating solo, will be Chaz, J.C., and Garrett." I let my hand fall against my leg as I looked up again. "Congrats to all."

Everyone applauded as Winter stepped forward, a proud smile on her face. "We felt it was only fair to reward you all with the hard work you've put in. You will all have your chance to spotlight in some way." She laughed and took my arm, as though I had everything to do with this decision. "I went ahead and reserved an extra studio in case you want to split the group up. What do you think, Theo? 'The Cure' partners in Studio B and soloists in here?"

I cocked an eye. *This is going to be a nightmare.* "Sure thing," I said instead.

She squealed and jumped, still hanging onto my arm. "Perfect. Let's get started. Oh. Lex, would you be a dear and teach the choreography for 'The Cure'? You know that one, right?"

What the fuck? "I can do it," I said.

Winter squeezed my arm in warning. "Don't be silly. Someone needs to teach 'What Do You Mean?'"

"But—'The Cure' is Theo's choreography. I just partnered," Lex said, wearing a confused expression.

I don't think Lex meant anything by her comment, but Winter sure as hell took offense to it. She drew back her shoulders, released her hold on me, then stepped forward to get in Lex's face. "I'm aware of whose *choreography* it is. Clearly, since I sign the checks around here." She laughed in an attempt to cover up her annoyance. "But Theo needs to be in here with the soloists." Winter narrowed her eyes. "Is that going to be a problem for you, Alexandra?"

Lex blinked then shook her head. "No, of course not."

"Great." Winter's condescending smile grew big again. "I'd love to see what you two cooked up." She raised a challenging brow at me. "Mind showing me?"

I stepped forward and clasped Lex's hand in mine. "Not a problem."

When we got to the center of the floor I pulled Lex into a hug like it was part of the choreography. "Don't hold back, Lex."

With my words, I felt her entire body relax in my arms, and if someone hadn't already cued up the music, I might have forgotten where we were, and what we were about to do. But now, I was ready to kill it, with Lex in my arms.

WATCH: THE CURE
smarturl.it/Gravity_TheCure

The moment the song ended, Reggie was stepping forward and placing his arm around Lex's shoulders. "Not bad. What do you say we go lead some choreo?" He looked over his shoulder and winked at Winter. "We've got this."

Her eyes flickered as if she'd been in some kind of trance. Then she smiled with pinched lips. "Great. Have fun, you two."

If the disappointment that crossed Lex's face told me anything, it was that she felt exactly as I did about the feature assignments. "The Cure" was ours. I didn't want her partnering with Reggie any more than she did.

I released the group for a fifteen-minute break before turning to Winter with all the rage I'd been feeling since she'd arrived. "How the hell did you make these decisions last night? I thought we were going to try out pairings today. You can't just throw two dancers together and pray they work."

She shrugged. "I was ready to make the decisions last night. Since you weren't able to join me, I had to get creative."

"How?"

"I might have had some help."

A ball of fire spun in my chest. "Help from who? Reggie? Is that how he ended up partnering with Lex?"

She let out a laugh. "Calm down. Reggie has been dancing for me almost as long as you've been choreographing for me. And right now, I can count on him more than I trust you."

I narrowed my eyes. "What are you trying to prove? Because I'm not following. I thought you gave me this job because you wanted my creative input, yet you're taking control from me when it matters most."

"I did give you this job for your input." She slipped off the speaker box and crossed her arms. "But clearly, your judgment has been lacking lately. Assistants and now backup dancers." She tsked as she shook her head. "I can't keep up anymore."

"That's not fair, and you know it. Lex is not Mallory. Not even close."

Winter's eyes widened before she rolled them. "The fact that you're so defensive over Lex worries me. You didn't see it coming with Mallory either." She released an aggravated breath. "I'm looking out for you. There's nothing you can do or say that will change my mind about the pairings. You need to be careful with that girl."

"There's nothing—"

Her nose flared, halting my lie in my throat. "You were with her last night."

"How do you—?"

She sighed heavily. "Reggie saw you two drive off in your car." She looked at me pointedly. "From her apartment."

Fuck, fuck, fuck. "She doesn't have a car. I just took her to the studio and we worked on some choreo."

"I'm sure you did."

"What the fuck, Winter? Stop being so damn dramatic."

"Okay." She shrugged. "Then no more partnering. No more alone time in the studio with Lex, period." Winter's eyes dug into mine. "I would never forgive myself if anything happened to you."

How could I convince her that Lex wasn't some obsessed psycho stalker? I couldn't. I knew any further pleading would result in more suspicion, and that was a risk I wouldn't take. Not for me but for Lex.

Winter patted my arm as she walked past. "You don't need me today. Get your shit straight, Theo. I'll be back Monday."

Chapter 30

LEX

Reggie's arms were like lead around me. They were heavy and forceful, as if he were trying to make up for my lack of passion with more of his own. It wasn't working. Nothing was working, and we'd been in the studio for the past four hours.

"You're supposed to mirror me here," I explained as I marked the steps, but he just shook his head.

"I don't like that. What if we did this?" He grabbed my hips, his fingers digging hard into my skin, and lifted me off the floor.

I gasped and kicked until he set me down, then spun on my heels to face him. The jackass was laughing at me.

"Seriously? Can you stick to the choreography?" I was convinced he was trying to ruin the entire dance out of spite for Theo. He'd been tweaking steps since we'd started, and even though I tried to correct him, the other dancers followed his lead.

By the time Theo walked in to observe us, I felt as if I'd yanked all my hair out of my head. My patience was worn thin.

"Let's see it from the top, guys," Theo called, his eyes skating over me.

I stared at him a little longer, waiting for him to acknowledge my presence, and maybe then I'd feel a little better about how the day had progressed, but no. I'd lost my solo and got paired with Reggie when I was adamant I didn't want to pair with anyone. I'd made an exception for Theo. It took time to build trust with the person who would be flinging me around the dance floor, and it wasn't starting out well with Reggie.

With an internal groan, I got into position and faced the mirror.

Reggie pressed against me from behind, and I shuffled forward an inch, as I'd done every other time. He was so close it was hard to breathe. His hand moved to my cheek, and I stiffened. I would have thought I'd gotten used to his touch by now, but I cringed each time I felt him near me.

"Ready, Coach," Reggie said with mock enthusiasm.

Finally, Theo turned in our direction. I could practically feel his eyes heat at the sight of us.

As soon as the music began, we executed the start of the number. It was slow and sensual at times, the way Theo and I had choreographed it. And just as before with Reggie, everything felt completely wrong.

Theo cut the music halfway through, his eyes moving over the dancers. "That's not my choreography."

Reggie stepped to my side. "I changed some things." He spoke boldly and unapologetically. I cringed as he continued. "It needed lifts to feel natural. It was lacking that extra oomph of intimacy." He winked at Theo. "That's cool, right, man? Figured since we're trying to get comfortable in pairs, we should make the changes that feel right for us."

Theo looked at Reggie as if he were crazy. "No, that is not okay. I didn't give anyone permission to change my choreography. If you can't make it work, then maybe you're the wrong partner for Lex."

"And who would be a better partner? You?" Reggie challenged, a grin spreading across his face.

Theo's eyes darted to mine and pinned me with his stare. "Do you like the changes?"

I opened my mouth, my chest swelling as I felt all eyes in the room on me. What was I supposed to say? If I told the truth and turned against my fellow dancers, I'd surely pay the consequences through their harsh stares and whispered gossip.

Reggie lifted a hand and rested it on my shoulder, then he squeezed harder than I thought he meant to. I winced under the pressure as he glanced at Theo. "The changes were mine, not Lex's. Lay off her."

When I failed to speak up, Theo's expression lost its fire. I expected him to fight back, to lunge at Reggie or something and remind him who was in charge. Part of me *hoped* he would.

Instead, he did the one thing I never expected. He lifted his hands in a sign that he'd given up, then he walked out the door.

I was still shaken by the time our group ended class for the night. Theo hadn't come back, I didn't have his address, and everything I cared about was in his car. I was pretty much screwed and starved.

Reggie and I walked to the curb in silence. Things had remained tense after

Theo had left, but we'd gotten through the rest of the number with the tweaks to Theo's choreography. It didn't take a genius to see that Reggie had overstepped by leaps and bounds, but the other dancers weren't concerned about who created what, they just wanted to learn the steps. I couldn't make excuses for Reggie. It was clear he was trying to create a wedge between Winter and Theo, and I hated that I was in the middle of it. And I couldn't understand why.

"You need a ride?"

I looked around. There was still no sign of Theo. "Thanks, Reggie, but I can walk."

"You sure? We could grab a quick bite. Your place is on my way home."

I thought about it, checked my phone again, and shot Theo a text asking where he was. When I didn't get a quick response, I sighed. "Yeah, okay. Let's grab a bite."

Reggie flashed me a grin, and he steered me down the sidewalk and around the building to the main parking lot, where his red Camaro sat. "There's a French café a few blocks away. They have the most amazing dips, if you're into that kind of thing."

"I could eat just about anything right now."

We arrived at the quaint café. It had a blue awning with yellow script lettering—Bonjour Deli. We ordered our food then found a table outside where we watched the Ventura Boulevard passersby.

When the waitress approached with two glasses of red wine, I held up my hand and noted her confusion when I said, "Oh, I didn't order that."

She set the glass down and smiled. "The gentleman ordered it."

Reggie looked up from his phone and spotted the drinks. "I've got this," he said with a wave of his hand, completely missing the point.

I sighed and handed the glass back to her. "I'm sorry. I can't drink this."

She looked between us, annoyance flitting across her features. "I'm afraid

I'll still have to charge you."

The sharp look Reggie cut me next filled me with unease. "I'll drink it." He pointed at a spot in front of him for her to set it down, never taking his eyes off me. She placed the glass in front of him and stalked off with a huff. Then he looked at me, an overly friendly smile appearing on his face. "It's against my nature to waste. Food, drink, whatever. I should have asked."

I watched as he took a swig of wine, wondering if I was supposed to ask him more about that statement. But I didn't want to ask. I wasn't interested in knowing the inner workings of Reggie's brain. At that point, I just wanted to leave.

But where would I go?

A full sandwich, a bowl of soup, and a half plate of French fries later, Reggie had rambled off every dance opportunity he'd ever been blessed with. I knew the guy had an ego the size of Texas, but I'd never quite known the shape of it until that night. "It's only a matter of time before I'm producing shows like this Vegas one. And I won't wait until two months before to start choreography." He chuckled, and I could almost pretend his comment wasn't a dig at Theo.

It continued on like that for the rest of dinner. Reggie, boasting. Me, unsure how to respond. By the time the waitress came around with the check, I was more than ready to leave.

I was silent on the ride to my apartment, checking my phone though I knew I shouldn't. A dull pang hit my heart when I noticed Theo had never responded to my messages. It had been hours, and I was beginning to think I wouldn't hear from him for the rest of the night.

Reggie pulled up to the front entrance, leaned in, and gave me a hug. "Think about that choreography over the weekend. We'll hit it hard on Monday. You'll pick it up in no time."

He winked and I returned it with a pinched smile. I hadn't even stepped onto the curb when he gunned the engine and sped out of the parking lot.

I sat on the bottom step, in no hurry at all to enter my hellhole of an apartment. How had today turned into a massive pile of crap?

A flash of headlights lit me in my spot, and then a black vehicle crawled toward me. My chest heated when I recognized Theo's car. Had he been waiting for me?

The tears that threatened earlier came back with a vengeance. I swiped them away and covered my eyes with my sunglasses before standing and sliding into Theo's car without a word.

He didn't speak to me, and I sure as hell wasn't going to speak to him. Instead, I let him drive to wherever he planned to take me. My energy was depleted, and the last thing I wanted was another argument. I would settle for one of his guest beds if that was what he offered. I'd even take the couch. It didn't mean either of us owed each other anything.

For the first time that day, I started to regret kissing Theo that morning. I'd complicated everything that was already complicated to begin with.

By the time we pulled into his driveway, I'd prepared myself for the worst. That the silence would continue until we were back to the way we were supposed to be. Just a choreographer and his dancer.

Satisfied, I reached for my bag, but Theo grabbed it first, his voice gruff. "I got it."

Air puffed out my nose in frustration. "Thanks," I shot back, just as cold.

He looked at me as if he wanted to say something but made the choice not to. And on the trek up the drive, through the side door, and up the stairs into his massive kitchen, I could feel my anger brewing.

I stopped in the hallway at the landing to another set of steps. "Where's your guest bedroom?"

Our eyes connected, and I felt the ripple of energy between us, energy that had never disconnected. My feelings for Theo were tearing me apart, tearing my dreams apart, and all I wanted was to lock myself in a room and have space away from him to clear my head. But I couldn't. I was trapped under his roof with this fucking energy zapping between us, tethering two opposites with steel chains.

He let out a breath and nodded for me to take the stairs. He followed, and I didn't stop walking until we reached the end of the hall and he pushed open the door to a room. "This one should work. Feel free to use anything in here. Kitchen too, but you already ate."

I slipped past, careful not to touch him, and placed my duffel on the four-poster bed. "Thanks." I glanced in his direction, attempting to drop some of my attitude. "Really, thank you. You didn't have to do this, but I appreciate it." I turned to the bed and unzipped my bag.

What else was there to say with this insurmountable tension between us? I refused to look at him again. I couldn't. The tears were already resuming, and I wanted him gone before the dam burst.

I tore my shirt off, leaving my sports bra intact. Then I kicked off my shoes and peeled back my socks. I expected him to leave when I reached for my leggings, but I could feel him behind me, waiting—for what, I didn't know.

I turned. "What do you want, Theo?"

His eyes blazed. "You don't want me to answer that."

I let out a sarcastic laugh. "Okay, fine. But can you leave? I'd like to shower and go to bed."

"How was your date?"

I whipped around. "What?"

"Reggie's into you. You know that, don't you? I know you know that. Everyone knows. And you went to dinner with him, anyway."

"I was starving. And you were nowhere to be found. Just disappeared like some goddamn jealous boyfriend. You didn't answer my messages. You never came back. Reggie offered to take me to dinner, so I accepted." I shook my head in disbelief. "What does it matter to you? Your career is already set. I'm the only one with anything to lose here."

"Is that what you think? That I have nothing to lose?" He stepped closer, but he was still several feet away. "I'm taking a risk here too. Don't insult me."

"I don't even know why we're fighting." Emotion clogged my throat. I turned again, swiveling on my foot so fast it caught on the carpet. I could feel my balance fail me before I had a chance to catch my fall. My foot twisted behind me, and I flew forward. My hands shot out, but Theo's arms wrapped around my middle, stopping me from crashing into the floor.

He lifted me and set me on the bed, then he sank to the floor to examine my ankle.

"I'm fine. It's fine," I pleaded.

I didn't know if he was concerned because of the show or because he genuinely didn't want to see me hurt, but the worry on his face did something to me.

"Just hold still and let me look at it."

His words broke the dam. Tears exploded from my eyes. It was the buildup from the entire day, my conflicted emotions, and the pain in my foot that threatened everything I'd worked so hard for. But none of that held a candle to what Theo's kindness did to me. The way he took gentle hold of my foot and applied pressure in the most tender of areas as he checked to see if anything was broken.

"You just tweaked it. You don't want it to feel stiff tomorrow." He stood up. "Stay here. I'm going to get you some ice. Stay off it and keep it elevated." He said all of this while picking me up and setting me against the headrest. He proceeded to stack a couple of pillows under my ankle before he left.

He was back less than a minute later, and as he tended to my foot, I couldn't help staring at his face. At the hard lines that seemed to melt away as he cared for someone other than himself. And I listened to the tone of his voice every time he asked me how something felt or if I was okay.

Those were the moments that tricked me into believing there was something real between us. That Theo could possibly care for me as more than a dancer or partner, more than something he needed to heal because his production depended on it.

I didn't know what to believe.

Chapter 31

THEO

I wasn't sure when I fell asleep, but I woke up with a crick in my neck and unfamiliar sheets in my grip. A moan wafted through the air. My heart pounded fiercely at the strange noise. It didn't come from me. *I don't think it did.* Another moan, this one followed by a rustle of sheets. My head snapped toward the sound.

Sometimes after waking, I'd feel suspended between dreaming and reality. Staring at Lex's matted caramel blond hair draped haphazardly against her delicate, olive skin, I wasn't sure which state I was currently in. I must have been dreaming. No woman like Alexandra Quinn would dare allow a man like me in her bed.

But she let me stay.

I quickly recapped the events of the day before. There was a lot of anger. Anger at Winter for making huge show decisions without me. Anger at Reggie for going off script with my choreography. And anger at Lex for going to dinner with that scumbag. To make things worse, I'd shown up at Lex's apartment just as Reggie was pulling away. He hadn't even waited until she'd made it safely through the doors.

My chest burned. Funny how that worked. How anger could expose true feelings and desires I hadn't even known were there. Or at least I'd done a good job of stifling them. It was why I had to walk out of that studio yesterday. Every second I stood there, I bled.

Fuck. I rubbed the skin over my heart, tearing my eyes from her sleeping form. That didn't help. I could still hear her, her breaths even and deep. I could still feel her, her ass pressed into my leg. I groaned when I realized my dick was hard too. It took everything in me not to work up a release right there.

I peeled my back from the bed and planted my feet on the floor.

"Theo?" a groggy voice called.

I stiffened before twisting my body to face her. One of her eyes was already cracked open. "Hey."

"You don't have to go."

The way she said it—with her small, gravelly morning voice—was a subtle plea for me to stay.

"I'm sorry about yesterday," she said. "About Reggie and the choreography." Her lids batted down as she spoke.

She was sorry? Was my behavior yesterday even redeemable?

I knew the tables had turned the moment Lex sank into the passenger seat last night, her small limbs already tense, her jaw hard, eyes facing forward, voice silent. It was too much to bear, yet I knew I deserved the silence.

An inferno raged within me, a ball of flames destroying me from the inside out. "Lex," I said, but I repositioned myself so I was fully facing her. "My issues with Reggie have nothing to do with you."

"But you were angry with *me*."

"I wasn't."

Her brows bowed down, and she shook her head. "I thought you weren't coming back."

I didn't think I could feel worse about yesterday. "I'm sorry. I was letting off some steam in the pool, and time got away from me. When I got your message, I went straight to your place."

The truth was, in the hours after I left Gravity, I distracted myself so I wouldn't beat the living shit out of Reggie. I unpacked her things in the guest room, then I threw myself in the pool, swam laps, and did nothing but count each stroke.

The moment I pushed out of the pool, *she* was everywhere. In my head, on my skin, in my fucking heart, and I didn't know how she got so close to begin with.

"And then you saw Reggie leave my place."

I nodded.

"Theo, he's my dance partner."

"I know."

"But you hate him." It wasn't a question.

I cringed and reached for the back of my neck, squeezing as if it were my last lifeline. How was I to explain any of this? I wasn't sure I could, not even to myself. "It's complicated."

"*Un*complicate it."

I'd been in this business a long time, and I knew the image Reggie portrayed versus the man he was behind closed doors. He was starting to show his true colors. But how could I explain that to Lex in a way that didn't make me sound threatened?

"Reggie and I go way back. Back to the foster care system. We ran in different circles but the same neighborhood, so there was a mutual respect at the time. He's a natural-born hustler. It sounds awful coming out of my mouth. I know firsthand what living in South Central LA can do to a kid, and it's not pretty. I was one of the lucky ones."

Perhaps we all played two different roles—one in the eyes of the public and one in private—but Reggie crossed the line when it came to using his assets to get what he wanted. He was a manipulator and a bully and a straight-up creep. I didn't want him around Lex. And it wasn't for the reason I'd initially thought. It wasn't because I thought he was after her. It was because I didn't want her to be a pawn in whatever game he was playing with Winter and me.

I'd been wrong about a lot of things in my life, but wanting to protect Lex was not one of them.

She tilted her head thoughtfully. "He seems to be doing okay."

I nodded. "Don't get me wrong. He's been through a lot, and he's come out on top, but sometimes his methods are … questionable. I don't trust the guy, especially when it comes to you."

"Why?" She was fishing for what she wanted to hear, and that made me want to smile.

I took a deep breath and let it out slowly, never taking my eyes off hers. "I think you know."

I could hear the hitch in her voice before she looked away. Then she scanned the room and lifted her arms then dropped them in defeat. "Should I be more worried about my ankle?"

Relief filled me. She was dropping the "us" talk for now. After a deep exhale to calm my racing heart, I ran my hand over the blanket and down her legs until I reached the small of her foot. "Can I?" I gesture toward the edge of the blanket.

"Sure." She watched my hand as I lifted the blanket and placed it over her other foot. I ran a finger from the bone at the top of her foot around to her ankle. I'd taken some sports medicine classes and knew her foot wasn't broken or even fractured. "You're not even swelling. You're fine. It might be a little stiff and tender today, so light exercises would be good."

"No dancing?"

"I'd give it twelve hours."

She smiled, her eyes softening. "Thanks, doc. What do I owe you?"

I scooted back on the bed and turned to my side to face her. "I know what I want. What are you willing to give?"

She blushed, and I thought about taking what I wanted right then—to feel her mouth on mine again. Her kiss from yesterday still made me lightheaded when I thought about it. Whatever came over her in that car, I wanted more of it.

"We should spend the day by the pool," she suggested. "I'm sure you're never home long enough to get much use out of it. And swimming should be good for my ankle, right?"

She didn't have to twist my arm. Not if it meant watching Lex prance around in a bikini.

"Let's do it."

Her smile grew wider, and it was so infectious, I could feel my mouth stretching in response.

"Let's do it."

Chapter 32

LEX

Something had changed. That was obvious from the moment I woke up to find Theo in my bed. What hit me instantly wasn't the fact that he was there—it was that he had stayed. After applying ice to my foot off and on for almost an hour, compressing my ankle with a wrap, and bringing me Motrin for any residual swelling, he still stayed last night.

I slipped on the only bathing suit I'd brought to LA. It wasn't anything glamorous or sexy, though in that moment, I wished it were. It was just a scalloped black triangle bikini. I used one of my long dance shirts as a swim cover-up and headed downstairs. As I passed by the kitchen, I grabbed an apple before slipping out the back door to the patio.

Theo's backyard was beautiful and private, with ivy spilling over aged brick walls and trees towering around the edge of the property. A large cabana sat on the far end of the water, and opposite it was a hot tub with a waterfall that plunged into the pool. As music spilled through the outdoor speakers, I smiled, knowing Theo had turned it on for me.

After shedding my cover-up, I tested the water with my toes. It was already warm from the morning sun, so I slipped into the water slowly and swam lap after lap, without trying to set a record. Instead, I focused on how the water felt as it glided against my skin. How my muscles worked against the water, making me feel weightless and lithe.

I became incredibly aware of my body when gravity was no longer a force against it. It was a lot like dancing—that freeing feeling that helps a dancer bend and twist and leap to music. If only I felt that way in life, but something always seemed to be holding me back.

I was half asleep under the cabana's shade when I glanced through my sunglasses and saw a shirtless Theo approaching. I swallowed as I took in the golden tan hiding his normally fair complexion. He was naturally athletic, and for a dancer, that meant conditioning the entire body. Clearly the man went above and beyond. He was lean and had defined muscle without being too bulky.

It was nice to see him this way too, without the leather jacket, his jaw relaxed, shades pulled up on his head, hazel eyes—which appeared blue today—sparkling against the sky.

"Hey," he said with a smile.

"Hey." I smiled back. "All caught up with work?"

He shrugged. "As much as I can be on everyone's day off." He sat on the lounge chair next to me and reached for the sunblock on the side table. "I got the final stage setup from Vegas. We'll have to make a few tweaks but nothing massive."

"What's that like?" I asked as he began rubbing lotion on his arms. "Putting on a huge show for someone like Winter?"

He let out a laugh. "A lot like putting a bunch of toddlers in a room with all the toys in the world at their fingertips and making them agree on which one they all have to play with."

I giggled. "That sounds … interesting. And not fun at all."

"Yeah, well, that's when my charm and negotiation skills come into play." He winked. "I win 'em over every time."

"I'm sure you do."

He grinned and reached his hand out. "Time to swim."

"I already swam," I whined while letting him pull me.

"But if I didn't see it, did it really happen?"

Theo still hadn't gotten into the water when I started to float on my back. Apparently when he said, "Time to swim," what he really meant was that it was time for *me* to swim. He, on the other hand, just sat at the edge with his long legs daggling, his palms pressed into the red and yellow tile rim, and his shaded gaze angled at me.

"The water's nice," I called out.

"Is that an invite?" he asked, flirtation buried in his tone.

I laughed. "Do you need an invite to get in your own pool?"

"Not usually, no. But I can't read you right now, Lex. I don't know if I should come closer or stay away."

My chest fluttered, and my mind reeled. "Come closer." I was well aware of the risks involved with my invite. That just yesterday I'd been grinding on his lap in an abandoned parking lot. But after the rest of the day had played out, I wasn't sure where we stood.

I heard a splash as Theo dove into the pool and proceeded to swim laps around me and under me. I was enamored by the way his dancer lines worked with the water, as though he was meant to swim too. I imagined Theo was good at a lot of things.

When he finally came up for air, he held onto the edge of the pool, an inquisitive look on his face. "How did you know you wanted to dance?"

His question was completely out of the blue but not an unusual one. Dancers loved telling stories about how they fell in love with moving to music. After all, it was what connected us, though our answers all varied. How did we find our place in the world when nothing else seemed to make sense? I'd probably answered the same question a hundred times, but I thought about it for a moment longer, wanting to give Theo more.

I pulled myself up beside him and rested my chin on my hands. "The hard parts felt easy, I guess. I'd wanted to dance since I was little. My parents were supportive of it then. You know, when it was an after-school activity that kept me out of the house a little longer and kept me in shape. Their support began to wane as I grew older. It confused me. If I was supposed to be ashamed of dancing, then why did I love it so much?"

"That's so sad," he said, and I heard the ripple in the water as he turned his body toward me.

I hated thinking about my parents and how I'd disappointed them, but what other choice was there? To conform to what they believed and miss out on a dream so many were too afraid to pursue? I could have been one of them. And I would have always known that I wasn't complete.

"It's sad, yeah, but that's not even the worst part." My eyes flickered to his, wondering if I should continue. His imploring eyes said yes. Besides, I still hadn't answered his question.

"I was sixteen when I thought I was going to die." I swallowed, my pulse racing through my veins. "I had just gotten my license and was driving home from Shane's house at night. We didn't live far from each other, just a few neighborhoods over, but it only takes a moment to change a life. I was stopped at a·light when a truck took a corner too fast and swerved into me, head-on. I remember my head smashing into the window so hard, I just knew I was going to die."

"Jesus," Theo muttered.

"Life didn't flash before my eyes like they say, but I do remember thinking that I would never be able to dance again. And that would have been the equivalent of death."

The water rippled as he moved behind me and wrapped my body in his arms.

"I wasn't hurt. A minor concussion, a few deep bruises, but that was it. The doctors said it was a miracle, and from the look of my car that got totaled in the accident, I believed them."

"It wasn't your time," he said, his voice hoarse and his lips trailing the back of my neck.

"Do you believe that? That everyone has a time and a purpose?"

"To be honest, I haven't thought about it much. But I believe *you* have a purpose, Lex. You have a gift."

I couldn't help smiling. "This coming from the guy who thought I was a lost cause from the moment he met me."

He sighed against my back, causing a flutter in my chest. "I wasn't capable of seeing you then. Not the way I do now."

"How do you see me now?" I asked, my amusement waning.

His lips moved to my ear. "As the center of everything."

Chapter 33

THEO

I didn't know what the fuck was wrong with me, following Lex around the pool like a puppy dog. Serving her. Finding every excuse fathomable to touch her uninjured ankle. Meanwhile, my need to touch her in other places was growing exponentially.

This wasn't supposed to happen. I wasn't supposed to get to know her. I wasn't supposed to care. But when I looked back on how all of it had transpired, I could only blame myself. I was the one who asked Lex for help, who crawled into bed with her in the staff room and brought her to my home studio to dance. I was the one who offered her a ride home and then barged into her apartment the next morning because something in my gut told me she was hiding something. And I was the one who invited her here to my house to spend the next seven days before we left for Vegas.

But why her? Why Lex? I'd never doted on any other girl. What made her different? I'd been surrounded by women my entire career. Confident women. Beautiful women. Sexy women. Limber women. I'd had them all with no shortage in sight. So why did life seem to stop when it came to Alexandra Quinn, the mousy, shy girl from Seattle? Why did I want to consume her in every possible way when there was more bad than good waiting for us on the other side?

After my rather bold "center of everything" confession, I began a new set of laps. And when I was finished, Lex was drying off by her lounge chair, her hair wet and stringy, dripping water down the lean curves of her back and waist, past the dimples above her more than perfect ass. It was hard not to look at her, and it was becoming a problem.

"How about we test that ankle of yours and go on an adventure?" I suggested as I toweled off.

"What kind of adventure?" Suspicion crept into her tone.

"There's actually a place I've been meaning to scout for a potential music video. I promise, minimal walking. We can even stop by a hot dog stand for dinner."

Her eyes lit up, and for some reason, that made me laugh.

"I'll go change."

Twenty minutes later, we arrived at the old LA zoo in Griffith Park. I ran around to her side of the car to help her out of the car. She said her ankle was fine, but I didn't want to take any chances. I held the door and took her hand with my free one then offered my elbow once the door was shut. She took it.

I'd never considered myself a gentleman, but it wasn't rocket science. It might have been bad timing. It might have been against the rules. But neither of those things stopped my heart from wanting to make Lex mine.

Lex was good, and sweet, and she had an innocence that made me want to teach her everything I knew and everything she was afraid to try. But there was also something more to her, an edge, a sass, and she challenged me.

"You should get back on the dance floor tomorrow. Maybe in the morning. We could go over a few tracks together if you're up for it." My suggestion was nonchalant, but I definitely had a hidden agenda. I wanted to feel the high that came with having Lex in my arms, supporting her, watching her, and moving in sync with her.

"Okay," she said, her eyes bright. She still hadn't moved her arm from mine. "Let's do it."

I smiled down at her, knowing that if anyone were to glance at us, they'd assume we were a couple. I liked it. A little too much.

We walked past the merry-go-round parking lot and started the hike toward the main section of the zoo. I'd been here before, so I had an idea where I was going. We grabbed a water at the nearest vendor cooler then continued our short trek across the space.

"What did you say this place was again?" Lex's eyes were filled with curiosity.

Rumor was, the old LA zoo was haunted, and after learning the history, I could understand why. "A zoo," I told her simply. I didn't know why I got off on her curiosity, but it meant I knew something she didn't, giving me something to teach her.

Lex laughed. "Where are the animals?"

I bit my lip and pointed at a set of metal cages. "It shut down years ago. They kept the property open for hikers and history, I guess. It's become a unique landmark. I'm sure a studio will buy it eventually, or they'll tear it down and build a shopping mall or some shit, but for now, it's a fun walk."

"A fun walk, huh?"

"Just wait and see."

I took her through the repurposed lion's den and found the doorway I was looking for, the words "At your own risk" colorfully painted there.

She froze in my hold. "Um, Theo. Should I be afraid?"

I chuckled. "No, absolutely not."

"I get the feeling these areas haven't exactly been tended to. What's in there?" She must have asked another dozen questions as she let me tug her along the pathway and down a flight of stairs. There, at the bottom of the stairwell, she saw it.

Traces of art appeared along the way, but this was the place I wanted to come back to, where graffiti—no, *art*—decorated every wall, every cage, every surface around us. We had just walked into an ocean of endless color, some abstract, some clearly meticulous in its design. Words like "Believe" and "Harmony" stood out among the rest.

"Wow" was all she said as we walked past concrete walls and rusted iron cages set on either side of us. "Is this where they kept the animals?"

"The big ones, yeah. After they abandoned it back in 1966, the riffraff went crazy tagging the walls, thinking it would all just get knocked down, but for some reason the city kept it. They turned it into a park and allowed the tagging to continue. Pretty smart of them, if you ask me. I hope they keep it open forever—as a reminder of where LA came from, what it still is, and how much it's also changing."

"Did you come here as a boy? When you were among the riffraff?" She smiled, and I smiled back. I loved that she cared about where I came from and wanted to know more, even if it wasn't the prettiest story.

"I did. It was nice to have a place to express ourselves, where freedom was allowed."

"Show me something you did."

"It's long gone now, covered up by someone else's masterpiece. I just visit to remind myself where I came from."

Her eyes lingered on me for a split second before she swung her head around the space. "This place is cool. It reminds me of an eighties music video."

Count on Lex to hit the nail on the head. "That's exactly what I was thinking. I'd love to use this whole space. The cages, the staircase, and maybe do a big dance number out in the main area with the carousel backdrop. You can see it too, can't you?"

She nodded. "Yeah, that would be epic. Who's it for?"

My vision was full-blown now, not just as a vague thought in my head. "Winter. She's going to love this shit." An idea sparked. "We should pitch her this concept."

She gave me a good-humored eye roll over her shoulder. "*We*? Nah. This is all you. Winter hates me, remember?"

I moved past her toward the cage and jumped onto the brick footer that the iron was wedged into. "She doesn't hate you. Winter can be protective, but she means well. She just doesn't know you yet. Trust me, when I show her this concept, she's going to forget all the drama of last week."

She nodded, a shadow overcasting her features. "Okay, what can I do to help?"

The ideas were spinning so fast, I couldn't keep up with my thoughts. "She's dropping her next single, 'Caged,' in three months. The video shoots in two."

"How is that going to work with the Vegas show?"

"It's going to be insane. We'll be in rehearsals for it around shows in Vegas. Casting for dancers in LA next month. And then shooting for two days only on Winter's days off. I haven't had time to focus on this with the show and everything."

"Can't you use the same choreography from the show?"

I nodded. "That's the plan, but I haven't gotten the gig yet." I let out a laugh. "She wants to see concepts this week."

"But it's *your* choreography." Lex's astonishment was refreshing. Sometimes I felt so bubbled into my own little world that I forgot what reality looked like.

"Yeah, well. It's kind of her tactic to make people work harder for her. If they always have that fear of competition, they're bound to."

I could almost see the gears shifting in Lex's brain. "So, then I'll shoot you running the choreo against the backdrop. You can show her what it could look like."

A grin stretched my face as I reached into my back pocket and started thumbing through my playlist. "Let's do it. I'll edit the footage tonight and send something rough over to Winter in the morning as a little preview of this week's pitch. You're a genius." I winked at her and caught her blush.

I'd been hesitant with Lex today, biding my time before I made another move. Yesterday was intense, and I didn't want to risk the rejection while wounds were fresh. But as my eyes traveled to Lex's mouth for the hundredth time that day, I didn't think I could wait much longer.

Chapter 34

LEX

We returned to Theo's house as the sun was setting, a little after six. The hot dog stands weren't open, so we agreed to make something back at his place. He led me to the kitchen, where he pulled out a stool from the island. He told me to sit, then proceeded to shuffle around his fridge and pantry.

There was something incredibly sexy about watching Theo work his way around the kitchen. He ignited the flame on the stove and filled a pot with water from the swivel faucet above him.

"Can I help?"

"You can open this." He set a bottle of red wine in front of me along with an electric corkscrew.

I stared at it as he walked away, and a fluttering erupted in my belly. I didn't know why. My normal reaction would have been to refuse to open it or to push it away. I searched for that dark feeling that usually crept through my blood at the thought of drinking with my peers. It never came. And I realized then, in a heart-stopping moment, that it was because I trusted Theo the same way I trusted Shane.

I reached for the electric opener and turned it over in my hands, then examined it as I tried to figure out how it worked. It seemed pretty simple: just cover the top of the bottle and push the button to drill the screw into the cork. Easy.

Theo turned to me once I had the screw spinning but with no luck. It attached to the top but was only digging a hole into the cork. A laugh bursting from his throat, he said, "Babe. You have to cut it." He took the opener from me and unlatched a horseshoe-looking device from the top, then he used it to hook around the top of the bottle and cut the foil.

Heat crawled up my neck.

"Have you ever used one of these things?" he asked as he reinserted the screw onto the top of the bottle and held the button. I watched as he pulled it away a few seconds later and removed the cork with another push of the button.

"I've never had wine before, so no."

The way he looked at me then, his eyes running over my face as though he wanted to memorize it, only made me hotter. He grabbed two wineglasses from the cabinet then set them down near the bottle. "Do you want something else? I have pretty much everything you could think of."

"Of course you do."

His eyes lifted, amused.

"Wine is fine. Just … maybe one glass."

♥

By the time Theo was finished cooking dinner, I'd poured myself a second glass. My head felt light, and giggles erupted from me when Theo leaned in to kiss my cheek. He'd taken the stool beside me after dishing our meals and placing them in front of us. It was a seafood Alfredo that smelled and looked amazing.

"You're cute when you're drunk."

I opened my mouth in mock astonishment. "How can I be drunk? This is only"—I looked at the inch of red liquid remaining—"not even two glasses."

"You overpoured. So it's more like four. And you're small."

I swiveled in my stool and placed my hands on the sides of my hips. "I'm not that small."

He grinned and shook his head. "You're perfect. But no more wine for you." He moved the bottle away, and I pouted.

After a few bites of seafood, I dropped my fork and looked at him. "This is fucking amazing."

He looked at me, his eyes darkening. "Did you just cuss?"

"Yes." I didn't see what the big deal was. "Doesn't everybody?"

He shook his head. "Not you. At least I've never heard you. It sounded … dirty."

I laughed. "That's what Shane says too. He tells me not to. I think he wants to believe I'm this innocent little thing forever."

"Aren't you? Innocent?"

How did Theo always manage to make me blush? "Maybe. But I cuss when the mood strikes, just like everyone. Anyway." I exaggerated the word to change topics. I'd had a point when I acknowledged his cooking. "Where did you learn to cook? When have you had the time?"

He set his fork down and turned to me, his knees on either side of mine. "The foster care system kind of forces you to grow up faster than most, I guess. My foster parents, who eventually adopted me, were never home, and there were two other kids, younger than me. I was responsible for making sure their lunches were packed, that they made it to school on time, and that they had food on the table every night.

"When I bought this house a few years ago, I promised myself I would use it and not just let it sit here, like some celebrities I've come across. I never wanted someone to cook or clean for me. To me, that stuff is just a part of life."

"But—" I couldn't stop thinking about little Theo raising two younger kids while he was trying to be a kid himself. "If you were taking care of the kids, when did you find the time to dance?"

"I did what every other thug did." He grinned. "Skipped school. But instead of crawling the streets, I hung out at the rec center. Took dance classes there and eventually got noticed by the man who basically saved my life."

"Who is that?"

"Rashni, the owner of Gravity."

My heart stopped. "You mentioned him before. Didn't he—?" I couldn't bring myself to ask. I'd heard a lot about Rashni. There were photos of him and groups of dancers all over the halls of the center, along with a plaque honoring his life. He died when he was thirty-four. I'd always wondered how. I knew that his wife owned Gravity now, but she was never there.

"He always walked to and from the rec center when he taught. Never wanted to be seen as different by the community that had practically raised him. He'd built Gravity from nothing when he was a boy. The way it blossomed over the years was all due to his hustle. Hustle he wouldn't have had if he hadn't faced some of the worst times growing up. He wanted a better life for himself and others. He wanted a positive outlet to feed his creativity. Just like the zoo housed a place for creativity, that's what Gravity became for others. To this day, I believe Gravity's success is due to the origin of it all. Due to Rashni's passion giving a home to others who needed that type of release. He beat the odds, and he wanted others to beat them too. That's why he took me under his wing. He saw something in me, and he offered me a place at Gravity to make something of myself."

"Sounds like he was an amazing man." I swallowed. "What happened to him?"

"Wrong place, wrong time. Some thugs were crawling the streets, looking for money. One man pulled a gun in a convenience store, and he happened to be buying smokes. His fucking worst habit he refused to break. He tried to talk to the robbers, but when that didn't work, he jumped the man with the gun and got shot in the chest."

I placed a hand on his knee and squeezed. "I'm so sorry, Theo. He would be so proud of you."

Theo's jaw tightened, then he nodded. "I hope so. Rashni's wife, Ananya, runs Gravity now, but she can hardly bring herself to come in." He rubbed his chest and shook his head. "Shit, that got heavy. You should think twice about asking me questions. I come from a dark place that's not always fun to go back to."

"Your past doesn't scare me."

He gripped my eyes with his. "Maybe it should."

Chapter 35

LEX

Theo excused himself after dinner and started editing the video we'd taken earlier today. After his swift departure, I wondered if leaving was just an excuse to be alone following our conversation about Rashni. My heart broke for him, for Ananya, and for everyone who considered Rashni the hero he was to Theo.

Before that conversation, I'd expected the night to go differently. I had wanted it to. We had had the perfect day, and I was starting to feel bolder around him, especially after some wine. I was desperate to feel Theo's lips on mine again, to feel him between my legs. His hot breath on my neck.

Flustered, I showered off our day at the zoo, feeling the effects of the sun that had stained my skin. The lightness I'd felt from the wine hit me again when I stepped out of the shower. I glanced at my reflection in the mirror. There was a glow to my skin, my eyes appearing brighter than before. My heart kicked, and I smiled. I felt happy, weightless, and free from all the insecurities that had clouded me over the years.

I couldn't stop thinking of Theo as I slipped on my rose-gold pajama shorts and matching tank. My hands swept over the silk, up my thighs, over my stomach, and stopped over my breasts, where my strained nipples poked through.

Heat flashed through me as I remembered batting him away when he tried to touch me yesterday morning. I knew if I had the opportunity again, I wouldn't bat him away.

I closed my eyes, imagining what it would be like to be with Theo. To be wrapped in his arms, skin to skin, his hot breath on my neck, gentle grunts in my ear, his length pushing into me, deeper and deeper, until I unraveled like an untamed spool of thread.

My eyes flew open, my breaths quick, and the space between my thighs heated as a full-body ache gripped me. I shook my head, pushing away my thoughts and letting out a breath. This was ridiculous. My throat burned as my heart pounded. *I need water.*

The hall was quiet and dark, with no sign of activity in the room across the hall, where Theo's bedroom was. I took the stairs to the main floor and entered the kitchen, flicking on the overhead light. I pulled out a water from the fridge and chugged it in long guzzles. After replacing the cap, I leaned against the counter, feeling restless and wide-awake. My eyes landed on the closed door that led to the studio, and I knew of only one way to expel the energy that flowed through me.

I descended the dimly lit stairwell on my tiptoes, as though I was trespassing, but when I entered the studio and saw the moonlight cast through the arched windows and lighting the center of the room, all anxious thoughts dissolved.

It took a few seconds to connect my phone to the Bluetooth speaker. I thumbed through my playlist and selected one of my latest favorites, "Confidently Lost." I loved everything about the soothing track. Sabrina Claudio's voice, the lyrics, the light percussion, and the highs and lows in the melody—it was all magic.

My muscles reacted as soon as the first note sounded through the speakers. That was what it was like when the music overtook me, when my soul spoke through my limbs and pushed my every move to the max. Every sensation within me was heightened, and I sailed through the song as if the lyrics were crawling through me.

As I stood in the center of the room and the final notes of the song faded, bare feet padded toward me, causing my heart to crash like cymbals.

I looked over my shoulder, our eyes locking on an invisible beat. "Oh." The word slipped past my lips at the sight of Theo approaching, his torso bare and his damp hair tossed wildly atop his head. My breath caught in my throat as I looked down at where his black sleep pants hung. They were just a drawstring away from falling to his knees, and I wanted to be the one who unknotted them.

A new track started. The first chords of James Bay's "Wild Love" surrounded us, and the intro sent a wave of chills over my body. He closed the distance, smelling of soap and mouthwash, as though he'd been on his way to bed. His arm eased around me, fingers skating along my gooseflesh until he reached my middle. Then he pulled me to him until my back was flush with his front.

I sucked in a breath and looked up into the mirror. I had a clear view of his hooded stare as he leaned in to kiss my neck. "Dance with me." His voice was gruff, filled with sleep and sex, making my stomach knot and my lids slam shut. Blood sped through my veins like wildfire.

He took my hand with his, and he guided my hips left, then right—

his palm still on my center. The thin fabric of his pants left nothing to the imagination either. He was hard and completely shameless about it.

As his hand slid from my stomach to my hips and then around to my ass, every conflicting emotion I'd ever felt between us swirled through me. Our first heated exchange in the theater. That horrible moment during the audition when I knew he didn't want me there. My shock when he barged into the staff room and caught me sleeping, followed by his request for help. Our almost kiss on the Santa Monica Pier, followed by our actual kiss in his car, one block away from Gravity. And now this. Him, dancing with me, for pleasure alone.

WATCH: WILD LOVE
smarturl.it/Gravity_WildLove

I'd never before danced with someone and felt the lyrics so wholly. Partnering made me vulnerable—it gave a man permission to invade the deepest parts of me.

And while one song transitioned to another, Theo still didn't let go. Our breathing was heavy, every inhale as intense as our locked gaze in the mirror. He spun me, pulled me to his chest, and settled both palms on my ass. He squeezed, bringing the material of my shorts higher.

My breath hitched and my palms rested on his chest, giving him unspoken permission to continue.

He leaned in, his nose skimming my ear before his lips landed just below it.

A moan slipped my throat. He kissed that too.

I felt myself shake. He held me tighter.

And then he was leaning me back, dipping me until my hair swept the floor. When he brought me up, his eyes roamed my body until they reached my eyes. "What are you doing to me, Lex?"

I leaned in, pressing a kiss just below his neck. "Probably the same thing you're doing to me."

Theo's fingers found my chin, guiding it up until he was peering back at me. Depth to depth, soul to soul. I'd never been so present with anyone in my entire life. "And what's that?" he asked.

"Breaking the rules." I shivered at the sound of my own voice, so foreign, filled with flirtation and want for a man I wasn't allowed to have. I worried that made me want him more, but deep down I knew that wasn't true.

He was nodding, a smile filling his mouth. Then he kissed me. A soul-stealing, heart-shattering, life-altering kiss that detonated everything I'd ever known inside of me. My mouth parted, and his tongue wasted no time tangling with mine. He lifted me off the floor, his hands back on my ass. My legs wrapped around his hips.

I didn't know where he was going when he started walking with me, our lips twisted together. But when my back landed against the mirror and his hips pushed into me through our clothes, nothing else mattered.

My mouth separated from his in a gasp. He took the opportunity to move to my collarbone, sliding his tongue across it before bringing it back to my neck. "Were you hoping I'd come down here and see you?" His teeth nipped my skin, and I could have sworn I felt him smile, knowing.

My body hummed. "Maybe."

"I know you were," he murmured.

So cocky. It made me even hotter, and I knew if he pushed into me right then, I would be slick and ready.

"Did you wear this outfit for me too?"

My heart was beating out of control. "Maybe." I swallowed and gasped when his hot mouth hovered above my hard and aching nipple. My eyes squeezed shut, anticipating his next move.

He brought his mouth down and wrapped his lips around me through the satin of my top, his tongue darting out and swirling in a slow circle. I gasped again when he bit down slightly, shooting sparks off within me.

This was how it was supposed to feel. Passionate in a breathless sort of way. And wrong in a way that also felt right.

"You aren't wearing a bra," he growled. "That wasn't very nice of you."

God, the things his gravelly voice did to me. I slid my fingers into his hair and ran my teeth along his ear then along his tight square jaw that I loved to hate. When I reached his neck, he pumped his hips into me so hard through our clothes, I thought they would tear off. He ground his hips and whispered my name.

"Fuck," I moaned as the ache grew stronger.

His fingers pressed into my jowls. He tipped my chin back, his eyes blazing as he stared back at me. "What did you say?"

I could barely breathe, let alone talk. But I tried. "Fuck," I whispered and watched as his expression grew fiery.

He shook his head. "Your mouth is too pretty for dirty words." He leaned in, his lips at my ear. My lids slammed shut as I sucked in another breath. "The next time you talk like that, I better be inside you."

Chapter 36

LEX

Theo swung me away from the mirror, our mouths never separating. He carried me through the studio doors, across the foyer, and up the stairs to the kitchen. My ass crashed onto the cool granite of the counter, his hands greedy as they gripped my thighs through my shorts then slid up to fill his palm with my breast.

"I shouldn't be touching you like this." He groaned the words as if they pained him. But if he was trying to stop himself, he was doing a shitty job.

"You really shouldn't be." My voice was dark and dripping with a challenge. "There are rules, Theo."

"Fuck the rules." His eyes opened on mine. "I want to break all the rules with you." He kissed me again, this time slowly, inhaling through his nose.

My heart was like a hummingbird in flight, whirring away. "Then what are you waiting for?" I swallowed, knowing exactly what I was giving him permission to do.

That was all it took. Permission. Words. His mouth crushed mine, his breath heating as I shuddered in his hold.

"I love your mouth," he spoke between kisses. "And your skin."

I gasped at the feel of his mouth sliding down my silk top between my breasts and over my stomach until he was at my waist. He peered at me as he played with the waistband of my shorts, his finger gliding between the fabric and my skin. I shimmied against the counter, helping him slide them over my ass and down my legs to reveal matching rose-gold silk panties.

A curse left his mouth when he saw them. "You're soaked, Lex." His gaze flew up to mine. "I haven't even touched you yet." His thumb moved over my wet opening, circling it slowly as he gazed drunkenly into my eyes.

Could someone like me really have this effect on him? It sure as hell appeared so.

I spread my legs, and he looked down to catch the movement. His jaw hardened—this time for a different reason. He hooked his finger around the thin fabric and tugged it to the side. "I'm going to make you feel so good."

The hint of the smile on his face had me curious. It was a warning, but it wasn't until his thick finger entered me that I registered what he meant. My head fell back at the intensity. He brought himself closer, wrapping an arm around my waist and crushing my chest to his. "Tell me you feel this." He sank deeper, making my insides flutter.

"I feel it," I gasped. "Don't stop."

His smile was at my neck. "Oh, I won't. Not until you scream."

Damn it. Why did he have to be so cute ... and arrogant ... and sexy. And—God, yes—he was good with his fingers.

He added another digit, the thickness filling me, stretching me. His mouth found my neck and tickled it with a graze of his lips until he reached my ear and nibbled. Too many sensations were knotting my belly, the tension so powerful I knew it wouldn't be long before I combusted around him.

His lips practically swallowed mine with his next kiss. It was just the way I'd always imagined kissing Theo, with those fleshy lips like two firm cushions devouring me. He was persistent yet patient as his fingers pumped me relentlessly, working me to a release.

But just as my muscles tensed and I started to feel the first hint of an orgasm, his fingers pulled out, and he shook his head. My insides screamed to feel him again.

"Patience, Lex." He stepped back, his amused eyes scrolling over me.

"What are you doing?" My breathing grew rapid as I wondered what form of torture he was planning next.

"I'm about to make you come all over my tongue. And then all over my cock."

And with those words, he tore my panties down my legs before flinging them across the room.

He grabbed my feet on his way back up and placed them at the edge of the counter. "Arch your back for me."

I must have hesitated too long, unsure of what he meant. His hands moved under my ass, guiding my pelvis into the air so my back was arched and only my shoulder and head were pressed into the counter. "Oh," I said as he pushed my knees apart, spreading them wide as he pulled me forward to the edge.

My head grew warm as I felt him breathe against my opening. "I love how flexible you are," he murmured before swiping me with his tongue. I closed my eyes, anticipating what was to come. Fearing it but wanting it more.

There was so much I hadn't told Theo yet. So much that hadn't come up in conversation. Like the fact that I'd never had sex before. I hadn't even had an orgasm that wasn't self-achieved. I didn't know how he would take that. I didn't know if it would completely ruin the buzz, and I sure as hell wasn't going to bring it up tonight.

His tongue tasted me again before his mouth closed around me and sucked on my clit. My toes curled, and my eyes went wide. "Holy crap."

He chuckled, causing a vibration that made my eyes roll into the back of my head. Theo was way too good at his … ministrations. I shouldn't have been happy about that, considering he'd probably had tons of practice, but in that moment, I was deliriously okay with it.

He took his time, using my reactions as a way to control the way he moved his mouth against me, teasing me.

"Theo," I finally begged. I was so close to the edge and so afraid he would pull away again.

This time, he didn't. His mouth stayed on me as he added a finger, curling and uncurling it inside me to a speed that matched my heart rate. I came hard, my back still arched, my cheek pressed into the light-gray granite, and my scream loud and unashamed.

He stood as my pelvis sank back down, my tired legs slipping off the edge of the counter. He pulled me to a sitting position, and our mouths crashed together. It took a moment for me to realize the new taste on his mouth was mine.

His hands drifted up my skin, bringing my top with it. It landed softly on the counter, leaving me completely bare for him. His eyes darkened as he took me in.

"Jesus, Lex. You are insanely beautiful." His fingers wove through mine as he stared back into my eyes. "How are you single?" Heat crawled up my cheeks.

I sank my teeth into my bottom lip, wondering if this was the time to tell him about my misfortune. That it wasn't easy to find a boyfriend when your best friend, an attractive male, was always by your side. Or that one fateful night had made me fearful of intimacy until recently.

I opened my mouth to say something, anything, but Theo shook his head and kissed me softly. "Never mind. It doesn't matter. You're mine tonight."

I tried not to let my mind linger on his last word, a word that made me wonder if that was all this was. A one-night thing. He swooped me up into his arms and carried me up another flight of stairs as though my weight was inconsequential and set me on the edge of his bed.

His pants tented where his erection stood, and I reached for him, dragging a finger across his skin where bare skin met the elastic waist of his pants. But as soon as I reached for his string, he stepped away with a smile and made his way to his dresser on the other side of the room.

I sat back on his bed and glanced around. French doors looked out over the pool, and a set of chairs decorated the corner of the room in front of the brick fireplace. Every bit of his room, from the plain navy comforter to the LA art on the mantel, screamed its need for a woman's touch.

"You are such the bachelor, aren't you?" My eyes swung toward him and caught on his naked form approaching, his length heavy in his hand. My heart started as I glanced behind him to see his crumpled sweats on the floor and an unwrapped condom in his other hand.

"C'mere." He sat on the bed beside me and took my hand, placing it on his cock. He used his fingers to wrap mine around him then squeezed as he groaned in the air. "That's better. I don't really want to talk about my poor decorating skills right now." He guided my hand in long strokes, squeezing himself with my fingers.

"Then what do you want to talk about?" I bit down on my lip, trying to contain my smile.

His lips brushed up my neck and landed on my ear, the effects rippling over my skin. "I want to talk about how loud you're going to scream, because

I'm pretty sure you were trying to set a record downstairs. I haven't even gotten started with you, Lex."

He stopped moving my hand and turned to push me down on the bed until he was hovering above me, his knees between my legs.

My laughter was weak, filled with embarrassment. "It wasn't that loud."

He grinned as he lowered himself, his warm skin crushing mine. "Don't get all shy on me now." He kissed my nose. "You're a screamer. I can handle that."

I placed my hands on his chest and pushed him away teasingly, but he brought himself back down with his strength and kissed me, this time on the cheek.

I melted beneath him, happily submitting to it all. His touch, his words, his lips. Theo Noska was not supposed to be sweet. He was supposed to be an asshole who was easy to stay away from. How had he crawled so deeply under my skin and awakened something within me—something dark but beautiful too?

I watched in fascination as he sat up, his knees wedged between my thighs, his length hard and in his hands. My heart beat faster as he rolled the condom on, the sheer material covering him completely. But I could still see every strained inch.

"Does that hurt?" The moment the question slipped out, I wanted to take it back. The fact that I was a virgin shouldn't matter to him, but it didn't feel right to announce it right then. Whatever was going to happen between us, I wanted it to happen naturally.

He eyed me strangely before letting out a breathy laugh. "Not as much as it hurts to not be inside you."

There was a moment of quiet as he brought himself down and held his weight on his elbows. He dipped down to kiss me, this time slowly, as if savoring every second. I feared that too. I feared the depth of my feelings for a man who couldn't be mine.

When his fingers moved between my legs, his breath skated over my chest.

"Your heart is beating so fast." He pressed his ear against it then glanced up, meeting my eyes. "Are you okay?"

He was worried. So was I. Not for what was about to happen but for what could potentially change when it was all over.

"I'm okay."

"Nervous?" His tone was intense and indicated he'd put a stop to the whole thing if I even remotely doubted being with him. "Tell me the truth, Lex."

"I am a little. Aren't you?"

"Fucking terrified." He kissed the spot between my breasts before peering back up through my lashes. "I want you more than anything, but I don't know what happens tomorrow or next week or next month. I can't make any promises. I don't want to hurt you. That seems like something I'm pretty good at."

I hated his words—how honest they were, how little hope he saw in our future. In himself. But I wanted him, anyway. I wanted him to be my first, no matter what the consequences might be. "I'm okay with the not knowing if you are." I reached a hand to his cheek and swallowed. "Now stop stalling and make me scream."

His eyes softened, and something clicked in my heart. "I think I might aim for something a little different tonight." He let out a breath and pulled himself up to kiss me. As he did, the tip of him nudged against my opening. I held my breath in anticipation of what would come next. How would he feel inside me? If it felt anything like his fingers, I might explode before too long.

We were in midkiss, our tongues wrapped around each other's, when he finally pushed himself forward. I gasped, my lids flying open as I felt myself expand for him.

"I knew you'd feel so fucking good." He sighed and skimmed my neck with his nose. "I could stay here all night."

I was so absorbed by the fullness of him, his words almost didn't register, but when they did, I smiled. "I don't think you'd last that long."

He pushed himself deeper inside me and groaned. My heart lurched as I stretched for him again. "Don't underestimate me, Lex."

Theo reached an arm under my back and pulled me off the comforter and onto his lap, so he was kneeling, and my legs were wrapped around his waist. When he pushed into me again, I noticed the difference in position. He hit me deeper, making my insides coil and retract like magic. He felt it too. His eyes squeezed shut, then he did it again. And again.

I could feel my impending release as his movements quickened. My thighs started to shake as my muscles clenched. My fingers curled into his back as my release catapulted through me. And on the brink of my orgasm, he held me tighter, moving me and swallowing my cries with his beautiful mouth, and then he came too.

My limbs were weak when it was over, but I managed to hang on to his neck in an effort to stay close to him. I pressed my cheek into his shoulder, letting my heart settle until his and mine were beating together.

With his hand through my hair and an arm locked tightly around me, he nuzzled his nose to my ear. "For the record," he rasped, sending chills through my body, "if I could rewrite the rules, I'd do it for you."

THEO

I want to break all the rules with you.

My own words drifted through my mind as rays of sunlight leaked through my lids.

My eyes were heavy after hours of familiarizing myself with all the parts of Lex I'd been aching to know, to taste, to touch. But instead of this quelling my desire, as I'd imagined, I'd slipped off to sleep a short while ago dreaming of more. More Lex. Fewer rules.

Fucking rules.

My hand drifted across the bed in search of Lex's firm body. I needed to feel her to convince myself it hadn't all been a dream. When my search came up empty, I sat on the edge of the bed, feeling as if I'd just been doused with cold water. Panic filled my chest as I looked around. She wasn't on the balcony. The door to the bathroom was open, the lights off. She was gone.

The first thought that hit me was that she woke up and regretted the entire night. My next thought was that she'd gotten what she wanted and left. It wouldn't have been the first time I'd been used in such a way, but Lex wasn't like that.

And then I heard the faint sound of a door opening, followed by footsteps in the hall. Lex appeared in the doorway of my room, her hair wet from a recent shower, her body covered by an oversized salmon-colored muscle shirt that did little to cover the sides of her breasts.

"Hey." She smiled shyly from the doorway.

"Hey." Something stirred in my chest. "You could have showered in here."

Pink crawled up her cheeks. "My stuff was in there. And I didn't want to wake you."

"C'mere." My voice was still filled with sleep, but my insides were wide-awake.

She walked to me, and I pulled her so she was standing between my legs. My hand slipped under her shirt, searched for her panties, and slipped them off. They pooled around her ankles, then I looked up. "Oops."

She laughed as I pulled her onto my lap, her thighs around my hips and her fresh pussy directly over my cock. I fingered the sides of her shirt next, opening the loose material and pulling it over her firm breast and exposing it. I looked into her eyes and placed my thumb to her lips. "Suck."

She was hesitant at first, as though she didn't understand my request. She would soon. Her mouth moved around my thumb, and her tongue darted out before she wrapped it around her lips. I flashed her a smile and pulled it away, moving it down to her nipple.

"I didn't know where you were," I said, rubbing her light-pink peak between my thumb and pointer finger. I could practically feel the clenching and unclenching of her insides in reaction to my touch. "I was worried you left."

"I didn't know if I should."

My eyes shot to hers, the panic that had set in earlier back with a vengeance. "Why?" She looked away, so I released her breast to turn her face back to mine. "Why, Lex? Last night was okay, right? Did I hurt you?"

She tilted her head. "Last night was more than okay."

"Then what's wrong?"

Her eyes searched mine, hesitating to deliver the truth. I could feel it, the thick cloud of tension weighing us down. "I didn't know where we stood today. Last night we agreed to no promises. I didn't want you to think I had expectations."

I frowned, understanding everything she was saying. When I woke up this morning, the first thing I wanted was to feel her beside me. But my wants and our reality were two different things. "I didn't mean that we should put an expiration date on it."

"Maybe we should." She said it gently, but something stirred in my chest. "If we know it's going to end, then it will be easier, right? No one gets hurt."

Would it be easier? Somehow, I didn't think so. All I knew was that I wasn't ready to let her go.

"What do you suggest?"

"We leave for Vegas in a week. I'll need to be completely focused."

"Then we give it the week." I searched her eyes, looking for the words she hid. Was this really what she wanted? "You stay here, you share my bed, then we fly to Vegas and focus on work."

"And then that's it. No more—" Her conviction at the finale of us heated my chest.

"And then we reevaluate things after Vegas. When the contract ends."

She smiled in a way that lit up my insides, as if I'd just given her hope. "Okay."

Relief whooshed around my chest. I kissed her and pulled away. "If I only have a week with you, I don't want to waste any time." My hand slipped down to her ass and gripped it, holding her to me as I reached over to the nightstand and grabbed a condom. I held it in front of her face. "Put this on for me."

She looked at it, confused, then took it from me, slid off my lap, and lowered herself to her knees below me. She took me in her hold, one hand at my base, the other gripping me firmly and stroking. I watched her hungrily while my curiosity spiked.

There was something different about Lex, besides the fact that she came off shy in the bedroom. I kept waving away the thought that she was exploring a man for the first time. That couldn't have been it. Lex was twenty-two and gorgeous. Any guy before me would have been crazy not to chase her. Not to say Lex would have given it up to just anyone. She wasn't like that. But my curiosity was piqued when she dipped down to taste the tip of my cock.

My abs clenched with pleasure, and I leaned back slightly to give her more room, watching in awe as her mouth moved down around me. She dragged her tongue up the underside, then moved it back down, cloaking it with her lips. She seemed to be so into it, exploring me, swirling her tongue around the tip, moving her mouth as deep as she could go without gagging. It was all so innocent and sexy as hell.

She pulled off of me, unexpectedly, looking up, her eyes unsure. "Was that okay?"

I chuckled and immediately regretted it when I saw the crushed look in her eyes. "Lex, you're killing me. Haven't you ever sucked a dick before? It's hard to get it wrong."

She didn't respond. Instead, the familiar flush crawled up her neck and cheeks, and my eyes opened in surprise.

"You haven't? Ever?"

She shook her head, and my curiosity from the night before came slamming back. "But when I went down on you last night, that wasn't your first time…" I didn't ask. There was no way, but the shake of her head told me different. "Fuck, Lex." Disbelief whipped through me. "You'd had sex before last night, though, right?"

She shook her head again, and I wanted to explode. Why hadn't she told me? Not that it would have made a difference. I still would have fucked her, but maybe I would have done things differently? Given her a bit more attention before going all the way. Asked her if she was okay a few dozen more times. *Fuck.*

"It was perfect," she said before answering any of my unasked questions. "I didn't want to ruin last night by making a big deal of it."

"You were a virgin, Lex. That's a big fucking deal."

She smiled, despite my outburst, and inched her way up my lap, taking my face between her palms. "I'm not a virgin anymore."

In that moment, I might have fallen in love.

Lex kissed me then, her soft lips firming against mine. She rubbed herself against my lap, coming dangerously close to inserting herself on my bare cock. I shifted her and took the condom from her hand and placed it around me. She stood and started to straddle me, but I stopped her and spun her around and bit down on my lip at the sight. "I just needed to look at you."

"At my ass?" she said with a breathy laugh.

"I love your ass." I squeezed her cheeks with my palm and then spread her wide. "Fuck." I moved a hand to her waist. "Sit down. Slowly."

She did as I asked, the back of her legs pressing against my kneecaps as she descended. I opened my legs slightly and pulled her down, groaning as her heat sank around me. She was so fucking tight, I knew I was stretching her wide, filling her full. And the fact that I'd been the first to ever make her feel that way drove me fucking insane. If I had felt possessive of Lex before, I sure as hell did now.

She started to move above me, and as she did, I caught her peach scent and groaned. Everything about Lex drove me so crazy, in no time I was fighting my release to wait for hers. I pushed aside the fabric of her shirt, exposing her breast again, pinching her nipple with one hand and finding her clit with my other.

"Come for me, babe." My words hit her one second, and she was screaming the next. I wrapped my arms around her as she rode out her orgasm, then I finally let go.

I pulled her onto the bed when we were finished. As I slipped out of her, I rid myself of the condom and wrapped my arms around her body. My heavy lids succumbed to exhaustion, but not before muttering into her soft skin, "For what it's worth, I'm glad I was your first."

Chapter 38

LEX

I forced an eye open just enough to see Theo standing above me in nothing but a pair of gray boxer briefs. He held something in his hand, and I had to squint through my blurry eyes to make out a mug with steam drifting from the top. I moaned and stretched, my body a tangle of satisfying aches. Coffee had never looked sexier.

When I glanced at him again, he had a sly look on his face. I'd quickly grown to love that expression, especially when it was aimed at me.

I was painfully aware that it was Monday morning and we had to leave our sanctuary, but it was the final week of rehearsals. My excitement grew at the thought of where we would be next week—on a plane to Vegas.

Sunday had been a wash. We'd wasted the entire day in bed together, exploring each other and sharing stories of our young dance years. He was fascinated by my boring life back in Seattle, just as I was fascinated by his rise to celeb choreographer status. Things almost felt ... normal. As though we could be an actual couple if it weren't for the damn contract.

And then his phone rang, bringing me back to reality, where I was a secret and he was supposed to be kissing Winter's ass. He pulled his phone off the nightstand and groaned before silencing it and setting it back down again. "I'll call her later."

"Winter?" Of course it was Winter. She'd seen the cut of the zoo video Theo sent her yesterday and wouldn't stop calling him. They were setting up a meeting to talk about it.

"I can't move," I croaked, trying to change the subject and my rapidly declining mood.

He laughed and set the coffee down on the nightstand before stretching out beside me.

Theo's dimple popped as he ran his eyes over me. "You gonna be okay?" he teased when he dropped the sheet. "Need me to call a doctor?"

"Does he make house calls?"

He smirked. "He does, and he's more than willing to take care of your aches and pains when we come home. Where does it hurt?"

There was something so intimate about his words. I loved them as much as they terrified me. I smiled as I reached between my legs.

His eyes blazed as he tracked the movement. "Maybe he can squeeze in an appointment right now."

Theo dropped me off in the parking lot behind Gravity, and I headed straight to the community area. I didn't expect anyone else to be inside yet. But Reggie, Amie, and a few others congregated there, downing waters and snack bars, their heads bent low as they chatted. Usually I was the first one in the center. But I supposed everyone was eager since it was the final week before we left for Vegas.

My smile stretched wide as I approached them, pushing down the memory of the tension from the previous week. The dancers seemed happy with the selections on Friday. I wasn't on their radar anymore. I hoped. "What's everyone doing here so early?"

Amie's head snapped up as though she was surprised to hear my voice, then she smiled. "Hey, Lex. Reggie was just showing me something he put together for a choreography pitch this week."

Reggie glanced my way, and his eyes lit up. He patted the seat beside him. "Come check this out."

Discomfort rumbled within me. That couldn't have been a coincidence. "Oh yeah?" I asked nonchalantly. I took the seat, leaving a few inches between us. He slid over to close the gap, pressed his shoulder into mine, and held up his phone. "What's this for?"

"Winter," Reggie said without even batting an eye. "She's looking for a choreographer for the 'Caged' music video."

"What about Theo?" The words slipped out before I could think them through. "I mean, he's already done the choreography, and he's working with Winter. I assumed that kind of job would go to him."

Reggie's eyes narrowed momentarily before he shrugged it off. "She's holding the pitch meeting this week, which means it's a possibility. Besides, Theo will be slammed with the show. I can't see him taking his only three days off to work."

"You can't?" I couldn't help my amused expression. Did Reggie know Theo at all? And why the hell would Reggie go after a job that was so clearly Theo's?

Reggie set down his phone and leaned back against the couch with a hard look on his face. "Theo Noska ain't the be-all and end-all of dance, Lex. He's hit his ceiling. It's time this industry experiences some fresh ideas. Like in our partner routine." He pursed his lips, as if making a point. "We took some creative liberties and made it ten times better. Isn't that right?"

When I didn't respond, he looked at Amie, who turned away and raised her hands. "Uh-uh. I'm not getting involved."

He huffed and stood. "Never mind. Y'all wouldn't understand." He walked off. "See you in the studio."

Amie and I exchanged wide-eyed looks at the same time. "What is he trying to pull?" I hissed it as I scooted toward her, minimizing the chance that someone could hear us.

Amie looked around as if to make sure no one was listening and leaned in further and whispered, "I really want to stay out of whatever's going on, but Reggie's been on edge a lot lately. He's been on this kick to get some other choreo work outside of the studio, but I don't know why he's got his target on Winter and Theo. There are thousands of other artists, and so many of them come through Gravity."

"It's like he wants what Theo wants. It's a little creepy."

Amie agreed with a sigh. "I hope he cools it before we hit Vegas. It's going to be a long six months if he plans to challenge Theo every step of the way." She looked around again before her brows bent in with worry. "And between you and me, I think he had something to do with the selections Winter made with the featured spots."

Dread filled me as her words sank in. Amie was only guessing, but Reggie's nonchalance Friday morning before the announcements made sense now. He'd already known.

Chapter 39

THEO

"**B**ring it under." I swept my right arm under my leg. "Swing out. And hit. Then pop, pop." I emphasized the chest pop as I did an angled slide pivot with my feet. My gaze traveled around the room to make sure everyone was following. It was the third time I had to go back to the beginning and slow down choreography for "What Do You Mean?" It wasn't that they weren't getting it, it was that I was starting to nitpick the shit out of everything. Now that they knew the routines, it was time to make them perfect.

I swiped a towel over my forehead and shoved it back between the elastic of my shorts and my body, picking up where I left off. We continued to run the entire routine before starting the music.

The energy was different today. A good different. Less stress and more focus. No one spoke out of turn or joked. The mood was intense, and it made the room boom with a vigor that crackled the air and made my heart pound in my throat. This was why I loved dance. This feeling right here.

"Take it from the top," I boomed over the intro while counting them off with four claps.

Winter walked in just as the guys started. She weaved through them, checking out their moves as she went. Her smile was bright, and she nodded with the beat, clearly loving what she saw. And I couldn't help feeling that everything was going to be okay.

"Looking good, Theo." She stared at the dancers as she said it, and that made me smile, because she was talking about my choreography.

"They've been working hard."

She glanced at me, her angry eyes from Friday nowhere to be seen. I could almost pretend it had never happened.

"I loved the video for 'Caged.' I've never seen anything like that before." She was gushing, effectively inflating my ego. The video I whipped together Saturday night before I found Lex in my studio was something I was proud of. I could only hope Winter liked it as much as I did. To hear that she did was a relief.

"You never fail to bring on the magic with your creativity," she said. "The concept is fresh and colorful and fun. It brings me back to the beginning of all this. When simplicity won out over all the pyrotechnics and costumes heavier than me."

"Glad you liked it."

She was right where I wanted her, loving the idea, back in her good graces. I decided to push for more. "You gonna cancel that pitch tomorrow and let me focus on your show now?"

She laughed. "And disappoint all the hopefuls? I couldn't."

I pursed my lips and narrowed my eyes. "For real, Winter? You and I know you're just wasting their time. The song already has choreography. And you already have dancers. You realize you're only saving yourself time and money by sticking with me."

She shrugged and bit her lip. It was the playful Winter I'd always known. "Glad to see you really want this."

"You know I love working with you." That was the truth. Despite our less than innocent history together, we were still friends, and I cared about her as much as I always had.

When she didn't respond to my earlier question, I considered the conversation settled and nudged her arm. "You want to jump in?" I nodded toward the dancers as I reached behind and brought forward her headset. "Let's see it."

My grin was wide, and hers matched.

One week until Vegas, then the real magic would begin. I was ready. So was she. The rest of the bullshit could fade into the wind. At least for now.

She took the headset from me, darted out onto the dance floor, and took her position. I stopped the track and started it from the beginning. "Back to the top. With Winter this time."

Chapter 40

THEO

A horn blared near Wicked Saints Records as a car moved around me, blocking me from leaving my metered spot. LA gridlock was the absolute worst at any time of day, but I didn't have the patience for this now, not with less than a week before Vegas and my dancers already in the studio without me. My hand slammed against the wheel, and another car blocked me in. "Fuck."

A shrill ring sounded through my speakers, and Winter's name popped up on the dash. "Hey," I answered into the air, finally inching my way out onto the street.

"Congratulations. You got the job!" Winter's excitement made me chuckle. She couldn't have chosen a worse time to tell me great news. Ninety percent of my concentration was on not fucking up my car. "That was quick. I literally just walked out from our meeting." I slammed on my brakes as another car moved around me. I ground my teeth. "You might need a backup plan, though. I'm about to murder someone in this traffic."

She barked out a sarcastic laugh. "Funny. But don't. I have too much invested in you."

Oh, so now Winter wants to admit it. It was because they loved my idea. I'd never seen so many suits with wide eyes and dropped jaws before.

"Look," Winter rushed. "We'll be a few minutes behind you to the studio, but I just wanted to give you a heads-up."

That piqued my interest. "Okay. I'm sitting down," I teased.

"Ha," she said dryly. "Reggie's pitch was before yours. I just called him to let him know he didn't get the gig. He wasn't too happy."

Great. "What did I tell you? You shouldn't have had the damn pitch to begin with. Now I'm going to have to deal with Reggie's attitude all fucking day."

"Yeah, well. I'm allowed to fuck up every now and then. I'll admit, I should have left this one alone."

"Just say it." A grin stretched across my face.

She was silent for a moment, either hesitating or confused by what I meant. "Just say what?" From the annoyance in her tone, she knew.

"Tell me I was right. Just this once."

A snort pushed through the car speakers. "Not going to happen. But before your ego bursts, I need to tell you something else."

I made a face, my gut telling me I wasn't going to like this news. "Spit it out."

"I offered Reggie a bone. I'm letting him choreograph one of the features for Vegas."

If I'd had anything in my mouth, I would have choked on it. I coughed out my next breath instead. "News flash. That's *my* job. Also, the choreography is done. That ass has already changed practically the entire routine for 'The Cure.' You're giving him another one because you feel sorry for him?"

Winter sighed dramatically. "I knew you'd freak out. Look, Reggie deserves a shot just like you did when it was your time. He's a good choreographer. Really good. I didn't trust him to choreograph an entire Vegas show, but that had more to do with experience than his talent. You need to give him a chance."

"This is bullshit. What song is he redoing?"

"None of them." She perked up as though this was somehow good news. "I have a bonus track I'm releasing midtour, but I want to intro it on stage early to create the buzz. It will be perfect."

Despite the rage spiraling through me, I decided to let this one go. Reggie could have his partner choreography and whatever this bonus shit was. Maybe Winter was right. Maybe he just needed his shot. Maybe then he'd get the fuck off my back.

"Okay."

"Yay," she squealed. I cringed and turned down the volume a couple of notches. "Okay, I gotta go. Let's do lunch today and celebrate, and I'll tell you more about the bonus track so we can figure out where it will fit into the set list."

Lunch with Winter. Discomfort snaked through me as I imagined what Lex might think. I couldn't blame her if she got angry, not after the way I acted the other night when she went to dinner with Reggie. Although that didn't exactly have an unhappy ending. I smiled.

But we'd decided that this thing between us, whatever it was, would be temporary. We agreed the job was our number one priority. And if that was truly the case, she shouldn't have an issue over my going to lunch with Winter.

"Yeah, okay. Lunch."

Chapter 41

LEX

I t was late morning, and the crew was standing around without direction. We'd just run the entire show, full out, from top to bottom, and Theo still wasn't there. Reggie strolled in halfway through and joined us, and from the bent brows on his forehead, I knew his pitch hadn't gone so well.

"Should we run it again?" Brenda asked.

We were all breathing heavily, and many of us shook our heads.

"We should save our energy for Winter. She's coming today, right?" Contessa was at the front of the room, wiping her face with a towel.

I glanced at Reggie, who shrugged and started to walk away. I caught his arm, and he turned back. "Hey, how was the pitch? Did they like your ideas?"

I was dying to ask Theo that same question, but for now, Reggie was in front of me, and I'd never seen him look so down on his luck.

He shook his head and waved his hand as though it wasn't a big deal. "Nah. They liked the pitch, but it just wasn't my time. You were right about the gig already being Theo's. Him and Winter are a thing—I need to remember that. It's all good, though." He flashed me a smile as I started to lose mine at the mention of Winter and Theo. "I got another opportunity out of it. And I still get to partner with you. I'm pretty stoked about that."

"That's true." My optimism masked that awkward feeling that crawled through me again, the sensation that something was off.

My eyes drifted around the room, looking for something to change the subject, when Wayne stepped up to the speaker. He shuffled through his playlist. "I say we take a break until Theo gets back. Let loose a little, if you know what I mean." He smiled around the room then pushed Play. When Kelly Clarkson's "Love So Soft" started to sound overhead, everyone clapped.

"Ah," Amie called out with a grin. "I feel a freestyle coming on."

The crew agreed, and Reggie nudged me toward the center of the room. "Lex volunteers as Tribute."

"Was that a *Hunger Games* reference?" I raised my brows at him in amusement as the Ravens laughed.

He placed his hands on my back and nudged me toward the center of the room. The crew's cheers grew filling my insides with that bubbly kind of excitement that could easily be mistaken for nerves. It felt good to finally be accepted as one of them. I'd definitely felt the shift this week. I now felt that I was surrounded by a dance family, one that could have moments like these despite the struggles and the insurmountable stress. I was grateful that last week's drama was far behind us.

"All right, all right." I held up my hands and laughed. "Wayne, you'll need to restart that for me if I'm going to do this right."

He gave me a nod and went back to his phone and restarted the track as Reggie waved the crew off the floor. "Let's give our girl some space," he boomed. "Contessa, you jump in next. We'll go girls then guys."

WATCH: LOVE SO SOFT
smarturl.it/Gravity_LoveSoSoft

I was midway through my freestyle, the energy in the room building with the crew's cheers and applause, when I caught Theo's eyes in the mirror. My face immediately grew hot as I continued to move, my gaze glued to his. There was something about the way his stare burned through me, as if he could be standing in a ball of flames and still not move.

I loved it as much as I knew I should hate it.

Theo didn't stop us from taking turns to freestyle until every single person had a chance to take the floor.

"Sorry about this morning," he said once someone cut the music. "We lost some time, but we'll make it up this afternoon. As soon as Winter gets here, we'll run the set from the top. Just mark the new dances the best you can for now."

If the rest of the dancers felt like me, they were more than ready for a full-out performance.

And that was what we did. Winter arrived a few minutes later, and we started the entire show from the top.

"It's looking good, Crew." Theo's compliment made me do a double take. *Why is he in such a good mood?*

Theo seemed far less intimidating than he had when I first met him. Perhaps it was the fact that I'd seen him bare or that, just this morning, he'd wakened me with his mouth, working me to an orgasm before running out the door for his pitch. But it was also possible he had softened some since we'd gotten to know each other.

Still, I had to remind myself that whatever affection I'd built up for Theo was only temporary. In four days, everything would change, and I wasn't ready to face that.

"I think we're ready to pick things apart a bit. Once we get back from lunch, be ready to run through the tracks, one by one, until we perfect each one."

"That's right," Winter said with a clap of her hands, shaking me from my thoughts of Theo. "And you get an extra-long lunch break today. Be back in two hours."

My eyes tracked Winter's playful nudge at Theo's arm and the way she hugged his bicep as if it belonged to her. My gut felt heavy at the exchange, though Theo simply allowed the flirtation without appearing to return it. It was a harsh reminder that no matter how sweet and cute Theo was with me behind closed doors, he wasn't mine to claim.

"It's beautiful today," Amie said with brilliant eyes and a wide smile. She looked between Reggie and me. "Let's take our lunch outside."

A few other dancers accompanied us to the concrete steps in front of Gravity. As we unpacked our lunches—mine a selection of cold cuts and cheese slices from Theo's refrigerator—a flash of white and leather caught my eye. My chest tightened before I looked up to see them, Winter and Theo, dashing down the stairs and toward his black Ferrari. My heart sank when he opened the door for her and glanced up at the lot of us on the stairs, his eyes connecting with mine.

I looked away first, hating the way my chest ached, knowing this was what we'd agreed to. This was our reality. Me, the background dancer he'd secretly opened his home and his bed to, and him, the famous choreographer with a superstar on his arm. It didn't matter that he murmured sweet words against my lips last night as he drove inside me or fed me bites of grilled cheese from his plate at dinner. Because in this moment, hearing the rev of the familiar engine before it drove away and listening to the crew whispering about the hot sex Winter and Theo were surely having, my reality was my burden to bear.

And I'd do it alone.

Chapter 42

THEO

Lights from the fireplace flickered against the wall as a wave of heat washed the air. Lex looked beautiful with her hair knotted loosely at the top of her head and tendrils of blond framing her heart-shaped face. She wore a thin gray sweater that fell off her shoulder, revealing bare silky skin I'd quickly become infatuated with.

I was falling for her.

The thought hit me hard today when I walked into Gravity and saw her dance. It was so much like the first time I watched her audition, except this time, she wasn't an amateur dancer with stars in her eyes. She was the best damn presence in my life. But she had a dream—a dream that I would ultimately be responsible for destroying if anyone were to find out what we were doing.

I couldn't let that happen.

She pulled the chopsticks to her mouth and took the helping of lo mein between her lips. When she looked up, she caught my stare and smiled. Her mouth closed around the chopsticks before sliding them out and swallowing. "What?" she asked, and I knew if I said the right thing, regardless of the dim lighting, I'd see her cheeks fill with color.

"Nothing. I just like looking at you."

Mission accomplished. Her cheeks glowed against the firelight. And I knew I shouldn't have said it. Affectionate words would only make our end more complicated.

"Aren't you hungry?" She pointed at the untouched box of Chinese in my hands.

"I had a big lunch."

Something fell in her eyes, and I wished I could have taken back the mention of lunch. "Oh, right. Of course."

I knew she was bothered when Winter got in my car, but she hadn't brought it up, and I was sure she wouldn't. Just as I'd refrained from mentioning how awkward she and Reggie looked today as they partnered during the full run-through. He threw her around the floor like a ragdoll, and I had to look away before I did something I'd regret.

"How is it? I should have gotten the noodles instead of the fried rice." It was my best attempt at changing the subject.

She clamped her chopsticks around a helping of noodles and held them to my lips with a soft smile. "Have some."

I took the bite, my eyes staying on hers. "Damn," I said around a mouthful. "I definitely should have gotten that."

"Trade me," she offered, holding out her box. I took it and handed her mine.

"So, what's this new routine Reggie was talking about today?" She looked up as she pushed her food around with the sticks. "I didn't want to ask him too many questions. He didn't look happy about not getting that music video."

Shrugging, I swallowed another mouthful of noodles. "It's a mystery at this point. He told Winter it will be ready in Vegas. It'll be a trio, that's all I know. I haven't even heard the track. It's some bonus song Winter's planning to release."

She stopped playing with her food. "How do you feel about all that?"

Lex was the only one who had asked me that question, stirring something in me. I tilted my head as I thought about what she was asking. It was no secret that there was a beef between Reggie and me, but he was still one of my peers. He hustled his way through the business, and I couldn't hate him for that.

"It's a good thing." As soon as the words left my mouth, I knew I meant them. "He might be a cocky son of a bitch, but he's a great choreographer. This way he gets a shot. And it will add a different flavor to the show. I think Winter made the best decision."

Something flickered in her eyes at the mention of Winter's name, and this time, I had a burning desire to tell her the truth. That lunch was only business and that Winter and I were nothing more than friends with a casual past. It was Lex I wanted now—always—but saying those dangerous words would only give her hope.

"You looked great during your freestyle today." I muscled up a wink through my unease.

Her eyes brightened. "Wasn't it great to see everyone let loose? We should do more of that. It felt great. And for the first time, I really felt like we came together as a crew."

She had a point, and I couldn't help seeing how it had helped the group with their focus. As if they'd fed their souls with the magic that would rejuvenate them. "It's a good suggestion. I'll keep that in mind."

After I'd finished the rest of the noodles, I took our containers into the kitchen and joined Lex by the fire. She had her knees up, hugging them, as she stared into the flames with a faraway look on her face. I sat behind her and leaned her body back into mine. I pushed a golden tendril over her ear so I could see some of her face. She was so beautiful, in a timeless sort of way. Something tugged at my chest. "You ready for bed?"

I was hungry for her and desperate to be inside her as much as possible before the week was over.

"In a minute." She looked over her shoulder at me. "I like this." Her eyes lingered on mine. "It almost feels real."

Shit. Her words were a blow to my gut. "This is real, Lex." I tightened my hold on her so she could feel how real we were together. Because in that moment of weakness, I wanted her to know I felt the same.

Her teeth sank into her bottom lip then released it. "You know what I meant."

I hated the feeling that stirred inside me, a fear that I would lose her any minute and never be the same. Except, that was the plan—to end things and go back to following the rules. At some point, I'd lost complete control of my emotions.

She was about to turn away when my fingers caught her chin. I brought my head to hers, letting my nose skim her lips. "I love your lips."

Her gaze softened. "I love yours. They're filled with so much … talent." She grinned then let a giggle slip from her throat.

Fuck. Every sound that came out of her pretty mouth drove me wild. "Talent, huh?" I teased with a grin of my own. "What are you trying to tell me?" I moved my mouth against hers. "Are you demanding a demonstration of my *talents*? I'm happy to oblige."

Her focus zoned in on my lips, then she leaned in, pressing her forehead to mine. "Maybe." Her eyes burned into mine.

"It's not a demand if you're unsure," I rasped, then I pressed a kiss to her plush lips and pulled away. "All you have to do is ask." My hand floated to her sweater, tugging it up and drawing circles around her belly button. When she sucked in a breath, I let my hand move lower until I was skating the edge of her panty line. "Tell me what you want, Lex."

Her hand moved to mine and pushed it lower until I was inside her panties, skimming her wet slit with my fingers. I swallowed as my length thickened in my shorts. I bit her earlobe and breathed deeply against her neck. "You make me insane, you know that?" My finger pressed against her clit and rubbed, debating whether I should get her off like this. But when her hips rolled against my fingers, I knew what she was too shy to ask. I pushed two fingers inside of her, and my mouth covered hers, capturing her moans.

It had been only a few days with Lex, and I already knew her body inside and out. I knew the intimate places no one had been before and how to touch her in a way that made her beg for more. I knew all the different sounds of her releases, because they were never ever the same. And I knew that one time was never enough. She was always ready for seconds before I was.

"I can't wait to be inside you." I groaned the words against her neck as I felt her tight cunt strangle my fingers. Her soft cries came soon after as she rode out her release on my fingers.

When she finally shuddered to a stop, I watched her lift herself from me and stand. I was in a complete daze as she peeled off her leggings, panties with them, then slipped off her sweater, completely baring herself for me.

"Fuck." I breathed before making quick work of my shorts. I freed my erection and reached for my wallet to grab a condom. But before I could get it on, her mouth was already around me, sucking with an intensity that made my eyes roll into the back of my head and my body fall back onto my elbows.

As I sat there, my cock disappearing between her full pink lips and her hair wrapped around my fists, I couldn't remember why I had to let her go.

Chapter 43

LEX

B y Friday night, my heart started to feel heavy.

There I was, my bare toes hanging in the brightly lit blue water of Theo's pool, the sun dipping below the trees and casting a brilliant purplish glow against the clouds, and I felt more alone than ever before.

Theo was inside getting ready for dinner with Winter and the music video director to discuss their plans for the shoot, and I was working up my courage to talk to Theo about what would happen in Vegas.

It had been a week of secrecy and sex in the sanctuary of Theo's home and his car. That was exactly what we'd promised each other, and we hadn't talked about anything more. I'd told myself I'd be okay with it and that putting my focus 100 percent on the Vegas show would cure me of Theo, banishing him from my system. I never expected him to climb into my heart too.

I knew people did this kind of thing all the time. One-night stands. Casual flings. But there was nothing casual about the way he curled his body around mine every night and peppered kisses along my back and shoulders. Or the way he'd had to bite back his rage while he watched Reggie and me dance.

Those things weren't casual, no matter how hard I tried to ignore them.

The sound of my phone ringing by my side interrupted my confused thoughts. It was Shane. I sighed, debating whether I should pick it up. I'd been avoiding him all week, knowing that the moment we spoke, I'd have to decide. Lie to him or tell him the truth about Theo.

"Hey." I pulled the phone to my ear. "I've missed you."

Loud music and laughter vibrated in the background of wherever Shane had called me from. "Where the hell have you been?" he shouted into the phone.

I smiled, feeling the ache in my heart as my loneliness only seemed to increase at the sound of his voice. "Busy."

He snorted. "Busy lounging by the pool? Where was that taken, anyway?"

I rolled my eyes. He must have seen my Instagram post from a few hours ago before the weight of reality began to settle in. "We leave for Vegas tomorrow," I said, ignoring his question. "Please tell me you're going to visit."

"That's why I'm calling." The background noise faded, as though he'd locked himself in a room. "I wanted to let you know. I talked to Dominic and got some time off. I wouldn't miss your opening night."

Excitement flitted through me. "Really?"

"Really. You better be ready for me. And I want the entire Vegas VIP treatment. Bottle service, fancy dinners, the works."

I laughed. "Nothing but the best for you, honey."

"Good girl." Something pounded in the background. "Shit, I gotta get back out there. Love you, Lex."

Just then, the patio doors to Theo's house opened, and he stepped outside. My heart shot up to my throat and felt jammed there. He looked incredible, far too incredible to be having dinner with Winter. The ugly claws of jealousy scaled the walls of my chest. He wore jeans so light they almost looked as white as his button-down shirt. His pants were rolled up above his ankles, calling extra attention to his gray loafers. His sleeves were pushed above elbows revealing thick forearms and bronze skin.

"Lex, did you hear me? I've gotta go." Shane was still on the line.

"Love you too, Shane."

We hung up, and I was left staring at the GQ ad approaching me. I set my phone down, my eyes shifting over to the clock on the back of his house. My heart sank. It was eight fifteen, and dinner was at eight thirty, which meant he couldn't stay.

He kicked off his shoes and sat beside me, then he slipped his feet in the water before kissing my cheek. "Sorry I have to leave. I shouldn't be out late. Wait up for me?"

I gave him a pinched smile. "Of course."

He'd been attending meetings and lunches and interviews with Winter all week, and it had never bothered me as much as it did tonight. My confidence in their "platonic" relationship was starting to wane. I'd seen hints of a relationship brewing, and the media tried to paint a picture of one as well. And there were no rules for their relationship, unlike with Theo and me. No boundaries, which gave Winter free rein to throw herself at him. And Theo would do little to stop it as long as he was working for her.

I got it. I did. But it killed me to know Theo and I never even had a chance.

"Lex," Theo said with a nudge. "You're too quiet."

I dared a look at him, knowing I'd fall victim to his sweet, caring face that was reserved only for me. I did. I melted as I gazed back at him. Tomorrow was only a few hours away.

How could he not be thinking about it too? About our deal. And then I remembered, I was the one who suggested the terms of our arrangement. Maybe he was just respecting my wishes. Maybe he didn't want us to end either. Maybe there was another way.

Hope sparked in my chest, and I sucked in a breath. I would talk to him when he got home from dinner. Everything would be okay. "I'm just nervous about Vegas, that's all."

Theo's expression lost its softness, and something else washed over him. I couldn't quite place it. Then his lashes whipped against the top of his cheeks. I wondered if he realized how beautiful he was—in a way that was exhilarating. Surely he knew he was gorgeous. Too many women fell at his feet for him not to know. But did he know that it was more than his striking eyes and sculpted cheekbones that had captivated my heart?

"Theo?" I laughed nervously, because he still hadn't said anything.

His eyes caught mine, and he smiled. "You're going to light up that stage, Lex. Everything will be perfect." He leaned in and placed a soft kiss on my lips. "I promise."

Flutters erupted in my tummy, and with a soft sigh, I watched as he stood up and disappeared around the corner. I chose to believe in his promise.

And prayed he wouldn't break it.

Chapter 44

THEO

"We look forward to seeing you again in a couple weeks, Theo." Rocky Maine, the director of photography, squeezed my hand and gave it a few pumps before he walked out the door with his crew.

We'd finished our meal along with the after-dinner schmoozing just past eleven o'clock. I was ready to dart out the door and get home to Lex when Winter gave me a look that made me sit back down.

"Give us a minute," she said to Alison, who proceeded to send me an apologetic glance. The next thing I knew, Alison was walking out the door with Winter's two bodyguards.

"Geez, Winter. You look like you're about to murder someone."

Her eyes narrowed into tiny slits, and her nose flared. "I am."

I glanced at her empty wineglass, wondering how many she'd had. "Maybe you should lay off the booze for the rest of the night. We have an early flight."

She crossed her arms and rolled her eyes. "I'm fine. How long, Theo?"

Her question didn't register immediately, but I felt the inklings of guilt for whatever she thought I'd done wrong. With Winter, it could have been anything. Did I forget to turn in paperwork? Did I say something wrong during dinner? "I'm not following."

She blew out a breath. "You and Lex. How long?"

Shit. My chest swelled with heat. My mouth fell open, but words weren't coming out. I needed time to figure out how to answer her. What could I say that wouldn't ruin everything? What *could* I say? If I admitted anything, Lex would get fired, and I couldn't let that happen. But I couldn't lie either. Winter already knew. *How long has it been going on?* I wasn't sure how to answer that. One week, I guess, but there had been something from the moment I laid eyes on Lex.

"Clearly, you've got me cornered here. I won't lie to you, but I don't feel comfortable talking about this with you either."

"Well, too fucking bad."

"How did you even find out?"

She let out a patronizing laugh. "Your girlfriend got a little sloppy on social media today." Winter pulled out her phone and swiped until she got to a certain photo then handed the phone to me over the table. "Anyone who's been to your house can recognize that's your pool. What the fuck was one of my dancers doing at your house?"

My heart had stopped beating at some point after seeing the photo. It was clearly Lex, giving a peace sign in the same white bikini she was wearing when I left her. A bikini I bought her. Only a portion of her was in the frame, but

Winter was right. The tile that rimmed the pool was an unusual red and yellow. *Fuck. Fuck. Fuck.* I reached for my phone. "I'll tell her to delete it."

"Already done. Deleted it without her even knowing. Covered your ass again, Theo. You can thank me later." Winter yanked her phone from me and set it on the table. "All dancers will be getting a reminder about the policies they agreed to follow by signing that contract. As will you." *Which means Lex isn't getting fired.* I hoped.

Her eyes narrowed again. I could practically see the steam billowing from her head. "From your expression, I take it you're aware she was at your house."

"Yes," I replied as I ground my teeth. "I knew."

"Well, that's better than my initial thought. I'd hate to think you have a hard-on for the stalker types." Her head tipped to the side, as if she'd just thought of something else. "Is she *still* at your house?"

Fuck. "She has nowhere else to go." I wouldn't elaborate. Even saying that was too much.

Winter threw her head back and laughed like a fucking lunatic. "Just like she didn't have a car to take her to the studio? You are such a gullible bastard."

I stood up, the tops of my thighs crashing against the table and spilling my unfinished wine. "Fuck off, Winter. Believe what you want. I'm out of here." I shoved my phone in my pocket and started for the door.

"You know," Winter began in a seething tone that halted me in my tracks, "I'd hate for Lex to miss out on an opportunity like this just because her choreographer couldn't keep it in his pants."

I swiveled around to face her. "So, what are you going to do, Winter? Fire her? Fire me?"

She stood and stepped closer. "Here's the thing. If I let her go, the other dancers are going to ask questions. Lex might talk. And we'll have a hole to fill. I don't want to fire her, but I will if you don't end it."

"It's already done." My chest felt hot and heavy beneath my ribs at the reality of my words.

Winter's face twisted. "That was fast. A little too fast."

"We made a decision before it all began that we would end it before Vegas. It's already done."

Her jaw hardened. "You better be telling me the truth. Look, Theo. You're a grown-ass man with needs. I get it. But the rules are there for a reason. The whole Mallory situation stayed private, thank God, but if something like that happened on my show, it would be everywhere."

Her words slammed into me. I couldn't argue with a single point. She wasn't threatening me. She was delivering the reality check that I desperately needed. Lex deserved this opportunity, and I couldn't be responsible for destroying her reputation as a dancer before it had even begun.

She was moonlight and magic when she danced, leaving stardust in her wake. And she was only getting started.

Which was exactly why I had to let her go.

Part Three

VEGAS

Chapter 45

LEX

The shuffle of feet padding across the wood floors. Running water from a shower. The rustling of clothes and hangers in a closet. All sounds were faint as my mind fought the exhaustion that had finally taken me hostage well past midnight.

My eyes peeled open, and I stirred to look at the clock on the nightstand—two in the morning. My heart rate picked up. I listened harder to track Theo's movements, wondering if he had ever come to bed, but I knew he hadn't. I was a light sleeper. I would have wakened instantly to the feel of his warm body pressing against mine.

He said he would be home early. My gut churned with discomfort as I played over every possible scenario that didn't include him and Winter together … all night.

Light poured over the bedroom as the bathroom door opened. A second later, the light flicked off, swallowing the room in darkness. Bare feet again padded across the floors, stopping a few feet from the door. And then silence. My eyes searched the dark as I forced deep breaths to calm my racing heart. I caught Theo's faint outline near the bedroom door, as though he was about to leave.

Why isn't he coming to bed?

I stirred, hoping to bring his attention to the woman between his sheets. The woman who had waited up for him for hours until finally succumbing to sleep. The woman who was desperate to be wrapped in his arms, to feel his whispered mutterings of how crazy I drove him and how he loved being inside me. I could already imagine his hot kisses peppering my back as his fingers played their favorite game inside me. I needed them on me—inside me—now.

"Theo," my sleepy voice croaked. I couldn't bear the distance anymore. "Come to bed."

Too much hesitation snaked through that moment of silence, and more negative thoughts made their way to the forefront. When he finally started to come to me, my heart went into my throat as I imagined him spending the night naked and tangled with Winter. The images became more vivid when he crawled under the sheets and didn't make a move to touch me.

"Sorry I woke you. Go back to sleep, Lex." His tone was gruff, cold, heating the backs of my eyes. Hot tears dripped down my cheeks, and I couldn't seem to stop them.

I could have asked him where he'd been. I could have asked him if he wanted me to leave his bed, his room, his home. I could have asked him if he wanted to continue breaking the rules in Vegas, because before I'd fallen asleep, I was ready to risk it all for him.

But as my heart began to crack in two, I knew I didn't have to ask any of those questions, because in the span of a few hours, something monumental had shifted, or maybe the truth was finally coming to the surface.

I was falling in love, and Theo didn't feel the same.

♥

I'd barely fallen asleep when the alarm went off. I hit Snooze and waited for Theo's arm to hook me and slide me toward him. That had been our routine for the past week, so we always set the alarm earlier than we'd needed. Last night, I had set it to give us a full hour before we had to get ready.

But when a few seconds went by and I didn't feel Theo's rough fingers, memories of last night barreled through my mind. I twisted my body in the sheets to find Theo's side of the bed empty. My chest was achy and swollen. My head was full of fog from exhaustion. And my eyes were heavy and puffy from my tears.

It should have been the happiest day of my life. I was waking up to fly to Vegas as a backup dancer for Winter's residency series, a dream come true. But my happiness dimmed at the finality of what Theo and I had shared this week. I hadn't wanted it to end.

I moved slowly to the bathroom to shower and get dressed. When I was completely ready, suitcases in hand, Theo came into the room, looking as though he hadn't slept at all. His eyes moved to my fingers, which were wrapped around the handles of my bags, and he stepped forward. "I'll take those."

His hands landed on mine. But when I wouldn't release my hold, he let out a deep breath and looked up, meeting my eyes. "Lex, I've got it."

None of this made sense. Him coming in late, not touching me, his cold tone. This was guarded Theo, the one I told off in the theater. The jerk. Not the man I'd grown to adore.

"I waited up for you. What happened last night?" I hated that I even had to ask. I didn't want to know the answer. Not the answer I feared, anyway.

His jaw hardened, and he looked away, dropping his hands from mine. "I should have called."

I waited for him to say more, but when he looked at me again and gestured for my bags, I knew that was the end of the conversation. Heat flamed inside me as he reached for the handles again. "Your ride will be here any minute."

A black hole opened beneath me and proceeded to suck me in. "My ride?"

He looked over his shoulders as he rolled my bags out of the room, not meeting my eyes. "We can't show up together. Everyone will be arriving at the same time, and there's only one small lot at the terminal. I don't think we should take any risks."

He placed my things at the landing of the steps and turned around. "Breakfast?"

My stomach rolled. I shook my head. "Not hungry."

He nodded and strolled past me into the kitchen, returning a minute later with a bottled water and handing it to me. "For the ride."

I couldn't stop the first tear that rolled down my cheek. As much as I wanted to be strong and hide the pain, I couldn't stop my emotions from unraveling right there in his foyer. "So that's it? You're just going to send me off in a strange car, and that's the end of us?"

"We said one week, Lex." He still wouldn't meet my eyes. "We're headed to Vegas. You have your career ahead of you. A job to do. That was the plan."

"Yeah. That *was* the plan. But plans can change, Theo. When two people feel the way about each other that you and I do, plans change. Unless it was only ever about sex for you."

His eyes finally met mine, and everything about his expression crumbled. "It wasn't. You know it wasn't."

"I thought I knew a lot of things that turned out to be wrong. I thought things were over between you and Winter, for one."

I watched as his face transformed into anger. "There's nothing going on between Winter and me."

I wiped my cheek and shook my head. "You were with her until two in the morning. You didn't even touch me last night. And you weren't there when I woke up. Where do you think my mind went? There isn't much you can say to me at this point to convince me of anything else."

His jaw went slack. "What the fuck? These were your terms. One week, and then you wanted to focus on Vegas. On your career. And now you're holding it against me. I was trying to do the right thing last night. Or would you rather have had me try to get one last fuck in before our flight? Would that have made you feel better?"

Rage filled me as his words spewed like lava, destroying everything in its path. Our history, our memories, and whatever potential future we had. My hand reeled back and shot forward, slapping him across the face before I could think better of it. I swiped the tears from my eyes as he reached for his face, his eyes wide—shocked—but I didn't stop to see if I'd left a mark.

I grabbed my things, moved past him, and yanked open the door just as my ride was pulling up the drive. "See you in Vegas."

Chapter 46

THEO

Winter slipped into the company car beside me with an unreadable expression. Her white hair was down, straight and around her shoulders, her oversized dark shades hid her eyes, and her complexion was absent of worry lines. As her assistant and bodyguards slipped into the row in front of us, Winter turned to me. "Your situation all squared away?"

I shot her a look through the shades that covered my swollen eyes—eyes that were now filled with rage for the woman I'd once called my friend. She had given me no choice but to hurt someone I cared about, and I couldn't forgive her for that. "I already told you. It's done."

"Good." She faced front, tensed, then faced me again. "Does she know

I know?"

I narrowed my eyes. "No." And that was all I would say. If Winter expected me to give her the dirty details of last night and this morning, she would be sorely disappointed. "Are we done now?"

Winter let out a frustrated breath. "C'mon, Theo. What is your deal with this girl? You told me it was already over. All I asked from you was to promise that you won't be pursuing things further, and to keep my name out of your mouth. I don't need her to know I'm involved and create drama with my Ravens. You don't need that kind of drama either."

"Lex doesn't create drama." I muttered it under my breath, but Winter sighed as if she'd heard me.

"This works out for all of us."

I glowered at her. "How the hell do you figure that?"

She shrugged. "No distractions. A great tour. Lex gets to keep her job. And if you still have a hard-on for the girl by the end of the tour, then you're free to act on it." She smiled as if she'd just solved all the world's problems, as if seeing Lex but not touching her would be easy fucking peasy for me.

I'd never felt so helpless in all my life. Resisting the urge to hold Lex close last night. Not telling her the truth this morning, especially when she'd assumed I'd slept with Winter. It all was slowly killing me. Hurting Lex was the last thing I ever wanted out of all this.

"Well, you get your wish."

Winter let out a sarcastic laugh. "If I didn't know you better, I'd assume you were in love with her."

"And if I didn't know any better, I'd think the reason you're really doing all this is because *you* are in love with *me*."

Her mouth wrinkled, and she turned her head away. "I've moved on, thank you very much. Not that I couldn't have you if I wanted to."

I chuckled over the fury that bubbled in my chest. "Not a fucking chance."

She let out a frustrated growl and whipped her head in my direction. "Listen to me. Before we get on that plane, you better come back around to my side of things. I'm sure Reggie will be happy to take over your position and lead the crew if you're going to continue being so … difficult. We're supposed to be partners. This show is as much yours as it is mine. So start acting like it."

Winter's arms crossed over her chest, and she puffed out a loud breath of air. "Besides, we wouldn't be in this mess in the first place if you had obeyed the contract to begin with and kept your dick in your pants."

"You certainly weren't complaining when you showed up at my house and sucked that dick."

I watched with satisfaction as Winter's face grew red. Everyone in the car could hear us now. Our argument was no longer private, but I had nothing else to lose. She was silent for the rest of the ride, and when everyone started getting out of the car, I thought I was in the clear.

"Wait." Winter stopped me before I could reach for the handle. "We need a second alone."

Alison shut the door behind her, giving us the privacy I desperately wanted to avoid. Winter pulled off her glasses and turned to me with pleading eyes. "Theo, I need you." Her tone was softer now, almost apologetic. "Not as anything more than what you signed on for. My producer, my choreographer, and my friend. You know it's in my nature to eliminate any threat in my way, and that's exactly what I did. For what it's worth, I'm sorry."

I shook my head and looked toward the window, and the crew was already starting to board. My heart pounded furiously as I searched for Lex. I needed to see her. I wanted so badly to say "Fuck the contract" and tell her everything, but I couldn't.

"I am sorry," Winter continued. "I respect you. We've practically grown up in this industry together. The last thing I want is to make your life unpleasant, but you've given me no other option. I protect what's mine. My business. My crew. And you're part of that world."

"Do what you need to do, Winter." I reached for the door handle again. "But in six and a half months, when this gig is over, mark my words, I will *never* work with you again."

Chapter 47

LEX

B y the time the crew began to arrive, I'd managed to stop the flow of tears and dry my face, but I kept my sunglasses on to hide my swollen and bloodshot eyes. After one trip to the bathroom, it was clear I looked exactly how I felt. Like absolute shit.

Reggie and Amie arrived just as we were being ushered from the terminal to cross the tarmac to our plane. I let them carry on most of the conversation as I sipped my scalding coffee. The burn felt good as it slipped down my throat, slowly awakening me from the spell I'd fallen under with Theo. That was all it was, one week of passion that my heart took too far. An illusion of something I clearly wanted out of life. But the thought of ever letting another man into my heart felt impossible.

"Lex, did you hear us?"

I looked up, my eyes wide. "Um, no, sorry. I'm kind of out of it this morning. All the excitement. Couldn't really sleep."

At least I wouldn't have to lie for much longer. With Theo and I no longer sneaking around, I had nothing left to hide.

Amie hooked her arm into mine as we stood in line to climb up the jet's stairs. "We're hitting the slots as soon as we get to Vegas. You and me. And then after the welcome dinner, we're going to the piano bar at Harrah's. You have to come."

I cringed, already feeling the strong need to gain whatever shut-eye I could before we walked onstage for rehearsals tomorrow. "Can I at least take a power nap? I feel dead."

Amie laughed. "No, girl. You'll get your second wind as soon as we land. I promise."

I'd had enough promises to last me until the next century.

"Hey." Reggie nudged my other side with his elbow. "You okay?"

My gut felt weighted with all the things I wanted to vent but couldn't. I literally had no one I could talk to now. I waved away his concern and forced a smile. "Yeah. Just kind of weird doing this without Shane. We always talked about the big opportunities we'd have one day. We were supposed to have them together. I guess I'm just missing him right about now."

Reggie flashed me a smile and wrapped his arm around my shoulders. "I get it. I'm no Shane, but I'm here if you need me."

Amie squeezed my arm. "Me too."

The plane had two main compartments, with luxury couches and tables in the front compartment and a much roomier, more traditional style of seating behind it. We were ushered to the back, where we found two rows of seats that faced each other. Reggie and I took the forward-facing row while Amie and

Wayne sat across from us.

Despite recent events, I felt the injection of excitement as the crew discussed the night's plans, basking in the fact that we didn't have to show up to the theater until later the next afternoon. Besides the night at Rooftop, this would be the first time our crew would be hanging out together outside the studio.

I was laughing at Amie's impression of a dueling piano player when something white flashed across my line of vision, pulling my gaze toward the front of the plane. Winter's hair was long and loosely flowing over one shoulder, and she had a big smile on her face as she greeted the crew. "Everyone excited?"

Many hooted and hollered and clapped, but I wasn't one of them. My chest felt heavy, anxious, knowing Theo would probably be close behind.

Someone nudged me in my side. "Look who arrived together," Reggie muttered, as if whatever he saw annoyed him.

My gaze shifted to the figure walking through the plane's entrance behind Winter. It was as if someone had punched me in the heart.

Theo was trailing Winter, his glasses over his eyes and his stoic expression back. It was moody Theo. The one with the hard jaw and the tunnel focus. It made me swallow hard over the lump growing in my throat. How had I lost him overnight?

Glutton for punishment that I was, I watched him take the seat beside Winter, as though it was the most natural thing in the world. Maybe it was. They shared a history my one week with him couldn't touch.

Something stirred in my gut, causing me to switch my gaze from Theo and toward Winter, and she'd already been watching me, studying me as if trying to read my thoughts. *Does she know?* It sure as hell felt as though she did.

I tore my eyes away and inserted myself into the conversation between Reggie, Amie, and Wayne.

"Wait. Are you talking about the music video for 'Caged'?"

They nodded. "Did you get the email? They're flying us all back to LA to be in the video. If we accept. Whatever spots remain, they'll be holding auditions for at Gravity."

"Wait. So, none of us have to audition? I thought Winter was big on auditions, no matter what."

Reggie shrugged. "She must have had a change of heart. Timing is a bit crazy. That week will be exhausting as fuck, but it'll be worth it."

Amie grinned. "Definitely." She looked between us then and raised her brows. "Hey, you two nail your partner dance down yet?"

Reggie looked over at me and shrugged. "It's coming together." He winked. "We had some disagreements with the choreographer. Slowed us down a bit, but we're good now." He slid an arm over my shoulder and pressed a kiss to my temple. "It's going to be badass, just you wait."

My heart danced as I felt familiar eyes on me. I glanced over without thinking, because I'd become good at feeling the connection Theo and I had in a crowded room. And even though his shades were still on, there was no question that his gaze was narrowed and set on me.

He was jealous. But he sure as hell didn't have the right to be.

Chapter 48

LEX

A mie and I separated from the rest of the crew once we got to Hard Rock. Her excitement was palpable, which was exactly the distraction I needed. And she was right. I had miraculously acquired a second wind once our plane touched down.

"Slots," she said to me as she tugged on my hand, her brows wiggling with eagerness. She dragged me past the lobby and into a maze of machines and lights until we paused at an ATM. "Here"—she slid to the side and pointed—"get some cash."

I opened my mouth and shook my head. It was one thing to watch Amie play the slots, but there was no way I was gambling away my hard-earned money. Money had been decent ever since the show checks started coming in, but that money would need to last me until I booked another gig, which might not be until well after Winter's show ended. No. I had to be smart with my money.

"C'mon, Lex. Just get out twenty dollars and call it your entertainment money. You have to experience this one time in your life, and I want to be the one you experience it with."

I chewed on my lip while studying the cash machine, debating just how stupid it would be for me to take a single dime out of my checking account. I wanted to make Amie happy, and if I was honest, I wanted to try something new. Something adventurous. Something risky.

"Amie—" I was still debating with myself and about to tell her no again when she reached into her pockets and pulled out a five-dollar bill. "What are you doing?" I asked.

She handed the bill to me. "*When* you win, you can pay me back." She threw me a teasing look. "But don't worry if you lose it. That won't even last you five minutes."

I didn't care if it lasted five seconds. The less time I gambled, the better. "That five dollars could buy me dinner." My annoyance was mere fluff, because at this point, adrenaline was soaring through me.

Amie looked at me as if I were crazy. "Honey, that five dollars wouldn't have bought you a small packet of French fries at the nearest fast-food restaurant. We're in Vegas. However, you can probably score a free drink if you make that five last long enough."

I didn't want to tell her that I probably wouldn't be drinking either.

We pulled up a stool at the nearest row of machines, and I watched Amie as she played, pushing buttons and achieving a loud dinging sound when she won something.

After a few minutes of playing, she leaned toward my machine and pointed at the buttons. "This is the bet," she explained, pointing at each button. "This is a quarter slot, so if you push 'One Coin,' you'll only gamble twenty-five cents. Just play that until you get comfortable." My guess was that "Two Coins" doubled my bet.

Yeah, I'd take her advice. "One Coin."

"After you select your bid, just hit this button." She pointed at the big round button on my right side that read "Spin." Then she flashed me a smile. "So easy. Basically, you just push buttons and pray you get lucky. Give it a try."

I couldn't help giggling when I pushed "Spin" for the first time. The symbols inside the glass started spinning so fast I couldn't read them anymore.

Shane would have gotten a kick out of watching me play the slots. We always talked about going to Vegas together for the first time. We talked about doing everything together for the first time. A pang hit my heart when I realized how much I missed him. Theo had done a great job over the past week of taking my mind off my best friend. And now... *Shit. No.* Not going there.

"Anything to drink, loves?" A waitress in a sexy black number walked up, her eyes darting between us, as though she was in a hurry. Her name tag read "Chelsea."

"Green apple martini, please." Amie smiled at the waitress then looked at me. "They're so good. Try one."

"Um." It wasn't as though I was going to be driving anywhere, and Amie was a safe enough person to be drinking with. And I could already tell it would take more than the distractions of gambling to take my mind off Theo. I smiled at the waitress. "Same for me."

Shit. My entire body felt alive already. *Why did I just say yes?*

When Chelsea came back with our drinks, I was already down to my last seventy-five cents.

The drink was sweet and sour all at once. And strong. I wrinkled my face, and Amie laughed as I pulled the cherry from the cup.

"You don't like it?" She giggled the question.

I let the liquid settle in my stomach before answering. "Actually, I kind of do." I took another sip and confirmed that I liked the taste. "Yeah, I love it," I said with a grin.

Amie laughed and shook her head. "I'm already rubbing off on you. Better be careful. You're going to wish they'd paired you with anyone else but me."

"I highly doubt that." It was not as though I'd never had a drink before. And the gambling thing, wasn't that natural when in Vegas? I was simply having an experience. It didn't mean I was going to do this every night.

I turned back to my machine and let my finger float over the "Spin" button. I had only twenty-five cents left. I laughed at my horrible luck, feeling lightheaded from the martini, and pushed the button.

When the spinner locked on three of the same symbols, the alarm on the machine started sounding. I jumped out of my chair, afraid I'd done something wrong.

"Holy shit." I heard Amie say the words when she looked over, but I still hadn't made sense of what had happened. I watched as her jaw almost fell on the floor. "Lex," she breathed, then she pointed at the machine that was still screaming.

"Did I win?" I looked at the machine again. The siren at the top was going off like crazy. The lined-up symbols all said "Ten Times Pay." Excitement whirled through me.

"Yes, you freaking won." Amie stood up and gestured at something at the top of the machine, where the same symbols were lined up three in a row beside another number that listed the payout.

My heart lurched into my throat. I stopped laughing. "Are you telling me I just won five thousand dollars?" I shrieked.

Amie threw her head back and howled. When she came to, she was still clutching her stomach, nodding. "Yes, Lex. You just won five thousand freaking dollars off my measly five-dollar bill. Did I mention that the five dollars came with interest? Looks like we're going shopping." She winked and stuck her martini glass in the air and gestured for me to grab mine. "To Vegas."

I grabbed my glass and clinked it with hers. "To Vegas." I laughed.

Chapter 49

THEO

I'd been pacing my hotel room for so long I wouldn't have been surprised if my feet had made permanent tracks in the suite's premium carpet. I hated the feeling that had been slinking around my chest all day. I'd only been trying to do the right thing, to protect Lex, to remove the only thing standing between her and her dream—me. Yet it felt as though I'd done everything wrong.

I hadn't been able to sleep since we arrived. Not with thoughts of Lex running wildly through my mind. I hated being in a strange city and unable to call her, see her, or even know where the fuck she was or what she was doing. But what I hated most was the fact that I'd be trapped in this form of hell for the next six and a half months.

And then what? Who was I kidding? After the way I treated her today, as if she were some side piece along the way to wherever I was going, she might never speak to me again. She wouldn't give a shit about me in six months. She'd move on. We were in Vegas, for Christ's sakes. Sin city. Every male with a dick and a brain would take one look at Lex and realize what I already knew. She was a fucking goddess. And she was single.

Fuck that.

Fuck Winter.

Fuck Vegas.

I didn't need any of it.

But Lex did.

And if I quit, Lex would be out, according to Winter. And if I spoke a word about Winter's involvement, Lex would be fired. My only option was to let her go and make her believe it was what I wanted, when it wasn't. Not even a little.

A knock at my door made my heart rate spike, and I practically sprinted to answer it. I swung the door open without checking the peephole first, half expecting to see Lex's beautiful, smiling face on the other side. But it wasn't her. It was the devil herself.

"You ready?" Winter wore a skintight sleeveless white dress and some painful looking heels. Alison stood behind her, sporting something similar, only her dress was green. Winter's bodyguards flanked them both, suited and ready for the mandatory night ahead.

There were so many excuses I could have made to avoid the private dinner for the crew, and I should have used any one of them to avoid being in the same space as Winter and Lex. But the urge to see Lex, even from across the room, was too strong.

"You have everything?" Winter's tone was already dripping with impatience.

Do I have everything? It certainly felt as if something were missing, but when

I took a deep breath against my heavy chest, I knew that *something* was Lex.

I slipped my phone into my pocket and checked behind me to make sure I wasn't forgetting anything. "Yeah. Ready."

We took the elevators to the first floor to meet hotel security, who escorted us outside to a private SUV. The distance between Hard Rock and Rio wasn't far, but since we had to cross the strip traffic, I had to listen to Winter whine about Taylor Swift's new single that was stealing her limelight. I practically sighed with relief when we reached the private entrance of Rio's parking garage.

We were escorted to the fiftieth floor, home of VooDoo Steakhouse, and as soon as the elevator doors closed, I hung back from the group and searched the room for Lex. I didn't notice Alison until I accidentally glanced at her, catching her in a stare.

"So." She started the sentence, and I already knew what she was about to say. "You and Lex, huh?"

I looked at her, only to receive a sympathetic smile. "She told you?" Winter usually told Alison everything, but I was under the impression my relationship with Lex had stayed between us.

"Does it really surprise you that I know? Winter and I are practically the same person. Except"—she twisted her face—"her paychecks are much larger than mine."

Despite my shitty mood, I chuckled. "You should talk to your boss about giving you a raise."

"Ha," she barked. "I do. Daily. She only agrees when she's wasted. Funny enough, she never seems to remember it in the morning."

I pinched my lips together to keep from laughing. Alison was beautiful, intelligent, and exceptionally talented at her job. Not just answering to Winter's beck and call. Far more went on behind the scenes that Winter trusted her with but would never give her credit for. Lucky for Winter, Alison was loyal.

"I don't know how to respond to that, to be honest." It was nice to confess to someone, I just wished it were under different circumstances. "There was something but not anymore."

"Winter told you to end it?"

"She reminded me that it never should have started."

"And how do you feel about that?"

I searched for Lex in the crowd again, failing to see past Winter's entourage. I sighed and turned back to Alison. "It wasn't supposed to be anything. I've only ever been good at the casual stuff. But with Lex—" I stopped myself and shook my head. *What the fuck am I saying?* "I shouldn't be talking about this with you."

Alison's eyes went soft, and they held something I felt deep in my chest. Hope. Though it was just a glimmer. "You can trust me."

"Does it really matter how I *feel*, Alison? I've never exactly been dating material." I groaned inwardly at my own admission. "Lex deserves someone great. Someone who's available in every sense of the word."

The look that Alison threw my way only made my chest ache more. "You're a good guy, Theo. Hardworking, talented beyond belief, and loyal to a fault. Believe it or not, those are qualities women look for in a man. Don't sell yourself short."

"If it would have worked with anyone, it would have worked with Lex." The conviction in my tone shocked even me.

Alison squeezed my arm. "Maybe it still can."

Perhaps Alison didn't know how clear Winter had made things. Or maybe she was insinuating that I challenge Winter. But I was certain about one thing— after my jerkish behavior, Lex wouldn't be waiting for me to figure it out.

As we stood there, I noticed that not a single crew member had stepped forward to greet Winter. The room was filled to capacity at 250 people, all crew. Everyone from the AV guys to the roadies to Winter's personal staff were there, taking full advantage of the open bar and endless appetizers. This was supposed to be her night, and her grand entrance was already ruined.

Alison must have had the same thought because she shot forward, took Winter's arm, and started to navigate her through the crowd.

I continued to search for Lex. When I spotted Reggie, tall and boisterous, on the other side of the room, I knew Lex wouldn't be far away. One glance to my right confirmed it. She was standing between Reggie and Amie, a wide smile on her face as she spoke animatedly with Brenda. And like a punch to the gut, I knew I'd made the biggest fucking mistake of my life. I just didn't know how to fix it.

I'd never seen Lex look so radiant. With glowing eyes, a sparkling smile, and infectious laughter, she looked more in her element than I'd ever seen her.

My eyes dropped, and I swallowed as I took in her outfit. She wore a fitted black top with a low V that left little to the imagination. Hooked over her shoulders were tiny straps that I could easily shred with my teeth. A thin black necklace dropped between her breasts, dipping into the lowest point of her shirt, near her belly button. Her pink skirt was shiny, flowy, and short, wrapped tightly around her waist and tied in a long bow at the front. She was sensational. And apparently, I wasn't the only one who noticed.

Reggie's arm slipped around her shoulders, and he leaned in and said something in her ear. My fists balled, and my entire body grew hot. As soon as his gaze dropped to her breasts, I started to move across the room, too livid to think about what I was doing or what I would say.

My heart led the way as I edged through the crowd until I was a few feet behind her.

Fuck me. Her back.

Her shirt was cut so low it reached into her shiny ruffle skirt, held together with a thin string bow in the back.

"Theo," Amie called when she spotted me. "You'll never guess who hit the jackpot."

My heart thumped, wondering if she saw the way I was just eye fucking her friend's spine. I had no clue who she was talking about but narrowed my eyes and pointed at her. "You?" I mostly mouthed.

She shook her head and pointed at the vixen in the two-piece dress. "Lex."

Lex caught the exchange and turned to me, our eyes meeting for the first time since they were shaded on the plane. Her entire face grew shadows at the sight of me. I could have died, right then and there.

I had two options. Either embrace the pain as my insides withered away or throw her over my shoulder and carry her as far away from Reggie, Winter, and Vegas as we could get.

In a perfect world, all of that bullshit with the contract wouldn't matter. In a perfect world, I would have her back in my bed, beneath my hips, where I could stare at the sapphire eyes that had captured me from Day One.

When her eyes flickered away from mine and she lost her smile, I died a second death. The images of us escaping Vegas faded fast. Still, I considered pulling her away from the crowd to get her alone, to explain my behavior earlier. But a figure in white flashed before my eyes, halting me.

My heart sank. I looked up. Standing a mere five feet away was Winter, watching, just waiting for me to fuck up. I was almost thankful when Reggie's boisterous laughter ripped through the air, distracting Winter's gaze.

I didn't even notice Reggie's eyes land on me. "Hey, Theo." His lip curled as he tugged Lex to his body. "Can you believe this? I leave my girls for five minutes, and Lexie over here is cashing in on five K."

My girls? Lexie? Since when did he give Lex a new name? And why the fuck was he grabbing her like that?

Fire raged inside me as I took the few steps needed to get to Winter, my eyes blazing on her as she cowered. I didn't care that everything about me frightened her in that moment. I leaned down. "I want new terms. Starting now."

Her face wrinkled. "You don't get to set the terms, Theo."

I glowered, my jaw practically shaking with anger. "New terms. Or I quit."

Winter let out an uncomfortable laugh but shook her head. "If you quit, then—"

"No more threats," I growled low to her ear, so no one else could hear me. I wasn't taking no for an answer. "Keep your boy Reggie off her. I don't trust him. Talk to him, Winter. Or I walk and take Lex with me. You think I won't find her another gig? I'll find her a *better* one and expose you for your threats." I took a shaky, rage-filled breath. "Are we clear?"

Winter's eyes were pointed over my shoulder at Reggie, and I couldn't help noticing something I couldn't believe I had missed before—jealousy.

Winter's eyes flashed back to mine, her nose flaring. "Fine. You have a deal."

"And one more thing." I had her. I might have even had the upper hand. "What Lex and I do behind closed doors is none of your damn business."

"I can't agree to that," she hissed.

I shook my head, ready to drive my point home. "You don't have to agree to it. You won't know about it. Got it?"

She turned her cheek in response.

And then I grinned, because it was time to fix something I hoped like hell wasn't already broken.

Chapter 50

LEX

Alison slipped through the crowd and approached Reggie. She gestured for him to lean down and spoke something in his ear. Whatever it was caused amusement to spread over his face, then he shook his head and followed her away through the partygoers.

My entire body relaxed the moment he vanished. Reggie was a flirt, and perhaps he tried a little too hard in social situations, but he was harmless. I knew that. Still, every time he became aggressive with me—while we danced and when we talked—I couldn't help shifting a little in my skin.

Amie took my elbow and pulled me through the crowd toward the bar, and the discomfort I'd felt only moments before disappeared. She ordered us appletinis, which we'd been casually drinking all night, effectively numbing me to the man whose eyes I could feel following me around the room. I couldn't understand why his gaze never seemed to leave. After what happened this morning, I expected to see him with Winter, playing his part in whatever game he thought he had to play.

"I'm totally borrowing that outfit," Amie said, her gaze sweeping over me. "You look hot, girl." Her eyes caught on something behind me and squinted a little. "Wow, Lex. I'm starting to think you have more secret admirers than Reggie."

I set down my drink and tilted my head. "Huh?"

She laughed, her gaze still trapped on something else. "I thought I was imagining it, but Theo has been staring at you since he walked in."

How did Amie notice these things? First Reggie, now Theo.

My cheeks flamed, and I blew her comment off with a laugh before taking a swig of my drink. "Trust me, Theo isn't interested in me."

She didn't look convinced. "I don't know. Now that I think about it, the rumors of him and Winter have died down. And you two have been dancing together a lot." She shrugged then flashed me a grin. "Maybe Theo is totally into you."

"Theo doesn't date, remember? He definitely doesn't date backup dancers. Besides, it's against the rules."

Amie's eyes shone with laughter. "Sounds like you've thought about this."

I gave her a warning glance and handed her my drink. "Find us a seat near the food. I'm starving, and I need to go to the bathroom."

She saluted me, drink in hand, and I walked off with a roll of my eyes.

The bathroom was situated behind the bar. It was almost as crowded as the restaurant. I waited my turn, my eyes falling on Winter, who drifted into the bathroom past me and slipped into the next available stall. She didn't even bat an eye at the rest of us waiting. Alison had followed her but stopped at the closed door to wait. She shot an apologetic smile to those of us in line. When her eyes locked on mine, her expression softened. "Hey, Lex."

I mustered up a smile. "Hey."

I wondered if she knew more about Winter and Theo and the extent of their relationship. The complexities of it, business and personal. She didn't say anything more to me. Instead, she continued to stand by the bathroom stall Winter had disappeared behind.

"Gorgeous dress," a woman behind me muttered, and I turned to find Desire McQueen, the show's head costume designer.

"Thanks, Des." Coming from her, I took that as quite the compliment.

Amie had insisted I splurge a little with my winnings, so I entertained the impromptu shopping trip at the Wynn. But other than a few new outfits, shoes to match, and manicures for both of us, the money was securely stored in the safety deposit box in the room.

When I left the bathroom a short while later, I was grateful to have missed an uncomfortable run-in with Winter. She must have slipped out when I finally got into a stall. I was walking down the dimly lit hallway when I heard my name being called.

"Lex."

I swiveled to find Alison near a glass elevator, and I approached her timidly. "Were you calling me?"

She shifted her body and glanced nervously around us, as though she was about to get caught.

Why?

Her eyes settled back on me. "Do you trust me?"

How could I answer that? I didn't know Alison well enough to trust her, but something in my gut told me to say yes. I nodded, and she pressed a button on the elevator.

"Go up to the fifty-first floor then take the staircase to the top."

"Why?"

"I'm asking you to trust me, not ask questions."

My heart fluttered, and I tried not to think about why she was being so secretive. Deep down, I already knew, but I wasn't sure what it meant.

I entered the roof, the glow of the violet neon lights flooding the floor and walls. There was another bar outside, a large dance area, and seating by the edge that looked out over all of Vegas. Not a soul was outside, but I didn't think the club opened until eight o'clock. The staircase she mentioned was a semispiral, and I took it up to find that floor empty too. I shook, waiting there with my hands gripping the rails as I gazed around me in awe.

In a place as loud and bright as Vegas, I'd never felt more at peace.

I heard the footsteps approaching and tensed, refusing to turn around. I knew it was Theo, and I wouldn't give him the satisfaction of seeing my face crumble when he stared back at me. I'd come, and that was enough.

He stood behind me, leaving a few inches of distance, but I could feel him in the air around me, vaguely catching the scent of apple cinnamon and leather that I now knew was a mix of his body wash, his jacket, and his shampoo.

I knew the scent well since he loved to take me in the shower, with my breasts smashed against the glass as he pumped into me, slick and determined. He loved to hear my scream reverberate off the glass walls at the intensity of each thrust. And when I came, his mouth always found its way to mine to swallow my sounds. And I missed it. I missed all of it.

I crossed my arms, begging myself to forget how he made me feel last week and remembering how he made me feel this morning. Alone. Afraid. Heartbroken. Why had he arranged for me to come here? Hadn't he done enough damage?

"I'm so sorry."

I swallowed and slammed my lids shut, trying to tune out the shake in his voice. He stepped closer. I could feel his warmth, his breath, but he still wasn't touching me.

"Last night, this morning. I was shitty to you, but I didn't think there was another way. Lex, I've never regretted anything so much in my life."

The air was cool, but that wasn't why my entire body shivered. "So, Alison knows about us."

He stepped forward again. This time his front pressed against my back, and his hands gripped the rails on either side of my hands. "She does."

I felt the lump in my throat grow. "So, I'm screwed, then. She's going to tell Winter."

Theo's hand moved to my cheek, brushing the hair away from my neck before he leaned down to press his lips to my skin. My entire body came alive with his touch, and as much as I loved it, I hated it too. Why was he doing this?

"It's not an issue."

I let out a laugh, my mind foggy with confusion and need. "Of course it's an issue. Nothing has changed."

He pressed another kiss to my neck, his fingers sliding up my arm to the strap over my shoulder. He slid it to the side and pressed a kiss there too. "She wants me to be happy. She knows Winter is trying to keep us apart, and she thinks it's wrong."

I froze, and he seemed to realize why immediately.

"Winter knows? How?"

He bit into my skin as if my life was not about to get fucked over by our actions. As if we had nothing to lose. And I wished we didn't. I wished he could push into me against this rail right now. I wanted his scent all over me, inside me. I wanted to scream his name into the Vegas wind as I came.

"You took a selfie at my pool. Winter recognized it."

Horror cascaded over me like lava. "Fuck."

He bit my skin again, this time harder, and my eyes rolled back into my head. I knew he was punishing me because I cussed. "I'm crazy about you. As in, being away from you—being near you—drives me fucking insane, and all I can think about is being inside you."

His hand slipped down my arm. His fingers threaded through mine, and he squeezed.

I turned my neck slightly to catch his eyes, a brilliant mixture of deep blue sea and mossy green, for the first time since we'd been up here. "If everyone knows, what am I still doing here?"

"Winter didn't want to fire you. She also doesn't want any of the dancers to find out about any of this. So she told me to stay away from you."

"But you're here." I bit down on my bottom lip and chewed nervously.

"I told her what happened between us was none of her business, and she agreed to stay out of it. I was just trying to protect you, but I can't stay away from you. Not even for an entire goddamn day. Not even going into the biggest job of my career and knowing being together could be one giant disaster. It's selfish, and wrong, but you're all I can think about. Touching your skin. Inhaling your scent. Kissing your mouth." He pressed my body into the rail, letting me feel him. "There's no one else. There never could be. Not after you."

I swiveled to face him and kissed him so damn hard I could practically smell the flames of the inferno we'd created together. He engulfed me in his arms, and I wrapped mine around his neck then slid my fingers through his hair.

"Stay with me tonight," he pleaded against my lips. "Be with me. Forgive me." He peppered kisses against my mouth, fogging my mind even further.

"Are you telling me Winter is okay with this?"

He let out a sarcastic laugh. "No. But do you really want to spend the next six and a half months apart?"

"No, of course not. But what do you suggest? More secrets?" My hand gestured around the skyline. "In Vegas? Someone is bound to see us. Then what?"

"Then we deal with it. Until then, we keep it a secret. I'll get us a room no one else needs to know about. It'll be just how it was back in LA, then at the end of the show, we stop hiding."

It all sounded so easy. Except, I knew there was more we weren't thinking about. "What about Amie?" She was the first person who popped into my mind. "I've already been keeping secrets from Shane. You can't keep expecting me to lie to the people closest to me."

He searched my eyes. "Then tell her. Tell Shane. I don't care. Just make sure it doesn't get back to Winter. The deal was, we mind our business and she'll mind hers. If we flaunt this, it ends."

"How can you be so casual, knowing what could happen if any of this comes out?"

He leaned in, his eyes closing and opening again as he took a breath and let it out. "Because. I know what it's like to feel that I've lost you, and I'd take any risk to prevent that from happening again."

He released me and stepped back. "I know this is your career. I'm not trying to mess with that, but you know where I stand. Now I'm leaving this decision completely up to you." He took another step away. "I'll text you when I secure a room. If you show up, then I guess that's my answer."

And then he left, leaving me once again to find my center of gravity. On my own.

Chapter 51

THEO

The knock on the hotel door came shortly after midnight. I'd already been to the gym, showered, and paced the floor a few hundred times to distract myself from blowing Lex's phone up while I waited. When I opened the door and saw my woman standing there in the same pink-and-black outfit she'd worn to the party, I knew the wait had been worth it.

I watched her as she walked in and took in the massive suite I'd secured for us. "Your key is on the desk. Come here whenever you want. Sleep here whenever you want. It's ours."

She flipped around, her skirt swaying slightly on her pivot. The smile she gave me next lit up my chest. "I can't believe we're doing this." Her finger landed on the desk and traced the outline of the key. "Amie passed out before

I could talk to her. I didn't want to risk her waking up if I showered, so I just left." She looked up, shyly, like the girl I'd first met in that theater. The girl who'd driven herself under my skin without any effort at all.

"I'm glad you didn't change." I stepped forward and brushed her arms with my fingers. "I've wanted to take that dress off you from the moment I saw you wearing it."

Her lips curved into a smile. "Is that why I'm here?"

My heart pounded. "You're here because you want to be here."

There was a seriousness in her eyes that I couldn't ignore. "Is that why you're here?"

I shook my head. "I'm here because I've fallen in love with you, Lex. Madly. And I can't imagine another day without you."

I didn't expect her to say it back. I didn't deserve the words after the way I treated her this morning, but I needed her to know how I felt. How I would always feel, together or apart.

Her lip quivered, and she slid her arms around me, pulling me close. "And I'm here because I love you too. I'll take the risks. We'll find a way." She looked up into my eyes with a sheen of emotion glossing hers, and a thickness rose in my throat. "Thank you for talking to me tonight. For explaining. I know you were only trying to do the right thing."

I pressed my forehead to hers. "Thanks for listening."

We smiled at each other, and for the first time in my life, I wanted to make love to a woman. Not just any woman. I wanted to make love to Lex. I wanted to feel every beat of her heart and come so deep inside of her, she would feel me everywhere.

I placed my hand on her cheek, stroking it softly with my thumb while my other fingers played with the thin silky bow of her skirt. "This outfit. I almost had a heart attack when I saw you tonight."

Her eyes shone with amusement. "That was kind of the plan when I splurged with my slot winnings."

I glared at her, a rumble igniting in my chest. As much as I wanted to be gentle with Lex, I also had the insane desire to fuck her like a madman. When she teased me like that, she sparked something in me. Something desperate and wild.

My hand fell from her cheek, and both palms gripped her ass, lifted her into the air, and dropped her back down on the desk. She gasped, and I brought my mouth to hers. I slid a hand under her skirt, skimming her thighs then gripping them. Her tongue lashed mine, and she groaned, the vibration hitting me deep in the chest.

I was trying to slow my heart rate when she opened her legs, placed her hands on my ass, and pulled me in. My cock slammed her hard through our clothes, and I growled before pulling my head back. She continued to roll her hips and grind against me, her panties wetting my slacks. I took one of her straps and slipped it down her arm until she pulled out of it completely. And then I released the other strap until the fabric fell, revealing Lex's perfect tits and firm abs. I slipped her skirt around her, lifting as the material slid over her ass and down to the floor until she was completely bare except for a pair of pink panties. She was trying to kill me.

I sank to my knees, checking out the heels that were strapped around her ankles, skimming her skin with my fingers. Everything about Lex was so beautiful. The velvety softness of her bronze skin. Her smell. I reached for one heel to unhook it when she stood, shaking her head. I watched as she turned so her back was to my front, and she leaned over the desk, her ass in the air and her pussy in my face. "Kiss me, Theo."

I shook my head, which was still in a fog. I thought I'd imagined her words. How innocent they sounded but how truly dirty they were.

My hands moved back up her thighs, unable to get enough of how she felt beneath my palms. With one finger, I slid her soaked panties away to reveal her pink lips, swollen and glistening. I swiped against them with my tongue. She shook. I swiped against them again, and she moaned. When I swiped against her a third time, my mouth stayed there, closing around her, and sucking before I began to whip her clit with my tongue.

She fought against the desk while her legs quivered above me. And then she came, loud and hard, and I thanked the stars above that I'd managed to get us a room on the other side of the hotel from the crew's tower, where she could scream my name without fear of exposure.

I stood and turned her around then wrapped her legs around me. I carried her to the bed and laid her down before stripping myself bare. My palm squeezed myself as I looked at her splayed out on the bed, breathing heavy as she came down from her orgasm. What I would have given to push inside her without a fucking rubber separating us. I wanted to feel her more than ever. Her warm, tight cunt slipping and sliding against me.

She reached out her hand. "Come here."

I squeezed my lids shut with a growl. "I need to go get condoms, babe."

"No, you don't. Come here."

"Lex," I said with warning. *What the fuck is she thinking?*

She sat up, her eyes pleading. "What if I told you I've been on birth control since I was seventeen?"

My heart leapt, and in that moment, I didn't have any questions. I heard the words I wanted to hear, and I climbed over her, positioned myself, and slid into her, slowly.

And for the very first time in my life, I made love to a woman.

♥

My fingers skimmed over delicate skin, from her arm, to her legs, and then up again. I loved these moments with Lex. Lying here, relaxed, and taking her in from every angle possible. We probably should have been sleeping, but knowing Lex, she was ready for round two.

"Why didn't you tell me about the birth control?" I made sure my tone wasn't accusing, but I was curious. I'd told her how much I wanted to feel her before, and she had mentioned it only today. Why?

Lex shifted a little, as though trying to get comfortable, and I knew something was off. There was something else she hadn't told me. Anxiety pricked at my chest as I thought about the morning after we'd had sex for the first time, when she'd confessed to being a virgin.

"I could give you the easy answer and tell you that we barely knew each other and that no matter what, I wouldn't have let you come inside me without a condom."

My hand slid up her waist and gripped it slightly. She got the hint and turned so she was facing me. I stroked her cheek with my fingertips, my eyes making a trail of the freckles that filled her face. "And what's the difficult answer?"

She looked away, and something about the fact that she couldn't even look at me stopped my heart. I moved my hand from her face and drew her closer before pressing my lips to her nose.

"I was dating this guy, kind of," she began slowly. I feathered her arms and stomach with the tips of my fingers as she told me her story. It was all I could do to tell her I was there as she shook around her words.

"Please tell me someone murdered the son of a bitch," I growled after hearing everything she was willing to share.

She smiled through her pain then laughed through her tears. "Shane was the one who found him on top of me. He beat the shit out of him. I wouldn't have been surprised if he had killed him that night. But it wasn't Shane who killed him."

Whoa. "Someone killed him?"

Lex shook her head, wiping a tear from her eye. "He got into his car drunk and drove it into a tree that night. No one knows why he left or where he was headed. I figured Shane scared him shitless."

"Sounds to me like he got what was coming to him."

Lex grew pale by my insinuation. "Death?"

The truth was, if this fucker were alive now, he'd be dead tomorrow. "You never know what would have happened if he was still around. You might not have been the first. You definitely wouldn't have been his last."

Another tear fell from her eye, gutting me. What the hell did I know? Lex was the one who suffered through a night with that monster. Yet she'd wanted to lose her virginity to me. Something clicked in my chest, and I reached up and swiped the tear from her eye with my thumb.

"I'm sorry. I don't know what I'm saying. I'm glad Shane was there that night. And I'm glad you trusted me to be your first."

Her eyes locked on mine, and she smiled. "Yeah, me too."

Chapter 52

LEX

"Let's get the band onstage. Cue the lights and fade to black. Good. Okay, now give it a ten-second count and then fade in the recorded intro."

I had never thought about what went on during stage prep for a concert when I signed on to be one of Winter's backup dancers, but I was beginning to get a glimpse of the chaos.

Backstage, the Zappos Theater in Planet Hollywood was an epic disaster. People were running like mad in all directions, shouting their demands, raising hell if something wasn't going their way, fussing over Winter. Everything was urgent and distracting, and I was supposed to be listening for our cue to take the stage.

My heart was beating so fast, and this was only Day One of stage rehearsals. We'd walked through everything with Theo a few times this morning as we familiarized ourselves with the stage layout and our placements in a bigger space than Gravity provided. Now we were expected to run through the number, full out, with the live band and lighting.

"Cue band. Cue dancers for the intro," boomed the event show caller, through the surround-sound backstage.

When the band started its intro, the stage manager escorted Winter from her dressing room to a narrow tunnel where she would be elevated to a high rise on the stage. I watched this, all while Desire—who had us fitted weeks ago—made her way down the line of dancers to measure us again.

"Not now, Desire," Theo said, tapping her on the shoulder. "They need to focus."

She sighed and wiped the sweat from her brow and threw up her hands. "Fine. But every single one of them needs to see me before they leave today. Some of these alterations are going to take some time. You've been starving these girls, haven't you?"

He threw her a playful glare. "How about I just tell them to eat a few doughnuts?"

She jabbed him in the chest while fighting her smile. "How about you eat those doughnuts while I do my job?"

He placed his hands on her shoulders and steered her away. "How about I buy *you* doughnuts tomorrow morning while you measure my dancers? They'll be beat after today, I'm making sure of it."

She giggled, and my heart melted on witnessing Theo in his element. Everyone respected him. Everyone listened. And I couldn't stop reminding myself that he was mine. I didn't even care that it was a secret anymore.

"Dancers, take the stage."

Theo charged to the front of the three of us. Three more girls were stage right, and the guys were climbing into the tunnel with Winter.

When I passed Theo, his gaze slid by me, but his palm landed on the small of my back. It was the lightest touch, but it spoke volumes. Last night had been one of the best nights of my life and the feeling seemed to be mutual.

The stage was still dark, our only navigation the tiny stage lights that wrapped the perimeter. I executed each move with confidence and precision, the intro choreo only a tease of what was to come.

I'd heard so many horror stories over the last month about working for other artists in the industry, especially those who couldn't dance, and having only the most basic steps for choreography. I could imagine how painful that would be when all we wanted as dancers was to let loose on the dance floor and challenge ourselves with every beat.

The run-through seemed to go well up until one of the interludes later in the set, when the stage went black. The interludes gave Winter and us time for costume changes and water. There weren't any costume changes today, but we still appreciated the short breaks.

We were backstage, waiting for our next cue to come back out, when Reggie hopped over to me. "Come with me for a second," he said, taking my arm before I could ask him why he needed me.

I went with him to the stage, where Theo and a few others stood below us, talking about something we couldn't make out from the distance. I noticed then that he had grabbed Wayne too. Theo looked up, his eyes landing first on me then on Reggie. "What are you doing?"

"The next song is the bonus track. I just wanted to talk placements before I teach them the choreography."

My eyes grew wide, and I reached to yank on Reggie's shirt. "What?" My heart felt as if it would explode with excitement, but I didn't want to get my hopes up.

Reggie winked at me. "I choose you, Lex. It's your solo with Wayne and me supporting you."

I couldn't believe what I was hearing. My eyes shot to Theo, who wore a deep-set frown. "Mind running that by your boss? Winter won't appreciate being the last to hear about your selections."

Reggie chuckled, and something about his tone made my insides curl. "She'll be fine with whatever I choose." He gestured at the stage. "We're center stage for this one, right? Did my placement plans get approved?"

Theo's jaw tightened and relaxed, then he nodded. "Yup. You're approved. Winter will be on a bridge, sitting right above the stage. Lex will be wearing the same outfit as Winter, dark wig and all."

Reggie nodded, the air thick with his arrogance. "Cool. The song is about a damaged relationship where the woman is in the process of letting go. I'm seeing … dark, haunting. Spot lighting. Lots of fog. Tattered clothes." He looked pointedly at Theo.

"We can make that happen. I assume you're ready with choreography?"

Reggie cocked his head at Theo, his lip curling at one end. "Sure am."

"Good," Theo said, pointing at the side stage, where the VIPs would most likely gather during the show. "Get Lex and Wayne up to speed and be ready to show me what you've got by this time tomorrow. I trust you three will catch up with the rest of us at that point."

Reggie nodded again, his shoulders back and his chest puffed out. "Sure thing."

I bit my smile and followed the guys off stage.

"Hey," I said to Reggie as I tugged his arm. "Thanks for this."

He shrugged. "I owed you."

I crinkled my brows, confused. "What for?"

Shaking his head, he waved a hand in the air. "Because you're good, Lex.

And you deserve your solo."

My expression eased into a smile. "Thanks, Reg. I won't let you down."

♥

"Room service and sex? Is that how the next six months will be?"

Theo grinned. "If I play my cards right."

We were curled up together on the couch in the sitting room after finishing off two steaks and indulging in a glass of wine while we chatted. It was the first time I felt we were an actual couple. Sure, we were still sneaking around, but there was no more guessing about what would happen when the hourglass emptied.

I chuckled and pressed my lips to his. "I'm not complaining. But we might want to get creative at some point. I was reading up on Vegas, and there's so much to do off the strip. Hiking. Lakes. The dam." My eyes lit up. "Let's go on an adventure."

"Whoa there, tiger," he said, moving a strand of hair from my eyes. "You're here for work, first. Maybe after the show gets going and we wrap the music video, we can afford to play a little." He moved his nose against mine. "However, if you'd like to see how adventurous I can get with you naked, I'm up for the challenge right now."

I laughed and pushed him away. Standing, I faced him with my hands on my hips. He'd started to strip me the moment we walked into the room, but he got only as far as my bra and panties before I begged for food. It had been a long day with only one long break for lunch. "I can't stay."

Theo's eyes narrowed at me. "The fuck you can't. You're staying."

I shook my head. "I still need to talk to Amie. I already bailed on dinner with her to come here. I can't miss our movie night too. She's my roomie. And she's my only true friend here."

Theo snorted and leaned back into the sofa, moving his hands behind his head. "What about Reggie? He seems to be winning you over."

I grinned. "Is that jealousy I detect?"

"Hardly," he growled. "I'm just telling you what I see."

"Well," I said, with a little shimmy of my shoulders. "He happens to think I deserve a solo, and I happen to agree with him."

Theo chuckled. "Might be the only thing I'll ever agree with Reggie about." Then his forehead creased, his amusement clearly fading. "Are you okay with the choreography? Reggie likes lifts, and I know you're not crazy about them."

My chest warmed at his question. "Reggie can be a little … awkward … at times, but I'm used to him by now. He's harmless. And the choreo is great."

"And if it ever gets weird, you'll let me know, right?"

My cheeks lifted in a smile. "Of course."

"Good." He cleared his throat. "So are you going to show me this mysterious routine you guys were working on today?"

"Tomorrow. You'll see it tomorrow."

"What about tonight?" he asked with a pout. "I had plans for you." His eyes scanned my body. "Big plans."

I bit my lip again to control the smile that was fighting its way onto my face. I reached for my leggings to slip them on. He stood just as I was reaching for my tank top.

"Not tonight," I warned, bringing myself up to my tiptoes. My lips met his, allowing myself to sink into his arms as soon as they wrapped around my body.

He sighed. "I'm pissed at you for leaving."

I slid my palms down to his ass and squeezed. "You'll forgive me tomorrow when you show me all the plans you had for me."

"Damn straight." He bit his bottom lip with a grin, stirring something in me.

"Looking forward to it." And with a final glance over my shoulder, I slipped out our door.

Chapter 53

THEO

"Let's see it, Reg." Late in the afternoon, I finally called an end to rehearsals and had the dancers and crew join me in the audience. Winter too. Whatever Reggie, Lex, and Wayne had been working on was a surprise since they found a quieter space to spend their day rehearsing. "Show us what you got."

I was surprisingly calm at the thought of allowing another man to choreograph a number in Winter's concert. But Lex had that effect on me. Knowing that I would have her in my arms after today's sweat session ended was enough.

Winter took the seat beside me and shot me a glance. "How you holding up?"

Even though Lex and I had worked things out, I hadn't forgiven Winter. Not even a little. "Rehearsals are going as well as expected. Some snags with timing and formations, but we seem to be working through them all right."

"I meant"—she leaned into me, pressing her arm to mine—"with the Lex thing. We made a deal, but what if something goes down and she starts to get a little obsessive? I can't stop thinking about it."

Heat flared in my chest. "I think you have other things to worry about." I nodded at the stage, where Lex was taking her position on the floor. "Your boy's about to show us what he's made of. You ready?"

She narrowed her eyes and leaned back in her seat. "Just start the music."

I chuckled and gave a signal to the AV tech running the stage sound. He returned my salute as he started the bonus track.

As soon as music streamed through the speakers, I remembered why I loved working for Winter. Her tracks were all influenced by different genres, making everything I got to choreograph challenging in some way. I loved playing the tracks over and over until the stories came to life in my mind, knowing she'd give me lots of creative freedom.

Watching Lex dance to the opening phrases of the song raised the skin on my arms. With the stage lights dimmed and blue and white spotlights beaming down on her, she looked fucking radiant and 100 percent affected by where she was performing—in the best possible way.

Every lyric was being portrayed in each of Lex's steps. I could feel the emotion as she moved across the floor—with each split leap, each glide, each contract and retract. One move flowed into the other like a perfect symphony of dance.

Even when Reggie and Wayne joined Lex onstage, she was still the focus of the performance. I could almost forget anyone else was there, supporting her, lifting her, tossing her to the floor in an epic move that left the entire crew gasping.

I turned to Winter, and my throat thickened as a tear slid down her cheek.

She was quick to wipe it away, never taking her eyes off the stage.

When the song ended, everyone stood, and though only a few dozen of us were in that room, the applause was deafening. The dancers, Reggie and Lex, especially, were showered in praise. Deservingly. I had to give the guy credit.

"Nice job, man." I extended my hand. "That was great work."

He glanced at my hand then raised his palms to me with a shake of his head and a laugh. "Nah, dude. I'm good." He turned so his back was to me, and I tensed all over.

Fucking dick. And there I was, proud of myself, knowing that the only reason Reggie got the opportunity in the first place was because he was challenging me. I thought I took the high road by telling him what he deserved to hear, regardless of his tendencies to be a piece of shit. After his response, I wished I could take it all back.

My blood boiled as I tapped him on the shoulder to get his attention. He swiveled around, a challenge in his eyes.

"What the fuck?"

Reggie raised his brows then rolled his eyes.

He is such a punk.

"What? I'm not going to shake your hand while you stand there and patronize me with your weak-ass compliments."

I let out an incredulous laugh and backed up, legitimately entertained by his superiority. "Fine. No problem, Maynor. Just do your thing."

"I will, Noska. Don't you worry about that."

It took everything in me to muster the strength to walk away, but I knew it wasn't the end of the conversation. Reggie had more to say to me—more aggression he'd built up over the years while standing in my shadow. He would detonate one day. It was only a matter of time.

Chapter 54

LEX

When the crew shuffled off to dinner, I stayed behind to have a moment alone. I sat on the stage, my feet hanging over the edge and my eyes sweeping the open-air venue. Whispers of the night broke through the surrounding air. The main theater lights were off, but there was enough illumination from the perimeter to give me a faint view of it all. Adrenaline still soared through my veins from earlier, and I could only imagine how intense that same feeling would be in front of a real audience.

Seven thousand. That was the seating capacity of Zappos at Planet Hollywood. That was how many people would be watching when I performed Reggie's routine on opening night—and every night afterward. Chills rushed over me. I let out a breath and smiled as I shook my head in amazement. It was all so surreal.

"Psst." The sound came from behind me. I swiveled my head to see who was trying to get my attention, but no one was there. A familiar chuckle came next, and I smiled. I couldn't see him, but I knew it was Theo calling to me from the wings, stage right.

"C'mere." His voice broke through the steady Vegas noise. With bars and casinos open twenty-four seven, there wasn't a dead hour of night.

I stood and adjusted my spandex shorts and long gray shirt. Then I made my way toward the noise, past the black show curtain, past the wood crates and massive walls of cords and switches, until I reached a cluttered space where all the props were stored. Pushed against the back wall was a giant hamster wheel Reggie would be dancing in during the song "Catch Me If You Can." There was a box made entirely of mirrors that Winter would be walking in and out of it with a costume change for her "Black Magic" number. Tons of shelving held a variety of accessories for the rest of us—glasses, canes, hats, and more.

An arm shot out from the dark, and my breath caught in my throat before I could scream. I felt myself yanked off balance until I was falling into a man whose scent had become my home. I giggled and buried my face in his chest. "What are you doing?"

I felt him lean down, his lips just a breath from mine as he slid a hand over my ass and gripped it. Chills burst from my skin, and heat pooled between my legs. "I can't stop thinking about your hot mouth on my cock."

"Shh," I whispered and narrowed my eyes. Even in dim light, he could see me as well as I could see him. He smiled. "Anyone could see us right now," I reminded him.

He wrinkled his nose and looked around. "Not a fucking person here, babe." He pulled me closer and leaned in again. "I couldn't wait until after dinner. I just wanted one of these." He pressed his lips to mine. The kiss was soft and slow as his mouth parted mine, and my head swirled at the feel of his warm tongue darting between my teeth. I curled into him, melting with each second. His palms moved from my ass to my back, and his thumbs made circle patterns against me. It was the perfect kiss.

He pulled away but didn't let me go. Thank God. I might not have been able to support my own weight. Not with my head spinning and my heart pounding like crazy. "You were a fucking rock star today, you know that?"

I bit my lip, feeling the giant smile that was about to blossom on my face. "It felt … incredible, Theo. If it felt that good today, I can't even imagine a live show."

"It'll be a thousand times what you felt today. With the crowd feeding you their energy with their excitement and screams. When I'm up on that stage, dancing is the closest thing I've ever felt to flying."

"I can't wait." I beamed and leaned in for another kiss. Then I pulled back, remembering something. "What was that about between you and Reggie today?"

Theo's eyes flitted away, as if he wanted to roll them but didn't. "He was just being Reggie. Nothing to worry about."

I wasn't sure I believed him. Their exchange looked heated, but I wasn't able to make out anything. "Okay," I finally said, letting the subject go. "But now we really need to get out of here."

He nodded and kept his eyes on me as I backed away. "You're coming to our room tonight?"

I bit my lip as I considered my plans. "Yeah, I'll figure something out. Maybe I'll finally have that talk with Amie."

Chapter 55

LEX

I didn't talk to Amie. Not that night, not the next, and the secrecy continued well into the next week. I was starting to get nauseated every time I made an excuse to step away from our room. There were only so many trips to the gym I could make while praying she didn't follow me. My best excuse was the one that tore me up the most.

"I'm going to step out to call Shane," I told her that night as she was getting ready to shower.

The disappointment on her face crushed me. "But your calls with him are, like, five hours long. We're going to Tao tonight. Remember? Reggie got us bottle service, and the whole crew is supposed to be there." She wasn't about to let up. "Can you just tell him you'll talk tomorrow?"

The acid in my gut was about to eat its way through my body. Shit. I'd totally forgotten about our crew club night. We'd wanted to make it a monthly thing where we'd pitch in and grab bottle service at one of the fancier clubs on the strip. Tonight we were supposed to head to Tao at the Venetian.

I let the door handle slip out of my hands and walked over to the closet. "I can't believe I forgot." I tried to hide my burning face. I could sense that Amie wasn't buying it. She crossed her arms in the doorway of the bathroom and narrowed her eyes at me.

"Lex, be straight with me. Were you really going to call Shane and talk for hours? I mean, I have a friend on tour with him right now, and that crew works almost every night."

My entire body felt as if it were going up in flames. Why had I put off telling Amie? I could trust her. The time had just never seemed right. I faced her, my shoulder sagging, and I could feel the air deflate from my chest. "I wasn't going to call Shane." I bit my lip, trying desperately to form the right words in my head.

"Where were you going? Is it a guy?"

I nodded, relief slipping through my veins. Maybe if she guessed, it would be easier.

She narrowed her eyes. "Is it someone I know?"

Her mouth dropped at the half smile I gave her. The words were not coming off my tongue.

"Oh my God. It's Reggie. You're sleeping with Reggie?" Her voice practically squealed with shock at a volume that had me muffling my ears.

"Be quiet," I hissed. When I finally felt safe enough to release my ears, I tried again. "You think I'm sleeping around with Reggie?"

Amie threw her hands up, a befuddled look on her face. "Who else could it be? He's the only straight male on the crew. Except for Theo, but—" Her eyes locked on mine at the mention of Theo's name. I felt my blush deep in my bones. Her jaw fell open. "Lex. Please tell me you are *not* sleeping with Theo fucking Noska." When I cringed and didn't respond, she threw her hand over her mouth before hissing, "Our choreographer?"

Maybe it was an awful idea to confide in Amie. She might have been my best friend on this crew, but I hadn't known her very long. And I was breaking a rule. I wasn't above the rules, and maybe she'd feel that the rest of the crew should know too. Suddenly I felt sick.

"I should have known." Her gaze wandering around the room, she was probably thinking about all the instances that should have tipped her off. "All the extra sessions together. You were helping him. He wanted to hand you that solo. Oh my God, Theo has been … nicer than ever before." Her eyes shot to mine. "You're fucking Theo?"

I cringed again and took a deep breath. "We're in love, Amie."

She barked out a laugh, as though she thought I was kidding until she saw my face. "You're serious."

I nodded. "We spent a lot of time together back in LA. We got close without meaning to. I was honestly just helping him, but—I don't know—it just happened."

Her expression was still amazed. "Holy shit. You could get fired."

I stepped forward and took her hands. I would have sunk to my knees and prayed too if I thought it would help. "You have to promise not to say anything. Theo and I were going to end it once we got to Vegas, but we couldn't. It hurt too much to stay apart, so we're still together, but no one can know. Especially not Reggie. I don't really understand the beef he has with Theo, and I don't want to give him any more ammo."

Amie groaned and pulled her hands from mine. "Lex. Reggie is my friend. And he likes you. Do you realize how upset he'll be if he finds out?"

"He won't." I stressed my words. "No one knows. No one but you and me and Theo." I purposely omitted the fact that Winter knew too. "Please don't breathe a word of this. When the concert is over in six months, we won't care who knows."

"This is insane. I don't think I'll ever be able to look at him the same again. Or both of you when you're in the same room." She shook her head. "I'm sorry, are we talking about the same Theo? I thought you hated him."

"I don't."

"Are you sure?"

How could I convince her without dragging her to Theo's room and performing a makeout session in front of her? That wasn't happening.

"I'm positive. Amie, you need to promise me you won't breathe a word of this to anyone."

She sighed. "Fine. I promise. Does this mean you'll stop lying to me about where you're sneaking off to? And will you spend tonight dancing with me instead of eye fucking your new boyfriend from across the room?"

I laughed and reached around her neck for a hug. "I promise. All of the above. I'm yours tonight."

She groaned out a laugh. "All right, you dirty little whore. Let me shower. You find something to wear. One of those fancy dresses you bought with your winnings would be perfect."

Amie shut the bathroom door behind her, and I grabbed my phone. As soon as the shower started, I called Theo. He answered on the second ring.

"On your way? I'm in bed. And I already did the hard part and took my clothes off. All you have to do is sit on me."

I laughed. Despite my talk with Amie and the harsh reminder that what Theo and I were doing was wrong, his cocky comment reminded me why it was all worth it. "You're not going to like me very much right now."

"No," he warned. "Don't you dare bail on me."

"I'm sorry, but I forgot that I'd already promised the crew I'd go to Tao tonight."

"Fuck, Lex. I really didn't want to do the whole social thing tonight. I just wanted you."

My chest grew warm at his words. "I didn't say you had to go. Maybe I can sneak into our room after Tao."

He snorted through the phone. "If you're going to Tao, so am I. Winter invited me earlier, but I didn't know it was a crew thing. Now I feel like a jackass."

"Well, don't. But I should also let you know that Amie started asking questions, and she kinda-sorta guessed that we've been hanging out."

"Hanging out?" Theo challenged. "I think we've been doing more than that, don't you?"

I rolled my eyes and walked to the closet to start scanning my limited selection. "You know what I mean."

"Did she say what tipped her off?"

I explained her questioning my calls to Shane and how she'd had a feeling something was off. I also assured him Amie promised to keep our secret. Theo didn't seem worried about it.

We got off the phone just as I found the perfect outfit, a strapless red tube dress, fitted at the waist and chest but loose in the skirt. It had the perfect amount of excess material to twirl in without showing all my ass. I hoped.

I took a quick shower after Amie then put it on. "I won't be bending over in this dress."

She looked at me in the mirror where she was applying her makeup. She nodded. "It's as perfect as the day I made you buy it. But yeah, definitely no twerking tonight." She turned her eyes back to the highlighter she was applying. "Now finish getting ready. I told Reg we'd meet him at the bar downstairs for a drink first." She quirked an eye. "That's cool, right? You hanging out with

Reggie? Theo and Reg don't seem to get along very well."

I shrugged and reached for my concealer. "I have no idea what the deal is between those two. I don't know if I want to."

Amie reached for her mascara and let it hover above her eyes while she looked at me. "Why do I get the feeling that by the end of this concert series, some major shit is going to go down?"

I let out an awkward laugh. "Let's just take it one day at a time, shall we?"

Chapter 56

THEO

It was past eleven o'clock when Winter and her entourage finally came by my room to grab me. I didn't want to deal with the hassle of getting into a club, so I called Winter to let her know I'd changed my mind. She was already drunk by the time she showed up at my door.

"Glad you decided to join us." She beamed, her eyes glossed over, as we were escorted from the SUV and through a private entrance at the Venetian.

"Figured it was time to let loose a little." That was a lie. I was only going because Lex would be there, and I wouldn't miss the opportunity to see my girl all dressed up.

"Good." Winter wrapped an arm around mine, tripping a little on her heels. "It'll be like old times. Maybe I'll even give you a lap dance later." She winked and giggled, and my stomach recoiled at the thought of Winter rubbing her ass on me, the show visible to all around us, including Lex.

I let out a good-natured laugh to hide my discomfort. She wasn't serious. I could feel it. Whatever had once connected Winter and me in a less than platonic way had faded completely over recent weeks. Still, I never knew what Winter would pull when she had some alcohol in her. Suddenly, I was craving my night in with Lex all over again.

Alison shot me a look, and I knew what she was trying to tell me with her eyes. With six various bottles of liquor sitting in front of Winter, it was bound to be "one of those nights." I sighed, because I agreed with Alison's warning. This was about to become a shit show.

Winter gestured for me to sit beside her, and I knew I couldn't say no. I came with her, after all, and someone would need to alert her guards as soon as she needed to be dragged out of there. Shots were already being passed around our table and over to the Ravens' table beside us. I sucked in a breath when I saw Lex among the crew. She was wearing a sleeveless short red dress with her hair down and flowing freely over her shoulders. Reggie stood beside her with his palm splayed on her back. I tensed.

"Theo, wake up." Winter was yelling at me and nudging me with her shoulder, knocking the liquid in my glass over the edge and onto my pants. "Oops." She giggled then turned back to the group. "To the best crew a girl could ask for."

The table cheered, but my attention was focused on Lex, even when I tipped the glass back and the liquid lit a fire down my throat. Reggie glanced over at me, his eyes narrowing slightly, and something about his look unsettled my insides. His gaze darted between Winter and me, and I could almost catch the confusion in his eyes. Why the fuck did he care?

"Shit," Winter said before turning to me and leaning in. "I need to tell you something."

From her tone, I knew whatever she was about to say had sobered her some. "What's up?" I shouted.

"I wanted to warn you before tonight, but I didn't think you were coming. Reggie is pretty pissed off. You might want to stay away from him."

My brows turned in, and I wanted to tell her that I didn't give a fuck what Reggie was angry about. I wouldn't be tiptoeing around him. But I knew better than to say it. "Why? What happened?"

She cringed and leaned in again. "The label wants to cut the bonus track from the show."

My heart dropped into my stomach. *Fuck.* She didn't wait for me to chime in before continuing. "They think it's good enough to be a starter single, so they want to save it for my next album. I called Reggie after rehearsal to tell him, but he wasn't having it. He even called the label and started yelling at the first person who picked up the phone, the poor receptionist." She shook her head as if recalling the conversation. "It was awful. I've never seen him so enraged."

A rage-filled Reggie didn't surprise me, and I wasn't concerned in the least over his feelings. It was good choreography, but his attitude after the performance had me instantly regretting my compliments. "So, Lex lost her feature?"

Winter narrowed her eyes. "Seriously? Are we back to her? This isn't about Lex."

I pressed my lids together, knowing I had to keep myself in check. "I know. Sorry. But Winter, that's the breaks of the business. You keep trying to protect Reggie's feelings, but that's not the way this works. He'll get his opportunity. That doesn't mean you have to be the one who gives it to him."

Winter reached for her glass and sipped from it, as though she couldn't deal with her own thoughts. I could already see what would come of tonight if I didn't take her drink from her, but I couldn't do it. It wasn't my place, and

I was more upset over Lex losing a part I knew she would have killed onstage.

There were many reasons I shouldn't have hooked up with one of my backup dancers, and this was one of them. Witnessing the rapid changes that happened in the industry, often to career-altering levels, was something I could handle. But watching these changes happen to the woman I loved made me want to step in and fix things for her, and I couldn't. Not if Lex were truly going to make it in this industry. She had to grow her own wings and experience the rise and fall on her own to truly succeed.

Reggie's jaw tensed when he saw me talking to Winter. I watched as he tugged Lex closer, jerking her body toward him. She looked up in obvious surprise as he stared down at her with a playful smile. Before I could stand and get her the hell out of his grip, Amie was pulling her away from the table and toward the dance floor. Maybe she'd witnessed what I had. Whatever the reason she was helping Lex escape, I was grateful.

Something crawled under my skin and festered as I watched Reggie pour drink after drink down his throat. All the while, his eyes never left Lex. Lex, Amie, and the other female Ravens were tearing up the dance floor, attracting eyes from all over the room. As much as I wanted to enjoy the show, I couldn't look away from Reggie. There was something about the way he'd grabbed Lex and the careless way he was tossing liquor back, as if he were trying to drown himself. I didn't trust him. Not for a second.

I tracked his movements as he stood and cracked his neck before making his way to the dance floor. Amie tried to dance with him, but he moved her to the side to get to Lex. What the fuck? I stood, inching my way to the side of the dance floor. If he tried anything, I'd get to him and break his neck faster than he could try to stop me.

"Theo, what the hell are you doing?" Alison gritted out as I started to take off. She must have been watching me watch Reggie. But she was steaming.

I could feel the heat of her words and the warning that came with them. In that moment, I didn't give a fuck. "Just going to talk to my friend here."

"You're acting like a jealous boyfriend," she hissed from behind me. "You think no one will pick up on it? Sit back down. Now."

Reggie didn't touch Lex when he started to dance. It actually looked pretty innocent to begin with, but I noticed what she didn't. That when Lex turned to dance with the girls, he moved up behind her and pressed his body into hers. I could see the shock that registered on her face and the way she immediately tried to fight it, but his grip was strong. Her eyes found me, and that was when I snapped.

Anger blew through me as I stalked onto the dance floor, slithering past dancers until Reggie and Lex were in front of me. I reached for her hand, tugged her toward me, then gestured for her to move away.

"Something bothering you, boss?" Reggie's eyes were filled with amusement and challenge.

"Just making sure you remember to behave yourself."

"Oh yeah? What's it to you?" He cocked a brow.

"Don't make me spell it out for you. If I catch you getting handsy with my dancers again, I will break you."

Reggie's eyes moved over his shoulder to Lex. She was watching us, her eyes wide and anxious. "Lex doesn't seem to mind my hands"—he winked— "if you know what I mean."

My fists curled at my sides. "Watch yourself, Reg. You never know when karma's gonna swoop in and fuck with you." I clapped him on the back and gave his shoulder a squeeze, adding some pressure to drive my point home. "Consider this a warning."

He threw my hand off with a shake and stepped up to me, so close I could smell the onions he'd eaten at lunch. "You really just float through life on your cloud of ignorance, don't you, Noska? I don't believe in karma. When I want something, I'll do whatever it takes to get it."

"Yeah?" My chest filled with dynamite, two seconds from lighting up. "How's that working for you? How's your bonus track?"

I shouldn't have antagonized him. I should have gotten Lex the hell away from him and left with her. Fuck the consequences.

His eyes narrowed. "Winter told you?" He looked over my shoulder and curled his lip. "That bitch."

Explosions went off inside me. I could barely see through the smoke. "It wasn't Winter's call. For Christ's sake, she was trying to throw you a bone and give you the shot you've been crying about." I shook my head. "If you ever wonder why you're still stuck where you are, maybe you should look back on this moment. The moment you called the one woman who's been looking out for you a bitch. Maybe then it'll sink into your brain. It takes more than great choreography to make it in this industry. It takes people skills, which I'm afraid you just don't have."

He moved in, so close his toes jammed into mine. "Everyone knows you screwed your way to the top, Noska. You think you're above the rules? You're not."

"What the fuck are you talking about?"

He puffed his chest and tilted his head as though considering his words, a rarity for Reggie. "Just stay out of my way. Try to stop me and I'll defend myself the only way I know how, the way of the streets, brother. You remember what that was like?" His top lip curled. "No, you probably don't. Let me tell you. I'll burn you, motherfucker. Until you're as good as a pile of ash, like your dead girlfriend."

All I saw was red and not the red from Lex's dress. Everything slowed around me—time, the bass booming from the surrounding speakers, the crew spotting our argument and freezing while they watched us. He knew. I didn't know how. But he knew the real reason Mallory had died. Because of me.

A gleam appeared in his eyes when he saw my expression. He knew he'd just hit me where it hurt most.

Suddenly, everything around us blurred except for Reggie—my target. I lost sight of the Ravens standing around us with shock and fear in their eyes. I didn't hear Winter and Alison running up behind us and shrieking for us to calm the fuck down. Nothing was going to stop me from serving Reggie my fist for dinner.

I reeled back with my right hand and clocked him so hard he fell back into a group of dancers. Blood rushed through my veins as I shook off the fog of rage.

Reggie popped up from the floor and ran for me, his elbow cocking back on the way. I didn't move. I would have let him hit me. And I wouldn't have fallen down like a pussy, like him. But Winter's bodyguards were on him and pulling him away before he could throw a single punch.

"You're gonna be fucking sorry, Noska." He thrashed his arms in an attempt to free himself from the grips of the men. "Just wait." He let out a belligerent laugh. "Just wait."

Chapter 51

LEX

I spent the weekend in tears, my heart heavy. Amie accompanied me in our veg-out session. With opening night less than a week away, we should have been watching our figures, but I would have done anything to take my mind off the drama that went down at Tao.

Reggie was acting crazy, which caused Theo to act crazy. Winter was pissed. And now the entire group of Ravens was making assumptions about exactly what was going on. Sure, the bonus track got pulled. I lost my feature. Reggie lost his opportunity. And there would be last-minute changes to the show. But now everyone was convinced there was a love triangle between Theo, Reggie, and Winter.

It made me sick.

I was avoiding Theo when I knew I shouldn't, but I needed my space to sort through the craziness of all that had transpired over the last few weeks. It all seemed to be happening so fast, and I hadn't had a moment to myself to breathe through it.

There was a knock at the door, and I jumped. Amie tossed off her covers and laughed when she saw my expression. "Relax, Lex. It's probably our pizza." She jumped out of bed, walked around the corner, and opened the door.

Whispered voices caught my attention. My heart jumped into my throat when Amie popped around the corner with wide eyes. "Um, Lex, someone's here to see you."

Fuck. I sat up, looking around for the clothes I tossed before I climbed into bed for an early night. I was wearing only my sports bra and underwear. "Hold on."

I just knew Theo was going to walk around the corner next, but when I looked up, I felt all the built-up emotion explode. "Shane!" My best friend stood there with a huge grin on his face. Tears sprang to my eyes, and relief flooded me all at once. I threw off the covers and took one leap from the bed and into his arms. And then I sobbed.

I didn't hear Amie leave the room. She'd snuck out quietly at some point during my cry fest. "Damn, girl. You sounded like shit on the phone last night, but I had no idea."

My breaths were staggered as I wiped my face and fell on the bed. I hadn't told Shane everything yesterday, just that it was all becoming so real and that I needed him. He was planning to be here for our opening show in four days, but he must have decided to come earlier after our talk.

"It's a shit show."

"All because of the bonus track? Was Reggie basing his career on the hope someone would see one choreographed piece and shit themselves over it? No offense, Lex. I'm sure you danced it brilliantly, but Reggie seems to have a huge stick up his ass." He lay back on the bed beside me. "Combined with this feud with Theo, I'm sure your partner routine is a disaster waiting to happen."

I groaned. "The disaster *did* happen."

Shane turned to me and crinkled his face. "I don't understand. I get that it's all overwhelming, but why do you care so much about their drama? Let Theo and Reggie have their cock war without you. You're walking your own path."

Then he saw my face, and his own reflected how transparent I was. He knew I was hiding something. "Lex, tell me."

I sighed before taking a deep breath and blurting it out. I told him everything, from Theo asking me to help him in class, since I picked up his choreography the fastest, to the night Theo spotted me dancing and we wound up sharing a bed in the staff room. And then how it all evolved. I wanted him to know it wasn't a fling, as we'd both planned for it to be. I wanted him to know that we'd been through the pain of trying to stay apart. I told him everything, leaving out Theo's personal stories about Mallory and his relationship with Winter. Those bits of the story weren't mine to tell.

"Shit, Lex." His eyes were wide, and he shook his head after my hour's worth of storytelling. I expected a lecture, a hard look to tell me to wake up and end it before I destroyed my career. I expected anything but the words that came out of his mouth next.

"You let Theodore Noska deflower you. I'm so proud."

And despite all the emotions that had been spinning within me, I laughed. I laughed hard as more tears streamed down my face, this time because I was thanking God Shane was with me.

"Can't I call in sick?"

Amie, Shane, and I were on our way to the theater when I stopped near the entrance and halted in my tracks. I wasn't ready to deal with any more drama. Theo and I hadn't spoken, but we'd texted each other a few times yesterday. He knew I needed some space to clear my head, especially with opening night approaching.

"I bet it's all died down." Amie was trying to reassure me. "Besides, no one thinks that night had anything to do with you. Let's just go in there and do our jobs."

I turned to Shane, hoping he'd steal me away, give me the reprieve I'd been searching for, but he just shook his head. "I didn't come here to save you, baby girl. I came to watch you fly. Get out there and get out of your head."

I took a deep breath and moved past them, through the backstage door, past security, down the cement and brick-walled corridor, until we were in the dressing room with the rest of the Ravens.

Shane took off to find a seat in the audience while Amie and I found our costumes waiting for us on the rack. We stepped into our two-piece pleather outfits, booty shorts, and a vest that crisscrossed our chests in front, leaving our midriffs bare.

"Maybe we should have laid off the pizza and ice cream," Amie teased as she twirled to check out her ass in the mirror.

I chuckled and smacked her stomach. "You look perfect. Let's go."

The Ravens were lining up on either side of the stage, then I saw Theo, a clipboard in his hands and a headset on. He was speaking into it when his eyes landed on me. Something somersaulted in my stomach. I missed him. I hated that we were back to this place, our careers threatened by feelings we couldn't stop if we tried. We had tried.

He tore his eyes from mine without so much as a smile. But what did I expect? I was the one who'd been keeping my distance. And we both had a job to do.

"All right, Ravens. Five minutes. Find your places," he yelled out.

Reggie passed me to enter the tunnel with Winter and threw me a look over his shoulder. I didn't think he meant to see me, because when our eyes connected, surprise crossed his features, then something else I couldn't quite make out—something that stirred like sludge in my gut.

"Lex, c'mon. Get your head in the game." Theo came up beside me and placed a hand on my back. "Pretend this is the real deal."

I looked at him, my eyes scanning his. Then I swallowed and nodded, forcing thoughts of Reggie to the back of my mind.

"You okay?" he asked.

"Yeah, I'm fine. Just—" I scanned the space around us, but too many people were within earshot. "Never mind." I wanted to tell him something felt off, but I didn't know why. My thoughts weren't completely formed, so I didn't know what to say.

He leaned in. "We'll talk tonight. I have some news." Then he smiled. "Good news."

I took in a breath, surprised by the calm that washed over me at his words. "Okay."

And then the five-second countdown to our entrance began.

I marched to the stage in time to the beat coming from the live band above us. A few dozen people were in the audience—show producers, set designers, investors—everyone who had anything to do with the production but who wasn't part of the live show.

The adrenaline was insane as we all let go and performed as we would in just a few nights. To think that only one month ago we were at Gravity, stumbling through the routines without a full picture of how it would all come together, was incredibly rewarding.

♥

The Ravens were all backstage during the only song where none of us were needed. We were changing into our fourth costume of the set. It was one of the few pieces where the audience would see us all onstage together.

"Hey, Lex," Reggie said, approaching from behind. He was dancing beside me for this one.

Anxiety shot through me at his nearness. I knew he was drunk the other night, but I'd never known him to be truly aggressive until then. I hated that I saw him differently. "Hey." I looked away, unable to hold his gaze for long.

"I just wanted to tell you I'm sorry about what happened at Tao."

I looked at him again, thankful for his apology, but I knew our friendship would never be the same. "I'm sorry the bonus track isn't happening. It was really great."

He nodded, his jaw tense. "Yeah, well, it wasn't you that pulled it. It was Theo's decision. Dude's had it out for me for years."

"What?" My heart freefell into my stomach. "Why would you say that?"

Reggie laughed. "Ask your boy. He feels threatened, I guess. We go way back, Lex. And you should know, he's not the guy you think he is. But he'll get what's coming to him. I'm just sorry you had to get caught in the middle."

What the hell? "Reggie," I started to remind him that it was the label's decision to pull the song, but then I heard our cue to take the stage.

Was he threatening Theo? And why would he think I was caught in the middle? Because of the other night? Again, I felt I must be missing something.

That feeling didn't last long.

We took our marks on the stage while the band transitioned out and the prerecorded interlude video faded in. It was supposed to be an interview Winter had recorded during our rehearsals at Gravity. It was a moment for her to introduce us individually to the audience. And then we'd have an eight count each to freestyle.

Almost as soon as the interview began to play on the big screen, the video faded out and cut to black.

All eyes were on the black screen as the image transitioned into a faint outline of the backstage area.

"Hey, turn that up," Winter called out.

The faint noise grew louder, but once my eyes adjusted to what was playing on screen, I didn't need to hear it for my heart to feel it was being squeezed to an early death.

I recognized the couple hiding among the stage props. Two silhouettes, in love, kissing, laughing, and whispering sweet words. And that was all anyone else should have been able to make out. Shadows. Outlines. But then the camera moved in closer. There we were, Theo and I, together in more ways than one. And someone had recorded it all.

My hand flew to my chest, and my eyes opened wide. Tears sprang to them, and if it weren't for Amie's hands landing on my shoulders, I might have fallen to the floor. I looked around, and the Ravens were in various states of shock, fury, and confusion as they realized what they were watching. Then all eyes turned to me.

"Cut the fucking video," Theo shouted as he stormed onto the stage and pointed at the AV guys in the back of the room. "Cut it now."

They did. But it was too late. Everyone had seen. Everyone knew. And my career was officially over before it had ever truly begun.

Chapter 58

THEO

I couldn't find Lex anywhere. Not backstage, not in our room, not in her room. Nowhere. Shane had darted off to look for her before me. Now, I couldn't find him either.

After our cover was destroyed by that video that no one fessed up to shooting, rehearsal was dismissed, but not before Lex disappeared backstage and Shane followed. Me? I was the idiot who went back to the venue to talk some sense into the furious Winter. She was seething—foaming from the mouth, practically—and once the dancers left, she tore into me.

"I fucking warned you," she growled.

I knew there wouldn't be an easy way out of this. "I can't control some peeping asshole who stuck his camera where it didn't belong."

"How long have you been in this business? That's exactly how this kind of thing works. You just had to have her, didn't you? What makes Lex so goddamn special to you that you'd decide to fuck with my show?"

I shook my head and held up my hands. "No one had any intentions of fucking up your show. Well, I take that back. Whoever put up that video might want exactly that."

A heat wave blew through me at the thought of someone invading our privacy and using it against us. When I thought of who might have done it, only one person came to mind. "It was Reggie."

She shook her head, in complete denial.

"You know it too," I tried again. "And how fucked up is that? He's friends with Lex."

"I don't care who put up the video," she screamed. "There wouldn't have been a video if you had abided by the stupid contract. You know I don't have a choice but to let Lex go now. I've already sent notice to her room. Her flight back to LA will be fully paid. But she's got to go."

My chest puffed as anger swirled through me. "You can't let Lex go. Let *me* go. The choreography is done, anyway. I'll step down from my producer role. The show starts in four days. You can't lose a dancer now."

Winter's face was red. "I can do whatever the hell I want. How do you think it will look if she stays? Everyone signed that contract. Everyone knows the rules. I allow this one to slip, then the rest of the crew thinks they can get away with anything. This is a business, Theo. One you used to be very good at. You, better than anyone else, should understand the consequences of fucking with me."

There was no reasoning with her. "Then I'm out too."

She visibly shook. "You can't leave," she screamed as the tears brimmed from her eyes. "You would seriously turn your back on me? After everything we've been through together? After all the opportunities I've given you? Don't forget who made you an instant celebrity ten years ago. What ever happened to gratitude? To loyalty?"

"What ever happened to free will, Winter, huh? You don't *own* me. We were partners in all of this, but you fucked up the moment you decided to control my life."

She let out a scream that echoed off the stage walls, and I couldn't help laughing before giving her a piece of my mind. I had so much more to say, but I needed to find Lex.

"And for the record, I'm not turning my back on you. You turned your back on me the moment you decided to control my happiness. Lex is it for me, Winter. And if you can't accept that—if you won't amend the contract and keep Lex in your show—then we have nothing left to say here."

She wiped a tear and nodded. "Fine. Then leave. You'll be paid up until the start of the show."

I sighed, and while Winter could easily change her mind and right all of this bullshit, guilt was chewing through my insides. She might not have "made me," as she claimed, but she had been a friend since the beginning.

"I don't care about the money. Believe it or not, I care about you and this show and the dancers. All of them. You don't need to do this. Let Lex stay, and I will too."

She shook her head as more tears spilled down her cheeks. "It's done. You made your choice."

"That's where you're wrong. You didn't give me a choice."

Chapter 59

LEX

When Shane and I arrived at my room later that night, the termination papers were waiting for me. Amie was already there with the envelope in her hands. The paper shook as she handed it to me. It looked as if she'd been crying.

"I talked to the other dancers," Amie said, still holding the parcel tight. "Everyone was shocked. *Of course* they were. But no one gives a fuck that you're dating Theo. Not to the extent Winter is taking it. She's really letting you go?" She held up the envelope. "That's what this is, right?" She shook her head.

Shane sat beside Amie and wrapped a comforting arm around her shoulders. Then he tugged the envelope from her grip and handed it to me. I didn't open it right away. I couldn't. The moment I read whatever was inside, everything would be over, as if the last two and a half months hadn't existed.

Shane and I had spent the entire day and night walking the streets of Las Vegas, dipping into different venues to eat, talk, and cry. I'd turned off my phone too, delaying the inevitable and avoiding Theo. In the two weeks I'd been there, I hadn't seen much of Vegas. I'd taken it for granted. It wasn't supposed to be over this quickly.

My heart was torn between my dreams and the man I loved. Part of me wished I'd been stronger. I could have avoided the humiliation and devastation by staying away from him. We could have waited out the six months, but it had felt so impossible. The truth was, I didn't know if I was right or wrong, I just knew it was over. All of it.

"Who the fuck played that video? That's what I want to know." Shane steamed as he stared out the window at the Vegas skyline. "That was some dirty shit." He looked at Amie. "What would the motive be for trying to hurt Lex like that?"

Amie looked at me, and our eyes locked, a mutual thought passing through our silence. We both knew who'd done it. But did it even matter? The issue wasn't who outed us, it was what we were hiding.

"Reggie," Amie said, gritting her teeth. "It had to have been Reggie."

"What?" Shane practically screeched. "Dude was into Lex. There's no way he would—" His mouth formed an O. "You think he was jealous of Lex and Theo?" His face crinkled. "That doesn't make sense. What would he get out of having Lex kicked off the show?"

I sighed and shook my head. "I don't think that was his motive. He and Theo have had a rivalry for years, dating back to their foster kid life. Reggie's always felt gypped of the opportunities Theo's gotten over him. After the bonus track got taken away, he completely lost it. I think he saw an opportunity to destroy Theo, and I got caught in the cross fire."

I remembered the cryptic message Reggie was trying to pass to me before the rehearsal today and told Amie and Shane about it.

"What a douche," Amie snarled. "I can't believe we were friends with him."

Shane's face had gone stony. "I feel like there's still something we're missing."

I ripped open the envelope and pulled out the thick stack of papers. "It doesn't matter." I waved the document in the air. "It's already done. Terminated without pay for breach of contract." I looked at Shane, my eyes stinging, but I had no tears left to cry. "I'm going home."

"To LA?"

I shook my head. "I'm going *home*, Shane. Back to Seattle."

Chapter 60

THEO

I knocked on Lex's door first thing in the morning, only to be greeted by a perturbed Amie. She looked as though she hadn't gotten any sleep all night. I pushed the door open farther and glanced inside. "Where is she?"

"Excuse me," Amie said, pushing me back out the door and wrapping her arms around her waist. "It's six in the morning. You shouldn't be banging on doors. You'll wake someone up."

"It's Vegas," I reminded her, and she rolled her eyes.

"Well, Lex isn't here."

My heart started to pound. "What do you mean she's not here? Where the hell is she?"

"She left with Shane. They were catching the first flight home."

I pulled my phone out of my pocket and checked to see if I had any missed calls or messages from Lex. Nothing. "She wasn't even going to tell me?"

Amie sighed and glanced around the hall before her eyes landed on mine. "She was pretty upset all night. I don't think she was trying to avoid you so much as trying to figure out what the fuck to do for the rest of her life. I'm sure she'll call you when she lands."

I backed away, tapping through my phone to find the first airline app that popped up. I wasn't going to sit around waiting for Lex to call me. "Then I'll go to her. It won't take me long to get to LA."

"She didn't go to LA."

Cold air swirled around us, but I could feel it in my bones. "What do you mean? You just said they were flying home."

"Yeah, *to Seattle*."

No. Lex was going to give up everything. And it was all because of me.

I felt physically sick as I ran to my room, without so much as a goodbye to Amie, and tossed all of my belongings into my suitcases. When I reentered the hallway, I debated taking the long route to the elevators to avoid passing Winter's door. But it was six in the morning. Winter wouldn't be awake.

I was almost in the clear when the door to her room suddenly opened. I had nowhere to hide, and there was still another hundred yards until I arrived at the elevators. So I stood there like an idiot, but it wasn't Winter who walked out.

Reggie stepped out as he zipped up his fly and stuffed his shirt into his jeans, all while Winter's door was shutting behind him.

I went absolutely still.

He looked up and his eyes widened to the size of a raccoon's. "Shit," he muttered quietly.

"What the fuck?" The boom in my voice was uncontrollable. Suddenly, everything started to make sense. My brain was working so fast, my head felt as if it were flying along the tracks of a wooden roller coaster.

Winter had been fucking Reggie. *"I've moved on, thank you very much."* That was what Winter had told me last week. *But with him?* How had I not seen that coming?

That was why she *really* gave him the bonus track.

It probably all started the night he helped Winter choose the feature spots. *Reggie saw you two drive off in your car.*

I shuddered as reality washed over me.

Reggie's shock had disappeared. He glanced at my bags and chuckled. "What would you call something like this? Karma?"

I released the handles of my cases and shoved Reggie into the wall so hard that it shook against his back. Then I cupped his throat with my palm and squeezed. "Listen to me, you son of a bitch. You fucked with the wrong person."

He swiped his hands up to grip my wrists and ripped them from his throat before gasping for air. "You're fucking crazy," he choked out.

"I don't think so. Crazy is peeping on my personal shit and broadcasting it for all to see. I get it. You've been jealous of me your whole fucking life. You can't help it. So you wanted to fuck with me. Get me off the show so you could take my place. It makes sense, and I'm not even surprised you would go to such lengths to take out the competition since that's the only way you'll ever succeed in this world. But why Lex? She's been nothing but nice to you."

He finally seemed to be breathing normally, but his eyes were pointed hard at me.

"And don't think I didn't figure out that you fucked with Winter's head when she was making selections for the featured spots." I motioned to the door he'd just stepped out of. "So this is how you take my job, huh? You sleep with Winter, show a video to get Lex kicked off the crew, and then you—what? Take credit for my choreography? Is that what you think will happen next?"

"I don't need to take credit for shit," he spit. "I'm a lot of things, but I'm no thief, Noska. And yeah, I *will* pick up the slack when you leave. As a matter of fact, I just sealed the deal on that." He winked, and I knew he was trying to piss me off further. It worked.

It was then that another question flashed through my mind. "Who told you about Mallory?"

His lip curled up on one side. "Who do you think?"

Winter. *Of course it was Winter.* But why? Because they were sleeping together? Was that their version of pillow talk? It still wasn't adding up. "So tell me this. Why would you pair yourself with Lex, and spend loads of time flirting with her, when all you really wanted was to fuck Winter for a few measly opportunities?"

Reggie laughed and shook his head. "Really? Aren't you the one that put the moves on Winter to get your first gig?"

"No, that's not how it worked at all."

He waved off my comment with a roll of his eyes. "Whatever. I actually liked Lex. Tight abs, juicy ass. What's not to like, right?" He wiggled his eyes as I fought back my rage. Then he shrugged. "But she wasn't into me. Winter, on the other hand—"

I cocked back my elbow and slung it forward, but he caught it before I could drive it into his face. "Hit me again and I'll break this hand, pretty boy." He gripped my fist as he twisted.

His jaw was clenched, and the smile that flashed across his face was so dark, I wouldn't have been surprised if he did snap my fist, right there.

The door behind him opened, stunning us both. Reggie dropped my hand, and though it throbbed, I didn't give him the satisfaction of letting on that he'd caused pain.

Winter stepped out, her eyes filled with fury. "What the hell is going on here?"

347

Stanley, Marcus, and Alison stepped into the hall almost as soon as she had. I shouldn't have been surprised. The three of them knew where Winter was at all times.

Alison's eyes narrowed on Reggie, and she stalked forward until she was right in front of him. "You are so fired."

He did a double take, apparently to make sure she wasn't speaking to me, then he barked out a laugh. "You can't fire me."

She tilted her head. "Actually, I can. But if you'd rather wait until Winter talks to the poor AV intern you paid to broadcast that private video of Lex and Theo, then sure, feel free to stick around." She rolled her eyes. "I knew you were a creep the day I met you. Glad I finally have proof."

Winter was shaking as her eyes darted between them. "You took that video?" She squinted at him as though she couldn't believe it. "Why would you do that?" She shook her head.

Reggie looked at her sideways. "Why would I do that? You were grateful the first time I outed this asshole. Don't change your tune now."

"I never said I was okay with exposing my choreographer and backup dancer the way you did, Reg. That is not the way it works around here. You could have come to me."

Logic. It was something Reggie so clearly lacked, and part of me felt bad for him as I watch confusion overtake his angry expression. I realized the system had failed him the way it had helped me. It wasn't easy growing up in the foster care system in our neighborhood. It was easy to fall in with the wrong crowd. While we both had frequented the rec center, I was the one Rashni pulled under his wing, not Reggie.

But none of that gave a person an excuse to be a shitty human.

And then it hit me. After ten years of dealing with the same bullshit with Reggie, I finally understood what made him tick. This wasn't about Winter or

Lex or Alison. This was about Reggie feeling that he got left behind at the worst possible time in his life and never feeling as if he'd been able to catch up. That was why he'd been tailing my career, trying to compete, and finally going to sad lengths to reach my goals instead of creating some of his own.

"You're off the show. Alison will arrange your transportation back to LA."

Winter blinked past the moisture building in her eyes.

Reggie stepped up to her, wrath filling his face. "Don't be stupid. The show is in three days, and you're already down one dancer. You can't lose me too."

"I think less is more in this case," Alison said with a wink.

He glowered at her. "Listen here, you stupid bit—"

Stanley yanked on his arm and bent it slightly, making Reggie wince. "Don't talk to a lady like that," he snarled. "It's time to go."

Marcus helped him pull Reggie down the hall, his legs dragging behind him.

Chapter 61

LEX

Shane and I stood at the hotel curb, suitcases in hand. And with a heavy heart, I watched as our driver pulled up and exited the SUV to greet us. Our flights were already booked—his to Atlanta to meet up with Dominic, mine to Seattle, where I would finally hear the words I'd been running from since I was a little girl.

I told you so.

I shivered thinking about my parents' likely reaction as I walked through their front door, defeat written all over my face. Would they even care what I'd been through? They probably wouldn't even ask. They'd chalk it up to young, immature Alexandra, who had finally seen the error of her ways.

The sour image of my future was broken up by Shane's hand resting on the back of my neck. "You ready?"

I shook my head and clutched my belongings tighter. "Just give me a minute." I met his eyes. "We're early, right?"

"There's no rush. Take your time." He stepped forward and talked to the driver, who proceeded to nod and walk back to his car.

I looked toward the busy Vegas traffic, but it was all a blur as I thought long and hard about my next move. My gut churned, telling me something was wrong. My decision to go back to Seattle was an emotional one and made in haste, a reaction to the heartbreak and confusion I felt yesterday after receiving that letter of termination. But maybe it was the wrong decision.

Shane approached again, this time stepping in front of me and forcing my eyes to meet his. "You don't have to go back there. This doesn't have to be the end of the road."

My throat burned. *Why did I think it was the best option?* And then, with an ache in my chest, I remembered.

"You read the termination papers. The contract I signed is active for one year. That means even if I keep taking classes at Gravity, I won't be able to audition for a single thing until that expires."

"That contract is bullshit, and everyone knows it. Winter can fire you for breaching the contract, but she can't fuck up your livelihood."

I swallowed, knowing what he was saying was probably true. "Still, I only have enough savings for the next four months. That's not enough time to find something else and earn a living."

"You know I'll take care of the expenses until you can pitch in. I'm making money now. We'll be fine."

I groaned. "I need to be able to support myself. You know that's important to me."

He nodded as he squeezed his eyes shut then opened them again. "There's got to be another option. There's nothing good for you in Seattle. That's not your home anymore. Your home is wherever you're able to live out your dream."

Despite the awful situation I was in, his words breathed hope into me. Winter could take away my money, but she couldn't take away my skills or my dream. If I decided to give up, that would be totally on me.

Dancers trained long and hard to find their center—*their balance*—in order to look and feel as light as possible on the dance floor. We were taught to be grounded, sturdy, limber, and weightless. So then why was I having so much trouble finding that sense of balance in my life?

"Have you tried to talk to Theo?"

I frowned, hating the guilt that tore through my chest. I wasn't being fair to him. I knew that. "He'll just convince me to stay, and I need to figure this out on my own."

"Okay," Shane said, peeling my bags away from my hands. I looked down, confused. "I'm not going to tell you what to do, but I am going to force you to think harder about your next move. So, I think you should cancel your flight."

"What?" Panic gripped me. "Why?"

"Because," he said, gesturing to the bellhop to grab our things. "If you really wanted to go home, you'd be on your way to the airport by now. Today we're going to live it up, Vegas-style. When you're ready to make a decision, you will."

Relief flowed through me at the thought of not having to make a life-altering decision right that second. "I do have some Vegas winnings I could splurge with. And there's so much more I've been dying to see." I looked up at him, excitement bubbling from within. "And I might also have comp tickets for Thunder From Down Under."

Shane's mouth spread wide with a grin. "There's my girl."

♥

The Vegas strip was as alive during the day as it was at night. Drinks were flowing, alarm bells were ringing, and roller coasters were zooming by.

Shane and I tried our luck at a game of blackjack, which ended up lasting a few hours longer than I'd anticipated. The five-dollar table we'd chosen at Imperial Palace was filled with supportive gamblers who talked me through each hand. Even the dealer stepped in to give me some advice. I walked away with the same forty bucks I'd started with, an apple martini in my hand, and a smile on my face.

"What's next?" I asked excitedly as we walked by Carnival Court at Harrah's.

He shrugged, his head still aimed down at his phone. I swore he never let that thing go. "This is your day," he said. "You tell me."

I didn't have to think about it long. The items on my Vegas wish list had been sitting stagnant since we'd arrived last week. "Okay. Then New York, New York, it is. I want to ride the roller coaster."

He gestured for me to lead the way. "After you."

We trotted through Vegas, riding the Big Apple roller coaster, playing in the arcade, then visiting random hotels along the strip and plopping down at the video poker machines along the way. We moved nonstop from one adventure to another without pause until the sun finally dipped behind the Paris Hotel.

When we arrived at the Excalibur for Thunder From Down Under, an Australian male dance show, Shane was practically frothing at the mouth. "Please tell me we have good seats."

I grinned and flashed him the tickets I'd received when claiming my comp seats. I had to upgrade them, but I knew Shane wouldn't be disappointed.

"Table five. That sounds good." He was nodding, then his face scrunched. "What's the Thunder Zone?"

I bit my bottom lip to keep my excitement at bay and pulled out a map of the seating chart I'd grabbed when I got the tickets. "That's front row center, baby. Pretty sure you're getting a lap dance tonight."

He squealed and pulled me into a hug and squeezed. "Your best friend card just renewed for another lifetime."

"Not long enough," I said, resting my cheek on his chest. "Our friendship will never expire."

♥

Near midnight, a very drunk Shane insisted we go to the Bellagio to check out the water show. I knew it would be our last stop of the night, and I considered turning my phone back on to finally face what I'd almost run from.

I reached into my purse, pressed the power button, then waited for the screen to light up. It was easy to get lost in Vegas, but no matter the thrills, thoughts of Theo still dominated my heart and mind. He didn't deserve my silence, though I still hadn't decided what I would do next. In fact, I hadn't thought about it all day. Distractions were much easier than making life-altering decisions.

I wanted to cry when I pushed the power button again and my phone's screen remained black. "No," I groaned. "It's dead."

Now that I was thinking about calling Theo, that was all I wanted to do. I was anxious to get ahold of him and see where he stood after everything had gone down. Why had I been so damn selfish?

Shane slung his heavy arm around my shoulders. "Can we just stay for the show?"

I looked up at the bright Bellagio lights shining down on a horizontal pond and nodded. After dragging Shane around all day, I couldn't take him away from the one thing he'd wanted to do. "Of course. We're here. We can head back when the show's over."

We'd been standing there only a minute when Shane slapped at his jeans pocket and pulled out his phone. He checked the screen and took a step back. "Sorry, Lex. I need to take this." He started weaving through the crowd before calling over his shoulder, "Give me two minutes."

As I held onto the rail, I felt anxiety ripple through me at all the unknowns I'd let mount throughout the day.

What would Theo do?

Did he get fired too?

What about the rest of the crew?

How would they forge ahead with a missing dancer in formation?

The reality of the entire situation slammed me before I could brace for impact. I hadn't just ruined my dreams, I'd caused a mess with the show too. A show we had all worked so hard on over the past several weeks.

By the time music started playing over the loudspeakers, signaling the start of the show, I was wiping tears from my eyes while battling the guilt inside me. When I realized the opening notes were to Elton John's "Your Song," my heart had grown too heavy to stay still any longer.

And in that quick beat, I knew exactly what I had to do.

I stepped from the rail, my pulse zooming through my veins. Before I could even turn around, I slammed into something hard.

"Going somewhere?"

My heart kicked at the familiar voice as I spun on my heels and saw him. The man of my dreams, the man in my heart, the man I couldn't have left if I'd tried.

Theo—*my Theo*—stood there, a hint of a smile on his face as he pulled me into his arms.

"Mind if I keep you company?"

I couldn't tear my gaze from his. I couldn't speak. I just stared as tears welled in my eyes. "Theo, I'm—"

He shushed me with a shake of his head and nudged me back to the rail. "We have a show to watch. And then we'll talk."

Chapter 62

THEO

"Thanks, man. I owe you one." I shook Shane's hand as he winked at me.

We were standing outside the Bellagio after the water show, my arm still around Lex. I swore I would never let her go after her disappearing act. The entire day had been a shit storm, between finalizing the new contract terms with Winter and trying to track Lex down through Amie then Shane.

"No. It's me who owes you. I should have never left Lex in that apartment alone."

He was right about that, but if it weren't for Shane keeping tabs on Lex all day and updating me, I might have gotten on a plane to Seattle.

"Wait," Lex jumped in. "You two planned this?" She looked at me, her eyes narrowed. "You didn't, like, just happen to show up and see me standing there?"

Shane chuckled. "You're not in a Nicholas Sparks movie, Lex. Things like that don't just happen."

She shot him a glare. "It could happen."

I tilted my head, a grin spreading across my face. "I'm not opposed to grand gestures."

She looked smug. "See," she told Shane. "It could happen."

Shane shrugged. "Cool. So if your love story gets optioned for film, then I get to play the dazzling best friend who concocts a scheme to reunite the long-lost lovers."

Lex laughed, and it was the most beautiful sound I'd heard all day. "You're ridiculous."

"And you love me," Shane said.

The affection pouring from Shane's eyes and tone had my own heart swelling.

I tightened my hold around Lex's shoulders and leaned in so she could hear me. "What's the plan now, Lex?"

She pushed her shoulders back and looked between the two of us. "I want to go back to Hard Rock. I'm going to find Winter tomorrow morning and talk to her. And then I'm going to beg for my job back if I have to. I'll talk to the others too. If everyone still wants me gone after that, then—" Her eyes found Shane's. "Then I'll head back to LA until another opportunity comes along. I'm not ready to give up yet."

Shane beamed at her, and I tugged her close to me. "In that case, I have some news."

Both pairs of eyes looked expectantly at me. "C'mon, dude. Don't do the suspenseful thing. Just tell us you quit on Winter and screwed her over the way she hurt Lex."

"Not quite." I grinned as they both waited. "Reggie was fired this morning for trying to sabotage the show. He admitted to sharing the video. He also admitted to sleeping with Winter just to get a few auditions, the music video and Vegas series being two of them."

Lex gasped, and Shane muttered something under his breath.

"So, Lex, you have your job back if you want it."

Lex clutched my side. "Really?" The hopeful tone in her voice made me fall in love with her even more.

I nodded, caressing her cheek with my knuckles. "Yup. Winter talked to the crew today. Everyone wants you back. Nobody cares that we're together. In fact"—I chuckled at the memory of my earlier phone call with Winter—"they said they've liked me better recently, and now they know who to thank for it. Apparently, I was some kind of *jerk* before."

She laughed as she slid her arms around my waist.

"Oh." I couldn't believe I'd almost forgotten. I turned to Shane. "And you're in too, dude. If you want the job."

Shane's jaw dropped. "What?"

"Someone needs to fill Reggie's spot, but it can't be me since I've got other commitments. Winter already knows about your gig with Dominic. She understands if you need to wrap that up first. I'm happy to fill in until you've learned the steps."

"Wow. That's—" Shane shook his head, his eyes wide and mouth agape.

"It's incredible," Lex gushed. "Say yes, Shane." She made steeple fingers in an effort to beg.

Shane laughed. "Do you think I'm fucking crazy? Of course the answer is yes."

Lex jumped into his arms, and when they finished celebrating, she found her way back to my side.

"What do you say?" I looked between Lex and Shane. "Ready to head back to the hotel?"

They both muttered an exhausted "Yes."

My gaze traveled to Lex. "By the way, I canceled our room when I thought you'd left. I wasn't staying here without you. But I still have my original room. And since we're not a secret anymore, you can stay with me there."

She scrunched her face. "The one down the hall from Winter? Are you sure that's okay?"

That was my girl. Still trying to be cautious. "It's all squared away. It's fine, Lex. Stay with me?" I was desperate to hold her tonight after an entire day of worry. Even when I knew she hadn't left for Seattle, I still didn't know what she'd do next. What if she hadn't wanted her spot back with the crew?"

"What about Shane?" Her eyes traveled to him. "We haven't talked about the hotel situation yet."

He waved a hand in the air. "Don't worry about me. I already told Amie I'm crashing her room tonight. She seems pretty stoked about it."

We all laughed, and I tucked Lex under my arm. "What do you say? Wanna be my roomie?"

She squinted up at me playfully then shrugged. "I suppose that wouldn't be the worst arrangement."

Chapter 63

LEX

As soon as we got back in the elevator after dropping Shane off at Amie's room, Theo was all over me. His fingers threaded my hair, his mouth slammed against mine, and his knee found its way between my legs. "I love you," he rasped between kisses. "I love you so goddamn much."

"I love you too, Theo. I'm sorry I was going to leave without saying anything." My chest ached as I muttered the apology. To think I would have missed out on this time with him because I was too stubborn and embarrassed.

He shook his head, his nose brushing mine. His eyes were soft. "You weren't going anywhere. You just needed time to figure that out on your own."

I smiled at how well Theo knew me already. There was a time I thought I'd never trust a man again, let alone fall in love. And here we were, unable to keep our hands off each other, stumbling down the hall toward Theo's room.

He placed me and my things against the wall while he searched for his room card. My chest heaved with impatience as he unlocked the door and opened it. "After you." There was a hint of a smile, his eyes darkening as they fell to take me in. My insides coiled. I loved the way Theo looked at me as though he could never get enough—and would never take me for granted.

I slid by him, the scent of leather and mint filling the space between us. I should have expected to walk into a king suite. He'd told me about it, but his words did no justice to the stunning sight before me—white leather sectional, a jaw-dropping view of Vegas at night, and a fully stocked bar in the corner of the room, blue neon lighting its underside. And through an arched doorway, a gigantic white bed.

"You like?" He approached from behind, wrapping his arms around my middle and placing his chin in the crook of my neck.

"Not too shabby." I grinned before spinning around to loop my arms around his neck. "I can't believe you were slumming it on the ninth floor with me when you could have been staying here every night."

He chuckled. "Kind of pointless without my girlfriend naked under those sheets."

I grew so warm with his words, I practically melted right there. "Did you just call me your girlfriend?"

He scrunched his mouth and nodded. "'Slumming partner' doesn't have the same ring to it. 'Girlfriend' will have to do. For now."

When he grinned, I felt fire light up my cheeks as my heart stuttered. "I think I like the sound of that."

He leaned in and grazed my nose with his lips. "You know what I like the sound of?"

I bit my lip to keep from laughing. Theo and his dirty mind. "I have a pretty good idea."

His palm patted my ass then squeezed. "The hotel should be up soon with your things. Why don't you make yourself comfortable while we wait?"

I pouted then backed away with a teasing bite of my lip. "Fine. I need a shower, anyway."

As soon as the hot water hit me and rolled down my skin, I relaxed. Vegas summers were no joke. My body was crisp and stinging from too much sun and not enough sunscreen. But I had an inch of sweat I needed to clean off before I could roll around naked with Theo.

After wrapping myself in the fluffy robe hanging behind the door and unknotting my hair with Theo's comb, I slipped into the hallway just as he was tipping the bellman.

"Thank you, sir." The man nodded. "Have a good evening."

Theo shut the door and turned to face me. "I have a feeling we will."

He closed the distance, grabbed my face, and ran his lips against mine. "How was your shower?" He grasped the bow of my robe and unknotted it. "Hot?" He teased before sinking his teeth into his lower lip as he eyed me. "Wet?"

I smiled as I reached for his shorts, tugged at his elastic waist, then slipped them down his legs. His blue boxer briefs too. "It was—steamy." I wiggled my eyebrows as I pulled open my robe.

He groaned as if he could combust right there then tore his shirt over his head. My palms found his chest, dragging my nails over hard and sculpted terrain. I pushed him down on the couch. His back slammed against it, and he looked up, grabbing hold of his erection. I stepped forward, and he stared at me with a sigh. "Goddamn, you're beautiful."

I climbed onto his lap, straddling his swollen shaft. Two fingers pushed into my opening, and I gasped. His lips curled into a smile. "Yeah," he murmured darkly, pushing deeper inside me. "That's going to feel good."

And then his fingers were gone. He shifted me to place me on his crown. His shoulders were my leverage as I sank around him, filling myself. He hissed out a breath.

His hands snaked under the robe and around to my lower back. He gripped me and moved, setting the pace.

We were like that for a while, leveled gazes, breaths mingling, sweat dripping, rhythmic and unhurried as we moved together in my favorite kind of dance, in a freestyle that had me soaring almost as high as I had out on that stage.

And I knew, without a shadow of a doubt, everything had played out exactly as it was meant to. It might have taken me eight months of focus and hard work, but I'd found my balance. My center.

My center of gravity.

Epilogue

SIX MONTHS LATER

Epilogue 1

THEO

The stage lights went dark, and a thunderous roar erupted through the theater. Glow sticks and phone lights danced through the air, and arms waved frantically as eyes strained to get a hint of what was to come. It was almost time.

I jogged the last few steps onto the side stage and flung myself against the rail. There, I had the perfect view of everything, but my eyes searched for only one person.

Two weeks. That was how long it had been since I'd held Lex in my arms, kissed her, breathed in her scent, watched her tear up the dance floor. And I couldn't wait to watch her soar again in the final show of the Vegas series.

The last six months had been a flurry of travel between Vegas and LA for music video shoots and spending every spare second with Lex. But that wasn't all.

One month ago, I got a phone call from Rashni's wife, Ananya, who was now running my old rec center. She was looking for someone to head up the dance program and thought of me. I couldn't turn her down. I just didn't realize how invested I would become in my old stomping grounds.

A shoulder nudged me, pulling me from my thoughts. "Geez, Noska. Couldn't even wait for me?"

I threw Janelle an amused glance. "And stop while you greeted and hugged every damn person you know? No, thanks." I stuck my tongue between my teeth and placed my elbow on the rail.

She rolled her eyes. "Shouldn't you be backstage wishing your *girlfriend* good luck?"

"She doesn't know I'm here. I'm going to surprise her after the show."

Janelle shook her head and laughed. "Wow. You really are whipped. You really like this girl, huh? Like, *really* like her?"

"More like *love* her." I grinned.

Her jaw practically crashed to the floor. When she picked it up, she narrowed her eyes, accusation brimming from them. "Isn't that interesting?"

I chuckled, running a hand through my hair and ruffling it a little. "Go ahead, Nellie. Just say it."

"This was all me. You realize that, right? If it weren't for me, Lex would have never auditioned. She sure as hell wouldn't have become a Raven. I think you owe me."

"Is that all you wanted to say?" I asked, amused.

"No." The biggest goddamn smile blossomed on her face, and she leaned in. "I told you so." She sang the words loud and proud, adding a little vibrato at the end.

Despite my defeat, I grinned back at her. "You did. And for once, I'm glad I listened."

Epilogue 2

LEX

The music from the theater thrummed through my ears as I sprinted backstage for a costume change. I had precisely three minutes to put on my next outfit—a black sequined bra, jean shorts, and a pair of white high-tops.

By now, I had this down. I knew I'd reach my entrance marker with around two minute to spare. I knew the rest of the girl Ravens would be right beside me the entire time, but for the sake of my focus during the immense rush of live performances, I didn't even see them. Not until I was safely waiting for our cue to get on the stage.

"All right, girls, take your marks. You're on in two."

The countdown began as we edged around the stage and prepared to join

Winter. From this spot in the wings, I could see the stretch of crowd that was eating out of the palm of Winter's hand as she chatted them up. They couldn't take their eyes off her.

But then why did it feel as though someone had eyes on me?

I felt it on the back of my neck—a tingling that raised my hair, a warmth that crawled under my skin and wrapped my chest. And somehow I knew Theo was there.

I searched the crowd until my gaze got to the side stage and slowed. My pulse raced as our eyes locked, and a smile slowly grew on his face.

I took off running. Left my mark. Tore through the twelve feet that separated us, over tangled cords and light poles and speakers. I leapt onto the rail of the side stage until Theo was directly in front of me. My heart felt as if it could burst from my chest.

"Surprise," he said, his eyes traveling to my lips. "Miss me?"

Seeing him there after an entire two weeks apart, his light eyes shining back at me, I couldn't resist him a second longer. My mouth crushed against his as my arms slid around his neck to hold him closer.

"Lex," someone hissed.

I ignored them.

"You weren't supposed to see me until after the show," he said before I kissed him again, inhaling his scent like a damn junkie. "But now that you've spotted me, you should know there are others here too."

I grinned over his shoulder at Janelle. "I already knew Janelle was here, silly."

He shook his head as his eyes moved toward the media pit below the stage. "I made sure to give them front row seats."

I cocked my head at him and narrowed my eyes. *Okay, something is up.* "Theo?" I questioned in warning. Then I turned in the direction his eyes were pointed and gasped when I saw my parents looking stiff and awkward, just as

I remembered them. They were here for me. Emotion felt packed in my throat as I turned back to Theo. "You did this?"

He bit his lip and nodded.

"I love you." I smiled with my words, just as someone hissed my name again. It was Amie, calling to me from the stage, where I knew time was running down to the final second.

Through the fog in my brain, I sucked in a breath, jerking away from Theo with a laugh. "Rain check?"

Theo nodded. "Definitely." He jerked his head up, gesturing behind me to the stage. "They're waiting for you. Time to kill it."

This time, I was the one who winked as I dropped back down from the rail. "Always do, Theo." I bit my bottom lip, my chest swelling as I realized in the moment just how far I'd come. "Always do."

And then I flipped around to take the stage, carrying my center with me.

It would never leave me again.

WATCH: LOVE IN THE DARK
smarturl.it/Gravity_LoveInDark

Surprise!

The extended epilogue can be found here:
www.kkallen.com/GravityBonusEpilogue

For My Readers

I hope you enjoyed Lex and Theo's story! If you have a few minutes to spare, please consider leaving a review on Amazon and Goodreads. Reviews and sharing your love for our stories mean the world to an author. You can also connect with me on social media and sign up for my mailing list to be sure and never miss a new release, event, or sale!

Website & Blog: www.kkallen.com
Facebook: www.facebook.com/AuthorKKAllen
Goodreads: www.goodreads.com/KKAllen
BookBub: www.bookbub.com/profile/k-k-allen
Instagram: www.instagram.com/kkallen_author
Twitter: www.twitter/KKAllenAuthor

JOIN K.K.'S INSIDERS GROUP, FOREVER YOUNG!

Enjoy special sneak peeks, participate in exclusive giveaways,
enter to win ARCs, and chat it up with K.K. and special guests ;)
www.facebook.com/groups/foreveryoungwithkk

WANT MORE?

You do not want to miss what K.K. is working on next ;)

Sign up for new release alerts to never miss a thing!

WWW.SMARTURL.IT/KK_MAILLIST

DANCE TUTORIALS

If you're into dance, or know someone who is, I highly recommend these dance tutorials! I am in no way affiliated with this product—I just thought it was really cool. Enjoy!

WWW.TMILLY.TV

Thank You

Every now and then there's a story that won't stop brewing in the back of my mind (especially when I should be doing other things, HA!), and Center of Gravity was one of them. For some reason, just the idea of trying to translate my passion for dance into the written word seemed daunting. I am so glad I listened to my heart, that I pushed through the doubt, and wrote a story that so many of you already love. Thank you so much for reading. Thank you for joining me on Lex and Theo's amazing journey.

Now, to pull the curtain back and show you all the folks who helped make this magic happen. My people. My tribe. My inspiration. If it weren't for the following rock stars, I do not know if this story would be in your hands today.

Kristen, Puck, Kris, Sis. I love you to the moon and back. I have so many amazing memories with you, which all came flooding back while writing this story. Always an inspiration, a gracious and loving soul, an amazing dancer, and an amazing friend. You are one of a kind, and I'm so lucky to get to love you.

To my fellow dance sisters and brothers, from the studio, high school, college, the gym, wherever we met, please know that a part of our time together is in this novel.

To all the dance studios, and choreographers, and dancers that throw their hearts on the floor and share it for the world to see on YouTube. And to the video production teams who capture that passion. You are such an inspiration for all, especially our younger generation, and I hope you continue to spread that joy. It's powerful, and beautiful, and as my readers now know, addictive AF. Shoutout to Jade Chynoweth, JoJo Gomez, Tim Milgram (T.Milly), Nicole

Kirkland, Blake McGrath, Kyle Hanagami, Nika Kljun, and Millennium Dance Complex for posting some of the most inspiring choreography and dancing I have ever seen. It was a pleasure to share your art in my story.

Lindsey, AKA, "The Boss of K.K. Allen" (snorts), I love you big. You are truly my rock, my friend, the greatest partner in crime. I cannot wait for the day I get see your beautiful face in real life.

To my incredible Badass Beta team. Sammie, you were rereading this bad boy until the very last second. In fact, you're still reading through this book while I'm writing these words. Thank you so much. I adore you for so many amazing reasons, but it's our friendship I value most of all. You, my babe, are my unicorn. Cyndi, I always love your feedback, your excitement over my stories, and our daily mommy chats. Thank you for always being there. Taylor, you are phenomenal. Your enthusiasm over Theo and Lex sparked something in me I will never forget. You brought me back to life at a time I needed it most. Thank you! To Thessa. Girl, I am so glad we met, and I cannot wait to hang with you in February. Thank you for stepping up at the last minute to read Lex and Theo's story. Now you'll never get rid of me ;).

To my early Alphas, who helped to steer this story in the right direction, Lauren and Sue. Love you both so much.

Lynn with Red Adept Editing, thank you so much for being an absolute doll and offering wonderful talent to work with me on this book. I am blessed to say that I've worked with your team. To Jessica, my lovely developmental editor. Your feedback was brilliant, and just what I needed to bring this story to life. To Angela, I am so grateful for your feedback and advice. I hope we can work together again.

Lauren Watson Perry from Perrywinkle Photography. It has been a dream to work with you, and I'm so glad we finally had the opportunity. This was the perfect project, and you gave me the perfect Lex and Theo. Thank you so much for everything. I cannot wait to work with you again.

Sarah Hansen with Okay Creations. You are such a joy to work with. I can trust you with anything, and I know you'll spin it into gold. Thank you for being consistently fabulous.

To my formatting guru, Nadége with Inkstain Designs. You blow me away, girl. I am so happy we finally get to work together in this capacity! Thank you for making my words look extra beautiful.

For this release I was blessed beyond words to work with Social Butterfly PR. Emily, thank you for always being there and holding me a little through our first release together. I adore you! And to Nina, thank you for everything you do!

To my babes from Do Not Disturb and 30 Days to 60K (can we please change this name now? LOL) Y'all were my rocks while writing this book, and I cannot imagine this author life without you all.

To my Angsters, for being the best, most badass street team out there. Thank you, babes!

To all my loves in my reader group, Forever Young. I love you all more than words. You make me smile on the daily, just by sharing space with you on the interwebs. You make this author life extra fantastic. Thank you!

To my family, thank you (as always), for supporting me, lifting me, and helping my dreams become a reality. None of this would exist without you. I LOVE YOU.

Lastly, and most important, thank you, dear reader, for spending your precious time with this story. I hope you were entertained, and if you didn't love dance before, I hope you have a special appreciation for it now.

All my love,
XOXO
K.K.

OTHER BOOKS

Tragedy had stripped Aurora of everything she once loved.
But now she's back in Balsam Grove, ready to face all she's
kept locked away for seven years.
Or so she thinks.
Aurora doesn't expect her first collision to be with the
boy she left all those years ago.
The boy who betrayed her trust with no regrets.
The boy who is no longer a boy, but a man with the same stormy eyes
that swept her into his current before she ever learned to swim.
She'd thought he was safe.
He'd thought their path was mapped out.

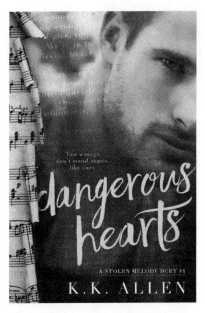

His heart beats for the music. She's his favorite song.

Lyric Cassidy knows a thing or two about bad boy rock stars with raspy vocals.
In fact, her heart was just played by one. So when she takes an assignment as
road manager for the world famous rock star, Wolf, she's prepared to take
him on, full suit of heart-armor intact.

Wolf is the sexy lead singer for the hottest rock band around with a line-up of
guaranteed one night stands. Lyric Cassidy isn't one of them. That's fine with him.
Women like Lyric come with fairytale expectations, so it should be easy to stay away.
Too bad she's hot as sin with a fiery temper and a mouth that drives him wild.

She's also got something to hide. Something he discovers. Something he wants ...

Sharing a tour bus, neither of them are prepared for the miles of road ahead and the
fierce attraction they feel toward one another--a dangerous combination.

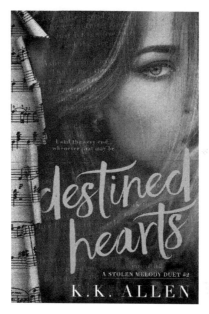

He stole her lyrics, and then he stole her heart.

Lyric Cassidy is off the tour, lost as to what her next career move will be, and certain that she'll never love again after Wolf. All because of a social media scandal that left her with no choice but to pack up and face the consequences. When she learns that the fate of her career is in her hands, she has a difficult decision to make. Step back on the tour bus with Wolf and deal with the mess she left behind, or end her contract early and lose her job at Perform Live?

Wolf's shattered heart finds no resolve in giving Lyric a chance to come back on tour. He can never be with her again. Not after she walked away. Conflicted with wants and needs, he struggles to remember who Wolf was before Lyric. That's what he needs to become again. Maybe then his heart will be safe.
Or maybe there's no hope for the damaged.

But with stolen dreams, betrayals, and terrifying threats—no one's heart is safe.
Not even the ones that may be destined to be together.

I wanted to tell him all my secrets, but he became one of them instead.

Chloe Rivers never thought she would keep secrets from her best friend. Then again, she never imagined she would fall in love with him either. When she finally reveals her feelings, rejection shatters her, rendering her vulnerable and sending her straight into the destructive arms of the wrong guy.

Gavin Rhodes never saw the betrayal coming. It crushes him. Chloe has always been his forbidden fantasy—sweet, tempting, and beautiful. But when the opportunity finally presents itself, he makes the biggest mistake of all and denies her.

Now it's too late . . .

Four years after a devastating tragedy, Chloe and Gavin's worlds collide and they find their lives entangling once again. Haunted by the past, they are forced to come to terms with all that has transpired to find the peace they deserve. Except they can't seem to get near each other without combatting an intense emotional connection that brings them right back to where it all started . . . their childhood treehouse.

Chloe still holds her secrets close, but this time she isn't the only one with something to hide. Can their deep-rooted connection survive the destruction of innocence?

One kiss can change everything.

Fun and flirty Monica Stevens lives for chocolate, fashion, and boys … in that order. And she doesn't take life too seriously, especially when it comes to dating. When a night of innocent banter with Seattle's hottest NFL quarterback turns passionate, she fears that everything she once managed to protect will soon be destroyed.

Seattle's most eligible bachelor, Zachary Ryan, is a workaholic by nature, an undercover entrepreneur, and passionate about the organizations he supports. He's also addicted to Monica, the curvy brunette with a sassy mouth—and not just because she tastes like strawberries and chocolate. She's as challenging as she is decadent, as witty as she is charming, and she's the perfect distraction from the daily grind.

While Monica comes to a crossroads in her life, Zachary becomes an unavoidable obstacle, forcing her to stop hiding under the bleachers and confront the demons of her past. But as their connection grows stronger, she knows it only brings them closer to their end.

It's time to let go.

To have a future, we must first deal with our pasts. But what if the two are connected?

On an Alaskan cruise in the dead of winter, Emma and Luke find each
other under the aurora borealis, a phenomenon that bonds them in the most
unlikely of ways. While Luke teaches Emma what it means to soar,
she gives him a reason to stay grounded, but as their journey nears
its end memories of a forgotten past surfaces,
challenging their future—if a future for them still exists.

About the Author

K.K. Allen is an award-winning author and Interdisciplinary Arts and Sciences graduate from the University of Washington who writes Contemporary Romance and Fantasy stories about "Capturing the Edge of Romance." K.K. currently resides in central Florida, works full time as a Digital Producer for a leading online educational institution, and is the mother to a ridiculously handsome little dude who owns her heart.

K.K.'s multi-genre publishing journey began in June 2014 with the YA Contemporary Fantasy trilogy, *The Summer Solstice*. In 2016, K.K. published her first Contemporary Romance, *Up in the Treehouse*, which went onto win RT Book Reviews' 2016 Reviewers' Choice Award for Best New Adult Book of the Year. With K.K.'s love for inspirational and coming of age stories involving heartfelt narratives and honest characters, you can be assured to always be surprised by what K.K. releases next.

More works in progress will be announced soon. Stay tuned for more by connecting with K.K. in all the social media spaces.

WWW.KKALLEN.COM

WORKS CITED

Milgram, Tim [Tim Milgram]. (2016, November 28). *Michael Jackson –
Heartbreaker – Choreography by Misha Gabriel & Maho Udo – Shot by @timmilgram*
[Video file]. Retrieved from https://youtu.be/5CBF1F9DiZI

Gomez, JoJo [JoJo Gomez]. (2018, January 17). *Demi Lovato – Confident
– Choreography by JoJo Gomez* [Video file]. Retrieved from https://youtu.be/
JHKpaBpRDYk

Kirkland, Nicole [Nicole Kirkland]. (2018, February 23). *Jhene Aiko – "New
Balance" | Nicole Kirkland Choreography* [Video file]. Retrieved from https://youtu.
be/ZhNk2owmpgI

Kljun, Nika [Nika Kljun]. (2015, November 14). *Justin Bieber – What Do You
Mean? – Choreography by @NikaKljun & @SonnyFp – Filmed by @TimMilgram* [Video
file]. Retrieved from https://youtu.be/x0n6BCmTv7A

McGrath, Blake [Blake McGrath]. (2017, April 21). *BLAKE MCGRATH | THE
CURE CHOREOGRAPHY* [Video file]. Retrieved from https://youtu.be/AwSjxweBsrA

Hanagami, Kyle [Kyle Hanagami]. (2018, March 23). *JAMES BAY – Wild
Love | Kyle Hanagami Choreography* [Video file]. Retrieved from https://youtu.be/
foR6taRL1IQ

DanceOn [DanceOn]. (2017, September 28). Kelly Clarkson – Love So Soft |
Blake McGrath Choreography | DanceOn Class [Video file]. Retrieved from https://
youtu.be/fWXDa_HnzCY

Milgram, Tim [Tim Milgram]. (2015, August 12). *Ellie Goulding – Hanging On
– Choreography by LindsayNelko | Directed by @TimMilgram* [Video file]. Retrieved
from https://youtu.be/P12H7xA0XrY

Hanagami, Kyle [Kyle Hanagami]. (2017, November 22). *ADELE – Love In The
Dark | Kyle Hanagami Choreography (Leroy Sanchez Cover)* [Video file]. Retrieved
from https://youtu.be/aeijJf-zjzY